In The Image of Man

Robert Roush

Tony and Christen,
Do not grow weary of doing good!
Gal. 6:9
And Remember,
Believing is Seeing!
2 Kings 6:17

Copyright © 2014 by Robert Roush

All rights reserved.

ISBN-10: 0-69202-802-1

ISBN-13: 978-0-692-02802-5

Hearts of Compassion Publishing

Holland, Michigan

The characters and events of this book are fictional. Any resemblance to actual persons or events is coincidental.

Scripture quotations are taken from the Holy Bible, New Living Translation, copyright © 1996, 2004. Used by permission of Tyndale House Publishers, Inc., Wheaton, Illinois 60189. All rights reserved.

Stories for Compassion is a program that directs net proceeds from book sales to fulfilling Jesus' call in Matthew 25:40 to provide clean water, food, clothing, and compassion to those who are in need.

This program provides a win-win opportunity: God-honoring stories for readers to enjoy and be challenged in their walk with God, all while investing in the welfare of children around the globe.

ACKNOWLEDGEMENTS

Special thanks to my loving wife Becky for her patience and tolerance. Without her encouragement and involvement, this story would never have reached its full potential.

This book is dedicated to my grandfather, Floyd Hydon, a true storyteller. Our thirty-eight years together helped to develop any creativity and humor you may find in this book. He is now telling stories in Heaven and can truly laugh at my attempt to portray the unfathomable spiritual realm which he can now witness in living color.

PROLOGUE

Saturday, June 3, 1995

Mael stood in the shadow of a modern-day castle. Roses, shrubbery, and white-stone statues lined the courtyard where a fountain bubbled in the center of a dirt walkway. An absurd image of a chubby angel perched atop the fountain. Humans possessed such a weak view of the heavenly creatures. If only his angelic opposition were so inept.

He stepped to the center of a manicured flowerbed and unfurled his mighty black wings. Beneath his deformed claws, raindrops pounded frail petals into the mud. A low satisfied growl echoed deep within his chest.

A presence approached. "My liege—"

Mael spun and scowled at the pathetic excuse for a demon. "Yes Leon, what is it?"

The disfigured assistant bowed to the ground. "The first has been born."

"The boy?"

"No my lord. The girl."

"Pity." Mael withdrew his electric-blue sword and etched a circle with a plus in the dirt. "I should have liked our plan to begin with a first-born Adam."

"If it please you my liege, I will dispose of her."

Mael swept his sword back and forth erasing the symbol. Indeed, it would please him. What would please him more would be to deprive his wretched assistant of such satisfaction.

Leon licked his lips as he stared at the decimated symbol. Drool ebbed from his snout.

Mael exhaled a long sulfurous breath. "No. We will find a use for her."

Leon bowed and stepped back. His lip began to tremble.

"Have the princes arrived?"

"Most my liege. They await your presence."

"Show them to the bone room."

Leon bowed then spread his black leathery wings and arose like an eagle soaring on a mountain wind. He vanished over the edge of the building to retrieve the others.

Mael descended into the ground. Rose bushes wilted as his wings passed through, leaving only thorny stems behind. Beneath the garden, he strode through dirt and stone until he reached a concrete wall. Beyond the twelve-inch foundation of the building, the pleasing aroma of death and decay greeted him. The perfect atmosphere to discuss Lucifer's plan.

~~~~~~~~~~

CHAPTER ONE

Friday, April 17, 2020

Just get out alive. Sergeant Chris Davis pressed his back against the wall.

Beads of sweat oozed between his palm and the cool grip of his Glock 22. He slid his left shoulder to the door frame. One final breath to dull the thumping in his ears.

Like most of the quiet middle-class neighborhood, the Hendersons had left for work hours ago. The house stood empty, or so he hoped. He aimed the gun at the gap separating the door from its frame. His free hand pushed the oak door. Black knuckles turned to tarnished bronze as his grip tightened around the Glock.

The door stopped.

A drip of salty sweat stung his eye. Was there someone in the room? He squinted into the darkness, letting his eyes adjust from the bright sunlight. "Arrow Springs Police! If you're in there, step into the open with your hands in the air. I will not ask again!"

No response.

Should he call for backup? With the mayor's cuts to the force, he'd have to wait for County to arrive. Dispatch reported a simple break-in. No reason to expect danger—except experience.

Through the crack between the door and its casing, he saw them.

A pair of tennis shoes rested against the door—devoid of an occupant.

He exhaled an overdue breath.

Gun barrel leveled, he willed himself through the doorway. A quick survey of the dining room to his right. Empty. His aim panned to the stairs. One floor at a time. He slid clear of the door and pushed it closed.

His pulse surged through his ears, roaring against the silence in the home.

After a final scan of the dining room, he moved across the hardwood and into the living room. Elegant end tables lay toppled with beveled glass crushing plush beige carpet. Magazines and DVDs littered the floor. A forty-two inch flat screen television remained securely fastened to the wall. Dents in the carpet gave evidence to the relocation of much of the furniture.

The kitchen revealed a similar story. White dishes smashed on the floor, oak cupboard doors flung open, even a cherry silverware case lay shattered at his feet. Forks, spoons, and knives formed an expensive game of pick-up-sticks on the countertop.

He approached a closed door at the far end of the kitchen. His legs began to shake, as he reached for the handle. The cold brass electrified his senses. He fought back the memories, now a dozen years old.

He pushed the door open.

The smell of iron assaulted his nose. Blood splatter covered the sink and a man's body lay sprawled across a throw rug—his brother's body.

He closed his eyes and pushed the bile back from his throat.

A quick breath for composure and he forced his eyes open. An immaculate bathroom, complete with brass trimmed faucets and the fragrance of apple-cinnamon, replaced the scene from his distant past.

His feet released him from the floor as cold beads of sweat trickled from his forehead. Fingers molded to his sidearm, he completed the sweep of the main floor and moved to the upstairs bedrooms. The first room appeared to belong to Mike Henderson, the eighteen year old who reported the break-in.

Clothes, papers, and a five-by-seven photo littered the floor of Mike's room.

The remaining rooms appeared untouched.

Back on the front porch, Chris motioned to Mike. The six-foot-one high school senior strode toward the house. His tussled brown hair showed the stressed signs of waiting through the half-hour search. Mike seemed like a good kid. They'd gotten to know each other the previous summer on a youth retreat.

"Officer Davis, what'd you find? Was it really a break-in?" Mike joined him on the porch.

"Afraid so. Ya did the right thing. Someone could've been there waitin' for you."

Mike's gaze fell to the porch.

"Hey, don't worry about it. I know this can be rough. Your home's been violated. It's okay to be scared." Chris slapped the boy on the shoulder. "Fear can be healthy. It's what keeps me alive."

Mike's lips quivered as he looked up. "Did they take—everything?"

"No," said Chris. "It seems they were lookin' for something specific. You up to looking through the house with me?" He could wait for the boy's parents, but if Mike agreed, he might learn more one-on-one.

Mike lifted his shoulders and cranked his neck, first left then right. "Let's do it."

Chris smiled and led Mike into the house. "It looks like the search ended with your room. Let's start there and you can tell me if anything is missing."

"Okay..."

Mike paused with each stair step, as if dreading what he might find at the top. He rounded the corner and looked into his room. "Oh man!" Mike threw his hand to his forehead.

"Look at this! Mom's gonna freak. She hates it when my room's a mess."

"I'm guessin' she'll go easy on you."

For the first time since they had entered the house a slight grin crept onto Mike's face. "Yeah, but if she gets ahold of whoever did this . . ." The grin disappeared. He began tossing more clothes and papers onto the floor.

"What is it?" Chris leaned forward watching the search. "Is something missing?"

Mike dropped to the floor and swept his hands through the debris. He scanned under the bed. "My camera. I don't see my camera." He threw his hand in the air. "I've only had it for a week."

Chris crossed his arms and studied Mike's expression. "Would there be a reason someone would want to steal your camera?"

Mike looked up. "Um—" His eyes blinked several times as he pondered the question. "I don't think so."

Chris leaned against the doorpost. "Did you have pictures on it?"

"Yeah, I guess so."

"Pictures of whom?"

Mike fidgeted with a battery he'd picked up from the floor. "A couple of friends at school and . . . my girlfriend, Stacy."

"Is anything else missing?"

"I don't think so."

"Alright, let's go check out the kitchen and living room."

Downstairs, Mike assured him nothing seemed to be missing from the kitchen.

They walked into the living room and Mike began to examine the room.

The intruder had stopped the search in the bedroom. The other rooms upstairs were untouched. Finding something missing downstairs seemed highly unlikely. Whatever they had been after they found in Mike's room.

Mike walked to an end table and knelt down. "What?" He reached for something. "How did this get down here?" He stood up, holding the unstolen camera.

"So we haven't found anything missing?" asked Chris. The teenager wasn't telling him something.

"Not that I—"

"Shh!" Chris held a finger to his mouth and drew his gun.

Footsteps. One, maybe two people.

A woman stepped into the doorway and shrieked.

"Mom!"

Sharon Henderson's mascara-smeared eyes locked on the gun.

Chris holstered the weapon. "Sorry 'bout that."

Ron Henderson joined his wife. "Chris. I'd hoped they'd send you."

Sharon looked caught between tears and screams. "What on God's green earth is going on here?" She scanned the mess. "Who did this? When I got your call—I was scared to death."

"We don't know yet," said Chris.

She turned to Mike. "Did you lock the door when you left? How many times—"

Ron pulled her close. "Hon, the door was busted. It's going to be okay. Just relax."

"I'm sorry." She put her hands over her face. "I just don't understand. Why?"

"Don't worry Sharon," said Chris. "We'll find out who did this."

"Did they take anything?" she asked.

"Just my camera," said Mike.

Sharon stared at the camera in her son's hand. "What's that?"

"When we checked his room, his camera was the only thing missing," said Chris. "We found it down here."

She shook her head in the way only a mother could. "He leaves that thing sitting all over the house."

"Mom, no! I know it was in my room."

She put her hands on her hips. "So, some mystery robber grabbed your camera and ditched it in the living room? Come on."

Mike's lips tightened, but he said nothing more.

Chris could feel the boy's frustration. "Perhaps it was just some kids. A simple case of vandalism." He walked to the couple. "The CSTs will be here in a few minutes to dust for prints and take your statements. If you need anything, just give me a call." He patted Ron on the back and tilted his head toward the door. "Can we?"

Ron followed him onto the porch. "Chris, thank you for all you've done here. This is all just a little weird. Is all this typical for you, or just a bad day?"

Chris shrugged. "Long as the Lord brings me out alive—it's a good day." He glanced to see if anyone followed them out the door. "Ron, I don't think this was vandalism. They were lookin' for something specific and they stopped searching in Mike's room."

Ron's eyebrows furled. "I'm not sure I understand."

"I don't either. Perhaps the techs will find something to tell us who did this." Chris checked once more to ensure they were alone. "Whatever they were lookin' for, they found it in Mike's room."

~~~~~~~~~~

Chris headed east on River Drive for one last patrol loop. The northern section of Arrow Springs sat nestled between the Lamine River and the Union Pacific railroad. The river flowed south along the western edge of town, turned east to separate the north and south parts of town, and then flowed back north toward the Missouri River. In the past few weeks, the oak and maple skeletons separating the road from the river had blossomed with fresh green growth.

The sun sat low in the amber sky. His polarized shades accentuated the brilliance of the encroaching clouds. Having skipped lunch, he decided to make for the new McDonalds on the south side and minutes later he parked next to another cruiser—Daryl's.

His mouth watered as a deep-fried aroma lured him into the building. He nodded at Daryl, who sat with his back to a burnt-orange wall waving a French fry.

With a Big Mac, fries, and diet Coke in hand, he joined Daryl. "Uneventful day?"

"Mostly." Daryl sipped at his soft drink. "Got a drunk-and-disorderly this evening."

"River's Edge?"

"Yep. Where else but Arrow Spring's finest?"

"Joe again?"

"Nope. A woman actually." A grin crept onto Daryl's face. "She was soliciting a little action from Mayor Richards."

Chris returned Daryl's smile and wiped a drip of ketchup from the black stubble on his chin. "Not from around here, I take it."

"Nope. License said she was from Kansas City. She didn't wanna tell me much. Said it was none of my business."

"Yeah. Did you offer her a place to think about *her* business?"

"Sure did."

Chris ate a couple fries and unwrapped his burger. The two all-beef patties staring at him from their special sauce were going to require some extra jogging the next morning.

"How 'bout you?" asked Daryl as he picked up another fry. "Anything of interest over on Oak?"

"Not really sure." He went on to tell Daryl about the break-in at the Henderson's and how he believed the search ended in their son's room.

"Drugs?"

"That's my thought." Chris paused as a young mother walked by with a toddler and entered the ladies' room. "Mike seems like such a nice kid though."

"Don't they all?"

"I suppose."

13

Daryl drew in a deep sigh and eased it out. "Have you ever wondered why you do this?"

Chris looked up from his burger. "Hmm?"

Daryl tugged at the shield on his chest. "This job. Arresting hookers, suspecting teenagers, protecting loyal citizens like Mayor Richards at the local bar—"

Chris shut his eyes and nodded. "I hear ya. Yeah, I have my days. I just keep tellin' myself I can make a difference."

"I used to tell myself that too." Daryl tossed a wadded napkin on his tray. "I wonder."

"Daryl, we do make a difference. Trust me. Even if Mike did have drugs in his room, if I can catch the thief and bring the issue to light, then maybe—" His voice caught.

Daryl's voice was soft. "He won't end up like your brother?"

Chris nodded.

~~~~~~~~~~

CHAPTER TWO

Sarah McIntyre pushed a cart stacked with research materials past the front counter of the Arrow Springs Library. Another Friday evening and she spent it helping students with their homework. She glanced at the clock above the entrance and back to Abigail, the one remaining fourth grader.

At seven-thirty, a soft chime from the counter announced the arrival of Abigail's mom.

"I'm so sorry." The woman glanced around the library. "She's the last one here?"

"It's no problem. I love helping the children."

"But the door says you closed two hours ago."

"Honest, it's okay. The others just left. I told them I'd keep the library open. Besides, Abigail's a sweetheart. She reminds me of myself when I was her age. I loved to read, especially the mysteries." Sarah held up a couple books from Abigail's stack. "Looks like she picked up a couple for fun reading as well as her research materials."

"Oh, there's a surprise." The woman placed her hand on Abigail's shoulder. "Come on Abby, we gotta go."

"Bye Abby. Enjoy that mystery."

The girl cast Sarah a contented grin. "Bye. Thank ya for helping me."

"It was my pleasure."

Abigail headed toward the door with her stack of books. Her mom paused and turned to Sarah. "Thank you Sarah.

God bless." She turned back and they vanished into the night.

Sarah walked across the empty lobby to another cart of books. She wheeled the cart to the reference section where the dusty smell of old books greeted her.

At eight o'clock she brushed book dust from her blue oxford blouse, slipped off her flats and replaced them with her jogging shoes, locked the front entrance, and strolled down the sidewalk. As she walked to the corner of Sixth and Birch, the last glimmer of sunset slipped beneath the western horizon. Ahead, a breeze ripped last year's most persistent leaves from a tree and hurled them across the road. She turned onto Sixth and glared at the still lightless street lamps.

To her left, a low growl resonated from somewhere in the dark shadows. She spun to face the yard, her blouse scratching against hyper-sensitized skin. A dark shadow shot across the grass and leaped toward her. A throaty guttural bark announced the creature's intentions.

Her knees buckled.

With her right hand, she broke her momentum toward the concrete. Her left hand flew in front of her face in a feeble attempt to stop the encroaching fangs.

The Rottweiler pulled up just before it reached the sidewalk.

"Bruce!" A deep voice came from somewhere on the home's porch. "Get in here!" The front door opened, unleashing a sliver of light onto the yard. "I hope he didn't frighten you." The beast disappeared into the home.

Sarah straightened her shaking spine and snatched her purse. "Just a little."

"His bark's worse than his bite," said the silhouette on the porch.

"I'll take your word for it."

Sarah's muscles ached as she journeyed down the sidewalk. She could almost hear her mother scolding her for walking alone at night. "There are bad people out there

Sarah," she'd say. But Sarah knew all too well. And now, she was always alone.

Overhead, a bird of prey screeched. She turned and headed west on Ash. The moist west wind chilled her face as red shoulder-length curls flapped in her eyes. With lips pursed and eyes squinting, she trudged homeward. Sarah rounded the corner onto Second and pushed south. Not much further.

A single shadowed figure roamed toward her.

Something inside her stirred.

A voice saying—no—yelling, "*Warning*! Run *now*."

Only twenty feet from the sidewalk to her small redbrick home, she found herself in a sprint across the grass, leaping the stairs to her front door. She pulled the keys from her purse. The key ring caught.

No!

She clung to the house key as her purse tipped and dumped her leather wallet to the front porch.

Time slowed.

Heavy footsteps pounded the sidewalk. Closer. Louder.

With one swift motion, she lunged for the door, unlocked it, and hurled herself through. She spun to slam the door. As the door latched shut, she registered a glimpse of the man who ascended the stairs. She slid the deadbolt securely into its locked position, and then resumed breathing. Something strange in those eyes, a hollow black veil, triggered fear she had not experienced for many years.

As fists pounded on the door, her slender tension-filled frame slid down the wall to the cold slate floor. Her mind raced with memories of that dreadful day. She'd spent the last ten years pushing memories of that single event further and further into the cold colorless corners of her mind. Within a few terrifying moments, the memories flooded back like the Lamine River on a rainy spring day.

~~~~~~~~~~

Chris wiped a renegade piece of lettuce from his deep-brown cheek. "I suppose it's time for me to run."

Daryl didn't look ready to leave just yet. "You headed back to the station?"

"Probably for a few minutes." Chris wadded the napkin and a few limp french-fries in his recycled-paper place mat. "You there 'til Joe comes in?"

"'Fraid so."

Chris stood and tossed the wad at the wastebasket. It bounced off the rim and onto the floor.

"Ouch." Daryl chuckled. "I see why you were an All-American wide receiver, and not a quarterback."

"Funny." The greasy smell of fries, so enticing when Chris entered the restaurant, encouraged him to be on his way. "See ya later."

Chris opened the glass door to the parking lot and held it for an elderly couple. In his cruiser, the radio jumped to life. "Hey Chris, you there?" It was Sally from dispatch. Her raspy voice bore evidence of too many years of smoking before she finally said enough was enough, and quit for good.

"Go ahead Sally."

"We just got a call from Mrs. Ferguson on the corner of Second and Maple. Said she saw a man chase her neighbor up the sidewalk and onto the young lady's porch. The perp was climbing the stairs when the woman slammed the door in his face." Chris sensed a chuckle in Sally's voice. "Mrs. Ferguson says, the man is still there pounding on the front door. The address is two-thirty-nine Second Street. Can you check it out?"

"On my way."

He sent up a quick prayer. "Lord, keep this nut outta her house 'til I get there."

With familiar blue and reds strobing steel girders, Chris' cruiser shot across the Lamine Bridge. The stoplight at the intersection with Oak flashed to red. Despite the strobes and siren he stepped on the brake to avoid risking an accident. He turned right onto Oak taking advantage of the slower speed, then left onto Second.

"Chris," Sally's voice crackled from the radio, "Daryl is a couple minutes from your location."

"Thanks Sal."

Still no sign of the man fleeing from the approaching siren. As Chris approached the intersection with Maple, he saw the suspect turn from the door and step to the stairs. Oblivious to the approaching squad car, apparently he'd given up on the idea of his prey inviting him into the house.

~~~~~~~~~~

"God, I hate you!" Sarah's chest heaved. "Where were You? If You're so all-loving and precious and merciful, then why didn't I deserve Your mercy?" She slammed her elbow back into the drywall and then buried her head in her hands.

She sat on the floor drenched in the tears of her painful reflections. How long had she been there? The pounding on the door had stopped, but the pounding of her heart continued.

With all the strength in her trembling limbs, she lifted herself from the floor and approached the door. Her right hand reached instinctively for the dead bolt as she leaned to look through the peephole. She had no intention of unlocking the door, but the motion left her totally vulnerable.

Pain. Intense pain flooded her senses.

The door burst in on her sending wood splintering from the deadbolt latch. She crashed back to the slate, as the intruder came smashing to the floor next to her. She brought her knees to her chest, rolled toward the wall, and let a scream reverberate through the open doorway.

~~~~~~~~~~

From his vantage point, as he threw the squad car into park, Chris saw the large Caucasian man hurl his body at the front door. Chris jumped from the car, sprinted across the lawn, and took all three steps in a single stride. He let his momentum propel himself into the torso of the man who was staggering back to his feet. The man lay face down next to the terrified young woman of the home.

Chris jabbed his knee into the man's back and wrested the intruder's right arm. With his left hand Chris pulled out his handcuffs and securely fastened one to the wrist. He reached for the other arm.

The man grunted and twisted tossing Chris from his back.

Chris let a cuss word slip and jumped back on the man. This time his knee went to the back of the neck. He yanked the other wrist behind the man and latched the other cuff.

Cuffs secure, Chris wrenched the man to his feet and shoved him out the front door.

Daryl approached the steps. "Everything under control?"

"Yeah." Chris shoved the man toward Daryl. "You wanna take him in? I got here in time to see him busting through the door." He put his hands on his hips and took a deep breath. "You got your digital recorder?"

"Sure do. Do you want me to Mirandize him?"

"No," said Chris. "Just don't question him. I'll take care of that in the morning. Let him talk. See what we get. I'd like to know why he did this."

"Will do." Daryl grabbed the man's arm. "Come on."

Chris headed back to the front door to check on the victim. "Ma'am, are you okay?"

His stomach tightened as he looked at the defenseless young woman curled up in the fetal position. She'd taken a nasty blow to the head and would probably need stitches. Blood from the wound matted into her auburn bangs. Her right hand hung limp at her side. Swelling already pushed a pink and white yarn bracelet deep into her skin.

"I'm Sergeant Chris Davis, Miss. Looks like we'd best call paramedics 'n get you looked at."

A subtle nod of her head caused her eyes to wince. When she tried to stand, he eased to her left offering his hand.

At first she pulled away, but apparent light-headedness caused her to take it.

He helped her to her feet.

She took one step and toppled into him. "Ow!"

"Let me help." He placed his arm around her waist to take the pressure off her left leg. Her muscles tightened at his touch. "Is there somewhere we can get you off that 'til paramedics get here?"

She nodded with a glance to an archway down the short hall and to the right.

Chris helped her limp to a floral sofa in the living room and called paramedics on his two-way. He glanced around the room. A recliner matching the sofa sat in the corner. The décor was simple yet elegant. Two large plants thrived on either side of a small television. Several books sat on a contemporary end table. Though he couldn't see any flowers, a floral fragrance wafted through the room.

The woman settled onto the sofa and Chris slid a burgundy throw pillow between her left leg and the coffee table. Her right hand lay nestled by her side.

He pulled a Leatherman from a pouch on his belt and pointed to the yarn bracelet digging deeper into her arm. "I'm afraid we'll need to cut that off Miss."

She closed her eyes and nodded.

Chris pressed his finger between her skin and the bracelet and then slid the knife up under it. He handed the bracelet to her.

She clasped it tight in her left hand. "It was a gift from Sophie."

Though necessary, He felt as though he'd just severed the sacred symbol of a friendship.

"The name's Sarah," she whispered. "Sarah McIntyre."

"Sit tight Sarah. The ambulance's gonna be here soon—you'll be fine."

Before the ambulance arrived Chris retrieved a hand towel and ice from the kitchen. He put pressure on the gash in her forehead, which refused to stop bleeding.

Two EMTs entered the living room with a gurney. "We'll take it from here."

Chris watched as they asked Sarah a few questions before lifting her onto the gurney and rolling her out of the house.

He pulled the front door to its broken frame and placed yellow police tape across the entrance.

Turning to descend the steps, he noticed a pocketbook and driver's license on the porch. He picked them up and ran to the ambulance. "Thought she might need these at the hospital."

"Thanks," said one of the EMTs.

The ambulance pulled away.

Chris made his way to the open door of his cruiser and flopped into his seat. He sighed and ran his finger between his neck and shirt collar. Such a sweet young woman. What did that creep want with her? Perhaps he'd slip and say something to Daryl. Either way, he'd be spending some time in jail.

~~~~~~~~~~

CHAPTER THREE

Mael knelt on the polished teak floor of the office of Maiya Mirinova. In the center of the large office, a ring of candles flickered as the sole source of light. The gothic ambiance of the room rivaled that of his dungeon at the base of the building.

"Casimir. Can you hear me?" Dr. Maiya Mirinova sat with her legs crossed on the floor in front of Mael. "Have I offended you? Why do you hide yourself from me?"

Mael eyed the woman. It had been three weeks since he last chose to reveal himself to her. He would need her obedience over the coming weeks. The time had come to move forward.

He breathed into her face.

Her nostrils flared and she raised her face in his direction. "My love? My lord Casimir, is it you? Have you come to me at last?"

Mael reached a black withered hand to her cheek. With the back of his talon-like fingers he stroked her albino-white skin.

She clutched a golden ankh resting against her black robe and breathed deeply.

She could sense his presence. Good. He marveled at how easily she submitted her senses to his control. At one time, when he first came to her during a séance in college, he had barely gotten her to hear him. Her essence, her very soul, had at that time been too hot for him to hold. Now she had given herself to him. As he caressed her being, he absorbed just a trickle of heat into his cold black hands.

"I am here," said Mael.

At his voice her hazel eyes opened in a near trance. "You've come."

"I have." He often considered revealing his true form, but he knew the illusion of the dashing Sir Casimir would garner her allegiance. "Why have you called for me?"

"I was afraid. Afraid my lord was displeased with me."

Mael drew back inhaling the worship and fear of the creature sitting before him. "Have I given you reason to distrust me?"

"No my lord." Her voice begged for his acceptance. "I love you."

"Have I not fulfilled my promises to you? When you struggled with your biology and ethics courses, did I not give you my wisdom?"

"Oh yes, and I am eternally grateful."

Mael knelt in front of her. "Indeed, and did I not bring you back here to your father, before his dreadful stroke? In time to ensure you took your rightful place at the head of his empire?"

Tears trickled from her eyes. "You have been merciful to me."

He leaned forward and licked at the tears with his bull-like tongue. "And I have promised you that you shall be a queen. Our plan is falling into place. Soon this land will be mine. I will be king. And you shall be my queen. I told you it shall happen." He reached his hand to her forehead and stroked a white strip of bangs amid her midnight black hair. "I gave you this as a sign of my promise."

"Yes my lord. I am yours."

He moved forward enveloping her in his massive form.

He could feel her muscles tighten in expectation.

He slowly descended through the floor, leaving her alone in the room.

"No! Please do not leave me!"

He could hear her pleas through the floor as he floated away.

"My lord—"

Mael was invigorated. He could still feel her fearful worship despite leaving her to wallow once again in his absence. When he needed her to act on his behalf she would be ready.

He descended into his dungeon at the base of the building. A black figure with a boar-like head awaited his presence.

"Legion! How are you?" Mael puffed out his chest. Such a pathetic creature, barely larger than a human.

"My liege. You know I no longer go by that name." Leon snorted and took a step backward.

"Oh yes, it is Leon now." Mael chuckled. His mood was too high to let a little backtalk spoil his evening. "I should remember when I gaze upon your ugly face. What happened to you Leon? You were a powerful demon. Yet you chose to cower before *Him*. A mere human."

"He was no mere human and you know it."

"You cowered and He cast you into a heard of pigs."

"You would have done no more."

"I did more!" Mael's voice thundered off the concrete. "I had him killed."

Leon crossed his arms. "And a lot of good it did. He did not exactly stay dead now did He?"

"Perhaps I could not defeat Him then, but the day is coming. You could at least have stood up to Him. But perhaps you prefer looking like—that." Mael spat sulfurous saliva onto a pile of bones beside him.

"I played my part," said Leon. "Without us, you would never have gotten Him crucified. Your control of the priests could only accomplish so much. You needed us controlling the masses. We got that crowd, who one week cried Hosanna, to demand his crucifixion." Leon wagged his head back and forth in defiance. "I am the best at controlling humans—that is why Lucifer chose me for this assignment."

Mael kicked a skull across the room and it cracked against the concrete wall. "Enough of this! You are earlier than I expected."

"So."

Mael wanted to put Leon on a spit and roast him like the pig he had become. "You were instructed to lay low in town until sunset before returning to the house."

"We walked fast."

Mael head-butted the concrete ceiling with his Cape-buffalo-like horns. "So you found it?"

"It was there, as I said."

Mael began to relax.

"We left the home in disarray to prevent any awareness of our intentions." Leon toyed with a small backbone with his foot. "We discarded it on the way out of th—"

"You what?!"

Leon jumped to the next level of the building. But, Mael grabbed his leg and yanked him to the floor of the dungeon. "Are you that addled?"

"I, we, ah, removed the contents."

Mael eyed Leon, but said nothing.

"I was fearful, if we were seen with it, someone might grow suspicious."

Mael closed his eyes and took a deep breath. "Are you certain no one saw you?"

"Of course no one saw me."

Mael ground his teeth together. "I know they did not see you, you idiot. Did they see him?"

"Oh, no, no one saw us. The entire family was away to school or work. I surveyed the area. They shall not link him to the break-in."

~~~~~~~~~~

Daryl escorted the perp into the police station on the south end of town. The front desk sat vacant as usual after business hours. He grabbed the man's elbow and pulled him toward the first of five desks in the main area. The chain on the cuffs rattled as the man contended with Daryl's grip.

Daryl pointed to a chair next to the desk that he, Chris, and the part-timers, used for booking suspects. "Have a seat."

The man grunted and started walking toward a woman seated at the third desk over.

"I said, sit down!" Daryl spun the man around and forced the chair into the back of his knees causing him to buckle into it.

At the commotion, Laura turned from her paperwork. "It's about time you got back. I got a hot date tonight and thanks to the make-up queen you've got in cell number one, I couldn't get out of here to turn myself back into a woman."

"What? You're a woman?" Daryl feigned a look of shock, but her form fitting navy-blue uniform made it abundantly clear.

"Very funny." She put her hands on her hips and cocked them to her left. "A woman that could kick your— Um," she raised her hand and pointed, "your friend there seems to have somewhere to be."

Daryl spun around to see the man walking toward the front door. "Hey! Get your ugly hide back here."

The man ignored him and kept walking.

Daryl jogged after him. The man didn't run, but he didn't stop either.

"Wonderful." Daryl caught the man by the arm and yanked him backward. "I told you to sit down!" Once again they walked to the desk and Daryl forced the man back into the seat.

"I really would like to split," said Laura. "You gonna be alright with him? Sean's out on patrol."

"I'm fine. I'll just get him checked in, and let him smarten up over night." Daryl raised his eyebrows and one corner of his mouth.

"Okay. Later."

Daryl turned back to the man. He pulled the digital recorder from his pocket and set it on the desk. "Alright bud, what's your name?"

The man just stared at him.

"Look. Let's just get this over with can we? Your name?"

The man tilted his head to the side and stared Daryl in the eyes.

Great. "Um, comprenda el ingles? Hmm, begreifen Sie Englisch? No? Sorry high school Spanish and German is all I got." Still no response. "Okay, well let's get some prints and we'll show you to your night's accommodations."

As Daryl reached for the man's shoulder, the perp thrust his head forward and attempted to bite Daryl's hand.

"Alright, now you're just tickin' me off." The muscles in Daryl's neck began to tighten. "Fine! If you don't wanna cooperate maybe you'll enjoy your cell." He clicked the button to stop the recording. *No need to waste electrons.*

He pulled the man to his feet and escorted him to the cellblock entrance at the far end of the office area. The station contained only two jail cells. Most of the time two cells were two more than they needed. This night they would both be occupied.

Daryl unlocked the steel cellblock door and pushed the man through the doorway. The smell of too much cheap perfume greeted them. "Looks like you're gonna have someone to talk to tonight," he called out to the woman in cell one. He opened cell two and gave a push. The man sank to the concrete floor and sat staring at the cinderblock wall.

"I don't want ta talk," said the woman who went by the call-name Candy. "Why don't you toss him in here so we can at least have some fun—talk's cheap." She crossed her legs showing off her oh-so-short leather skirt.

Daryl forced his gaze up to her eyes. "But isn't that what you claimed you wanted from our honorable mayor. 'Just wanted to talk,' you said. How come that talk was going to be so expensive?" Daryl chuckled at his own witty retort.

Silence.

He looked up to see why she hadn't offered some smart or not-so-smart response.

The woman sat on the edge of her cot weeping, as if her obstinance had just slithered away.

~~~~~~~~~~

Alex sat at the foot of Sarah's hospital bed. His large white wings formed a canopy over the sleeping woman. A tear trickled down his cheek falling to the pale blue sheet that covered her. So much pain. More than any human should have to endure. He pictured her as the red-curly-haired six-year-old who bore a wide grin which distorted her peppering of equally red freckles.

When he first met Sarah, she sat on the family's couch in the arms of her mother and father. She had made a commitment to accept Jesus as the Lord of her life. She bounced with excitement in their arms. An intense light burned in the center of her being. He was assigned to her. He was her guardian. For ten years he grew to adore the burgeoning teenager on fire for God. Then it happened. In a single day, her innocent youth shattered like crystal on concrete.

No longer white hot, the light in her heart now flickered the faintest amber. He despised the pain and the enemy who caused it.

Next to the bed digital displays and blinking lights indicated all was well with Sarah. But there were no displays, no graphs, no x-rays capable of showing the critical level of her soul.

Alex lifted his eyes to Huw, his long-time friend from Wales. "Do you think she remembered?"

Huw's wings stretched over Sarah. "Ah yes, she remembered." His accent bore a heavy Welsh influence. "After all these years blamin' God for what happened to her family, I just hope she can begin to trust once again."

Alex nodded his head. "It is hard to see."

"To see what my friend?"

"Why He permitted it. How it should fit into His perfect will."

Huw closed his eyes. "We can only trust Him. We have cast our eyes on His perfect love in many uncertain times."

"Yes, yet she must trust without the advantage of seeing." Alex drew a deep breath. "You have a great task before you, my brother. She has amassed ten years of bitterness and anger."

"And fear," added Huw. "Only if she is willin' to lay her anger and fear before God will she ever find true freedom from the oppression which plagues her."

Movement at the doorway caught Alex' attention.

A deformed black face emerged through the closed door followed by black talons.

Alex withdrew his wings, spun to the floor, and rose to face the intruder. "You shall be on your way. You are unwelcome here. Take your mischief elsewhere or discover your residence in the Abyss." The muscles in Alex' left arm rippled as he pulled his flaming red sword from its sheath.

The demon's green cat-like eyes popped large and round before disappearing back into the hallway.

"Such a pity," said Huw.

"That he did not remain to be put to waste?"

"On the contrary. Such a pitiful existence. To have once known the love of God as an angel of light. And now he roams in darkness and despair."

"So I would have shown him favor through his demise."

Huw grinned and shook his head. "Warriors. You are all the same."

"Are we now?"

Huw chuckled with satisfaction. "All in jest my friend. You are a worthy protector. As you demonstrated tonight. I fear for what might have become of her had that man entered her home before it was time."

"Just giving you opportunity to perform your duty." Alex looked directly into Huw's eyes. "Did you see the demon with him? The one who left only moments before the attack?"

"Indeed I did, but who was he now? Not the demon I mean, but the man."

"That I do not know," said Alex. "But I suspect we shall."

"The enemy in this burg is up to somethin'," said Huw. "I wonder—what are we up against?"

"All in due time my friend. We will know when *He* wants us to know."

~~~~~~~~~~

In the subterranean level of the facility, Mael reviewed the plans with Leon. The infiltration progressed without flaw. His long awaited revenge on the *favored creations* drew nigh.

A black snake-like creature bolted into the room.

Instinctively, Mael grabbed the invader by the neck and sent it sprawling. The creature landed in a heap in the corner of the rough poured concrete.

A wry smile crept onto Leon's face.

"Lech! How dare you enter my presence uninvited?" Mael lifted his right wing and reached for his electric-blue sword. "You miserable worm. Have you forgotten your place? No one enters my lair uninvited."

"Forgivvve meee." Lech was a small yet formidable demon of lust and desire. "But I brrring you newwws of signiffficant immporrrtancce."

"Do not hiss at me you insolent excuse for— What news?"

"I come from the police station in Arrow Springs."

Mael's nostrils flared. "I have no concern of your ability to get your whore thrown in jail."

"Nooo buuutttt— Sorry, my liege." He started again. "I believed you would find interest that while I was there, they brought in a familiar individual—one who comes from this facility."

Leon began to edge toward the opposite wall.

"Lech, what are you babbling on about?" asked Mael. "Who is at the jail?"

"It is really none of my business, but I recall a certain demon of manipulation accompanying this particular individual just tonight at the River's Edge." The wry smirk now belonged to Lech's twisted black face.

"Do not toy with me!" Mael tired quickly with the games of the lesser demons.

"Perhaps you should inquire of Leon about the individual," said Lech.

The realization crashed upon Mael. "Leon, you have ten ticks of time to explain how your charge ended up in the local jail, beginning five ticks ago."

"I—I—I left him just two blocks from the house. He should have traveled straight home. I do not understand." Leon scowled at Lech. "Why did they arrest him?"

The snakelike creature just shrugged.

"You know the rules," said Mael. "Do you think this is a game? You may have compromised the entire project. If they discover his origin the enemy shall descend on this place. I should have known I could never trust you Legion."

"No my liege. Please have mercy on your servant."

"That may have worked with *Him*, but I am not so weak as to show mercy to the undeserving. I would suppose you would have me send you to wallow with the pigs once again?"

To his credit, Leon said nothing.

Mael closed his eyes. After a breath and a deep swallow, he reopened them. He controlled his voice. "Leon. If you were so harried to report to me on your mission, could you not have assigned one of your minions to take your place for a short while? Perhaps your second in command. What is his name?" Mael's throat tightened in expectation.

"Tudur?"

"Yes, Tudur." Mael sprang on Leon. A giant blue arc split him in two. In a sulfuric cloud he vanished to the Abyss to await the time of judgment.

"Bring me Tudur!" Mael commanded Lech.

In an instant, the snake darted on his way to find Tudur.

Mael paced in the black stillness. "What now?" he thought aloud. "Lucifer cannot hear of this debacle. It must be dealt with." He knelt and picked up a tiny human skull. He stared at it until a thought occurred. "Of course. Mors. This would be a perfect job for him." He crushed the skull in his palm and laughed as the powder seeped from his fingers.

~~~~~~~~~~

Lech ascended from deep beneath the building. Level after level passed before his eyes. Satisfaction surged through his being. He could feel his form grow with the betrayal of his fellow demon. Darkness surged through him. In just moments, he passed from the top floor and through the roof.

He paused.

Something had caught his attention. He slowly lowered himself back into the facility. In the middle of a large office lay a slender woman in the midst of a circle of candles. She lay face down on the hardwood. Her body shook as she wept.

So pathetic these creatures. So weak.

He longed to stay. Green drool seeped from the corners of his mouth. A forked tongue swiped his lips. He could not stay. Mael would be furious if he delayed his mission.

Lech's wings flapped slowly and he rose toward the ceiling.

The woman's face turned in his direction. The glow of the candles danced in the tears on her cheeks. He willed himself through the ceiling and into the night air.

The building grew smaller and smaller as the river bend which surrounded it came into view. Under the moonless midnight sky the river appeared as a black rat snake curled around the facility to the west and around the northern section of Arrow Springs to the east.

The cool night air invigorated him. He breathed deeply almost absorbing its steely blackness. Hundreds of feet below, only the convenience-store-gas-station on First Street and the River's Edge Bar illuminated the landscape. He had met Tudur earlier in the evening at the River's Edge. Tudur had treated him none too kindly. A low hiss passed from Lech's nostrils as he turned to the south.

He could see his destination—an intimidating figure perched like a humungous fruit bat atop Mayor Richards' elegant traditional two-story home at the end of the cul-de-sac. Lech dove toward the house like an osprey, pulling up just in time to alight next to Tudur.

"What do you want Lech?"

"Pleasure to see you again, Tudur." Lech wrapped his tail around his legs.

Tudur stared at Lech's torso. "You seem different."

"You mean the scales?" Lech lifted his left wing. "Nice addition, would you not say?"

"It makes you less . . . slimy. At least your appearance."

"Yes. Well it has been a beneficial night."

"Really? Just what have you been up to since you insisted on drawing such undue attention to the mayor tonight?"

"It is of no importance," Lech replied with confidence. "I have come from a meeting with Mael, and he demands to see you—now."

"Why would *you* be meeting with Mael?" Tudur snorted. "You are just a measly run-of-the-mill troublemaker."

"Perhaps." Hateful words would not spoil the exhilaration of the night.

"I thought Mael met with Leon tonight," said Tudur.

"I suggest you stop pestering me, and report to Mael before he takes out his frustration on you."

Without another word Tudur swung down through the roof.

Moments later Tudur emerged from the side of the house and darted into the night.

Lech unfurled his wings and sniffed the night air. He needed to return to the police station. He needed to be with her.

~~~~~~~~~~

Daryl stood with his back against the tan cinderblock wall of the cellblock. He stared through galvanized bars at the man who sat in eerie silence. Talk about mood swings. Chasing women, literally, breaking down doors, getting up to walk out of the station, not run—just walk, attempting to bite an officer, and now sitting on the concrete like he'd lost his best friend. It didn't add up.

Daryl turned to his left and walked toward the steel door leading back to the station. He paused as he walked by cell number one. The middle-aged woman, who'd given him the name Candy, sat sobbing. He couldn't recall a prostitute making a more drastic one-eighty after being arrested. Sure, they'd try to act innocent, but she seemed truly remorseful. No claims of innocence, no pleas for her release, simply repentant sobs. It seemed the sudden realization of her destructive lifestyle washed over her like a tsunami, leaving her drenched in a waterfall of her own tears.

"What's your real name?" Daryl asked softly.

"Cindy."

Her unoriginal "working" name now made sense.

"Where are you from Cindy?"

"Lived in Kansas City. Grew up in Dallas, but moved to Kansas City at 17." She blinked to rid her eyes of their tears. "Getting a little too well known with the police in K.C., so heading to St. Louis to start over."

Daryl leaned against the cold steel bars. "Start over? As in a new life—or just a new location?"

Her shoulders twitched. "Not sure."

"Based on your actions tonight, I'd say you aren't exactly off to a great start. How'd you end up at the River's Edge?"

She sniffed and shrugged slightly. "Don't have a car. So hitched a ride with a guy from this area. Said he was headed to the local bar, so thought maybe, could earn some cash to get back on the way to St. Louis."

Daryl put his hand to his forehead, closed his eyes, and shook his head. "So you decided the mayor would be a good candidate?"

"Didn't know who he was. He came up and sat on the next stool at the bar—he certainly seemed interested."

It kind of made sense. Daryl never liked Arrow Springs' new mayor, and he certainly didn't trust him.

Lightheadedness swept over Daryl. Guilt and despair pierced deep within his brain releasing a stream of regret which flooded his soul. He staggered back to the concrete wall.

This is how you lost Marilyn.

Where had that thought come from? He wasn't flirting with Cindy. He cared for her well-being. Still he couldn't resist the guilt. As with most every day since the divorce, his thoughts returned to his unfaithfulness to Marilyn.

He missed her so. She was his high-school sweetheart. Their marriage reigned as the best thing to ever happen to him. Sure, it wasn't perfect. They'd had their disagreements—she had a fire and he occasionally got burnt. What he wouldn't give to be burnt by her once again.

Then it had happened.

He travelled to Chicago for a few days on police business. The last night of the trip he met *her* in the hotel elevator. He'd never been a ladies' man—so easily drawn in by the batting eyelashes and banter of that young twenty-something.

The image of her perfectly toned figure as she stood in that elevator, only partly concealed in the latest style of clothing, would remain forever burned into his memory. Despite three years of trying to wipe the seductive images from the hard-drive of his brain, she still haunted him.

In the distorted reflection of the elevator doors, he had seen himself as the fit black-haired twenty year old he used to be, rather than a slightly overweight thirty-two year old with a receding hairline and glasses. She started the small talk. Or was it him that started it? It didn't really matter. It quickly shifted from small talk to a seductive banter.

When he entered the elevator the thirty-fifth floor button was lit. But she stepped off the elevator with him on the twenty-third floor. She followed him down the hallway, and to the door of his room.

"Mind if I join you?" she had asked.

No! Why couldn't he have just said no!

It wasn't until the next morning, when he awoke to the door of his room shutting, that he realized the implications of his response. That was the first time he experienced the piercing pain of guilt and despair.

He didn't even know her name.

There was no way Marilyn would forgive him.

He questioned his worth as a husband. He questioned his worth as a police officer. He questioned his worth as a human being.

He had considered running—never returning to Arrow Springs. He felt a shame that redefined him. He was unforgivable.

He'd contained the horrible secret for one week. Somehow Marilyn knew. He didn't know how, but the intimacy they once enjoyed haunted him like a distant memory. Resisting unbearable despair and guilt, he'd confessed the affair to Marilyn. He sought her forgiveness, but his violation of her trust exceeded her ability to forgive. His shame was great and their marriage was dead.

~~~~~~~~~~

Mael paced his underground lair. He swept his wings across a pile of dried bones. It had been nearly a year since new matter had been added to his collection. Perhaps the time had come.

Behind him he heard a throat clear.

"You called, Master Mael?"

"Tudur—I began to think you had ignored my request." He turned to face the bat-like demon. "That perhaps you inherited Legion's foolishness."

Tudur bowed at the waist. "My apologies, my lord. I delayed to ensure my charge slept. I did not want to leave him at risk of discovery."

"Wisdom Legion clearly lacked."

A tremor rippled across Tudur's wings. "What has happened? If I may ask."

"You may." Mael snorted. "I banished him to the Abyss. He failed me for the last time. He left his charge walking down the sidewalk to come and boast to me." Mael took a deep breath. "Now his charge resides in the Arrow Springs jail. Had it not been for Lech's timely presence, we may not have known until he jeopardized our operation."

Tudur nodded apparently pondering the situation. "Surely he will tell them nothing."

"Indeed. As you well know, he cannot—not without his overseer. Still, that is what concerns me." Mael paced to the other side of the room. "I fear his silence and demeanor will raise suspicion. Perhaps even medical scrutiny."

"Would that be a problem? Can they detect it?"

"I do not know. Doctor M'Gregor is good. But we shall not take chances. The human biological system is a complex mechanism. Through the millennia I have learned that when we assume we have all the contingencies covered, *HE* steps in and disrupts everything."

Tudur wrapped himself in his black leathery wings. "What do you desire from me, my lord? I cannot leave Trenton unattended for long."

Mael turned to face Tudur. "I have a mission for you tonight. Are you aware Mors is in Arrow Springs?"

"I have heard."

Mael despised Mors, but he had his place. Mors personified death. Humans often referred to him as the Grim Reaper. His nine-foot-tall human-skeleton-like frame with eternally decomposing flesh was only overshadowed by his black full-length robe and an eight-foot scythe. Still, Mael could not imagine appearing in the form of a weak human even if it did reflect death. He preferred his powerful combination of Cape buffalo and of course the king of all beasts, the lion.

"You want me to convey to Mors that you should like to speak with him?" asked Tudur.

Mael could hear the quiver in Tudur's voice. He placed his foot on a ribcage which sat on the floor. "That will not be necessary." He let his weight crush the bones. "I wish for you to communicate my instructions."

"Why me?"

"Are you not capable?" Mael leaned toward Tudur and let out a growl. "Would you prefer to join Legion?"

Tudur stumbled backward. "What shall I tell him?"

"Inform him of the situation with Legion's charge. Tell him his master Mael wants him to deal with the situation as he does best."

~~~~~~~~~~

Lech descended into the cellblock at the police station. An officer dressed in tidy navy-blues conversed with Lech's charge.

"I saw an opening at the gas station on First. Maybe you'd be better off getting a job here and staying out of the cities."

Lech burned with anger. Joe Friday sought to convince Cindy she did not need him. He descended to the cot next to her. He wrapped his wings tightly around her chest as he dug his talons into the center of her being.

Candy was back.

"I bet you'd like that. Wouldn't you?" Candy turned away from the policeman. "You should be ashamed of yourself, coming on to a prisoner in your own jail. I should press charges." She crossed her arms over her chest as if attempting to protect herself.

The officer's face twisted. "I did no such thing! I just don't want to see you ruin your life."

A small black demon hovered next to the man. "His wife left him because of adultery. Her name was Marilyn."

Perfect. Lech went for the jugular. "Is that what you told Marilyn when you cheated on her?" Candy echoed the words with a glint in her eyes.

The officer's face filled with horror.

Lech watched the demon sink talons into the man's skull.

"You are doing it again," whispered the demon. "You are pathetic."

The man stumbled toward the steel door, his knees barely capable of carrying him through it. The door clanked shut.

Lech could feel Candy flinch at the sound. "Yes sweetie. I am back."

~~~~~~~~~~

CHAPTER FOUR

Saturday, April 18, 2020

Eran watched as Chris awoke at six o'clock to the radio alarm clock on his nightstand. The phrase "all You ever do, is change the old for new" echoed across the bedroom. Though his eyes weren't open, he was clearly awake because his head began to bob to the beat. The song drew to a close.

Chris' eyes opened. He rolled to his left and shut off the radio before the deejay could interrupt the melody he began to hum.

Eran couldn't help but smile. Despite the growing opposition of the enemy in the town, Chris continued to grow in his love and trust of the Almighty. He had accompanied Chris since his days at the academy outside St. Louis when his training officer revealed the most important truth any young policeman, or human being, could ever learn.

Officer Young had told Chris, "True strength only comes through a trusting relationship with Jesus Christ. Men—they'll fail you. Your own strength—someday it will fail you. But God—now He won't fail you." Over the following year, Officer Young taught Chris that there would be times when it would seem God had turned his back on him, or on others he served. Only God could fully comprehend His plans. "That's where the trust side of the relationship comes in," Officer Young would point out.

Eran adored Officer Young.

One of the hardest days of Chris' still brief career as a policeman came one week after he hired into the Arrow Springs department. A call came from a precinct in St. Louis. A drug dealer had shot and killed Officer Young when he responded to a domestic dispute.

He had feared for Chris' faith.

Though truly challenged, Chris proved his relationship with Jesus to be one of trust, as he struggled through understanding why God had allowed such a godly and influential man to be taken from them. Eran learned a great deal about trust from Chris throughout those weeks.

With the dawn of the new day, Chris rose energetic and full of life. He hummed his way to the bathroom and shaved a day's worth of stubble from his rugged chin.

Eran couldn't help but admire the confident stature of the man. He stretched his wings across the bathroom and breathed deeply of a spiritual breeze that flowed through the room. He could feel his dark hair dancing to the unheard melody echoing in Chris' soul. This man had proven to be one of Eran's favorite assignments in a millennium. Sure he was not perfect, but his commitment to daily worship left Eran aglow in the power of the Spirit. Many of his fellow warriors in Arrow Springs were not so blessed. As the power from the presence of the Holy Spirit washed over him, Eran's wings began to swirl with the colors of a rainbow.

Dressed in grey jogging shorts and a blue sleeveless tee, Chris settled into the meager living room couch in his Cape Cod home. He lifted his Bible from the coffee table and began to read. At first he read to himself.

"Aloud," whispered Eran. He loved to hear God's Word and especially the Psalms.

Chris read aloud from Psalm Chapter Three.

"O Lord, I have so many enemies; so many are against me. So many are saying, 'God will never rescue him!' . . . But you, O Lord, are a shield around me; you are my glory, the one who holds my head high. I cried out to the Lord, and he answered me from his holy mountain. . . ."

Chris set down the bible and headed out the front door. He started to jog down the sidewalk. As he ran, Chris began to pray aloud. "Lord, I don't know what You've got in store for me today. Thank You for givin' me breath for yet another day. Help me make a difference for Arrow Springs—for You. Help me make sense of yesterday's break-ins. Give peace to the Henderson's despite the violation of their security. And Lord, I don't know what Mike's got himself into, but protect him."

The sidewalk thumped beneath his feet. Eran grinned as Chris stepped to his left to avoid stamping out a small green shoot of life that struggled to find its existence in a miniscule crack in the concrete.

Chris wiped the corners of his eyes with his palm. His pace quickened. "Please Lord bring healin', both physical and emotional, to Sarah McIntyre. Lord, this is one of those times when I just don't get what's happenin'. That man was strange. Like I was wrestlin' an animal."

A row of maple trees passed by, one after another after another.

Eran hovered effortlessly beside the sprinter. "Daryl," he whispered.

"Oh and Lord, I know Daryl's been strugglin' since Marilyn left him. Please Lord—remind him how much You love him. Give him the strength he'll need to make it through yet another weekend without her."

After forty-five minutes of running and worshipping God, Chris stepped back into the house. His nose rose into the air. The aroma of fresh brewed coffee drew him to the kitchen like a mouse to cheese. He took a quick shower, put on his uniform, and headed to the kitchen where he downed his usual peanut-butter toast and another cup of coffee.

Five minutes later Chris climbed in his squad car and headed to the station with Eran riding shotgun.

~~~~~~~~~~

Sarah awoke from the most peaceful night of sleep she'd experienced in years. After the half hour ambulance ride to Regional Hospital in Columbia, she spent three hours getting x-rays of her wrist and ankle, seven stitches in her forehead, and a cast on her right wrist. She finally settled into her room at one in the morning. Could've been exhaustion or maybe just the medication, but she slept like her grandpa on Thanksgiving afternoon.

Her mind reviewed the events of the prior day like a DVD in fast-forward. First, the chilling walk home, then the voice prompting her to run, followed by the maniac who burst through her door. She paused the review where the handsome black-man dressed in a dark-blue uniform tackled the intruder, removed him from her house, and cared for her until the paramedics arrived. She had trusted him. Why? She knew better. He was a man. But he seemed so kind. He was a police officer. It didn't matter. They all seem kind at first. What did he say his name was? It all happened so fast. She couldn't remember.

She swung her feet off the bed to visit the restroom. Once her ankle dropped below her heart, blood rushed to it, causing her to whimper. The ankle pulsed, her wrist throbbed, and her head pounded as she moved. Perhaps she didn't need to go that bad after all.

Peace washed over her like she was back in the fields of Scotland. She could smell the soft barley fields after the spring rain. It was a vacation she'd always remember. The last they took as a family. She could almost hear a Scottish voice encouraging her to lie back. No need to rush. Just rest.

Her eyes began to mist over as she lay back down.

~~~~~~~~~~

Chris rolled down his window as he drove to the police station. The brisk morning air washed over him. The amber morning sun flooded onto the serviceberry bushes, reflecting brilliant white off their popcorn-like blossoms. His nose tingled as he drew in a deep breath—only a hint of their light flowery aroma. The bushes lined his subdivision, a perfect expression of God's provision. In just a couple months the white beauty would yield to purple berries capable of feeding the local birds and squirrels.

Minutes later, he approached the station. The bright sun set the white concrete trim afire against the fresh red brick walls. He parked the car and walked up the steps leading to the front door, still softly humming and bobbing to an inaudible worship chorus. He walked through the front door. A chill sank deep within his spirit. The sun, which washed the exterior of the building, seemed forbidden entrance despite fully open blinds.

He walked through the main office area. No sign of Joe. In fact all five desks were empty. Light seeped from the office next to his own.

Daryl must have stayed all night.

He found Daryl quavering behind the desk in his office.

"You okay?" asked Chris. "Man, ya look like you went ten rounds with a prize fighter and I don't think ya won."

"It's been a long night." Daryl's cheeks puffed out as he exhaled through the corners of his mouth.

Chris pulled a chair up to the Daryl's desk and sat with his forearms resting on the fake-oak surface. "What're you still doin' here anyway? Where's Joe? Wasn't he supposed to relieve you at four?"

Daryl nodded, his eyes wrought with deep lines and dark circles. "His wife has the flu. He stayed home to take care of his daughter. I told him I'd cover."

"Well, I'm here now. You need to get some rest."

Daryl rubbed his eye with the heal of his hand. "Thanks. I suppose some sleep would help. I've just been doing a lot of thinking that's all."

"About Marilyn?" Chris glanced at the photograph still hanging on Daryl's bulletin board.

"Yeah, you probably think I'm obsessed. After all, it's been three years."

So much guilt and shame. Chris' jaw began to tighten. He'd heard the judgments. Mutual Christian friends condemned the man for his unfaithfulness. So quick to forget their own failures. Perhaps his failures kept him from such free-wielded judgment.

Daryl set his elbows on the desk and rested his forehead in his palms. "My sister thinks I should just get on with my life. I'm better off without her. She thinks Marilyn overreacted—that everyone sleeps around once in awhile."

Chris hesitated until Daryl looked up. "What do you think? Did she—overreact that is?"

"No. She had every right to leave. I only wish there was a way to make it right. I feel so helpless."

"Daryl, have ya asked her to forgive you?"

"I did—she said she couldn't. Frankly, I don't blame her." Daryl diverted his eyes, the familiar confession of guilt. "What I did was unforgivable."

"Nothin' you've done is unforgivable." Chris fought back tears. "Oh, you're right—Marilyn had every right to leave. But you can still be free of your guilt—and your shame. You don't have to live with it the rest of your life."

"If only." Daryl sighed.

"Listen to me—you can." A tear crept from Chris' eye. He wiped at his cheek with his palm. "Tell ya what. Pick ya up on my way to church tomorrow? Might cheer you up."

"Sure, why not? Beats sleeping in." Daryl offered a contorted smile.

~~~~~~~~~~

Eran watched as Daryl began to relax. The demon of guilt and despair that continually plagued the man found reason to be elsewhere when Eran entered the room. Daryl chose of his own will to entertain the pest. But Eran would have liked nothing more than to send the rat permanently packing.

Chris was a good friend. He offered the man an oasis in his personal desert.

"You really do need your sleep. Go on. Get out of—" Chris' eyes grew large and round. His body shook as if he'd just felt a cold February breeze.

Both men sat in silence.

This was no ordinary chill. Eran could feel it. A presence. Not in the office, but not far away. Somewhere in the station.

A woman's scream shredded the thick silence of the station.

Eran followed Chris and Daryl to the holding cells.

The woman in the first cell gripped the bars and stared at the man in the next. "He was shaking and having convulsions. Now he isn't moving!"

Eran froze.

The assailant from the night before lay face down on the concrete floor in a pool of foamy saliva.

Daryl approached the man's cell. "Probably drugs." He grabbed the keys to the cell.

"Don't go in there. It might be a trap." Chris' voice bore a concern Eran's eyes could confirm.

Daryl proceeded unaware.

Eran knew this demon—Mors.

They'd met before, in Auschwitz during the month of January, 1945. Eran and several of the heavenly host engaged Mors in a fierce battle. The battle raged for three weeks, leaving Eran and his angelic soldiers severely wounded.

They accomplished their mission. They detained Mors long enough for Soviet soldiers to liberate the concentration camp. It was Mors' most horrific effort in history. Mors had finally retreated and the battle torn angels were content to let him go. After the battle, Eran spent a year in the presence of his Creator before healing enough to return to the Lord's service among men.

Now once again they stood within twenty feet of one another.

"Just fly away," challenged Mors. "This is not your fight."

"You know I cannot do that."

A grin revealed his boney teeth. "Attack!"

Pain surged through Eran's left arm. He had been attacked. A cloud of sulfur assaulted his nose, as hideous arms wrapped tight around his neck. He could smell the traces of guilt and despair encompassing the demon. Another blow this time to his ribs sent him to the floor. He struggled to reach his saber.

A dragon-like face appeared before him. It drew closer, its lizard tongue swiping from side to side. The creature pounced onto Eran's chest. He could feel talons sinking deep into his ribs.

"Pathetic," said Mors.

Eran rolled his head to the side in time to see Mors enter the man lying on the floor. The man crashed into Daryl. As Daryl fell to the floor unconscious, the man pulled his sidearm from its holster and turned it on Chris.

No! Not Chris. Eran thrust his shoulders forward, tossing the demon of guilt to the wall. His next target was the dragon-like demon. He head butted the dragon in the nose. A tail wrapped around Eran's head and whipped it back. He was helpless to protect Chris.

"Lord help us!" Chris called out to God.

"Good for you Chris," said Eran.

An evil grin formed across the lips of the man. "God will never rescue you."

He pulled the trigger.

The room flashed with an intense light.

"Ah!" The demon atop Eran covered his eyes with his talon-clad hands.

"Nooooo!" a woman's voice echoed off the concrete walls.

Chris fell to the floor.

Energized by the intense light and enraged by the certain demise of his charge, Eran surged from the floor. He pulled his fiery saber from its sheath.

The demon of guilt charged him once again.

With the hilt of the saber, Eran sent the demon shrieking through cinderblock. He swirled the saber over his head. His left hand joined his right on the hilt. His jaw clenched and his biceps flexed to stone.

The dragon swung its tail above its head to protect it from the blow. It provided little resistance as the saber cut him in half. A cloud of blackness and sulfur enveloped the creature before it vanished to the Abyss.

The intense light of the Holy Spirit temporarily blinded Mors. Like a vampire hit by the sun's rays, he wrapped himself in his cloak and disappeared.

Eran's gaze turned to Chris.

~~~~~~~~~~

His ears still ringing from the gunshot, Chris rolled to his right and rose to one knee. He pulled his Glock from its holster, and fired off three rounds to the man's chest, and one to his head.

The man crumpled to the ground.

Chris' heart tried to beat through his chest. Nothing, not even his simunition exercises, could prepare him for what he'd just gone through. He lowered his head to his arms still pointing the gun at the cell.

His head snapped back up. "Daryl!"

He sprang to his feet and crashed through the steel cell door. Daryl lay motionless on the floor. He searched his neck for a pulse.

Thump thump. Thump thump.

His shoulders and neck released their tension. *Thank you Lord.*

Next he checked the man lying in the middle of the cell. No pulse.

The series of events ran through his mind. He should have been shot. He looked straight down the barrel when the trigger was pulled. What?

In the screen of his mind he saw the woman in the next cell throw herself into the path of the bullet.

A faint moan filled his ears.

He grabbed the cell keys and ran to open the door. Speckles of blood spotted the sheet on the cot. The woman lay shaking in the corner of the cell. He grabbed her body and rolled her toward him. The bullet had hit her in the chest. Her immodest pink top stained red. He laid her body on the cot and placed pressure on the wound. With his free hand he called dispatch, and demanded an ambulance *stat*.

"Why?" he asked, not intending it to be aloud.

"Because I don't deserve to live, and you didn't deserve to die." Her voice grew faint.

Her eyes fluttered and her cheeks drew back as she struggled for a breath. He could hear a gurgle from her lungs.

"That's not true. Don't believe that lie." Tears poured from his cheeks. "Everyone deserves to live. Jesus died so you could live and so you could find love—true unconditional love."

"No one's ever loved me—" Another deep gurgle. "that way."

"*He* does."

A soft smile smoothed her hardened face. Her eyes stilled.

~~~~~~~~~~

By the time the ambulance arrived, Chris saw Daryl beginning to stir.

One of the EMTs, a young man, hustled to the cell where Daryl sat. After verifying the man on the floor was deceased, he examined Daryl.

"I'm fine," said Daryl. "Chris! Is Chris alright?"

"I'm okay." Chris looked to the EMT. "He okay?"

"Looks like a possible concussion," said the paramedic. "He'll be fine."

A second paramedic, a young woman, made her way into cell one. She pulled up three feet from Chris. He glanced down at his blood covered hands still covering the bullet wound in the now deceased woman's chest. "Are you hurt?"

Chris stared into the face of the young EMT.

"Sir, are you hurt?"

He dropped his chin and swung his head from side to side. "That—that should've been me. He shot at me. She jumped in the way." *Why would she do that?*

"We called the Coroner's office," the young man said. "They'll be here in a few minutes. We should get this one to the hospital for tests," he said pointing to Daryl.

"Will you be okay 'til they get here?" the woman asked.

"I'm fine." He looked up at his friend, now standing outside the cell. "Daryl, I'll meet you there soon as I can."

"Take your time. I'm okay. Really."

Moments later, Chris was alone, again. "Why God? She was just beginning to understand. She would've accepted You. Why take her now?"

Slowly, the pain began to disperse like fog pierced by the sun on a cold March morning. Perhaps she had accepted Him. Maybe she was now in a better place. He would get to the bottom of these mysterious events. Her death would not be in vain.

"Hello?" The voice came from the front of the station.

"In here."

The door opened and in walked a balding man in his late forties and a young woman in her late twenties.

"Officer Davis, looks like you've had a rough morning."

"Hey Don, glad you're here." He'd met the Cooper County Coroner on several occasions over the previous few years, none quite so disconcerting as this. The woman he had not met.

Don followed his gaze. "Oh, this is Samantha. She's my understudy. Comes from the Mizzou Forensic Medicine program. A pretty bright one she is."

"What've we got," said the young woman.

"This one was arrested yesterday on a drunk and disorderly," said Chris. "She was here to sober up and would have been on her way this morning. Over there, he was in for attempted assault and breaking-and-entering."

He gave them a rundown of the morning's events.

"We can take it from here Sergeant," said Don. "Go get yourself cleaned up?"

Chris looked down at his blood-covered uniform. "I guess that'd be a good idea."

He turned to leave the cellblock. "Hey Don, there was something strange about him. He didn't speak from the time I arrested him last night 'til just before he pulled the trigger. He just sat absent in the middle of the floor of his cell—kinda like an animal that'd lost its master. We need to know why."

"We'll do all we can."

~~~~~~~~~~

CHAPTER FIVE

Lights, storage cabinets, a handrail, and even a clock orbited Daryl. His heart pumped pain through his temples. The ambulance bounded its way toward Columbia Regional.

Once again pangs of guilt and despair pierced his head. *It's all your fault. You never should have opened the cell. Chris tried to tell you. It nearly cost him his life. Now Cindy is dead.* He closed his eyes, but the world continued to swirl out of control.

You have a real way of destroying women.

"Why didn't he just kill me?" asked Daryl.

"You can't blame yourself," said the young paramedic. She sat in the seat next to him.

Why not?

She leaned forward to check his pulse. Her white blouse brushed his forearm.

Hey, she is cute. You are pathetic. The assault continued.

"Ahhhh!"

"Easy," said the young woman. "Your blood pressure is spiking."

His heart tried to push a cannonball through his brain. *Oh no, gonna—* "A bag . . . something." Too late. Nausea overtook him.

Well, that ought to impress her.

He gasped struggling to breathe. The rancid air seared his raw sinuses initiating a repeat performance.

"Try to relax," said the paramedic. "You've got a pretty bad concussion. You need to rest." She laid her warm latex armored hand on the back of his neck. "You're blood pressure's up. It's increasing your symptoms. I'll add an Acetaminophen drip to your IV. It should take the edge off."

He coughed out a "thank you."

"We'll be there soon."

~~~~~~~~~~

Chris stood in the shower at the station watching drops of crimson drip from his hands. The hot water washed over him driving the last vestiges of the woman's life-force down the drain. If only his guilt were so easily removed.

After his shower, Chris buttoned up a fresh shirt and wiped steam from the mirror. He gazed beyond his own image and into the dark shadowed eyes of the assailant. The way he smirked as the bullet exploded from the gun. The sound of the shot jerked Chris back to reality. He stared at the mirror as a fog overtook his reflection.

Fifteen minutes later, he trudged to his car and started for the hospital. He should check on Daryl. He also needed to speak with Miss McIntyre. Could she enlighten him about the homicidal maniac lying dead in his jail cell?

The day had warmed to a pleasant sixty degrees. Sixty degrees that in the spring felt so much warmer than in the fall. The warmth soothed the ache in his soul. He turned left and accelerated down the ramp to East I-70. With the squad car at seventy-five by the end of the ramp, he merged in front of a semi-truck going at least seventy. Not his jurisdiction and much more important matters to attend to.

"Lord, I don't get it. I've never seen such evil."

So many enemies, God will never rescue you.

He'd read it in his devotions. Had it really only been a few hours?

A chill ran up his sleeve and into his brain.

Not just what he'd read—the taunt of a murderer.

He shut the car window.

But the Lord answered my cry.

He shivered. It was true. "Lord, you did answer."

He glanced at the roof of the car. "Why did You have to take another life to preserve mine? I don't understand."

As he drove past the exit ramp to Boonville, his thoughts turned to the attractive young woman from the night before. He envisioned her lying on the cold slate floor, pain and fear shivering through her body. The stray lock of red curly hair, which she probably brushed to the side often, matted to her forehead. Blood from the gash connected freckled dots around her eyes and down her cheek.

Her eyes—they said so much. They cried for help. Yet flashed fear at the offer. He could still feel her warmth as she fell into him. He wanted to see her again. Needed to talk to her. To be sure she was okay.

He parked the squad car in a reserved spot and approached the building of brick and glass. Automatic doors granted him entrance. To his left several people waited in a room with composite seats and vinyl flooring. Three teenage boys sat on one side. The right cheekbone of the one in the center was purple and swollen—likely the result of the youthful abandon that accompanied the first warm days of spring.

In the chair closest to the reception desk, a woman not more than twenty sat holding a screaming infant. The cries came out hoarse and labored. The woman's eyes were shut and her lips mouthed soft whispers. As he approached the desk, the woman's eyes opened and locked with his. They pleaded for him to not judge her for her obvious failure as a mother. His heart sank within his chest and he nodded an it-happens-to-every-parent smile.

"Can I help you sir?" A grandmotherly woman sat behind the registration desk.

"Officer Daryl Williams? Came in within the last hour or so?"

"Let's see. Ah yes, he went back about twenty minutes ago. I'll get Dr. Deupree." She motioned to the waiting area. "You can have a seat over there. It'll be just a minute."

True to her word, a moment later a tall man in his mid-fifties approached. "You must be here for Officer Williams?" He stuck out his hand. "Daryl suffered a grade three concussion. The headaches and nausea should reside after a few days. Mostly, he'll just need some rest."

"Can I see him?"

"He's getting a CT Scan right now. You can wait here. I'll let you know when he's back in his room."

"That's okay. I've got someone else I can visit while I wait. How long do you think you'll be keepin' him?"

"I want to keep him here a few hours for observation. Why don't you check back around one."

"Will do. Thanks doc." Chris turned and headed back to the pleasant woman at the desk. "Can you check a room number for a young woman who came in last night? Sarah McIntyre."

"Let me see, M-a-c- . . . No, um M-c- . . . Yep there it is. Room 426."

"Thanks much." Chris turned and strode to the elevator.

At the fourth floor he stepped from the elevator and approached the nurses' station. An overweight middle-aged nurse busied herself behind a desk.

"Mornin'. I'm Sergeant Chris Davis from Arrow Springs. I believe you have a young woman here, Sarah McIntyre? She's the victim of an attack I'm investigatin'."

"Ah yes, a real sweetheart. Pretty beat up though."

"How's she doin'?"

"Oh, she'll be fine. Sore for awhile, but fine."

"Would it be alright if I spoke with her?"

"Well now, that's really up to her." The woman looked at him with a twinkle in her eye. "She's slept most of the morning so I think she should be up to it. Just try to keep her relaxed. Don't you go getting her all worked up. You hear?" The caution came with the motherly point of the finger.

"Yes ma'am."

The nurse nodded. "I'll go check on her and make sure she's ready to talk. Give me a couple minutes."

"Thank ya kindly ma'am."

"Oh, you're quite welcome young man." She walked down the hallway and into a room on her left.

~~~~~~~~~~

Sarah lay in her hospital bed weighing the pros and cons of another attempt at visiting the bathroom. Her head told her she didn't have to go that bad. The cramping of her bladder told her otherwise. She looked at the red call-button lying at the corner of her pillow. Surely the nurses had better things to do with their time. Besides, it was only ten feet to the small bathroom. How bad could it hurt? She laid her left hand on the bed next to her hip and pushed. As she began a slow roll toward the edge of her bed, a voice caused her to jump.

"Good morning!"

Sarah looked up to see a middle-aged nurse wearing a light-blue top crowned with a wide smile. "Oh! Hi."

"So sorry, I didn't mean to startle you. How ya feelin'?"

"Like I was hit by a truck."

"Well, I gotta say you look a bit like it too."

"Great. Thanks."

The nurse chuckled. "You have a visitor. Are you feeling up to it?"

"A visitor? Who?" She had no one—no family, no friends to speak of.

"A police officer from Arrow Springs. Said he had some questions."

"Ow." More cramping.

"Would you like me to have him come back later?"

"No, no, that's okay. I, um, would like to speak with him. He might have saved my life yesterday." Still he was a man. She couldn't trust him.

"Alrighty. I'll go fetch him then." The nursed turned to leave the room.

"Wait! I, ah, need to use the little girl's room." Sarah winced. "Could you help me? Last time I tried to get up, the pain nearly made me pass out."

"Well certainly. That's what I'm here for." The nurse flourished her hand in front of her and bowed. "Besides, you should feel better this time. I gave you a fresh dose of painkiller half an hour ago. It'll take the edge off." She walked around the bed and took Sarah's hand. She was right. The throbbing only produced a dull ache.

"If you need anything just holler. I'll be right here."

In the bathroom Sarah nearly jumped at the mess that stared back at her. After dealing with the more pressing issue, she ran a brush through her hair. What was she doing? Did it really matter what she looked like? She dug through her purse which the nurse must have set next to the sink. She found her coral-red lipstick tube and brought some color back to her lips. Who was she trying to impress? He certainly wouldn't be interested in her.

She opened the door and stepped back into her room. It seemed brighter than before.

"Feel better?" asked the nurse. "You look better." A twinkle in the nurse's eye revealed the great restraint it took to keep from laughing.

"Would it be possible to put on some real clothes?"

"Oh, well, your slacks have blood on them. And your blouse, well, I'm afraid they had to tear it to work on your arm. But let me see." The nurse walked to a set of cupboards. "Yes, here we go." She returned with some pajama pants and a top. "I think we can get these over that ankle without too much trouble."

"Thank you. You must think I'm just silly." *Now there's an understatement.*

"Nonsense, a girl needs her dignity."

Sarah took the pale-blue pants and pulled them over her bad ankle. After shedding the gown she'd been wearing, she slipped into the white top with small dark-blue flowers. The nurse helped her to the chair next to the bed.

"I'll go get the officer."

"Did you happen to get his name?" She didn't want to admit to him she'd forgotten it.

"Oh, well now, let's see." The woman looked as though she flipped through a file cabinet within her head. "Yes, there it is. I believe it was Chris, um, Chris Davis." She smiled sweetly as she left the room.

He was just there to ask her questions about the case. Why was she getting all smitten? She knew better. But she'd sure prefer to have him see her in the PJs than in that breeze-in-the-back thing. Her feet were still bare. Given the state of her ankle, there wasn't much she could do about that.

A slight rap on the door.

"Miss McIntyre?"

"Come in."

The tall and handsome policeman walked into her room.

"You may not remember me from last night."

"Of course I do." Breath seemed harder to find. "How could I forget Officer Davis, my hero?" Did she sound as much like a schoolgirl-with-a-crush as she felt?

"Chris is fine."

Definitely. What was wrong with her? She knew better. Her heart ached as past betrayals flashed through her mind. She was damaged goods.

"Do you mind if I pull up a chair?"

"No, of course not."

He grabbed one of the guest chairs from the foot of her bed. His dark bicep flexed and pushed against the restricting navy-blue shirt sleeve. Thankfully, she wasn't hooked up to the heart monitor they'd put her on earlier. Her heart rate must have doubled in the last sixty seconds.

The memory of her appearance in the bathroom mirror began to haunt her. She felt like an ugly duckling in the presence of this handsome drake. She was pathetic.

~~~~~~~~~~

Taken aback by the simple beauty of the young redhead, Chris subtly sucked in his gut shifting the air into his chest. Even with a shiner covering much of her forehead, her sapphire blue eyes took his breath away. He flashed a shy smile and set the chair in front of Sarah. Even her bare feet were attractive.

"How's the leg?" Best to break the ice before getting into serious questions.

"Not as bad as the wrist. But still pretty sore. Doctor said it's a moderate sprain. Gonna need a splint for a few days." She rubbed the fingers of her right hand. "The wrist will be in this lovely cast for several weeks."

He couldn't tell if the cute little scrunch of her nose showed pain in her forehead or distaste at the white cast on her arm. "And your head?"

"Looks worse than it feels—at least when I'm medicated."

"I don't know. Sure it's a little black and blue, but it draws out the blue in your eyes."

"Right." Her tone was sarcastic. Her nose scrunched once again.

He'd overstepped his bounds. "I'm sorry. I didn't mean to make you uncomfortable."

"No, no. It's okay. Seven stitches above the eye, and a severe headache, but it wasn't even a concussion. The doc was really quite surprised. Said I must have one tough guardian angel." A smile formed in the corners of her cinnamon-red lips.

"Mine must be gettin' quite a workout today." *No don't go there. Not yet at least.*

"Rough morning?" Despite all she'd gone through in the last twenty-four hours her lips pursed together in concern.

"Yeah." He took a deep breath. "I need to ask you some questions regarding the assault last night, if you wouldn't mind."

"I don't know what I can tell you," said Sarah. "But, I'll try."

Chris pulled a notepad from his pocket. "Had you ever seen the man before last night?"

"No."

He watched her nonverbals. Nothing changed. No excess blinking, no perspiration on her smooth delicate skin. *Stay focused on the task.* She still rubbed her fingers, but nothing to indicate there was more than she was telling.

The pause must have made her feel she should elaborate. "I don't think I've seen him around town or anything."

Chris nodded. "Can you tell me what happened? Anything you can remember may help us figure out who he was." *Is, not was.* He needed to focus.

She continued to answer his questions. Thankfully, without more of her own. "I was walking home from the library where I work. When I turned onto my street, I could see the man heading toward me on the same side of the road."

"Okay, now you were coming from the library, so you were heading south on Second?"

"Um," She glanced to the top of the window to her left. "Yes, that's correct."

He jotted a couple of notes. *Suspect was walking north on Second. Possible lived locally?* Had he seen any unfamiliar cars in the area? Perhaps at the River's Edge, it was straight south of the scene? *Check out River's Edge.* Even if the suspect hadn't left a vehicle, perhaps someone saw him.

He realized she had paused for him to jot his notes. "Please continue."

"Well, I was at the corner of my yard when I heard—"

She seemed to struggle with what to say next. Was she about to lie to him? "Heard? Go on, it's okay."

"I probably shouldn't say heard, more like felt a voice urging me to run. I'm not sure why. It wasn't like the man was running at me or anything like that. He just stared at me. I guess that's what spooked me, I'm not sure." She fidgeted with her fingers.

"Maybe it was that guardian angel you were talking about."

"Maybe." She gave her shoulders a quick shrug. "I learned many years ago not to ignore that voice." She closed her eyes as if envisioning some past horror. After a few moments she reopened them and continued. "I ran to the front door. I hurried through and slammed it." She stopped rubbing her fingers and crossed her arms in front of her chest. "He was close. I could smell cigarette smoke as the door shut." A shiver ran through her body. "His eyes. His eyes were—I don't know how to describe it—evil!"

Chris understood all too well. "You must've been frightened."

"I was. At least at first. Then I felt a strange peace mixed with anger. It seems odd. The man hadn't stopped pounding on the door. Yet I felt I was safe. Safe enough to be mad. Mad at the intrusion. Mad at my parents. Mad at the world. And mad at—" A soft tear formed in the corner of her eye and then glistened across it.

"At?"

"Mad at God." Her body rocked back and forth in her chair. "I sat on the floor of my entryway. The fear stirred memories from my past. Memories I never wanted to relive or remember." Anger seemed to tunnel just beneath her surface the way a ground mole moves through a yard. "I'd prefer not to discuss it."

Chris nodded content to let it pass. "What happened next?"

She went on to tell him about going to the door and how it crashed in on her. "Next thing I remember is the man lying on the floor next to me with you handcuffing him. You really are a hero you know."

He drew his lips between his teeth and diverted his gaze to the floor. *Too late as usual.* If the man had broken through any earlier, she'd probably be dead like the woman at the jail. "Anything else you can think of?"

"Afraid not. Were you able to get anything from him? A name? ID?"

A murder. "No." Chris returned his gaze to her eyes. "Sarah, I need to tell you something."

"What? He didn't escape?" Her eyes drew large and round. He could see the surface of her pajama top begin to rise and fall in rapid succession.

"No, he's dead."

Sarah's eyebrows vee'd upward. "How? . . . Suicide? . . . What happened?" Despite her concerned questions, her breathing began to return to normal. Clearly she wasn't heartbroken.

Chris told her about the events of the morning.

"Oh my!" Her left hand covered her mouth.

"I had no choice but to shoot him."

"Were you hurt?"

"No." *I should've been.* "He shot a woman in the cell next to me. She died this morning before paramedics arrived."

She gasped. "Oh no!"

"Sarah, do you know anything else that might help?"

"No. I'm so sorry." It was too much for her. She began to heave out sobs. "You don't even know who he was? Why did he attack me?"

"I don't know." Chris stood and put his hand on her shoulder. "I promise you. I'll find out."

~~~~~~~~~~

"It was Mors," said Eran.

The declaration knocked the breath from Alex. He sat on the bed next to Sarah observing the conversation between his charge and the charming police officer. Not so much what was said, but what was not. There was an attraction between them. He could sense it. "Mors is here?"

Eran just nodded.

Huw looked up at Eran in disbelief. "In Arrow Springs?"

Sarah had endured so much. Now, Alex would have to protect her from one of the vilest most evil beings to walk the earth? "What on earth is the mighty slayer Mors doing in such an out of the way little town as Arrow Springs?"

"Something big is happening," said Eran. "I can only tell you that his mission this morning was to kill the man who attacked Sarah."

Alex tried to make it compute. "Why do you think he was trying to kill him? Is it possible he was trying to help him escape?"

"No." Eran just shook his head. "I think in his bloodlust Mors was trying to take as many lives as he could, but he clearly wanted the man dead. He could have run out of the cell as soon as he knocked Daryl to the floor. But he just stood there and took aim at Chris. I think he was as surprised as anyone when the woman jumped in front of the bullet. Yes, he might have killed her too at some point, but that bullet was for Chris."

"Why do you think she took the bullet?" asked Huw.

"When Mors attacked, I was jumped by two demons. The larger was a vile demon of adultery. I would suppose that with his absence, she was faced with the reality of all she had done with her life. She chose to make a difference."

Alex still could not see it. "If Mors wanted Chris dead, it would not be like him to give up after a single shot. Why did he not keep shooting?"

"Prayer!" Eran began to bounce. "Chris sought the Lord's protection, and the light of the Holy Spirit flooded the room. Mors was stunned long enough for Chris to get off a few shots. That was all it took. I dispensed with the two demons that jumped me and then turned to face Mors. Content at having completed his mission, Mors just left."

"This does not make sense." Alex slid to the edge of the bed. Sarah engaged the officer in light conversation. "I do not get what Mors would want with some nobody in Arrow Springs." He turned a questioning look to Huw, who now bore a wide cat-that-ate-the-canary smile. "What?"

"Maybe Eitan will have some answers tomorrow," said Huw.

"Captain Eitan?" Eran's gaze snapped to Huw. "Eitan is here?"

It was too much. Huw was Alex' friend, his confidante. Yet he had kept such a wonderful secret from him. "You have known this and did not tell me?"

"I was instructed to tell both you and Eran at the same time," said Huw.

"Any other surprises we should know about?" asked Eran.

"Actually, yes. We believe Mael is here as well. Though we have not been able to confirm it."

"Is this a joke?" asked Eran. "The dark prince of Rome and the dark prince of Brittany are both in Arrow Springs?" Eran began to pace beside Sarah's bed. "Not to mention Eitan?"

"We will have to wait and see what Eitan knows when we meet with him. We meet at the church after the service. Until then we are just to act like business as usual. Can you make it Alex?"

He would not miss it. "I should be able to get someone to watch Sarah for a few hours. Yes. I will be there."

~~~~~~~~~~

Chris glanced around the small hospital room. Despite its nothing-but-ordinary appearance, the room possessed a warmth he'd never felt in a hospital room. Perhaps it was the beautiful yet fragile rose that sat in the chair across from him. He felt he could stay and talk with her forever. "I Suppose I should go check on Daryl, and let you get some rest." He couldn't let himself get too close. It could hurt too much.

"I really appreciated your company," said Sarah. "I think I'm going to go insane here 'til tomorrow." There was that scrunch of the nose again. "I feel fine, but the doctors want to keep an eye on me. They want to make sure I don't show signs of a concussion."

"Do you have someone to call for a ride home tomorrow? Any close relatives or friends in the area?" *Boyfriend? Husband? Significant other?*

"Not really. I can call a cab or catch a bus."

"Nonsense, I can pick you up after church."

"Oh, that's not necessary. You've done so much already."

Chris stood and stepped behind his chair. "I've just done my job."

"I don't want to bother you." The look in her eyes—did it say, "I don't trust you," or, "Don't give up now."

Take the risk. "It's no bother. I'd be honored if you'd allow me the privilege."

The corners of her lips crept upward. "When you put it that way, how can I turn it down?"

He'd guessed right. "Twelve-thirty, one o'clock?"

"That'd be great."

Chris pulled the chair back to the wall.

"Could I impose just a bit more?" asked Sarah.

"Sure?"

"Could you swing by my house and make sure everything's okay? I talked with my insurance agent and she's supposed to get someone there to fix the door sometime this afternoon. But, I don't like my house being open to the world until then."

He couldn't imagine anyone wanting to harm her. So sweet. He loved the way she'd lit up when they talked about her job at the library. She loved the children. "No prob. I'll check it out."

"Thanks—for everything."

"See ya tomorrow." He turned and willed himself to walk from the room. The smell of mashed potatoes and disinfectant met him in the hallway.

He passed by the nurses' station and thanked the middle-aged nurse. He guessed she only pretended not to notice him finally coming out of Sarah's room.

"You're very welcome. I told you she was a sweetie."

Chris neared the elevator and turned back to her. "Guess I'll see you later."

She was gone.

~~~~~~~~~~

CHAPTER SIX

A warm spring breeze lifted sermon notes from Reverend David Thomas' desk and fluttered them to the floor. A deep breath of misty air softened his rigid muscles. Outside the window screen, green maples budded to life. Beyond the trees, the river splashed against its banks. His eyes drifted back to the papers lying on the floor—like them, his message had been tossed about in the wind of the Spirit.

As the pastor of River of Life, a small Arrow Springs church, he'd established a general routine from which he seldom deviated. Monday was his day to recover from the rigors of Sunday services. Tuesday began his study, preparation, and scripting of the coming message. By Friday he would refine the details and presentation of the sermon. Not that his schedule didn't vary. Over the past three years he'd spent time doing other things. Attending prayer meetings, visiting shut-ins, enduring board meetings, praying with parishioners in the hospital, he'd even attended his share of football and baseball games when students from the youth group were participating. But all-in-all his routine remained largely unchanged. This week had been no different. Everything was ready. Or was it?

During his morning devotions uneasiness began to envelop him. He sensed the Spirit directing toward an entirely different subject. Would God really wait until Saturday morning to change His mind about what he wanted David to preach? God was immutable. He didn't change.

Maybe he could convince God that he needed to preach on discipleship as he'd planned.

He'd planned. Now there was a joke.

He pushed the remaining pages off the edge of the desk and closed his eyes.

"Lord, I trust it's You leading me to this uncomfortable situation so late in the week. I certainly don't get Your timing. But it doesn't matter. Please just give me your wisdom as I prepare."

"Chirp." A sparrow bounced along the window sill. "Chirp, cheep, cheep."

He inhaled another deep misty breath and picked up his Bible.

"So God created human beings in his own image. In the image of God he created them; male and female he created them." He studied the words from Genesis 1:27. He turned to his computer and typed in the keywords "Image of God." The hard drive spun to life, whirring in search of references in both scripture and biblical commentaries. The computer screen listed over a dozen commentaries on the passage, as well as cross references, quotes in the New Testament, translation comparisons, Hebrew and Greek word studies, and even related sermon slides and songs. Some significant speed reading would be necessary.

A sweet voice from the entrance to the study drew his undivided attention. "What're you up to in here?" asked Trina, his lovely wife.

"I wish I knew. I feel God wants me to change the subject of tomorrow's message and I'm none too happy about it." His heart danced as she massaged his shoulders. "I thought the message on discipleship was exactly what the congregation needed."

"Well maybe you can do it next week. I'm sure God has a reason for this new direction. Somehow," her voice took a playful turn, "I think it just might be best to talk on the subject He wants you to."

"You see, that's why I married you. You have a way of making complex situations seem so simple. You know, I really love you." His eyebrows rose apologetically. "I've just got so much work to do in so little time."

She patted him on the shoulder. She understood. "God will provide. He always has. Remember the church building."

"I know. But even in that—I didn't understand His reasons. It was clearly His intervention and timing but you have to believe He would've preferred that Saint Andrews had survived despite their struggles."

"His ways are perfect," said Trina.

Such a sweet woman, surely he didn't deserve her.

~~~~~~~~~~

In the small study, two enormous angelic warriors overlooked Pastor Thomas. Yora, the man's protector knelt on one knee beside the window. Every angel dreamed of an assignment like this. Pastor Thomas' devotion to the Lord filled Yora with the power of God. A power he needed often. He dealt with attacks from the enemy on a near daily basis. A situation all too familiar for a guardian assigned to someone in ministry. Despite his own refined physique, a result of daily basking in the glory of the Lord, Yora gazed in awe at the presence of Captain Eitan.

The captain towered above him. Despite humility in his words, and compassion in his eyes, no one could question his nature as a warrior. He had accompanied King David during his reign in Israel. He had legs like cedars, and arms not much smaller. Atop his brilliant white tunic he wore a golden breastplate adorned with an embossed sterling lion. An enormous helmet of white gold sat on the corner of the desk.

Eitan's shield lay against the edge of the desk. Like Yora's own, it was made of silver, with a golden cross overlay. Yora recalled when he first received his own shield. Over four millennia had passed since that day. He had stared without understanding at the symbolic overlay. At times it brought warmth to his being. Yet at others it nearly brought him to tears. Why had God chosen this strange symbol to represent His warriors? Nearly a millennium later the Persians began using crosses for crucifixion. It made sense. The cross was a symbol of God's justice—the punishment of those who did evil. Centuries later he wept and tried to tear the image from his shield as he watched God Himself tortured and killed upon the very symbol which adorned his shield of protection. Only after Christ arose from the dead did he recognize the cross as the symbol of faith.

The clickety-clack of the keyboard indicated Pastor Thomas had resumed his study.

"He is going to need an extra day to recover from this one," said Yora.

"He is a good man." Eitan's voice rolled like thunder in the small room. "Many so-called teachers of the Word today are too busy *serving God* to hush themselves enough to hear the still quiet voice of the Spirit."

"He desires to be used by God." Yora stood and placed his hand on the man's back. "He prays continually for God to use him to make a difference in this town."

"He has, and He will."

"This has not been an easy town to minister in."

Eitan raised his eyes from Trina to Yora. "Lady Thomas commented on the acquisition of their church building. What happened?"

"The enemy was busy. Three years ago Pastor Thomas, Trina, and the girls moved to Arrow Springs. They brought a passion to see the good news about Jesus spread in this little town. The first two years the church burgeoned. Under the teaching of Pastor Thomas, River of Life grew to eighty-four regular attendees. Pastor Thomas directed River of Life to a purpose of bringing new life to the hurting and broken of this town."

"What was she referring to regarding the building?" Eitan's voice was patient.

"Right, well, over the last several years the enemy has continued to gain a presence here." Yora needed to keep it short. The Captain was too busy to babble on. "The building used to belong to Saint Andrews, a well established church taking a biblical stand on most issues to arise in the community. A few years back they hired a young pastor—quite a gifted communicator. Unfortunately, he knew it."

"The enemy began to gain a foothold in his preaching through the inflation of his ego and a spirit of pride. Then a year ago the Spirit of God brought a personal revival to his life. His messages bore evidence of the transformation and the enemy grew uncomfortable. By the time of this revival, most of the people who remained in the congregation were unwilling to stick with their newly impassioned preacher. By last fall, Saint Andrews had declined to two dozen members—far too few to maintain the ministry."

Eitan nodded. "I have seen it too many times to count. The building belonged to Saint Andrews?"

"Yes. Last fall Arrow Springs suffered a suspicious and dirty mayoral campaign. Two days before the election, Trenton Richards gave a speech in which he detailed an affair between incumbent Mayor Johanus and the Junior High principle, Mrs. Freeman. The following day, The Arrow printed the story complete with photos to back it up. In the aftermath, Trenton won the election by a landslide."

"Rather convenient timing."

"Rather." Yora could still see the look on Tudur's face. The mayor's personal demon had reveled in the victory. "Trenton's first action as Mayor was to prevent River of Life from meeting at the Elementary School. He claimed the arrangement violated the 'Separation of Church and State' principle. It took only two months for Judge Burns to rule against River of Life. The following Sunday they were without a place to meet."

Eitan walked to the window and bent down to face a plump little sparrow sitting on the sill. "Trying times for a young pastor."

"Undaunted by the development, Pastor Thomas called together the entire congregation and challenged them to enter a time of prayer and fasting."

"A tough proposition for most American Christians."

Yora put one hand on Pastor Thomas' shoulder and the other on Trina's. "Pastor Thomas told them, 'if we are willing to trust God, I believe He will provide.' And provide He did! Two days after the fast began, the board at Saint Andrews called Pastor Thomas to inform him their congregation had voted the night before to donate their beautiful building to River of Life." He looked at Pastor Thomas. "It was the only time I have ever seen him speechless. He wept for two hours in awe of his God. Then he called Trina and told her the news. That evening the congregation met in their new building and broke the fast together."

"That must have been quite the celebration."

"In my time on Earth I have yet to experience a more incredible time of praising God. Much to the displeasure of the enemy, River of Life continues to grow and impact this community."

Eitan unfurled his luminescent wings. "God's favor is clearly on this local body of believers."

Trina put her hands on her husband's shoulders and rubbed with a sweet compassion. "Is there anything I can do to help?"

"How 'bout a nice tall ice-tea?"

"Coming right up." She patted his arm and turned to leave the study.

He turned an apologetic look to her. "And can you tell the girls I'm sorry we won't be able to go for our spring walk today?"

Yora turned back to Eitan and smiled. "This should be a good sermon."

~~~~~~~~~~

Chris dropped Daryl off at his home on the south side of the river and headed to Sarah's. He slowed as he approached the house. The scene so mysterious in the nighttime blackness now appeared sweet and subtle. Only the yellow police tape he'd left across her door betrayed the previous night's events. He turned the squad car into her driveway and pulled up to her garage door. Like many of the homes in Arrow Springs, the house was made of brick. Unlike the older redbrick homes, this was a newer mottled arrangement of red and browns.

He turned off the engine. A shiver rose from his knees to his head. Memories of the previous night's arrest coupled with thoughts of the madman at the jail flooded his mind. He needed to get a grip. There was no one there. No reason to get all worked up. *The man wasn't gonna be botherin' anyone again.*

He climbed from the squad car and headed for the front door. A slight breeze wafted an early lilac fragrance across the lush green yard. Sarah must have taken great pride in making her home a pleasant site for the neighborhood. Her bushes were well manicured, and flowers poured from large black pots strategically located along the front of the house. The occasional dandelion or patch of clover served to show a lack of obsession with the lawn. It looked lovely nonetheless.

He ascended the front steps and instinctively knocked on the front door. *What would you do if someone answered?* A grin pulled at his lips. Thankfully no one did. He entered the house. Everything looked just as it had the night before when they left. He started his sweep of the house with the living room because it was familiar. She'd been there with him. Everything was as it had been. Books on the table and next to them the yarn bracelet he'd cut from her wrist.

He turned to leave the room, but a painting caught his eye. He hadn't noticed it the night before. Behind the couch, a beautiful island castle reflected in subdued waves. The brass plate at the bottom read "Eilean Donan Castle – Scotland." Beyond the castle yellow-browns and olive-greens formed rolling mountains. The terrain looked rugged, maybe even harsh. Yet at the center stood the castle. Peaceful, strong, age-tested. A road and bridge led from the island to her living room. Had she stared at the painting envisioning the prince riding from the castle to rescue her from the harsh environment which surrounded her? She seemed so sweet. So likable. Yet cautious and reserved. What drove her fear?

She'd called him her hero. Had he been that prince?

He walked to the kitchen, resisting the urge to investigate her refrigerator to see what he could learn about her. He was there to check the house out for her. Not to pry. On the door of the fridge were numerous magnets holding up school photos of students of all ages. Perhaps even the one who had made her the bracelet. She said she had no family or friends. That wasn't the story before him.

He checked her bathroom. All clear, and very neat. His heart pounded the inside of his chest as he stepped into her bedroom. This was sacred territory. He stepped softly on the carpet the way one would at a gravesite. Everything looked neat and orderly. Her bed was made, no clothes on the floor, no papers sitting haphazardly on her dresser. The only thing separating this bedroom from a showcase in a furniture store were three books sitting diagonally on her night stand. A picture on her dresser showed a red-haired teenager, obviously a younger Sarah, standing with an older couple, her parents perhaps, under the Arch of St. Louis. Where were they now? Were they dead like his? Or had they had a falling out? He made his way back to the front door. All was quiet in the home.

When he stepped down from the porch, his foot caught on something sending him to the ground. His face came to rest in the soft grass next to an evergreen branch. *That was sure clumsy.* Thankfully, Sarah wasn't there to see it.

~~~~~~~~~~

Eran stepped from Miss McIntyre's house with Chris. A black flash darted from the bushes.

An ambush!

Two brazen demons charged him at the top of the steps. A swirl of light and darkness fell to the yard like a zebra fallen prey in the African savannah. Fangs and claws gnashed at him in an attempt to survive the attack. Only a third his size, they had to know their chances of surviving the confrontation were slim. Why did they attack him?

The answer appeared out of the corner of his eye.

They were a diversion.

Four demons circled the corner of the house like a pack of wild hyenas and headed for Chris. Eran grabbed one of his attackers by the neck and hurled him head over tail at the four demons. The makeshift cannon ball crashed into three of them. Black wings and bodies tumbled through a green sulfurous cloud and into the house. The last of the four attackers threw himself at Chris. He landed on the porch and grabbed Chris' right foot. Chris stumbled and fell to the ground.

Eran saw the demon draw his dagger and lunge for Chris' brain. "A stroke will do you well."

In a flash of white, Eran snatched the demon out of the air. Grabbing him by the wing, he flung the demon into the clouds like a black kite spinning out of control. "Not on my watch."

One demon remained in the yard. One of the first two that attacked.

Eran drew his fiery saber from its sheath and raised it above his head. This one would pay the price for attacking Eran's charge.

Oomph!

Before he could bring down the saber, the four minions charged from the house and straight into his chest.

He heard a clanking noise behind him.

No. His saber. The force of the impact sent it flying from his grip. They would be on him before he could reach it.

Emboldened by the sudden turn of fate, the demons righted themselves and pulled daggers. Three demons advanced on him. The other two turned toward Chris.

Despite his best efforts, a grin crept onto Eran's face.

A duet of screams—then silence.

The trio of demons flinched at the sound. They spun to see another massive angelic warrior brandishing a scimitar still aglow from banishing their companions.

Eran collected his saber from the driveway.

Fighting and clawing to get ahead of one another the three demons streaked into the clouds in pursuit of their comrade.

"Gida!" said Eran. "Nice to see you again."

"I know you could have handled yourself." The dark-haired warrior grinned. "But I surmised if the enemy would send six minions to attack this charge of yours, there must be a good reason to defend him."

"Where did you come from?" asked Eran.

"Across the street, keeping watch over Mrs. Ferguson. Fifteen years she has been my charge, ever since Mr. Ferguson passed on. She is a sweet woman of God. A tad nosey, but a real prayer warrior. I should probably get back. I do not suppose those four will be back."

"Unlikely." Eran struck his chest with his fist. "If they would be so bold, I will be ready. Thank you again my friend."

~~~~~~~~~~

Chris pushed with his left hand and rolled to his side. His eyes locked onto several items lying under a shrub. Must have been more items from Sarah's purse. He rose to one knee and picked up several coins, an ink pen, two pictures, a credit card, and a few other items. He climbed the porch once again and took the items into the house. In the kitchen he set them on the counter. At least his klutzy header off the porch accomplished something of worth.

Exiting the house he tried to get the front door to stay shut. A useless task.

Behind him, tires ground their way into the driveway. He turned to see a pickup pull up.

"Is this 239 Second?" asked a man in his fifties. Concern danced across his face at the presence of the squad car in the drive. "I have a repair request for a Sarah McIntyre."

"Sure is."

The man climbed from the truck wearing grey coveralls. What remained of his black hair flopped here and there atop his round head.

"I was just checkin' on the house for her." Chris stuck out his hand in greeting. "Any idea how long it will take?" The man's grip was firm and friendly.

"Well let's take a look—good, it's a thirty-six inch door. I brought a couple different doors hoping I'd have the right one. The deadbolt and handle are damaged so I'm gonna need to replace 'em. Do ya know how I might get the new key to her?"

Chris straightened his back. "I'm pickin' her up at the hospital tomorrow afternoon. I can give it to her."

"Great." The man seemed pleased. "Well let's git 'er done."

Twenty-five minutes later the man finished the job and his story about his aunt who had someone break into her house twenty years ago. "It'll need to be painted to match the old door, but that can wait. Here's the key. Thanks for yer help."

~~~~~~~~~~

Dusk began to set on Arrow Springs. A storm was gathering. Despite the sun hanging low, the western sky grew blacker by the minute. The storm surged around the facility west of the river.

Within the facility, Mael sat on his haunches in the candlelit office of Maiya Mirinova. Fury flowed from his being. He had come to bask in her worship while he waited for the others to arrive. The practices which normally pleased and empowered him only fueled his ferocity.

The gaunt female seated before him shivered. She could sense his mood. They had been together long enough. She could feel his presence, though he refused to reveal himself to her.

He released a loud growl and thunder from the gathering storm ripped through the building.

A shriek echoed through the office. Fear danced in Maiya's eyes.

Despite thousands of demonic beings which enveloped the building, he sensed the arrival of one specific demon. The last of the twelve. Well, eleven now that Leon would not be attending.

He reached for Maiya's neck and squeezed just enough to invoke panic as she struggled to breath. Another clap of thunder. As he released her, he swept his wings across the circle of candles. The room fell into utter darkness.

Another scream.

He was ready. He descended to meet his guests in the lair below.

Mors and the nine lesser princes stood once again around the circle of bones. Just as they had done twenty-five years earlier.

"Good, everyone is here." Mael turned to the gap in the circle. "Leon will no longer be joining us. You need not leave a space for him."

The two demons on either side grinned and slid toward each other.

"Better. Despite Leon's inept handling of this project prior to my return, everything now proceeds as planned." He turned a glare to Mors. "At least until your incompetent handling of the situation at the jail."

Anat ruffled her bird-like feathers and one of the demons standing next to Mors took a step backward.

"You dare accuse me of incompetence," snarled Mors. "You have been trying to bring this measly town under our control for three years, and what have you accomplished? I would say you are more a detriment to our cause than its savior."

"What?" Mael let his hand slide to the hilt of his sword.

Mors took a step into the circle and toward him. "You think we have not heard? Leon is not the only of our numbers you have seen fit to banish. Just today you banished four of your lackeys because they could not rid you of the pesky Officer Davis. In your rage *you* have destroyed more than has the heavenly host."

Though the thought of ripping Mors' ugly bones apart tempted him, the confrontation could not progress beyond a verbal volley. They were equally matched and as the enemy so aptly pointed out, "a kingdom divided is headed for destruction." He pulled his hand from the sword and growled. "Lucifer put me in charge of this mission. I shall not allow the failure of others to bring his wrath upon me."

"I accomplished my task," said Mors. "Yet, you prove you cannot keep track of the *ones*." He stepped back to the circle, clearly recognizing an encounter would benefit no one. "I have come here to clean up your mess."

"You have cleaned up nothing! Because of your thirst for blood, you have now drawn attention to the *one* who was arrested. Autopsies will be performed, tests will be run, investigations will pursue." The others began to fidget. The discussion could not continue. He needed their loyalty.

"What did you expect me to do, make him disappear?"

Mors would not have the last word. "A simple suicide would have sufficed. Cut and dry suicidal maniac—no questions asked. Instead you tried to kill Officer Davis." He shook his head. "You fool! Chris Davis is one of the few prayer warriors left in Arrow Springs. You realize the angelic warrior known as Eran is assigned to the protection of the deputy? I believe the two of you have met before, have you not?" He grinned as he let the jab roll from his tongue.

Mors exploded with rage sending one of the gathered demons tunneling through cement, rock, and clay. "Perhaps if you spent more time dealing with your opposition than fearing them, your little secret here would not be in jeopardy." Mors' tone softened. "It is clear, that if God is so interested in protecting this individual, we need to find a way to lessen his impact, perhaps even remove him from the picture completely."

Mael reeled in wings he had not realized he had spread. "Yes, I must agree." He turned to Anat and two others.

"Follow Chris. It is clear a frontal assault will not work. We need a way to remove him. Find his weaknesses, his little dark secrets, even unfounded suspicions we can exploit to discredit him or persuade him to leave town. Do not attack him! Remain in the shadows and observe. You shall not fail me."

When they left he turned to the remaining six lesser princes. "Go! Empower our faithful followers. Unleash your cronies. Barrage the bars. Fuel the feuds. Prep the peep shows. Declare to the enemy—this is our town."

~~~~~~~~~~

CHAPTER SEVEN

Sunday, April 19, 2020

By four o'clock the thunderstorm reached its full fury encompassing all of Arrow Springs. Lightning ruled the ionized sky with bolts arcing from cloud to cloud and then crashing to the ground. One energized bolt pierced the electrified air like a harpoon through the ocean in search of its prey. With an intense clap the bolt struck a large maple tree in Daryl's back yard. Fragments of wood sprawled to the wind shuddered lawn. At that precise moment, Marilyn's right hand smacked Daryl's cheek in utter disgust.

The clap of thunder and intense light flooded the master bedroom at the rear of the transitional style home. Daryl jolted from the recurring nightmare. For three years it taunted him most every night. Guilt, anger, bitterness, shame, and despair had become his sleeping partners. He rolled to his stomach and buried his face in the sweat soaked pillow. His chest ached to wake once more in the absence of Marilyn.

Unlike the hundreds of others, this dream offered a unique twist leaving his heart stinging with disappointment. It started as usual, happy times with Marilyn. Walking through the St. Louis Zoo, laughing as a swinging monkey crashed into the glass in front of them. Popcorn, pop, and two straws at the Forum 8 in Columbia. Then came the dreaded skip in time to the hotel room and a realization of his unforgivable betrayal of the woman he loved.

But he didn't wake up. The dream continued. He sat once again with Marilyn, her soft hands caressing his palms. With tears flowing from her eyes, she said the words he longed to hear, "I forgive you Daryl." Joy and relief overwhelmed him.

Then it happened—again—time skipped, same hotel room, different woman. He found himself in the arms of the young EMT from the ambulance. The event never happened. The dream wove together familiar people, places, and feelings into a new torture.

"How could you?" Marilyn screamed.

His mind moved to the next act of this personal tragedy. "I forgave you! I trusted you! I opened my heart to you, again!" Then came the deserved slap.

He lay on his bed transported back to reality to ponder the torment of this new nightmare. His heart pumped pain through his throbbing head. Tears mixed with the sweat in the pillow. Anguish writhed deep within his soul.

Then it caught his attention. Flickering like a candle flame against a forest fire of negative emotions burned a glimmer of hope. For the first time since the divorce, he'd actually envisioned Marilyn forgiving him.

Was it just another cruel trick of guilt and despair? Or was it possible? Was the kind of forgiveness Chris spoke of possible?

He raised his head and glanced at his alarm clock. There were no glowing green numbers. The storm had taken out the power. He reached to the night stand and picked up his cell. Four-twenty. Chris was going to kill him. But he had to talk to someone.

~~~~~~~~~~

Chris' eyes flicked open. At least he thought they were open. His bedroom lay in complete blackness. No blue glow from the alarm clock. No red LED shining from the fifteen-inch TV. Even the blue charge LED from his cell wasn't illuminating the ceiling. The power was out. He vaguely recalled hearing thunder but he'd slept on. Something had woken him. Was it the sudden silence of the power outage?

"Hmmmmmmmmmm . . ."

It finally registered. He reached above him and plucked his cell from its charging cord. "Hel—" He cleared his throat and tried again. "Hello?"

"Chris, man, I'm sorry to wake you—"

"Daryl? What's goin' on? You okay?"

"I think so. I needed to call somebody." Daryl went on to tell Chris about the dream.

"Daryl, I've tried to tell you. What you did, it wasn't unforgivable. It was just one of the many sins we've all committed." There was a lengthy pause. Had he overstepped?

"Hey Chris?"

"Yeah?"

"Is that invitation to church still open?"

He'd remembered. Even after Saturday's horrific events. He'd actually remembered. "Certainly. Do you think you'll feel up to it?" asked Chris.

A couple minutes later, Chris flipped the phone shut and stared at the ceiling. At least he would have, if he could see it in the blackness.

He lay on the bed, unable to go back to sleep. He thought about Daryl. About the murderer in the jail, and Cindy, the woman he'd killed. Then his thoughts drifted to Sarah. He reached to the shelf atop his headboard and felt the key the repairman had given him. He felt the cool brass against his skin. The ridges that would provide her access and security in her home. His thoughts drifted to the painting of the castle. Could he be her shining prince?

The blackness chased away the image. Or would she be one more in a long line of people he'd cared about who ended up dead? Could he even afford to get close?

Grey light began to make its way into the room. It had to be nearing seven.

The weather outside wouldn't be conducive to jogging. He climbed out of bed and went across the hall to the second bedroom, which doubled as his study and exercise room. He lay down on a blue mat and began doing sit-ups. When his abs began to burn, he rolled to his stomach and rattled off fifty pushups. Next he spent twenty minutes on the treadmill. Not nearly as enjoyable as running outside.

He showered and put on a burgundy button up and blue jeans. He'd add the gray sports coat before he headed to pick up Daryl.

In the kitchen, he toasted two pieces of bread, dark brown but not burnt. He covered them with crunchy peanut butter and strawberry jam. After pouring himself a cup of rich blend coffee, he headed to the living room. Opening his Bible, he read aloud from Psalm 30.

"I will exalt you, Lord, for you have rescued me. You refused to let my enemies triumph over me. O Lord my God, I cried out to you for help, and you restored my health. You brought me up from the grave, O Lord. You kept me from falling into the pit of death. Sing to the Lord, all you godly ones! Praise his holy name. For his anger lasts only a moment, but his favor lasts a lifetime! Weeping may last through the night, but joy comes with the morning."

"Lord, You did rescue me yesterday," he prayed. "I'm concerned about what's going on in this town, but I'll trust You. You will bring joy once again to this little town." He continued to pray for several minutes.

At nine-fifteen the clouds from the night's storms began to retreat from the skies. He walked to his Jeep Wrangler and headed for Daryl's house.

At nine-forty-five they pulled into the parking lot of River of Life Church. Two familiar faces from the congregation approached Daryl and welcomed him. Chris could sense Daryl's uneasiness begin to relax.

They entered the foyer. The stale dark air revealed a lack of electricity at the church as well. After a couple more "hellos," they entered the auditorium where they had no trouble seeing. Light flooded through stained glass windows on the east end of the auditorium. He'd never paid the windows much attention. With light streaming through, he saw how beautifully they told God's story—from creation, to the death, burial, and triumphant resurrection of Christ. A light vanilla fragrance wafted through the auditorium from strategically placed candles.

He looked around the auditorium and saw several familiar faces—Mrs. Ferguson, the Hendersons, Trina Thomas, and then another, not a regular at River of Life. *Oh boy.* Marilyn Williams.

"You didn't tell me she went here," said Daryl.

"She doesn't. At least she hasn't." He looked at Daryl, turned his palms upward and raised his shoulders. "I thought she was attendin' a church on the southeast side of town."

"Maybe it would be best if we just sit down and hope she doesn't notice me." Hesitation crept into Daryl's eyes.

They found a spot on an ornate carved wood pew near the back of the auditorium.

The plan didn't work.

In a few moments Marilyn approached them with a friendly yet inquisitive look on her face.

"Good morning. Chris, I knew you went here—" She turned her eyes to Daryl. "I hadn't heard you were coming here." A tone of kindness and civility wrapped her words.

"First time," said Daryl. "After yesterday, I figured it couldn't hurt."

"I heard about the shooting at the jail. Two people killed?"

"Afraid so," said Chris. "The shooter and a woman in the next cell. We can't get into it yet. I hope you understand. The investigation's still ongoing."

"Of course, I'm sorry. I didn't mean to pry."

"Oh, it's okay." Daryl about tripped over himself getting the reassuring words out.

"Well, it's great to see you both." She turned and walked to the other side of the auditorium to find a seat.

"Honestly, I didn't know," whispered Chris.

"It's alright." Daryl raised his eyebrows and took a deep breath. "At least she talked to me. That's an improvement from the last time."

~~~~~~~~~~

Eran glanced around the auditorium as the worship leader began a time of musical worship. Over one hundred angelic warriors had gathered for the service. Many of them, like himself, were personal guardians. He saw Yora with his silver shoulder-length hair and dark-olive skin. Across the room stood the massive warrior Gida with wings of marble. Behind him, Eran heard the elegant rich voice of Adiya. Adiya had accompanied Marilyn. It was their first time at River of Life.

In addition to the guardians, others were in Arrow Springs on special assignment. In addition to the mighty Captain Eitan, he had noticed Miguel, Teman, and Zeke. He had yet to see Alex and Huw.

Most of the angels floated above the pews. The glory of God shone throughout the auditorium. Angels spread their wings basking in the manifest presence of their Creator.

Wings rustled beside Eran. He turned to see Alex and Huw settling into place.

"Glad to see you could make it," he said.

"Would not miss it," said Alex. "Sarah is resting. There are many guardians at the hospital. She will be safe until our return."

The unplugged musical worship continued. All around him, Eran saw angelic warriors begin to return to their full glory. Alex's opalescent wings glowed like a new snow on a sunny day. The iridescent rainbow of color swirling through his wings made him a sight to behold. Each warrior reflected the light of God's presence in a unique way. Some glowed like neon under a black light, others like intense glow-in-the-dark figures. His own pearl-like figure glowed ever more intense with the infusion of light from the True Source of Light.

For many of the angelic warriors the preceding week brought drought and desecration. This time of worship in the presence of God's glory provided a welcome and needed relief. In the temple of old, God's manifest presence dwelt in a single location. In the modern church each believer glowed like a lantern radiating the light of the presence of God.

Eran saw several people gathered that didn't possess the Light of Life—including Daryl.

~~~~~~~~~~

Daryl sat amazed at the passionate worship of Chris and the others around him. His soul parched like a jellyfish washed ashore in the sun without the protection of the sea.

"Brothers and Sisters," opened the pastor, "I'm afraid today I haven't had a chance to prepare all of the slides, videos, and imagery we would normally have for a service." A huge smile formed across his face, "but I guess it doesn't really matter now. Does it?"

Several in the congregation chuckled. Chris' pastor had a sense of humor? People actually laughed in church? It didn't fit Daryl's image of church.

The pastor continued. "I had a message all prepared, but yesterday God redirected me to the message I'm going to share here this morning." After an opening prayer and some additional comments, he had the congregation turn to Genesis 1:24.

Daryl just sat and listened. He didn't have a Bible. And though there was one in the back of the bench in front of him, he wouldn't know where to look in it anyway.

"Today we're going to look at the sixth day of creation." The pastor raised a Bible in his left hand and read. Then he looked up and glanced around the room. His eyes seemed to lock onto Daryl. "What does it mean to be created in God's image?"

Daryl closed his eyes. He certainly didn't have an answer. He reflected on his own image—dark and hollow on the inside, chubby and balding on the outside.

For thirty minutes Pastor Thomas discussed how many teachers would present the image of God in man as man possessing speech, reason, personality, and even a spiritual nature.

"While to one degree or another each of these may be present in the intent of the word here, it would not seem this is primarily what is being implied."

Daryl listened intently as he went on to explain how in most kingdoms of the ancient world, kings would create images or statues of themselves as reminders of their kingship.

"When God created mankind in his image, He created us as His representatives. Adam and Eve were His first representatives in the created kingdom. They were vassals of God."

Did he say vessels? No, it sounded more like vassals. He was unfamiliar with the term, but he continued to listen, intent on understanding.

"The only way a vassal can properly represent his or her king is to reflect the quality and character of that king."

Okay, it's a representative. Why didn't he just say that?

"You see as 'Images of God' our responsibility is to properly reflect the quality and character of God. This is only possible because God created us with some of the attributes I mentioned at the beginning of the message—reason, personality, and a spiritual nature. Most importantly, a representative of God must be holy and righteous." The pastor paused and looked around the auditorium as some of the people wagged their heads back and forth. "There in lies the problem. You see, Adam and Eve messed up—through their disobedience they eliminated themselves as proper vassals for the perfect God."

Now that's me, Daryl thought to himself. A screwed up, imperfect, adulterous image bearer. God sure doesn't want me bearing His image.

He listened as the pastor read from something called Second Corinthians Chapter Four:

"Satan, who is the god of this world, has blinded the minds of those who don't believe. They are unable to see the glorious light of the Good News. They don't understand this message about the glory of Christ, who is the exact likeness of God. You see, we don't go around preaching about ourselves. We preach that Jesus Christ is Lord, and we ourselves are your servants for Jesus' sake. For God, who said, "Let there be light in the darkness," has made this light shine in our hearts so we could know the glory of God that is seen in the face of Jesus Christ."

Daryl's heart thumped within his chest.

"You see Christ is the perfect image of God. He's not a vassal, not a reflection—He *is* God. Jesus Christ came to earth to live as a human to pay the price required for mankind's disobedience. Last week we celebrated Jesus' death, burial, and resurrection. It's because of this death that we have any shot at being His image bearers."

He'd heard this before, from Chris.

"Through his blood those who believe can once again be—as we see here—effective representatives for God. God's light can be seen in the world because Jesus came as the perfect God image, and now all who believe are His servants, His vassals."

That's what he'd seen in Chris, the light of God.

"Are you willing to begin today a Lord-Vassal relationship with Jesus Christ? This requires you to be willing to trust Him with your life. Adam and Eve wanted full control of their lives and it cost them their unflawed image of God. Are you willing to relinquish the independent self-focused control of your life? Are you willing to become His vassal?"

The pastor closed the message and the congregation sang a song of response.

Daryl remained in his seat. He couldn't sing. He couldn't even stand. He needed a heart-to-heart discussion with God. "Lord, is it possible You still desire for me to be Your image bearer? Would You really be willing to forgive me?"

"You are already forgiven." He heard the nearly audible voice. "The question is will you give your life to Me? Or will you reject My perfect gift?"

A charge surged through Him. He could truly be free! Free from the guilt. Free from the despair. Free to live the life he knew God wanted for him. "I am forgiven!" He cried out in his spirit. "I will follow you Lord. Make me Your image bearer."

~~~~~~~~~~

Mael paced atop the facility. Since daybreak he and Mors had not spoken a word. Oh, how he hated Sundays. A constant reminder of their failure. Of their lack of true power. Millennia had passed since the fall of mankind, and still so many worshipped. So many found forgiveness. He hated it. He hated them. But most of all he hated *Him*. They did not deserve His love, or forgiveness.

A nuclear explosion of intense light erupted from east of the river. The spiritual shockwave slammed through the cloud of minions surrounding him. Black shadows spewed into the countryside for a mile. The wave propelled Mael and Mors off the roof. Flailing, they smacked into the ground.

He hissed and cursed. "What was that?"

"The glory of God," Mors spat. "Something terrible has happened."

~~~~~~~~~~

The angelic host gathered at the church rejoiced exuberant. Nothing brought excitement like a new believer coming to faith and trust in Jesus as Lord and Savior. This celebration would fuel the host for days. None more than Eran. His charge was instrumental in the life of this new believer.

The music ended and people began to talk and exit. Eran watched as Daryl turned to Chris and whispered with tears in his eyes, "I'm an image bearer. I'm finally forgiven. I know the Jesus you've been trying to tell me about."

Eran thought Chris would start jumping up and down. "Oh man. That's awesome. You gotta meet Pastor Thomas."

They headed for the back of the auditorium where Pastor Thomas stood shaking hands and thanking people for coming.

"Pastor Thomas," said Chris.

"Chris, it's great to see you."

"I've got someone I want you to meet. This is Daryl a fellow officer and good friend. He's got somethin' to tell you."

Pastor Thomas stuck out his hand and smiled. "Nice to meet you Daryl."

Daryl began to look a little apprehensive.

Eran floated down, and laid his left wing across the man's shoulders.

"Thank you. Pastor, I want you to know how much this service has meant to me." Daryl took a breath and swallowed. "For the first time I understand Jesus made it possible for me to be forgiven. I'm a new image bearer for Him."

Yora and Eran locked hands in a high-five celebration.

"That's awesome Daryl." Pastor Thomas pursed his lips and nodded. "You've made this whole weekend worthwhile. I'd love to hear a bit of your story, if you have a minute."

Daryl turned to Chris, "Well actually I rode with Chris."

"Go on," said Chris. "I'm in no hurry. I'll just catch up with some friends."

~~~~~~~~~~

Eitan watched the other angelic warriors still abuzz from the morning's events. He silently thanked God for the infusion of inspiration. They would need it.

He cleared his throat and prepared to address the gathering. "Before you leave, we need to discuss a few things." He paused as the celebration died down and faces turned toward him. "I wish I could tell you more about what is going on in this town, but for now the Lord has seen fit to keep the situation a mystery."

"In case any of you have not heard, both Mors and Mael are in town overseeing the enemy's efforts." A wave of murmurs passed quickly through the angelic crowd at the mention of the two mighty foes. "Eran had a run in with Mors and a couple others yesterday morning, and another half dozen demons in the afternoon."

"Gida showed up to help," said Eran.

"Like you needed it," said Gida.

Eitan cleared his throat once again. "Anyway, one thing I can tell you is that these attacks are just the precursor of much larger things to come. Alex informs me there was a hollowness about the man who attacked Sarah McIntyre. I do not know who or what he was, but he was not *in the image*. We need to proceed with great caution. We will discover more about what is transpiring as Officer Davis continues his investigation."

He looked at Eran. A sorrow tugged at his being. "The enemy is obviously aware of the significance of Officer Davis to the Lord's work here in Arrow Springs. They have three shadows following him everywhere he goes. They are in fact waiting just outside this building for him to reemerge. We need to guarantee his safety."

Eitan scanned the crowd until he found Zeke. "Zeke, I need you to assist Eran with Chris' protection."

The angel nodded his agreement.

"The enemy has us well outnumbered so we need to be wise about our actions. Do not initiate confrontation—not yet. However, do not hesitate to use force to defend your assignments." He paused to let a couple side conversations die down. "In addition, stay away from the building west of the bend in the river. The time may come for an assault on the enemy entrenched there. For now stay clear."

Eitan walked among the gathered angels, until he stood next to an angel who appeared as wise as he did fierce. "Now on to more exciting business." He patted the angel on the shoulder. "Asa, we have a new believer to protect. I think you are the perfect angel for the job. Mr. Williams is in much need of healing. God has gifted you in this area."

He went on to give Asa some background information on Daryl—his marriage to Marilyn, his adultery, and his three years of torment by a demon of guilt and despair. "Your first assignment is not an easy one. You need to let Mr. Williams deal with the demon of his own accord. Do not allow physical harm to come to him, but only as he is set free through the love of Christ will he truly be free from his guilt and despair." He nodded toward the closed door of Pastor Thomas' office. "Even now Pastor Thomas is giving him instruction that will be instrumental in overcoming the shame and forgiving himself."

He returned his gaze to the gathered host. "Go in the strength of the Father, Son, and Holy Spirit. Be strong and courageous in the face of the enemy, and know that we serve the God who will one day put an end to this war once and for all."

At that, the angelic host began to rejoice and praise God anew.

"Congratulations, Asa." Eran approached the angel. "Daryl is a good man. I am excited to see what God has in store for him."

"Thank you," said Asa. "I think I will go listen to the discussion between Pastor Thomas and Mr. Williams. See you on the ride home." He winked at Eran.

Eitan smiled, even as concern arose within his being.

~~~~~~~~~~

Chris stepped into the foyer. Waiting for Daryl would give him a chance to talk with some friends. He walked around a large-leafed plant in a golden planter.

"Chris . . ." The age-weakened voice rang with inner joy.

"Hey Mrs. Ferguson."

"Is it true?" Her cheeks wrinkled with an unfamiliar frown. "The man who broke into Miss McIntyre's house shot someone yesterday?"

He couldn't leave work at work for one day. "Afraid so."

"But why? Do you have any idea why he did it?"

He took a deep impatient breath through his nose. "Which, the break-in or the shooting?" She was just trying to be kind. He turned his shoulders to face her. "I'm sorry—no, we really don't know anything about him, much less his motives."

She lifted her glasses and rubbed her eye. "Well, I think I've only seen him once before."

"You have? Where?"

Her face lit. "Oh yes. A group of us from Saint Andrews were going door-to-door inviting people to attend our church. You knew that last fall the church was going under? Well, we were trying everything we could to bring people to our precious little church. I so liked Saint Andrews. Not that there's anything wrong with River of Life mind you. I just had so many memories tied up in Saint Andrews. Did you know Betty? Betty VandenDorf?"

"No, I don't believe I had the pleasure. You were saying about the man?"

"Oh, yes, like I said, we were going from house to house on Ash Street, and that man lived there. The conversation was really quite short, in fact he just laughed at us. Called us weak minded—if my memory serves me."

"Do you remember where on Ash?"

"Yes, yes, it was the pale yellow house, not much of a gardener, the grass was pathetic, certainly not the beautiful landscaping of Miss McIntyre's house, and nothing like my Frankie." She tilted her head. "I miss him. He so loved his gardens."

Chris made sure to keep his voice calm. "Where on Ash?"

"Oh, on the right side of the road before you get to Second St."

"Thank you so much. That will help us."

"Just glad I could be of assistance." She raised her chin and made a beeline for one of her elderly friends. No doubt to share how she'd broken the case.

He heard another female voice behind him calling his name. He turned to find Marilyn approaching. "Hey Marilyn."

"It was good to see Daryl here." Her lips smiled but her eyes reflected an inner pain. "Is it true what I heard? He made a decision to turn his life over to Christ?"

"Wow! Word sure travels fast, doesn't it?"

"Well this *is* a church foyer." She flourished her hands. "The ladies need to have something to 'pray' about don't they?" She folded her hands and bobbed her head. "I really am happy to know he found Christ. I know it's made a huge difference in my own life."

"He's a good man," said Chris. "I'm excited for him. I don't know how he handled bein' an officer without a relationship with Christ. I couldn't do it."

"You've been a good friend to him Chris. You stuck with him through everything that's happened. I respect you for it."

Chris paused. Should he push on? "Marilyn, what he did was wrong. He knows that. The last few years have been incredibly rough on him."

Her olive skin pulled tight across her cheek bones. "Not just on him. Chris, I know this is going to sound very un-Christian-like, but, I don't know if I will ever be able to forgive him. I know God forgave me for as much and probably more. But He's God. I'm not. Daryl hurt me—deeply." A moist sheen rippled across her deep brown eyes.

He closed his eyes, and took a deep breath. "Marilyn, I won't pretend to ever know the hurt Daryl caused you. I'm certainly not gonna tell you what you should or shouldn't do." His heart screamed with empathy. "I do know Daryl is just as aware of how wrong his actions were. If God wants you to forgive Daryl, He'll give you the strength you need. Right now I just hope God can help Daryl forgive himself." He paused to see if she'd respond. Nothing. "You know," he continued "Daryl really does love you. He did then. He still does. For three years I've watched him beat himself up over his unfaithfulness to you. I can't ask you to forgive him. Just give him a chance as a fellow brother in Christ."

"I'll try." Mascara seeped from the corners of her eyes. "But I can't make any promises. I should probably get going. I don't think I want to be here when he gets out of his meeting with Pastor Thomas. Please tell him I said congratulations."

He bit down on his tongue. He'd sure handled that well.

~~~~~~~~~~

Chris pulled his Wrangler out onto West River road. They sat in silence. Daryl probably just needed to process all that happened.

A couple minutes later Daryl turned and faced him. "Did you get a chance to talk to Marilyn?"

"Briefly." Chris kept his eyes straight ahead. "She wanted me to tell you congratulations on your new relationship with Christ."

"She heard already?"

"Guess so." He forced a smile to his face. "That's what happens when ya get a group of people together that treat each other like family. How was your conversation with Pastor Thomas?"

"Good, really good. Seems like a nice guy."

"He is."

"I feel like a load's been lifted from my back. It's hard to believe considering all that happened yesterday. I can now understand how you've always seemed so joyful."

"Well I wish I could tell ya you'll always feel that way. It ain't always easy. God doesn't promise life as a believer's gonna be smooth sailin'. But He does promise to be there with us."

Daryl nodded. "That's pretty much what Pastor Thomas told me. He said the enemy would do everything they can to keep me from living as a child of God."

They pulled into Daryl's driveway.

"We talked a little about my past with Marilyn. He told me I need to realize God has forgiven me. What remains is to forgive myself, and eventually to seek Marilyn's forgiveness."

Chris turned off the ignition and turned to face Daryl. "Ya know that's not gonna be easy for her."

"Oh, I know. Right now I'm just going to bask in Christ's forgiveness of me, and work on trying to forgive myself." He closed his eyes. "Though, I must admit I'd love to think that someday Marilyn and I might have some sense of restoration to our relationship. Even if it is only as brother and sister in Christ."

"Only time will tell." Chris didn't want to dash Daryl's hopes. But, Marilyn made her position pretty clear on the matter.

Daryl opened the door and stepped out. "Thanks again Chris. For everything."

~~~~~~~~~~

Asa could see the menacing demon of guilt and despair trailing the jeep just above the treetops. "Looks like we have company." He looked at Eran and Zeke. "It is going to be difficult to just stand by and watch him mess with Daryl."

"Eitan knows what he is doing," said Eran. "You just have to trust the power of the Spirit." A chuckle rippled across his wings. "I suspect that pathetic little demon is in for quite a shock."

"I know. But it still will not be easy."

As Daryl walked toward the front door of the house, Asa made his way to the corner of the house. He was to stay vigilant but out of site—at least for the time being.

Chris' Jeep Wrangler pulled from the driveway and the demon dove for the house to be united with his prey.

Asa smiled as he thought of the surprise in store for the scrawny pest.

~~~~~~~~~~

CHAPTER EIGHT

Chris eased his squad car into a shaded parking spot. Songbirds in the trees greeted him as he walked to the deep-red brick building. The bright afternoon sun warmed his face. He'd driven around the block twice to pass the time until twelve-thirty—the time he told Sarah he'd be there. Didn't want to come across as anxious. The fresh spring air thrilled his soul. Or was it his destination?

He couldn't remember looking forward to a hospital visit more. Since leaving the hospital a day earlier, he couldn't wait for his chance to return. Of course it wasn't like she'd have a mutual interest. She had been kind, though he had sensed a reservation. *Sure she was kind. You're a police officer. What else could she do?* He came to her rescue. Perhaps she thought he could protect her. Only, he knew better.

He arrived at room 426 and knocked politely without turning to enter.

"Come in."

Her sweet invitation made his skin tingle.

He entered the room. They locked eyes. For a moment he actually believed she was happy to see him. "Hey. Y're looking better already."

She rested her head back in her chair. "Are you saying I looked bad yesterday?" A pout washed her face as hurt welled in her eyes.

His heart sank. He'd hurt her already. That must have been a record.

Her button nose began to twitch and her freckles began to tug at the corners of her lips. Like the sun burning through morning clouds, a grin pushed through the pout. "I'm sorry. I'm just messing with you. I've seen myself in the mirror. I know what my face looks like with this nasty thing on my forehead. But it was nice of you to say just the same."

Beautiful and a sense of humor. He couldn't decide if he wanted to hug her or run from the room. For now, neither.

Her eyes gave him a once over. "I must say, it's nice to see you in regular clothes. Not that you don't look good in the uniform, but this seems less, um, policey."

He walked to the chair and held out his hand. "You ready to go?"

"I think so." She took his hand and stood favoring her left ankle. "The doctor told me I was free to check out whenever I was ready. I'll give the nurse a call and see if there's anything else I need to do."

~~~~~~~~~~

Moments later a candy-striper pushed Sarah down the hall to the elevator in a wheelchair. At first, she protested the wheelchair but the teenage girl insisted it was hospital policy. Though Sarah hated to admit it, a long walk on her new air-filled splint made her nervous. The tightness of the splint pushed the swelling to her calf and foot. She spent the first fifteen minutes with the splint convincing herself she really didn't need to itch her ankle. Her broken wrist throbbed, so crutches were out of the question. Chris had run ahead to pull up to the Patient Pick-Up.

The moment her chariot emerged into the fresh air, she raised her left hand to shield her eyes. Oh the beautiful sunlight. She knew—even before she could see the driver that the metallic green Jeep had to be Chris. It just looked like the kind of vehicle an off-duty police officer would drive.

Chris walked around the Jeep. "Probably not the easiest to get into." He opened the door. "Let me help ya."

Warmth flowed from his hand, sending pulses up her arm. His grip was strong yet gentle.

She looked into his eyes. "See, I knew chivalry wasn't dead."

Chris jogged back to his door and climbed into his seat. He turned his head toward her as he looked for traffic. "Have ya eaten lunch?" They pulled from the hospital drive.

"No, I just didn't feel like another hospital meal. Don't get me wrong the food was fine—the atmosphere left something to be desired."

Chris bobbed his head. "I know this nice little bistro outside Boonville. Definitely a better atmosphere than Regional. Would ya let me buy you lunch? I didn't get a chance to eat yet either."

"Sounds nice. Thank you." He was too good to be true.

~~~~~~~~~~

Chris hoped the bistro would meet with Sarah's approval. There were few places in central Missouri more breathtaking. Yet the prices were reasonable. He didn't want her to feel uncomfortable with the gesture. At one-thirty he escorted her into the quaint little bistro overlooking the Missouri River.

"This is so beautiful," she said.

He took a sip of his water and watched her take in the setting. Her eyes looked to the beautiful tongue-and-groove wood ceiling.

"Have you been here before?" he asked.

"No. I didn't even know it existed. This view—" She looked to the river to their north. "It's incredible."

The wind and rain from the night before left the river area fresh and pure under the day's bright sun-lit radiance. Her eyes seemed glued to the beautiful farmland across the river. Land that thrived as a result of the river's provision.

He silently admired her beauty. The edge of her ear peeked out from behind red curls. Somewhere she'd gotten hold of a black sweater which complimented her figure. Her eyes gazed somewhere beyond the floor-to-ceiling glass.

"God's quite the artist. Ain't he?" said Chris.

"I'm sorry—what?" Her eyes turned toward him.

He forced his gaze off her and out the window. "I'm just saying—no matter how hard man tries, he just can't compete with the beauty of God's creation." Had she noticed he was more captivated by her beauty than the view outside?

"I suppose." Uncertainty swirled through those two simple words.

"Can I take your order?" asked a young waitress who had approached unnoticed.

"Oh, I haven't even looked at the menu yet." Sarah flipped open the menu.

"Could you give us a couple of minutes?" Chris studied his menu, but he already knew what he would order. No reason to rush her.

A few minutes later the waitress returned. Sarah ordered the baked Tilapia fillet sandwich, a side of French onion soup, and lemonade. He ordered the Chicken Marsala and an iced tea.

He waited until the waitress left. "I checked your house yesterday. Everything was fine."

"I know. I was just being paranoid."

"Not at all. If I hadn't stopped by, how would you have gotten this?" He set the key to her home on the table between them. "The repairman arrived as I was leaving. He asked me to give it to you."

"Thank you so much. It sure makes me feel better knowing the door is fixed. I don't think I could handle going home to a house with the front door swinging—" Her voice trailed off. "So, what made you decide to be a police officer?"

She practically swallowed back whatever she had planned to say.

He honored her change of direction. "Well, that's not such a pleasant subject. Out of high school I went to Mizzou on a full-ride football scholarship. By my sophomore season I was an All-American wide receiver." *That sounded arrogant.* "One night, everything changed. I got a call in my dorm room.

There'd been an accident. A drunk driver crossed the yellow line, and hit my mom's car. She was killed instantly."

Sympathetic tears began to seep into her eyes. "I'm so sorry."

"The man walked away from the crash—only minor scratches."

"Did you have any other family to walk through it with you? Father? Brothers or sisters?"

"No. I never knew my father. Some twenty year old college student who hadn't planned on a family, just a night's fun with an eighteen year old high school senior." He could feel his jaw tighten. "Nope, that drunk took all that remained of my family."

"Were you ever able to confront him?"

"The drunk?"

She nodded.

"Twice. The first time was at his trial. I wish I could say I conducted myself respectfully—the judge threatened to have me removed from the courtroom. But at least he was convicted. He's still in prison."

She tilted her head. "You said you confronted him twice?"

He took a deep breath. "Two years ago. I went to the prison to meet with him. In the year following the accident, I met a man who taught me what it meant to have a relationship with Jesus. I went to the prison to forgive the man."

A look of horror flooded Sarah's eyes. "How could you? He killed your mom?" She spat the words like bile. "He broke the law and it cost you your family."

He'd known that kind of pain. That kind of bitterness. "I realized no matter what was said or done, I would never have my mom back." He shook his head. "The grief, bitterness, and anger I harbored were crippling my walk with Christ."

Sarah let out a huff.

"I didn't want to live that way. I saw what that kind of anger did to my younger brother." Images flashed through his mind. "Because of his anger, I found him dead in our bathroom. He'd bled out from a gun-slapper's bullet. He didn't make the football team like me, instead he turned his anger to the streets. I found that same anger beginning to tear me apart. If Jesus could forgive me, I could do the same."

She rubbed her hand across her face. "I suppose you're a better man than me."

"I certainly hope so!" They both smiled and he felt the tension drain from the conversation.

She lifted her eyes from the table to look him in the face. "So you're a police officer, why?"

"Oh, yeah, after the death of my mom, football became an empty pursuit. I left college and went to the academy in St. Louis. I pledged to do what I could to keep guys like that off the streets. To keep others from the pain I've experienced."

"I must say I'm glad you made that choice. I know the last couple days have been a nightmare for you, but you were literally a knight in shining armor for me the last couple days."

He tried his best Joe Friday impersonation. "Just doin' my job, ma'am."

Sarah shook her head and wrinkled her cute little nose.

~~~~~~~~~~

Sarah watched the perky brunette set down her French onion soup.

"And here's your salad." The waitress smiled at Chris. "Is there anything else I can get you?"

He looked around the table. "Not right now. Thanks."

Sarah waited as the waitress pranced back to the kitchen. She closed her eyes and took a deep breath of the steam rising from her soup. The warmth and spice of the onion aroma eased the tightening muscles around her stomach. She was falling for him. How? She'd been hurt too many times.

He seemed different. He wanted to protect her.

It was his job—not her.

No, he was different. Different from the others. He really did want to protect her.

But would he?

Would he protect her from himself?

She watched him. Watched a strong black hand lift his glass to his deep-red lips. He possessed a quiet strength, with an edge. An edge emerging from the many pains that chiseled his character into the knight sitting across the table sipping his iced tea.

"What about you?"

No, please don't ask.

"What's your story?"

She stood at a cliff's edge. In ten years she'd shared her ordeal with less than five people. She longed to jump. To open her heart and let the truth cascade from her soul. She couldn't. She needed to run. Run to the safety behind the barriers. The safe answers came so natural.

Perhaps she could. Perhaps he'd catch her if she jumped. But what if he didn't? Could her heart survive another crash to the rocks? But he wouldn't allow it. He was strong, caring. He'd catch her.

But what if he didn't?

She swallowed at the lump forming in her throat. "Well, I'm afraid mine's not too pleasant either." She closed her eyes, feeling her eyelashes meet.

"It's okay," he interrupted. "Ya don't have to talk about it. You've been through a lot this weekend."

"No, I think I do need to talk about it. I was sixteen . . ."

~~~~~~~~~~

Saturday, July 3, 2010

One week after her sixteenth birthday, Sarah attended a youth praise gathering with a group of teens from Webster Groves Community Church. Tim and Angela dropped her off at the curb.

She bounded to the sidewalk and turned her carefree head back to the SUV. "Thank you for the ride."

Angela leaned out the window. "Sure thing. See you tomorrow at church?"

"Of course," she'd replied. "And then we're having family over for a Fourth of July party. It's gonna be so much fun."

She started up the brick sidewalk to her parent's newly constructed Victorian home. Skipping to the front door, the sun warmed her face. Another beautiful summer day in the suburb of St. Louis.

She paused at the front step. Something was wrong. The ornate door swung back and forth, back and forth, as the southern breeze pulsed against it.

She heard that voice. "Don't go in! Run back to the car."

Instead she stood, frozen by indecision. Her head turned as Tim's emerald Trailblazer pulled into traffic and disappeared. Alone with her fear, she overruled the voice. She convinced herself there was nothing to fear but fear itself. How wrong she had been.

She ventured into the house.

A stale dusty smell replaced the floral aroma of the yard.

She heard creaking from the second-story floorboards, somewhere beyond the winding oak staircase.

"Mom, is that you?"

At the sound of her voice, stillness fell over the house. Even her thoughts couldn't be heard in the deafening silence that enveloped her. She ignored the voice that all but screamed at her to run? Instead she ascended the stairs, walked the hall to her parent's room, turned to her left, and stumbled through the open door.

Time ceased.

The scene before her seared into her retinas.

Dresser drawers on the floor, glass from her parents' bedside lamp on the bedspread, speckles, spatters, pools of blood—the lifeless bodies of her mom and dad lay at the foot of the bed.

Thump-thump, thump-thump, the sound of her heartbeat in her ears retreated. Thump-thum—Her world faded to black.

~~~~~~~~~~

Sunday, April 19, 2020

"Oh Sarah. I'm so sorry," said Chris.

She opened her eyes and gazed into his deep compassion.

She finally found the courage to continue. "They were still there."

"The killers?"

"Yes. I'm sure they intended to kill me too." She looked down at her soup. "I think they thought I was dead. I probably would've been if Tim and Angela hadn't returned."

A large tear splashed on the table in front of her. Chris reached his hand across the table with his palm facing upward.

She rested her left hand in his. His grip tightened around her hand. Saying, "I won't let you go."

He caught her. His strong biceps kept her from plunging. Plunging to the rocks at the base of her soul. She'd jumped and he caught her. She told him—almost everything. But would he have caught her, if he knew?

"Angela told me at the hospital, she'd felt a sense of dread shortly after dropping me off at the house. She talked Tim into returning to the house. As they walked to the house from the driveway, they heard people in the house hollering and stuff breaking. When they entered the house the back door slammed from the intruders' escape. The police arrested them a week later, when they broke into another house."

Sarah searched the deep brown eyes staring back at her. Could she really trust him? "Angela found me unconscious on the floor of my parents' room. I found out later that she rode to the hospital with me and stayed there 'til she knew I was going to recover. She felt guilty for what happened to me. They had no way of knowing—like I said, I'd probably have died if they hadn't returned."

"Are they still in St. Louis?"

"As far as I know. I haven't talked with them for a few years. After the attack I suppose I kind of turned my back on God. I just can't understand why He would let something like that happen. My parents were good people. They were active in their church. They even spent time doing short-term missions. So I stopped attending church. With my absence from church and the guilt Tim and Angela felt, we drifted apart."

"Man. I'm so sorry. I see why the attack Friday was so traumatic. You must've been scared to death."

"Sort of. I flashed back to the events of that day, but not so much in a scary way, more of a reflection. I realize now how much pain Tim and Angela must have felt through all that happened."

"Maybe you should try 'n get a hold of 'em." Chris wiped salad dressing from the corner of his lips with his napkin. "Let them know how you're doin'. Maybe even thank 'em for helping you when you needed it most." His hand felt nearly as warm as his soft glistening gaze.

"You know, I just might do that."

Chris tilted his head to the left. "You said they caught the guys. Were they convicted?"

"Yes. The trial was quick. They didn't find any fingerprints in the house, but based on DNA evidence at the scene, they're all in prison." She pulled her hand back. "I won't be visiting them to offer my forgiveness anytime soon."

"Fair enough— How's the Tilapia?"

"Very good. At least the bite I've taken so far." She let out a quick laugh, relieved at the break in the tension of their conversation. She felt a cool moist sensation on her lip and scrambled for her napkin. That just had to look lovely. She wiped at her lip and then excused herself to the Ladies' room to freshen up.

When she returned, they finished their meals and engaged only in small talk. An hour and a half after arriving, they climbed back into his Jeep and headed for Arrow Springs. In her driveway, Chris opened the passenger door of the Wrangler and helped her climb out.

Sarah lingered beside the vehicle. "Thank you so much for lunch. It was lovely. You've been so kind to me." *Why?*

He shifted his weight to the right. "You're an easy person to be kind to."

"I bet you say that to all the damsels you rescue." Her heart slapped at her ribs.

"Hardly. It really was my privilege. Here—here's my number. Please call me if ya need anything."

"I will. Thanks."

He leaned slightly and stared at her face, as if trying to determine if she meant it. "Promise?"

"Promise." She leaned forward and sealed the promise with a peck on the cheek.

His eyes reflected his embarrassment as he climbed back into the Jeep.

Maybe she shouldn't have done that. He probably didn't see her that way. Was she like a little sister to him? Had she blown it already?

She put the new key in the pale gray door and opened it. Safely inside, she watched him pull away. Her cheeks tightened. Would he be back? Or, was he riding off into the sunset never to be seen again?

~~~~~~~~~~

CHAPTER NINE

The smell of an apple-cinnamon plug-in greeted Sarah as she stepped into her home. Had it only been two days? It seemed like weeks since the attack. The memories of Friday night loomed like a distant mountain on a foggy morning. She knelt to slip her shoe off her throbbing left foot. She paused staring at crimson spots on the slate. Blood. Her blood. She reached to her forehead and fingered the stitches. Perhaps it had only been two days.

She headed to the kitchen to check her answering machine. A red digital readout told her she had zero new calls. No surprise there.

A pile of items that belonged in her purse sat on the sandstone countertop. Though she didn't remember him saying so, Chris must have picked them up from around her porch. She picked at the items. Change, credit card, ink pen, oh no— Her cheeks itched as blood flushed her face. Wouldn't it figure that *that* would be one of the items to fall out of her purse. She eyed the small pink package. Even a single man would know it contained a personal feminine product.

Her eyes swept to a small piece of plastic sitting among her change.

~~~~~~~~~~

Chris crossed the Lamine Bridge into southern Arrow Springs. Fresh green trees reflected off the river, while azure skies reflected his mood. A beautiful girl. A beautiful day. A murder to investigate. Well, that was short lived.

"Do-da-dee-da-do do-da-dee-da-do."

He glanced at the small screen on his cell-phone. *That was quick.*

"Hello?"

"Hey Chris. It's Sarah." Her soft voice resonated through his being.

"Is everything okay at the house?"

"Yeah, I'm fine. Sorry to call so soon." She paused. "You're probably looking forward to gettin' some rest after your wild weekend. I can call you tomorrow."

"No, it's okay. I asked you to call. What's up?"

Another pause. "I just wanted to ask, did you pick some stuff up off my porch?"

"Oh yeah, I forgot to tell you. Sorry. I found a few things that had fallen under one of your shrubs." He prayed she didn't ask what he was doing crawling under her shrubs.

"Did you perhaps lose a small memory card?" she asked. "I was looking through the stuff and there's a small memory card. It's not mine so I thought maybe it was yours."

"Nope, not mine." *Memory card, why would I carry a*— "Wait a minute!" The realization jarred his brain. *Could it be?* "Sarah, I think I know what it is. Be there soon as I can. See ya there."

After calling dispatch for the number he punched in the phone number for Mike Henderson. "Come on answer."

"This is Mike."

"Mike, hey, it's Chris Davis."

"Yes?"

"Did your camera happen to be missing its memory card?" A long shot at best. He had no reason to believe the murderer from the jail had anything to do with the break-in.

"Yeah, how'd you know?"

Jackpot! The cruiser's tires squawked as Chris headed back toward Sarah's. "I think I may have found it. Would there be a problem with me hangin' onto it for a few days? I'd like to see if the pictures shed any light on why someone would break in to steal it."

The boy's voice was hesitant. "Um, sure. I guess that'd be alright."

"Thanks Mike, I'll get it back to you as soon as I can. Later."

When Chris pulled back into Sarah's drive, freckles and a bright smile awaited him in the doorway. "Hey there. Short time, no see."

"I really hope that card's what I think it is."

She led him to the kitchen and offered him a barstool at the counter. "Can I get you an ice water or a soda?"

"Water—please."

She grabbed a pitcher from the refrigerator and poured the water.

Their fingers brushed as he took the glass sending tingles up his arm.

He filled her in on the break-in at the Henderson's.

"So you think it was the same guy?" Her eyes grew wide and concerned.

"Honestly, I hadn't put the two together 'til you called. I assumed Mike just forgot where he left his camera. But now it looks like our man may have removed the card and ditched the camera."

"You think the card has a picture on it? Something that'll show why he'd steal it?

"See there, you're good at this detective work."

Sarah smirked. "Funny. But what could it have to do with me? Why would he break in here?"

He wanted to hold her. To tell her he'd protect her. To reassure her that it probably had nothing to do with her. "I don't know. Perhaps we'll find some clue on that card."

Her face lit up. "You know, our printers at the library have card readers. I think they could read this." She handed him the memory card. "People use them to print photos. Maybe you could stop by tomorrow and see what's on it."

"Sounds like a plan. What time?" Anything to spend more time with her. "Wait. You're plannin' on going back to work—already?"

She shrugged her shoulders. "Why not? I'll just go insane here." She rested her cast on the counter. "I can get someone to do the laborious tasks like stacking books and such. My mind still works. I can still help people find what they're looking for."

He didn't doubt that. "Okay then. I'll see ya sometime tomorrow mornin'. I'm guessing it'll be fairly early—I'll be anxious to see what's on this."

He could think of a half-dozen different places to get the card read—Sarah wouldn't be at the other five.

~~~~~~~~~~

Dr. Wilhelm M'Gregor stared past the screen of his television—oblivious to the infomercial claiming to have the world's best tool for preparing fresh food. He rested the bit of his pipe against his white-bearded chin. His mind taunted him with reflections of his past glory. He was a scientist. He had accomplished what no one else dared dream. He made a difference for mankind. Then five years ago *she* returned.

Maiya was the daughter and only child of Dr. Jurek Mirinov, his late business partner and co-founder of their business. He first met her when she was just ten. Her brown saucer eyes danced with life. Over the years he watched with amusement as she used them to manipulate Jurek into almost anything she wanted. She was a typical teenager. Her jet-black hair and toothy grin used to make him laugh. She was only an infant when her mother passed away. Jurek did the best he could raising a daughter as a single parent.

Jurek had beamed with pride when she went off to the East Coast to attend a prominent university. She returned two years later during spring break. Never, either before or since, had he seen Jurek so irate.

Her appearance and demeanor sent shivers down his spine. Her already light complexion had faded to a pale white, and her brown eyes acquired a reddish tint that intensified with her moods. He overheard her arguing with Jurek about the snow-white streak that adorned her black hair. Her father accused her of dying the streak white and said it looked ridiculous. She responded in anger that the streak had simply appeared there one night while she slept—something about a gift from her spirit guide. After working with her for the last five years, he now believed she had told Jurek the truth. He no longer felt comfortable in the same room with her.

He drew deeply on the pipe. How had it come to this? He felt like a prisoner at his own company—and under surveillance everywhere else. Perhaps he was just paranoid. At sixty-four years of age the two to three hours of sleep he managed each night left him weak both physically and emotionally. Never before had he questioned the direction of their research. But she continued to push. He grew more uncomfortable by the week. He had tried questioning her. Even threatened to leave. Though she never overtly threatened him, he knew Maiya wouldn't allow him to walk away from the operation.

Why did he ever leave Scotland? The call and excitement of America now served as his prison—if he were to leave Arrow Springs and the company, it would be in a pine box.

~~~~~~~~~~

Daryl sat at the round oak table in his dining room with his head buried in his hands. His temples throbbed from twelve hours of the usual attacks.

You are pathetic. Adulterer. Loser. God could not love someone like you. Rather than coming as his own thoughts, the accusations rang like echoes of stinging phrases, emotional arrows shot at him from some unseen stronghold.

Pastor Thomas and Chris both warned him—the enemy wasn't going to give up without a fight. The barrage of memories—his unfaithfulness to Marilyn—hurt twice as much as before.

The increase in pain came from a fresh perspective. In the past he realized how much he had hurt Marilyn and how one act had messed up his life. Now he saw his sin in light of the perfection of Christ. Like the way old socks don't really look old until placed next to a new pair of perfectly white ones—Daryl's best efforts at pure living now looked dark and dingy.

Pastor Thomas had said, "Daryl, as a follower of Christ, you died with Him, and were raised up as a new creation. You don't need to live defeated. He took your guilt and he wants to remove your shame."

He stared blurry bloodshot eyes at the section he'd just read. For almost four hours he hadn't moved. A large Bible, a gift to him and Marilyn for their wedding, sat on the table. He had read all of the book called Matthew, and now came to the end of Mark. His mind struggled with the story of Jesus' having died and then appearing to his followers alive. Though his mind struggled, his heart did somersaults. He could now live for this risen Savior.

~~~~~~~~~~

Asa stood in seclusion just outside Daryl's dining room. His muscles strained to hold back his amusement as he watched the demon of guilt and despair.

At first the demon tried his usual tactics—sinking talons deep within Daryl's skull to stir memories of past sin and failure. A look of horror flushed his mangled face as he pulled back smoldering talons.

The demon stared at his charge in disgust. "I knew I should never have let you enter that church."

Asa could see the glimmer of light blooming at the core of Daryl. His faith grew.

The demon circled Daryl as if he'd find an angle from which he could attack. "Fine we will do it the hard way. I will destroy your faith, render you spiritually impotent."

As the verbal assault intensified, so did Asa's distaste for this foe.

Asa nodded when Daryl began to read from the gospels. His charge would find freedom from the oppression he had lived with for years.

The demon began to fidget. The sight of his project delving into the Word of God clearly infuriated him.

Behind Asa a clock began to chime. One, two . . . eleven, twelve.

As if the declaration of midnight was the bell at the end of a fight, the demon blew up in a fit of rage. He pulled a serpent shaped dagger from his side. "If I can't have you, no one will." He screamed and swung the dagger down toward Daryl's head.

The dagger halted as if it hit a wall of steel.

"You no longer have any business here," roared Asa. The time for action had finally come. He held his fiery red sword between the dagger and Daryl's head. "Leave now, or be banished!" He pushed the sword forward sending the demon sprawling out of the dining room.

The demon charged. "He is mine!" he hissed through yellow sulfur covered teeth.

"Not anymore." A giant red arc split the demon top to bottom banishing him to the Abyss. Asa sheathed the sword and approached Daryl. "Rest dear friend." His wings formed a canopy over the battle worn human. "You can now rest in the peace of the Lord."

~~~~~~~~~~

CHAPTER TEN

Monday dawned and Chris awoke to the coos of Mourning Doves and the occasional warbling song of the Orchard Oriole. Despite the horrific events of the weekend the beauty of creation lived and continued as if nothing happened. But, his day would be dictated by the events of the weekend. His mind raced with anticipation of the day's tasks.

Based on the information provided by Mrs. Ferguson, it appeared the attacker lived near Sarah's house. Even though he didn't need to check the River's Edge for a vehicle, there might still be value in knowing if the man had been there prior to the attack. Perhaps Pete noticed something to give insight into the man's strange behavior.

In addition, the attacker's house needed to be investigated. He needed to follow up with the coroner's office to see if they found anything unusual about the perpetrator. Besides the obvious psychopathic tendencies. He should also touch base with Mike Henderson to let him know they had apparently found his memory card.

Despite the importance of these tasks, one item dominated the top of his list. He'd never been so anxious to visit the library.

Days like this provided the greatest temptation to jump headlong into the day, to blow off his normal exercise and quiet time with God. Until six months ago, he would have flown out the door ten minutes after the alarm clock went off. These days his body just didn't feel the same if he didn't get his morning run. Likewise, he quickly became sluggish both spiritually and emotionally if he didn't spend some time in prayer and God's Word.

Chris set his coffee mug on the oak end table next to the couch, sat down, and picked up his Bible from the table. He turned to Ephesians Chapter Six and read:

"A final word: Be strong in the Lord and in his mighty power. Put on all of God's armor so that you will be able to stand firm against all strategies of the Devil. For we are not fighting against flesh-and-blood enemies, but against evil rulers and authorities of the unseen world, against mighty powers in this dark world, and against evil spirits in the heavenly places."

"Lord," Chris prayed. "I know today's gonna be a busy one. I'm sure it'll have its struggles. I realize the enemy's workin' here in Arrow Springs. Please Lord—help me remember how much I need You in all I do. Not to attempt everything in my own strength and effort. But to trust in You, in Your strength. In my weakness I'm strong. You delight to use my weakness for Your glory."

"And Lord—about Sarah, I really liked the time I spent with her yesterday. Thank You for bringing her into my life. Give me the wisdom to know how to best interact with her. I know she's suffered great pain, beyond the mere breaks and bruises of this last attack. Help her be aware of Your peace. Protect her from the attack of the enemy. Give her strength as she returns to her job at the library. Help her to not overdo it—to know her own limitations."

"Lord, to You be the praise and glory for what You've done this weekend, and all that You're gonna do today. Amen."

After his run and a quick shower, he left the house and walked to his squad car. The unmistakable scent of the neighbor's lilacs danced on the swirling wind. Within an hour, he entered through the screen door of the River's Edge where the stench of stale cigarette and spoiling beer twisted his stomach.

The River's Edge closed on Sunday—not in an attempt to abide by some seemingly antiquated rule regarding working on Sunday, but because the business simply didn't warrant paying the help. The same could be said of Monday morning, but Pete and Fran, his wife, came in to get the place cleaned up before the lunchtime crowd arrived. Not that any turnout at the River's Edge constituted a crowd—with the exception of the evening drinkers of course. The food justified an occasional visit for lunch, but being Arrow Spring's only real bar attracted their most loyal customers.

"Hey Pete," Chris said to the quite large and not so fit owner. "Mornin' Fran."

"Officer Davis—got no drunk and disssorderlies for you to pick up this earrrly in the morning."

Chris shook his head. "That true Fran? Ya sure Pete's been behavin' himself?"

"Heyyy now, I'm the best thing that everrr happened to 'er. Ain't that r-right babe?"

Fran's eyes rolled up into their sockets. "I think I need to go clean up in the kitchen. You two boys enjoy yourselves." She spun and strolled toward the swinging gates. She paused but didn't turn. "Oh, and Pete don't forget to mop up that floor. Your buddy the mayor made quite a mess."

Pete turned his leer from her and looked back to Chris. "He's no buddy, but he is a good tipper. The waitresses love to see him come in."

Pete motioned to a seat at the bar and then perched next to it. "He that free flowing with your pay raises?"

"I wish! I don't see him much. He don't seem too fond of the station." Chris joined Pete at the bar. "In January, he called me into his plush office to give me a token pat on the back and a cost of livin' increase on behalf of the city council. That's about it. Sounds like you see more of him than I do."

"Yeah he's a regular." Pete stared at the glasses hanging from a rack over the bar. "I'd offer you a drink, but I don't take you as an on the job drinker."

"No, not exactly." Especially at eight-thirty in the mornin'.

Pete slapped his palms to the bar. "Well, I'm sure you didn't come in just to chat. Not that I mind, mind you. What's up? What can I do for you?"

"I need a favor," said Chris. "Friday evenin' someone broke into a house a couple blocks from here. We got the call round eight-thirty. The owner of the house said she saw the man walking up the sidewalk from this direction." He reached into his grey folder and pulled out a mugshot. "I was hopin' maybe he'd been here that night."

"I'll help if I can. Let me see?"

Chris pushed the mugshot down the counter.

"Oh yeah! He was here alright. He comes in every once in awhile. Don't know his name though."

This was good. "Did you notice anything strange Friday night? What was his demeanor? Did he meet with anyone? Did he appear to be on anything? You know that sort of stuff."

Pete rubbed his jowls with his hand. "Well let's see. I don't think he really met with anyone. Though he did take a shine to that tramp that was in here." Pete raised the right corner of his lips into a knowing smile.

Chris' neck began to stiffen.

"I hadn't seen her before," said Pete. "I think she was from out of town. Officer Williams came in and got her not too long after your man there came in."

"She's dead," said Chris. The words squeezed through his constricted throat. "Shot by our attacker there." He took a deep breath. "She saved my life. Took a bullet intended for me."

"Oh my G— I'm so sorry. I had no idea. I—I didn't mean no disrespect. I can see now why you want more info on this guy."

Chris moved his head from left to right hearing crackling in his ears. "Anything else you can tell me about him, about what happened Friday?"

"Well let's see, as I said he liked that—um—young lady. She seemed to have her eyes set on Mayor Richards." Pete eyed him to see if he was going to react. "She was pretty boisterous, definitely had too many beers. Not here mind you! We're careful not to over serve our guests."

"Right, and?"

"Yes well the Mayor didn't seem to mind her advances. They were quite—well—cozy." Pete tapped the photo. "Then this guy here comes up to them and starts chatting with the Mayor like some long lost friend. His presence made Mayor Richards quite uncomfortable. Then the—young woman got really mad at the man and started swearing up a cuss word tornado. That's when I called the station to come pick her up."

Chris' stomach twisted at the discussion of her actions. She may not have been a saint, but she still saved his life. "How about this guy. Anything strange? Unusually quiet? Perhaps emotionally unstable?"

"No, after that little incident he seemed normal. Quite pleasant actually." Pete's eyes roamed the bar as if he were watching the man interact with others throughout the bar. "He talked casually with several people at the bar, and then left just after eight. I remember the time—it's kind of an odd time to leave our establishment. Usually those who are still with us at that time of night end up staying quite a bit later, if you know what I mean."

"Could he have had too much to drink? The personality ya describe don't sound anything like the man we arrested." He watched Pete for signs that he was lying to him.

"Oh he wasn't drunk." Pete's face was sincere. "In fact he only drank 'bout a quarter of the beer he ordered. He seemed to get along with just 'bout everybody. He laughed with the happy ones, spoke empathetic with the ones trying to drown somethin', and kept up with the most profane in the crowd. He really seemed to play the audience."

It just didn't connect. "Sounds like we're talking about two different guys. You're sure this is the guy?" Chris pointed to the picture lying on the bar.

"Oh that's him! No doubt 'bout that one."

"I assume he walked here, but did ya happen to see a car? Perhaps after everybody left?"

"Well we had one pickup left here Friday night but they came to get it Saturday morning. Probably just a case of someone having too much to drink and one of their slightly sober friends takin' 'em home."

Chris reached into his pocket and slapped a business card on the bar. "Pete, I appreciate your assistance. If ya think of anything else give me a call." He picked up the photo and returned it to the folder.

"I'm glad to help. Anything I can do to stay on the good side of the local police force, you know."

Chris wagged his head and headed for the exit. "Catch you later."

"I hope not!"

~~~~~~~~~~

Daryl held his silver coffee mug and leaned against a white laminate table. The station's fax machine churned to life atop the table. He snapped up the piece of paper and sat in one of the briefing chairs. At the top of a brown tack board hung a picture of the lifeless body of Cindy. Pangs pierced his side as he reflected on their discussion only a couple days earlier. She was starting over. A chance at a new life, snuffed out.

Next to her picture, hung a mugshot of the man who ended her life. Lines spread down from the photo. One pointed to the address of Sarah McIntyre, where he'd been arrested. One pointed to the Henderson's, where he'd apparently broken in to steal a memory card from a camera. A third line revealed the address they'd received from Mrs. Ferguson. He read the address and then examined the piece of paper in his hand. He rose from the chair and pinned the sheet under the address.

A quick call to the Department of Motor Vehicles had produced a return fax confirming the man had used the suspected address when he registered for his driver's license. The casual appearance of the man in the photo was unsettling. He certainly didn't look like a homicidal maniac. Daryl's trust in that face had resulted in Cindy's death.

His gaze locked onto the name on the license, Leon Burgos. He finally had a name to put with the sinister face bound to haunt him for years to come. He pulled his cell from its clip, flipped it open, and spoke into the microphone. "Chris Davis." He heard the automated female voice, "Calling Chris Davis," followed by a series of beeps and clicks.

"Hey Chris, I thought you'd wanna know. We've got a name for the perp. Your tip from Mrs. Ferguson was right on. I just received a fax from the D.M.V. of a driver's license for a Leon Burgos, age 20, address, 130 Ash Street." he waited several seconds before Chris finally responded.

"That's good." Chris sounded lost in his thoughts. "Can you check out the address? See what you can find."

"Yeah, I was about to call Judge Burns to get a warrant to search the premises. I'll let you know if I find anything of interest."

"The warrant should be a no brainer," said Chris. "Stay safe."

"You too, talk to you later." Daryl folded the phone and put it back in the clip.

He walked back to his office and sat down in the black leather chair behind his desk. He'd dealt with Judge Burns several times in the past. It never seemed the judge liked him much. He took a deep breath and pulled up the contacts folder on his computer. He clicked on the Judge's name. The phone next to the computer jumped to life.

Moments later a receptionist's voice came across the speaker, "Judge Burn's office."

After talking with the receptionist, and then waiting several minutes, the judge finally answered the phone.

"Um, yes, good morning Judge. I'm sure you heard about the shooting here at the station Saturday morning?"

He listened to the man on the other end.

"Yes, that's right Sir, he did use my gun." His temples began to tighten. "That aside Sir, we've tracked down his address, and I would like to request a warrant to search the house for any information regarding his motive."

Daryl rubbed the back of his neck as the man asked about the address.

"Well Sir, we obtained a copy of his driver's license from the D.M.V. based on a tip we received as to a possible residence. According to the license his name was Leon Burgos."

Why was this man so irritating?

"Yes Sir! I'm positive it's the same guy. I was the one who brought him to the station, and took his mugshots."

He needed to stay calm. The concussion made his head tender.

"Yes, and I was the one who opened the cell. Sir, can I get the warrant or not."

"Thank you sir, I'll look for the fax."

Daryl swore at the phone as he hung up. Was it the judge's young age, or just his arrogance that made him so annoying? Burns achieved appointment to the county judicial seat straight out of college at the age of twenty-two. Many of the people Daryl talked with at the courthouse thought the judge was a pompous jerk. At least he'd agreed to the warrant.

Now, if he could just lose the headache before the fax came through.

~~~~~~~~~~

Sarah sat at the front desk of the library staring at a stack of books Marta left for her to catalog. She picked up an older looking one. People regularly donated books to the library. Some like the one she held in her hand were gems. This book possessed a red cloth cover, with gilt lettering on the spine. There were a few scuffs on the front. She opened its cover. Published in 1957, this was the earliest edition of The Fellowship of the Ring she'd ever held. It was beautiful.

A bell dinged under the counter, indicating the front door had opened. She looked up with an ear-to-ear grin as Chris approached the front desk. Pulling the book against her chest, she asked, "Is there something I can help you with officer?"

"Why yes." He was attempting an official police voice. "I was wondering if you would be so kind as to help me with some detective work?"

She returned the effort with a southern bell. "Why officer, I'd be glad to help." Laughter pulled at her cheeks. She finally gave in and broke out laughing. "Over here." She laid the book on the counter and walked to the bank of computers to her right.

His tall muscular frame stepped up next to her. She inhaled deep the fragrance of his woodsy scent. He handed her the small memory device and she plugged it into the narrow rectangular slot in the printer. The computer sprang to life excited at the opportunity to interact with a new friend.

"I really hope we get somethin' useful off this thing," he said. "Seems like there's gotta be some reason the guy would go to so much trouble, just to steal a memory card from a camera."

She didn't want to disappoint him. "You know it's possible he only suspected there was an incriminating photo. You can't always tell what somebody took a picture of you know."

"Yeah, but it's sure worth a shot."

"Uh oh" Not what she wanted to see.

"What?"

"There's something wrong with the card."

He read the message from the screen. "Memory Card Corrupt - Unable to Access"

She tried the card on another machine—same result. "It appears the card is damaged." It looked perfectly fine. Then again not all damage was evident from the outside.

"Maybe it got moisture in it from sitting outside all night Friday." He set a reassuring hand on her shoulder. "It was worth a try."

She wanted to melt, to collapse into his strong arms. She wanted to run.

Chris took the memory card from her. "I have a friend in St. Louis. We went through the academy together. Maybe she can get the information off this."

The mention of a former friend—a woman—made Sarah's stomach flip. They hadn't known each other long. Certainly he must have other female friends. She was falling for this prince charming.

"Hopefully something can be done," she managed without sounding jealous.

"Oh I almost forgot." He turned his chiseled cheekbones toward her. "We got the name of the man who broke into your house. His name was Leon Burgos. Daryl's gonna head over and check out his house."

The man's vacant eyes flashed through her mind. "That's good, at least there's progress."

"Hopefully." He didn't look convinced. "So, how ya feelin' today? Ya sure you're up to bein' here?"

"Hey, don't worry about me." Though she certainly didn't mind. "This is really a peaceful job, especially in the mornings. I'll just be here when people need help, and let Marta do all the lifting and putting books back where they belong."

"Right—sure you will." Chris tapped the red book on the counter. "I bet soon as I walk out that door you'll be reachin' for the top shelf with your good hand to put away some twenty pound dictionary."

"Who me?"

Dimples sunk into the center of his cheeks. "Well, I should probably be goin'. I've still got a few things to look into today. Call ya later?"

"I'd like that. Bye."

~~~~~~~~~

CHAPTER ELEVEN

Mael sat atop the white building. Demons scurried to and fro, intent on his bidding. He hated the spring. New life a constant reminder of *His* provision and restoration. Except for him. For him there was only regret, defiance, and certain destruction. Well he was sick of it. Sick of them, *His* cursed creations. Soon he would do something about that!

Behind him he heard a high feminine voice. "Get out of my way!" Followed by a small demon flailing past him.

He smiled and turned. "Anat, what do you bring me?"

She wrapped her bird-like wings across her chest and bowed her feline head. "I thought you should know. Officer Davis is with the woman at the library."

"What? He is with a woman!" His voice echoed high and mocking. "You disturb me with that!"

"No—it is the woman from Friday night. The one Leon's charge tried to attack."

"So?"

"There is more."

"I certainly hope so. Go on!"

"They were reading a memory card from a camera. Perhaps the one Leon stole. The one with the pictures." She thrust her head up convinced at the value of this information.

Leon—he would rip him to shreds. If he had not already done so. "Are you sure?"

"I left before they looked at the pictures. But they sure were anxious to see its content." She quivered like a bird stepping out of birdbath. "He asked her if she wanted to help him investigate."

"So the mighty detective has a lady friend to help him." Mael unfurled talon-like fingers. "Did there appear to be an attraction between them?"

"Oh yes, quite so." He could see the joy in her marbled eyes. This was her arena, her specialty. "Yesterday, after picking her up at the hospital, they had a nice dinner at a quaint little restaurant on the river. I would say they are quite smitten with each other."

The enemy had a weakness. "Perhaps we can use this to our advantage." He laughed a low rumbling laugh. "If we cannot get to him, then maybe we can get to her."

"Um, my lord, she does have a couple of protectors with her as well."

"Anat, you of all beings should understand that there are more effective methods than a frontal assault. That time may come. But for now we must avoid bringing attention to this town. We chose this location for our operation because of its relative obscurity. The enemy cannot know the magnitude of our actions here. No—use her. Use this attraction as a distraction."

"She is a believer. It may be difficult to influence her."

Perhaps he had overestimated Anat. "He is a man. She is a woman. You need not influence them. They are already falling for each other. Find ways to use it against them. Issues from their pasts that can be used to drive a wedge between them, or perhaps this newfound romance can be used to renew past fears, disappointments, or sins. We need more information. For now just do your job."

She dipped her right shoulder. "Yes lord Mael."

"Oh, one last thing—we do not need this woman nosing around for information. The library is Tudur's arena. Tell him to get her out of there."

~~~~~~~~~~

Chris returned to the River's Edge for lunch. He sat outside the worn building which desperately needed a fresh coat of brown paint. Though the smell inside had greatly improved. Still he preferred the deck which overlooked the Lamine River. The temperature had only climbed to fifty-five, but his jacket provided the warmth he needed. He finished his taco salad and sat back sipping a lemon tea.

He retrieved his phone from its clip and dialed the Criminal Science Lab in St. Louis, surprised he still remembered the number. He dialed it often during the six months he and Leilah had dated. Lei, as most of her friends referred to her, held a position as a forensic specialist with a focus on electronics and image-enhancement. He'd only passed his courses in computers and electronics as a result of her assistance.

"St. Louis forensics, this is Leilah."

"Hey Lei, it's Chris Davis."

"Chris Davis . . . hmm, let me think. The name sounds familiar. I used to know a guy by that name. He was a real ladies man. But I haven't heard from him in like three years. He got religion or somethin' and didn't feel our kind of relationship was appropriate. You wouldn't happen to be *that* Chris Davis?"

Hidden behind the sarcasm, he heard the pain. He'd fled from her like a rabbit from a forest fire. He had to, but she didn't understand. Why would she? "Suppose I deserved that. I know the last time we talked didn't go so well, but I could really use your professional help."

"Oh I see. Ya need a favor."

He felt like he'd been stabbed in the abdomen. "Lei, just listen for a moment. We had a prisoner this weekend that got hold of a deputy's gun, shot at me, and killed a prisoner, a woman."

Her voice softened. "What do you need?"

"We believe the same guy broke into a house earlier on Friday. The only thing he took was a memory card from a digital camera. We recovered the card yesterday, but when we tried to read it today, it wouldn't respond." She was listening. Perhaps she'd actually help him. "It sat outside over night Friday, and we're thinkin' maybe it got wet. Do ya think you could get the pictures off it?"

"Hard to tell." He could picture her with her thumb and forefinger on the bridge of her nose. They way she always pondered a situation. "Moisture shouldn't affect the memory chip. Most likely, it'd simply create a bad connection. If it's truly damaged it's more apt to be from trying to access the information with the connections messed up. But, I'd guess the information's still there."

Time to grovel. "Would ya be willing to take a look at it for us?"

"Just mail it to me. I can tell ya in a couple days what I could get off it. But it'll cost ya."

No. The mail was too slow. He wanted answers. "I'd rather not mail it. It's too important. I can drop it off this afternoon." He didn't want to ask the next question. "What's it gonna cost?"

The temptation he remembered so well returned to her voice. "How 'bout dinner Friday evening? That'd give me enough time to get any pictures off it."

No, definitely not a good idea. He couldn't risk being that close to her again. "Okay, sure, you've got a deal. Can I drop off the card today?"

"I'll be out of the office this afternoon. But you can leave it with Sue at the front desk. She'll make sure it gets to me."

"Keep me informed." He sighed. He wouldn't have to see her for at least a couple more days. "Later."

"See you soon," she replied. The phone went silent.

He felt like he'd just made a deal with the devil. His relationship with Lei lingered as the one aspect of his past he'd rather forget. His new friendship with Sarah made him regret his indiscretion with Lei more than ever.

~~~~~~~~~~

Much to Daryl's irritation the fax containing the warrant to search the house on Ash didn't come until two in the afternoon. The wait elevated his blood pressure, and now his head throbbed.

"That judge has no concern for justice." He murmured to himself and walked to his squad car with the warrant. He grabbed some fast-food and headed to the house on Ash. Doug, a Crime Scene Technician from the county Sheriff's had been waiting on standby for his call for much of the day. The best in the region at finding potential evidence at a scene, if there was anything to find, Doug needed to be there.

Relief washed over him when the county's Mobile Crime Unit pulled in immediately behind him. Younger than he'd expected, Doug appeared to be only a few years out of college.

"Good afternoon." The technician approached with his hand out. "The name's Doug. You must be Sergeant Williams. I wasn't sure I was going to hear from you today."

Daryl puffed out his cheeks as he exhaled a day's frustration. "Don't get me started. I'd like to say I patiently awaited the warrant, but I didn't. Now I got a screaming headache. Hopefully, it will subside once we get started."

"How do you want to proceed?" Doug asked the question out of respect for Daryl's obvious seniority.

"This is your arena. Let me know what you want me to do and I'll do it."

"Alright." Doug looked toward the disheveled ranch house with little grass and no landscaping to speak of. "Well, it doesn't look like anybody's home. But you never know. You stay here at the front door. I'll take a walk around the house to the back. Give me thirty seconds and then knock."

He had to smile as Doug waved his hand while giving the instructions. First, he held up three fingers then made a zero, followed by a knocking motion.

Doug continued, "If anybody is here we don't want them escaping out the back. If no one answers, force your way in. Sweep your way to the back door. Be careful not to touch anything. Let me in and we can get started looking for clues to your deceased perp's motives."

He gave Doug a quick thumbs up and a grin. "Got it. Watch yourself."

He waited thirty seconds, and then knocked loudly on the door. "Arrow Springs police, open up!"

No one answered. He waited a few seconds and then rang the doorbell. When he still didn't hear any movement, he knocked one last time even louder than the first. "Arrow Springs police. We have a warrant. Open up or we're coming in!"

Still no answer. He stepped back from the door, pulled his Sig P229, and gave the door a swift kick. The wood around the latch splintered and gave way allowing the door to slam against a stop on the inside wall. His pulse quickened. The throbbing pain in his forehead faded.

He worked his way from the entrance through the near empty dining room, then through the kitchen to the back door. Being sure not to turn his back on the seemingly empty house, he reached up and slid the deadbolt. The door opened and Doug joined him in the kitchen.

Daryl's nerves relaxed at having Doug in the house with him. "It hardly looks like anyone even lived here."

Systematically, they made their way through the entire house, verifying its vacancy. Neither he nor Doug understood what they saw. The house looked stripped clean. There were no valuables. The only piece of electronics, a small twelve-inch TV, sat on the carpeted living room floor. A cheap straight-back wooden chair made up the extent of the living room furniture.

A matching chair sat in the dining room next to a bar-style counter. The entirety of cooking and eating utensils found in the kitchen could have been packed in a picnic basket. A phone sat haphazardly on the counter, no notepads, no phonebook, no pens, nothing. The bedroom proved just as stark. A few clothes lay on the floor, and a few others, apparently the clean ones, were thrown in a laundry basket.

No dresser, no nightstand, no pictures, nothing but a single sized mattress lain on the floor covered with a single blanket and no sheets.

The scene proved difficult to comprehend. "This guy obviously wasn't into the finer amenities."

"You can say that again. I can't say I've seen anything like this. It's like this guy was homeless in his own home."

A brief survey of the man's bathroom revealed two bars of soap, one on the tub and one on the sink, a toothbrush but no toothpaste, a single towel, no washcloth, and a half-roll of toilet paper. The medicine cabinet was empty. He saw no evidence to indicate the man might have been on drugs—nothing to explain the odd behavior. The man acted like an animal, and apparently he lived like one too.

"See anything useful?" He asked Doug in a defeated tone.

"Not really. Did you bring a copy of the man's prints? I can dust for other fingerprints. Maybe it'll lead us to someone who can shed some light on your guy."

"Yeah, I have them in the cruiser. I'll bring them to you and then see if any of the neighbors can tell us anything about this guy. He gets stranger and stranger by the day."

"Sounds good," said Doug.

Over the next fifteen minutes Daryl talked to two next-door neighbor ladies. Both gave the same story. "Seen him once or twice. Never saw anyone else come or go. He was polite but definitely kept to himself."

He decided to check across the street.

~~~~~~~~~~

Sarah sat behind the front desk surprised at how much her wrist and ankle inhibited her usual activities at the library. The dusty smell of the older books bothered her more than usual, maybe it was the blow to her head, or perhaps just her inactivity. A cycle of recurring thoughts flowed through the computer inside her head. Why would somebody want to break into her house? Ten years ago, she at least told herself the murderers came to steal their possessions. Had God protected her Friday night? Where was He ten years ago? Why didn't He intervene then? Or did He? Did He bring Tim and Angela back to the house to save her life? A life lived with irreparable pain and scars.

After the fifth time following the same line of thought, she decided she needed to do something, anything to break the chain. Perhaps she could do some detective work of her own. She rolled her chair to the computer at the left side of the front desk. The library possessed a powerful search engine useful for various areas of research. She began typing keywords. L-e-o-n- -B-u-r-g-o-s. She typed the name followed by "Arrow Springs, MO."

The search engine returned surprisingly few links. A few times in the past she'd performed research on different people, some relatives, some in politics, and even the men convicted in the murder of her parents. Normally, the screen filled with pages and pages of links. This time the screen showed only three. The first link pointed to a white pages listing of the man's phone number and address. The second contained a mismatched link where the provinces of Leon and Burgos in Spain were mentioned as travel destinations for a tourist from Arrow Springs.

The final link left her in awe at how fast information made its way onto the web. The link recorded a search warrant issued that afternoon for the house of a Leon Burgos in Arrow Springs. She'd have to ask Chris if they found anything of interest.

"It's five o'clock Sarah."

Her heart slammed into her lungs. She spun to see Marta approaching the front desk.

Marta stopped next to the desk. "I'm sorry. I didn't mean to startle you."

"It's not you. I'm just a little on edge." She bent down to retrieve the computer's mouse which had bounded to the floor.

"It's no wonder. Look at you." Marta's voice embraced her, sweet and compassionate. "You were assaulted. Girl, what are you doing here anyway? I can handle things here."

Sarah glanced at the clock. Five o'clock? Where'd the hour go?

"Thank you Marta. I need to take my meds and get this ankle elevated. Both the ankle and the wrist are starting to throb again." She longed to kick back in the comfort of her sofa.

"Sarah, why don't you stay home for a few days? This isn't really a busy time for the library anyway."

"I don't know. At least here I'm not sitting around focused on my aches and pains, or the events of the weekend." *Only a small lie.* Much of the day she spent thinking about those very events. "Oh, by the way, please don't shut down this computer when you leave. Sometimes it can be a real pain reconnecting it to this new search engine after it's been shut down." This time she told a half-truth. The computer did fight reconnecting. But she might want to log on from home if she decided to do some more digging.

Marta locked her in a knowing motherly gaze. "Get some rest."

"I will! Don't you worry about that."

~~~~~~~~~~

Marilyn Williams stood in the kitchen with a pan of vegetable soup and a sizzling skillet cooking a ham and cheese sandwich when the doorbell rang. No, she didn't want a magazine subscription. She turned down the burners. This would be a quick discussion. When still married, her job as a receptionist at the insurance agency in Boonville provided them with some discretionary income. As a solo income, it barely provided for the necessities of a single woman living in a matchbox home. After the divorce, she learned saying no to salespeople wasn't as hard as it used to be.

She stomped through the living room and to the front door. Her breath caught as she opened the door. "Daryl? What are you doing here?"

His face reflected her surprise. "Marilyn! I had no idea you lived here." He tripped over his words. "I knew you sold the house and moved. I thought you were in some apartments in Boonville."

Did he expect her to believe that, as a police officer in town, he didn't know where she lived? "What are you doing here?"

Pain seemed to flicker through his eyes, providing a strange satisfaction.

"You remember the guy from the station, the one who shot at Chris?" he asked.

"Sure. What about him?"

Daryl pointed to the house across the street. "That was his house."

The blood in her arms and chest turned to ice. "Are you kidding me? My neighbor was a murderer?"

"Afraid so." He paused and then continued with hesitation in his voice. "Do you have a couple minutes? I'd like to ask you some questions."

"Um, my supper's burning on the stove as we speak." Her neighbor? A murderer? She had to help. "I mean—of course. I'll help if I can. I'm sorry, come in. Do you mind if I eat while we talk?"

"No, not at all. I'm sorry to bother you."

"Can I get you something?" She led him to the small table in her small kitchen. Why did he have to come? Her house was an embarrassment, proof of her struggles without him.

"Oh no, that's not necessary."

"Not even an iced tea?" Why'd she ask that?

"Okay sure, that'd be great. Thanks."

She could feel his look even with her back to him.

"I'm surprised you have tea. Not exactly your favorite."

"Bought the tea one time when I was grocery shopping. I guess some habits are hard to break." A burning sensation in her nose and behind her cheekbones evidenced a losing battle to keep a trickle of tears at bay. She took a deep breath. "So how can I help?"

Thankfully, he let the subject drop. "We're trying to learn everything we can about your former neighbor. So anything you can tell me might be useful." His voice remained professional.

Clearly he didn't feel the pain and loss the way she did. *Stay composed. You can get through this.* "Not much to tell, I'm afraid. I've seen him a few times. Definitely the quiet type. I said "hi" to him once at the mailbox. He might have returned the greeting, I don't even remember. I've only been here a few months." Surely Daryl knew that already. "He drove that car there in the driveway once in a great while, most of the time he walked to wherever he was going."

She could hear him scratching notes on a notepad. "Did you ever see anyone else at the house? Any deliveries?"

She turned and walked to the table with her food. "No, I don't think, oh wait, there was a young woman there once in a while. They would show up together in the car then they'd leave a few hours later. I don't think she ever stayed overnight. In fact they didn't seem that cozy."

He continued to jot notes. "Okay, I don't know if that will help, but at least it's something. Thank you for taking time to talk with me."

"Daryl . . . I heard you made a commitment to Jesus yesterday at church."

"Yeah, I felt like Pastor Thomas was speaking directly to me the entire message. I must say, I had a pretty rough afternoon yesterday. It seemed like a war took place in my head. I went to bed with a sense of peace I haven't felt for three years." His face turned pale. "Marilyn. I'm so sorry for what I did to you. I hope someday you can forgive me. I know I don't deserve it."

"No, you don't." She almost yelled it. Though not her intent, it felt good. "Let me know if there is anything else I can do for the investigation."

"I will thanks." Daryl acknowledged the end of the conversation, got up, and headed for the door.

She didn't want to appear bitter so she walked him to the door. "Take care," she offered as she closed the front door. She wanted to scream. Anger welled up inside her heart, anger not focused at Daryl, but at herself. She actually felt sorry for him. She had yet to experience this emotion since his betrayal, and quite frankly, it infuriated her. How could she ever soften to the man who had laid her heart bare and shattered it like tempered glass? Was it possible God would actually pick up those tiny pieces and put it back together?

Did she want Him to? Even if He did, it would never be the same.

~~~~~~~~~~

CHAPTER TWELVE

Tuesday, April 21, 2020

Chris pulled his squad car into a parking spot next to the hundred-year-old redbrick building. He entered through a large wooden door and strolled down a short hallway to the office of Don Hanson, Cooper County Coroner.

He knocked on the half-open door. "Hey Don."

"Chris! Man you look better than the last time I saw you." Don stood and shook Chris' hand.

"I'm sure that's true. Sally said you'd called. What ya got?"

Don peered over his glasses. "Well, if you're up for it, I think it would be best to talk downstairs."

Chris had been to the building before but not to the morgue on the lower level. "Okay?"

"It's not pretty." Don walked to the corner of his desk. "On the other hand, I'm sure you've seen worse."

The image of his brother flashed in Chris' mind. "Let's get it over with."

Don picked up the phone, "Sam, can you meet us in the examination area? . . . Great." He hung up the phone and headed into the hallway. "Sam has some information you will be interested in as well."

As they entered the cinderblock stairwell that led to the lower level, a chill crawled down Chris' spine. They approached a large steel door. What lie ahead would, no doubt, be the low point of his day.

Clank, clank, clank.

The sound of the upstairs door latching echoed off the walls causing his heart to stomp on his stomach. Would the door to the morgue open with a horror-film creak?

In stark contrast to the well-furnished, even cozy office upstairs, the lower level felt cold and dark, like some medieval dungeon.

A warm female voice thawed the frigid air. "Officer Davis, welcome."

Don waved his hand toward the woman. "Chris, you remember Samantha Clark from Saturday morning?"

"Certainly." Chris snatched a brief glance of the young assistant. "Nice to meet you again." In the chaos of their first meeting, he'd barely noticed her. She'd pulled her brunette hair tight into a bun. Probably a prudent choice given her line of work. She gleamed with a mix of intelligence and elegance.

Chris watched as she covered a wedding ring with medical tape and snapped on latex gloves. "So, what've you got?"

Don glanced at Sam. "Why don't you start with the wrists." He clearly didn't mind letting his young apprentice handle the dirty work.

"Okay." Stepping up to the body lying on a table, she pulled back a white sheet. "As you can see he sustained significant cuts on both wrists. We cut the cuffs away, but he had broken the chain, giving him the mobility he needed for the attack."

Chris hadn't even thought about the cuffs. "Those chains are supposed to be unbreakable."

She nodded. "Nearly—the intense level of pain this would have inflicted should have sent him into a state of shock." She pulled the sheet off the legs of the corpse. "It would appear based on these lesions down here that he used his knee as a lever to apply pressure to the chain. This would nearly double the force on the chain. An x-ray showed that the kneecap is completely dislocated."

Chris' stomach churned at the thought.

Sam replaced the sheet and picked up a blackened wrist. "It would seem your guy wasn't much for succumbing to pain. The bones in his wrists are chipped in several places."

"In summary," said Don, "this man demonstrated strength ten times what would be expected based on his muscle structure. Not to mention an ultra-high tolerance for pain."

"Drugs?" asked Chris.

"Afraid not," said Sam. "We tested him for all known narcotics, both legal and illegal. Tests revealed no evidence of chemical substances in his system."

"Somethin' that got out of his system by the time ya took the samples?"

She shook her head. "I don't see how. Based on the amount and location of the blood in his cell, he broke the cuffs right before the seizure. He died only minutes later. The body didn't have time to process any chemical substances prior to death, and it wouldn't happen after death. Anything that was in his system should still be there."

Chris crossed his arms and shifted his weight to the left. "Is it possible we're dealin' with some new, undetectable narcotic?"

"Anything's possible. We can only look for the things we know of, but there were *no* foreign substances." She formed a zero with her thumb and forefinger. "Not even an aspirin."

Don chuckled. "With that kind of pain tolerance, why would he need painkillers?"

Apparently not a lot of use for humor in the coroner's office. There had to be something Chris could learn. "You said he broke the cuffs before the seizure? I assumed he faked the seizure—to get us to open the cell."

She nodded her head. "That was my thought too, but I did a CT Scan." She tapped a manila folder sitting on a stainless table. "It appears he had several seizures. There is evidence of a significant one shortly before his death. It's possible the intense pain of freeing himself from the cuffs caused him to go into a seizure."

"Yeah, or the drug." He was stuck on the theory. Growing up in western Chicago, he saw more than his share of drug related crimes. "I just don't see how anything else can explain it. He subjects himself to incredible pain, has a full blown seizure, and still has the presence to disarm Daryl and take a shot at me?"

"As I said, it's possible." She removed her gloves and handed him a paper from the folder. "But there's something else you should see."

He shouldn't have taken college biology in the morning. "Afraid my med trainin' stopped way short of anything like this." He lowered the paper and looked at Sam. "Explain?"

Don patted Chris on the back. "She's just showing off."

Sam retrieved the document, a tinge of red filling her cheeks. "This is a DNA report. I sought to determine the source of the seizures. There are several genetically traceable diseases, which could cause this type of seizure. Massive amounts of stem-cell research have been done since the authorization of government funds to learn more about such diseases."

"But this one," she shook the paper, "has me puzzled. His tests don't show signs of any of the known genetic defects."

This information wasn't helping. He didn't need more questions. He needed answers. "There're other causes for seizures, besides genetic illness, aren't there?"

"Oh certainly—many. As I said, this last seizure could've been due solely to the pain. What has me puzzled isn't the source of the seizures. It's the unique genetic defect his tests do show. I doubt I ever would have detected it if I hadn't been looking specifically for a genetic disease."

Chris stared at the white draped body. "So what does it mean?"

"I'm not sure," said Sam. "If I had to guess—I'd say we've stumbled onto a new genetic disease yet unknown to the medical community."

The evil grin of the attacker flashed through Chris' mind. "A disease that turns someone into a homicidal maniac immune to pain?"

"I'm as lost as you are on this one."

Chris turned to Don.

"Same here."

~~~~~~~~~~

Eran stood in the cold dark morgue. He hated the place. Its very existence served as a reminder of the second great fall. It had not been enough that Lucifer had led a third of his brothers in a rebellion against their Creator. In anger and humiliation he seduced the treasured creations of God, and with them all of mankind, into defiance of their Creator.

He still remembered that dreadful day. Pain flooded his being. He could hear the tear stained voice of his Creator declare to the man and woman. ". . . to dust you shall return." This room, a memorial to the death of mankind, echoed the declaration.

"I feel it too, my friend." Uriel, Sam's guardian, patted Eran on the shoulder. "Everyday." Uriel's olive skin glowed with intense light contrasting his black curly hair.

"I do not know how you do it." The remarkable presence of the Spirit exuded from his being despite his surroundings.

"Sam is a faithful servant. Do not forget, my brother, it was through death that life was given to all mankind."

"And yet death still comes to all."

Uriel glowed ever brighter. "With it—life to so many." He walked around the body lying on the table. "You were there were you not?"

"Yes."

"It was not drugs, was it?"

"No. Demonic possession."

Uriel nodded. "But in the sophistication of twenty-first century America such things are not a consideration. People would prefer a physical explanation."

At the thought of the encounter, his left hand fell to the hilt of his saber. "This was unlike anything I have observed. Mors was in complete control."

They paused to listen to more of Sam's explanation of her DNA testing.

Uriel shuttered his mighty wings. "It would appear there are many mysteries surrounding this fellow."

"Indeed."

~~~~~~~~~~

Sarah sat at the front desk of the library with her back turned to the counter. She had pulled up another chair on which she rested her ankle. A cold wind blew up her spine and down her arms.

"What are you doing here!" The male voice startled her and she lost her balance.

In an effort to catch herself, she swung her right hand to the counter. Protruding from their cast, her fingers smacked the surface. Sharp pangs darted through her wrist.

With dampened eyes, she turned her chair to face the counter. "Mayor Richards? What brings you here?"

"I asked you first."

"I—I work here."

"Sarah—" He spoke in an I-know-what's-best-for-you voice. "I heard you were here. You were in the hospital just two days ago. Do you honestly think this library cannot survive without you for a week or two? Look at you."

The tears in her eyes were not helping her case, yet they continued, more from frustration than from pain.

Marta. It must have been Marta. Only the day before she'd told her how tired she was. Marta must have felt she wasn't ready to be there. At least she could have let her make the decision.

"Really, I'm fine. I've got nothing to do at home. At least here I can use my mind to help people with their research."

"Sarah, it is for your own good. Take a couple weeks off. We all know you have earned it. Besides, when was the last time you took some vacation time?"

What did he care? He'd not said two words to her since taking office. Now he was supposed to be her father or something. "I took some time on the Fourth of July."

"You took one day! Nearly a year ago." He crossed his arms. "This is not really up for discussion. Do not make me get the city council involved. You realize if you hurt yourself further, the city would be culpable?"

"Oh come on!"

"No! End of discussion."

"Fine!" She didn't wait for a response. She turned her back to him and left the counter.

She stormed past Marta on her way to the back of the library to retrieve her purse and car keys.

"What was that all about? What was Mayor Richards doing here?" asked Marta.

"You should know." She continued to the back as fast as her limping would allow.

"Sarah?"

She drove the several blocks to her house, thankful her left ankle was sprained instead of her right. She cursed her newly acquired cast each time she needed to change gears using the auto-on-the-floor shifter. At least she didn't have a manual.

She parked the car, marched into the house, and slammed the newly hung front door. She limped straight to the bathroom, and washed off her attempt to cover the yellowing bruise around her right eye. There—least now she looked like she was just beat up.

~~~~~~~~~~

"Write the letter," whispered Huw. Sarah needed the restoration. She needed friends. Most important, she would need their support. He looked to Alex and shrugged.

She spent the next hour trying to find some way to entertaining herself. She tried the television—all that aired were shows about people who were not so young anymore, but still very restless.

"That will not help you sweetie. Those relationships are fake. Not what you need."

She shut the TV off and clanked down the remote on her coffee table.

"There you go."

She picked up a stack of books from the table. One by one she set them back down.

Alex walked up next to her and laid his hands on her shoulders. "Write child."

She limped to the kitchen, picked up a notepad and pen, and began to write:

Dear Angela and Tim,

I know it's been a long time since I last talked to you, but the events of the past few days have reminded me just how special you both are to me . . .

~~~~~~~~~~

Wilhelm M'Gregor sat behind his large cherry desk. The opulence of the beige walls, giant bookshelves, and teak flooring no longer brought pride. It all closed in on him, mocking the arrogance of younger days.

"Dr. M'Gregor!" The air chilled at the icy voice of Maiya Mirinova. "May I have a word with you?"

"Yes?" He pushed back gray wiry hair from in front of his eyes. "How can I help ya?" As if the day hadn't been long and unpleasant enough.

"You could start by making sure you're less sloppy with your work."

There she went again. "Pardon?"

"Do you realize a genetic defect was found during an autopsy of Leon?" She glared at him with cat-like eyes.

"Autopsy? Leon is dead?" The news brought surprise but not exactly heartbreak. Leon always demonstrated a defiant spirit. For all he'd done for him, Leon only returned grief and disappointment. "What type of defect? How was it discovered? For that matter, how did Leon die?"

"He was shot Saturday morning in the Arrow Springs jail after he killed a fellow prisoner."

"Leon murdered someone?" The thought sent tremors to his core. The sole purpose for his research centered on life. To discover his work resulted in the loss of a life. No. It just couldn't be.

"Oh, pull it together! She was just some no-name hooker from Kansas City. Focus on the real issue here. How is it possible such a genetic defect was found?"

Heat flared from his collar. "I don't care who she was! It was still a life!" Maiya thrived on these games. "As for how a defect was discovered, that's a really good question. It seems to me perhaps, ya are slipping in your duties. Is it not your responsibility to monitor the patients? You are in charge of ensuring that something like this doesn't happen, are ya not?"

It was Maiya's turn to redden. While her cheeks remained a pale ivory, her eyes shifted from hazel to a McIntosh red. He'd observed the phenomenon many times since she returned to take her father's place. Nonetheless, it unnerved him.

She pointed a skinny finger in his face. "I sincerely hope for your sake they do not succeed in tracing him back to this facility." She turned to leave the office.

Stopping at the door she turned back to him. "If they do make the connection, I would suggest you think up a believable explanation. If this mission fails, I guarantee you your research will be finished, and I don't just mean here."

He jumped from his seat and followed her into the hallway.

"Are you threatnin' me?"

"You're a smart man doctor, you figure it out."

She stepped into her opulent office and shut the large wooden door in his face.

Only once had he entered the office since she moved in—the day after her father died of a stroke.

He walked back to his office, but the walls were closing in on him. He needed to get out—out of his office—out of the whole mess. Such an action would require meticulous planning. Until then, he would settle for a visit to his favorite patient.

He exited the elevator on floor S-1 and walked down a cool gray hallway. He rounded a corner and stopped outside a room with a handful of children.

"Top o' the mornin' to ya Ima. How ya doin' today?"

"Uncle M!" The eleven-year-old blond with round blue eyes ran toward him with arms wide. "Did you bring me anything?" she asked, before catching herself. Like most eleven-year-olds she still needed some work on her manners.

A wide grin crept across his face. "But of course." He held out a fist and unfolded it to reveal a butterscotch candy. In contrast to most of his patients, Ima often sported a wide smile on her innocent and slightly rounded face. Her eyes were like the sky on a clear March afternoon. She was the one bright spot that still existed in his job. She brought a true sense of joy.

He couldn't let his thoughts wander to her near certain future.

~~~~~~~~~~

Thursday, April 23, 2020

Chris sat at his desk. He rather enjoyed the evening shift when things were quiet. It seemed like all leads in the Burgos case were dead ends. Through the large glass window of his office he could see into the briefing room. For the last three days the briefings had been just that—brief.

He leaned back in his black leather chair and stared at his desk. He'd reviewed his notes a dozen times. He had to be missing something.

Friday night he would meet with Leilah to review the images she'd recovered from the memory card. It was the only good news he'd received all day. But even that seemed like a trap waiting to be sprung. Leilah had not been good for him. Though he hadn't realized it at the time. She was nothing like Sarah.

Memories of his lunch with Sarah on Sunday wafted through his mind like the subtle vanilla tones of her perfume. The way her freckles scrunched together when she smiled. The little wrinkle of her nose. The red pipe-curl that insisted on dangling in her face. His chest warmed at the thoughts.

Then another thought, the memory of the fear in her eyes as she recalled the death of her parents. How long had it been? Ten years? He hadn't moved to St. Louis yet at that point.

Was it possible one of his fellow officers had worked the investigation? Unfortunately, even a double murder wasn't big enough news for him to have heard about it a few years later.

Perhaps.

No. There was no justification.

He'd be prying into her personal life.

But she'd already told him. She hadn't hid it from him.

He logged into the Missouri crime database and began typing.

St. Louis, 2009-2011, McIntyre.

Several links popped up on the screen. The first was a police report. The rest were warrants, arrest records, court proceedings, and even parole hearings. He clicked on the police report link. As he waited for the file to load, he read the link description.

His stomach turned to concrete. *No. Please Lord no.*

"Webster Groves, St. Louis, July 3, 2010, double murder and sexual assault of a minor." His nose and throat burned.

The link disappeared and a verification screen replaced it. "Confidential – Law Enforcement Only Access. Please enter authorization code."

He had no right. But he had to know.

He typed in his code.

The police report appeared on the screen. An officer Johnston had responded to a 9-1-1 call from an Angela Gonzalez. He arrived on scene to find the bodies of Don and Virginia McIntyre. Both assaulted and killed in an apparent robbery.

Chris struggled to read the tear blurred words on the screen.

"Found teenage daughter, Sarah McIntyre, lying on the floor. She had been covered with a sheet by Miss Gonzalez. Clear indications of aggravated and sexual assault."

He clicked the X in the corner of the window. The report disappeared from the screen but not from his memory.

He buried his head in his hands and wept.

~~~~~~~~~~

CHAPTER THIRTEEN

Friday, April 24, 2020

Friday evening came much too soon for Chris. He drove east on I-70 toward St. Louis. He'd decided to take the cruiser rather than his Wrangler. It made his meeting with Leilah feel more official. It was strictly a business dinner, nothing more.

They would meet at none other than Francisco's. He'd been to Francisco's once before—when they celebrated their six-months-of-dating anniversary. He broke it off shortly after that dinner. It seemed Leilah hoped to pick things up where they left off. That simply wasn't an option.

Though he hated to admit it, a part of him still longed to return to the excitement of the relationship he once shared with Leilah. But for the most part, that part no longer called the shots. Against better wisdom, he spent the drive to St. Louis reviewing details about the case rather than dealing with his thoughts regarding Leilah.

~~~~~~~~~~

Eran sat next to Chris. He had to get through to him. "How will you respond to her advances?"

Nothing.

"You know she does not have a pure motivation for this meeting. Set your limits. Establish your boundaries."

He glanced at Zeke sitting in the back seat. Chris was not listening. For the first time in years, he was rejecting offerings of wisdom.

"He needs prayer," said Zeke. "This will be one of his greatest tests to date."

Eran closed his eyes and nodded. "And we must not interfere. This is a test of obedience. One he must pass on his own."

~~~~~~~~~~

Chris continued to focus on the facts of the bizarre case.

Perpetrator: Twenty years of age, demonstrated superhuman strength, apparently impervious to pain, no traces of foreign substances known or unknown, genetic defect, possibly a genetic disease. Oh yes, don't forget psychotic, homicidal maniac.

His home: Void of normal comforts, three sets of prints found, one belonged to the perpetrator, one male, and one female, neither showing up in the crime database, currently processing through the national birth-record database.

Like a broken record player, the thoughts ran through his mind until he pulled into the parking lot of Francisco's.

He'd arrived fifteen minutes early for their seven o'clock meeting.

At least he could have some control of the situation. He would arrange a table withdrawn enough to discuss the contents of the memory card, but not too isolated. He could use the remaining minutes to collect his thoughts.

"Chris Davis, party of two," he said to the Maitre d'.

"Ah yes. Your lady friend arrived a few minutes ago. This way please."

So much for controlling the situation.

He followed the Maitre d' to a discrete table nestled in the back corner of the restaurant.

He approached the table.

The astonishing beauty of the woman rising to greet him left him speechless. Leilah was always beautiful, but the years since he last saw her had done nothing but enhance her beauty. Her perfect formfitting dress was stunning. The deep-red-rose strapless gown appeared held up only by her near perfect bust. He'd always appreciated her five-foot ten-inch form—never one of excessive thinness, but a well-exercised fit figure with just the right amount of curve in just the right places.

No. He was definitely not the one in control here.

She floated to her seat on the left side of a U-shaped booth surrounding a dimly lit table. He dropped into the booth across from her. Ice water sloshed from narrow stemmed glasses as he bumped the table with his elbow.

Moments later a young waiter in a black tuxedo broke the awkward silence at the table. "May I show you our wine list?"

Wine? No that probably wouldn't be a good idea.

Leilah looked up. "No need, we'll have a bottle of your finest Pinot Grigio"

A little wine wouldn't hurt. He nodded.

The waiter returned with a smile and poured them each a glass of the copper white wine. "Our specials are the Vitello Marsala, or the Ravioli Di Aragosta. Would you like a few minutes?"

"That would be fine," said Chris.

The menu could provide just the distraction he needed to take his focus off the beauty sitting across from him. However, it proved difficult to divert his gaze to the menu.

The soft glow of the candlelight sparkled off her eyes and teeth in beautiful contrast to the dark glow of her ebony skin. A petite pearl cross hung low from an elegant silver chain drawing attention to the deep-cut neckline of her dress. Had she worn the Christian symbol to put him at ease, or to keep his attention securely fastened to her beauty?

Either way, it worked.

"I think I'll have the garlic-basil scampi over olive oil torchietti."

He raised his eyes to her face.

"And you—" Her tongue moistened her glossy lips. "What would you like tonight?"

"Oh, um, well let's see." He sounded like a clumsy schoolboy on his first date. Picking up his menu, "I think I'll go for the Pollo Cappellini."

"Nice choice. You know they use dark meat in their chicken dishes. You always were one for the dark thighs."

A blush of heat flowed to his neck and face.

~~~~~~~~~~

Sarah's fingers flew over the keys as she scanned the computer screen. She sat at her dining room table with her laptop and portable printer. A remote connection to the library provided access to the powerful search engine. She envisioned the computer sitting on the research desk with its keys mysteriously depressing and the mouse scurrying frantically across the mouse-pad in pursuit of some invisible curd of cheese.

Why did she feel so rushed? No one would be at the library for hours. But deep within her, she heard that voice. Not the way she had a week earlier. More subtle. Like a whisper. She needed to get as much information as she could before the door of opportunity clicked shut.

She started with the same search she'd performed a few days earlier. Leon's name returned several new hits. Most were links to news reports about the murder at the Arrow Springs jail. Perhaps the property database would produce something of interest. She typed in Leon's address on Ash Street.

Something wasn't right.

She picked up the notepad she'd scribbled the address on. 130 Ash Street, Arrow Springs. She had the right address.

The screen told her the house belonged to CeSiR Technologies. CeSiR Tech was a prominent business in Arrow Springs, yet she knew very little about it. The large gates and armed guards discouraged anyone from taking much interest in the place. And though Arrow Springs was as gossipy as the next small town, very few of CeSiR's employees actually lived in Arrow Springs.

From what she could dig up about the company through the search engine, property rental didn't seem to fit the business. For nearly a half hour she mined data on the company. Rather than reading all of the information as she went, she downloaded most of the it to the laptop. Occasionally, when she ran across a significant piece of information she would also send it to the printer.

A question popped into her head. *Did CeSiR own any other properties?*

Returning to the property deed database, she performed a search on the property holdings of CeSiR Tech.

~~~~~~~~~~

Chris began to relax as the savory flavor of mushrooms and tomatoes drenched in a white cream sauce danced lazily across his palette. The empty glass of Pinot next to his plate helped to ease his nerves as well. Francisco's was one of the nicest restaurants in St. Louis' famous Italian district known as "The Hill." Candlelight danced with the pleasing aromatic mixture of garlic, basil, and oregano—this was one of the few fine-dining experiences he thoroughly enjoyed.

He swept up the last piece of tomato onto a buttery piece of garlic bread and slid it into his mouth.

"Would you like to see what I've brought for you?" asked Leilah.

He about choked on the bread. "Pardon?"

"The pictures. You remember—the memory card. Do you want to see the mastery of my technical genius?" She reached under the table. "Or did you have something else you were interested in seeing?"

"Definitely. I mean the pictures that is."

She pulled a folder from her briefcase, sat it on the table next to him, and slid around the u-shaped bench. The alluring floral-chypre scent of her perfume mingled with the warm wood-fire aroma of the restaurant.

His heart began to race—a mixture of the intimacy of the new seating arrangement and the suspense of the pictures lying on the table before him.

One by one, he studied the pictures. Most were of Mike Henderson's family and friends. "These in the order they were taken?"

"Yes, I believe so."

A hint of garlic wafted on her breath to his nose.

The last several pictures were of Mike's girlfriend. She wasn't from Arrow Springs, though he had seen her on occasion at church on Sunday mornings.

"She's quite attractive," Leilah interjected, as he dwelled on one of the pictures. "No wonder he looks so happy."

"Not like you're implying." He balanced on the tightrope strung between his irritation with the comment and his physical attraction to Leilah. "He's a great kid. He's not like that."

"*All* men are like *that*."

He tried to ignore her and flipped to another photo of Mike's girlfriend.

"What's this?" The picture showed the beautiful young woman standing at the old bridge embankment overlooking the Lamine River to the north. He pointed to the photo. "There in the upper-left corner. That's the entrance to the CeSiR Tech facility." He could make out the gated-entrance. "There's a car turnin' toward the camera."

"Really?" She snuggled closer to him to see the car in the image. "I never would have seen that."

"Would it be possible to blow up that section of the photo?" His heart skipped with expectation. "Perhaps whoever's in that car didn't want this picture seen."

She leaned over the picture. "Possibly." She turned her head toward him. "What would that be worth to you?"

His abs tightened as he glimpsed her necklace suspended over the table.

Why had he agreed to the dinner? He knew better.

The pictures. He needed to stay focused. He began thumbing through the remaining pictures to see if anything else would account for the theft of the memory card.

"What?" He stared at an impressive enlargement of the automobile from the earlier picture. "Never would have seen it huh?"

"Well maybe I did happen to notice it." Her coy smile enticed him. "The camera had impressive resolution and the pictures were in raw format so there wasn't any compression error. I tried to bring those two faces out better—that was the best I could do." She leaned her right arm on the table and faced him. "Any idea who they are?"

"The one on the left is Leon Burgos—the man who shot the woman at the jail and the one we suspected stole the memory card. I can't tell who the other one is, the glare from the sun's right in his face."

"Figured as much."

He studied the photo. "Based on the location of the sun I'd say this photo was taken 'round eleven in the morning. There's a BMW logo on the front? You can also see part of the front plate of the vehicle."

"Looks like it says F24." She tapped the photo. "You can't tell what position the letters are in because of the branches from that tree."

"Certainly not enough to run the plates. At least it's another avenue to investigate." He smiled as he turned his shoulders toward her. "You're great Lei."

"I was hoping you'd feel that way." She laid her head on his shoulder.

His heart told him to get out—his mind and body were sending a very different message.

~~~~~~~~~~

Eran stood inside Francisco's with a tear trickling down his cheek. Chris sat with his arm around the temptress, ensnared by the beguiling influence of the demons of lust and seduction.

155

Slimy black faces smiled with glee. "He is ours now."

He longed to brandish his saber. To rip the pathetic creatures limb from black deformed limb. He could not. Though he did not understand his instructions, he would obey.

"Man has always fallen to the influence of a seductive woman," sang the demon of seduction. "Did you honestly believe this one would be any different?"

Truer words were never spoken by demonic beings. Eran had watched when Balak used the Moabite women to lead the men of Israel astray. As a result of their seduction, Israel began to worship the demon lord of Peor. Samson had wasted his God given strength to the weakness of his lust. David committed adultery and murder because of his. Even Solomon the wisest man to live let his desire for women lead him away from God.

Now he watched as one more man of God fell to seduction and lust.

~~~~~~~~~~

CHAPTER FOURTEEN

*D*ear *Angela and Tim,*
 I know it's been a long time since I last talked to you, but the events of the past few days reminded me just how special you both are to me.

First let me say how sorry I am that I never showed the two of you the appreciation you deserved for all you did for me. You were true friends when I most needed it. After the attack I was mad at God, and I fear I took it out on the two of you.

Last week Friday, I once again found myself under attack. You may have even read about it in the papers. This time was different from last time. I don't know if I ever told you, but ten years ago when I went into the house that day, I heard a voice telling me to get out. I ignored that voice and paid for it dearly. This time I also heard the voice, but I didn't ignore it. I ran and made it into my house only seconds before the attacker began beating on my door.

As I sat behind the door, with the attacker attempting to get in, I was reminded of those events ten years ago. For the first time in ten years I began to sense God was there with me. I went to enough Sunday School classes to know He's supposed to be everywhere all the time. But that certainly doesn't change the abandonment I've felt for the last ten years. I still hold God responsible for what happened to my parents. This time, He really seemed to be present.

Even as I type this, it is taking much longer than it should because my right wrist is in a cast. I also have a brace on my left ankle. Still somehow, I feel I was protected. Had my night-in-shining-armor not showed up exactly when he did, I would likely be dead now. His name is Chris Davis, the knight that is. He is a sergeant with the Arrow

Springs police department. I must say—I'm finding myself smitten. As I'm sure you know, since my attack ten years ago I've had little trust for men. But Chris is different.

I know you'd really like Chris. He is a godly man, one of the few I've found that seems trustworthy. He's been a model gentleman, taking care of me, protecting me, even giving me a ride home from the hospital after the attack. I realize we haven't known each other very long but I think he might just be the one.

He's currently investigating the attacker to determine what drove him to such grievous actions. Oh, I forgot to tell you the rest of the story about the attacker. It turns out the same man broke into a house in town just hours before the attack. Then something that still scares me to death happened Saturday morning. The man overpowered another police officer, took his gun, and fired at Chris. Instead of hitting Chris he hit and killed a woman in the next cell. It turns out that once again my attacker was also a murderer.

So far, the police have determined the man's residence, but not much else. They hope something at the house will shed some light on his volatile behavior. Chris seems to think it was somehow drug induced. Something in his eyes that night tells me there's more going on than a simple drug induced rage.

Pray Chris will be able to find more information.

Anyway, I've had some very meaningful discussions with Chris. One of those discussions made me realize how much I valued your friendships. I realized if you had not come back that day, I would probably have been killed right alongside my parents. This isn't a new realization. In fact it's what caused me to be mad at you after the attack. I spent weeks wishing I had died with my parents. I held you guys responsible for my being alive. What an irony, it's that very fact that now drives me to a deep sense of appreciation.

Nothing I can say or do will ever repay you for all you guys did for me. In fact, it can't even make up for the way I have hurt and rejected you. What I can do is restore the relationships I so carelessly destroyed, and ask you to forgive me. I really would like to get to know you and your family. I feel bad that I missed your wedding, and now I hear you have a little one. I can only imagine how special this child must be to you. He couldn't ask for better parents.

Well, I suppose I should let you go now. I find myself with an excess of time on my hands. Due to my injuries, I was told to stay home from the library where I work for a few weeks. I'm thinking I might spend some time doing some investigation and research of my own.

Please pray for me, first that I won't go nuts being home all day, second that I will have wisdom in my relationship with Chris, and third that whatever is behind this strange attacker will be brought to light. Pray for Chris too, especially for his safety. The very thing that brought us together, his occupation, is also the thing that makes me most nervous about getting involved with him. I'm not sure I could take losing one more person I love.

I have included my contact information. Please get with me when you get a chance.

Love,
Sarah McIntyre

Tears flowed from Angela's eyes as she finished reading the letter. It tore her heart out when Sarah began rejecting their love. She could only thank God—that He was drawing Sarah back to Himself.

"What's wrong?"

She looked up to see Tim's concern at finding his wife weeping at the table.

"It was her!"

"What? Who?"

"Sarah!"

His expression remained confused.

"You remember the attack you told me about in Arrow Springs? The one where an unidentified man busted through the front door of a house, and then killed a woman at the police station?"

"Yes?"

"It was Sarah."

A look of horror flooded Tim's face. "Sarah's dead?"

"No, no! It was her house." She wiped at her nose. "He was trying to attack Sarah when the police arrested him. Here—read this."

After a few minutes, Tim looked up from the letter with his eyes misty. "Wow, seems God is going to great lengths to get her attention."

"I miss her." A new wave of tears washed her eyes.

"I feel like we should pray for her. Like she could be in danger."

Angela just nodded.

"Dear Lord," Tim began as he took hold of her tear dampened hands. "You know we have often prayed for an opportunity to restore our relationship with Sarah. Now it would seem You are answering that prayer. For this we give You our thanks."

"Please continue to encourage Sarah and draw her to Yourself. She's been through so much—seen so much pain, physically, emotionally, and even spiritually. I know she still blames You for what happened and I'm not going to pretend I understand why You allowed it either. You don't tell us only good things will happen, but that all things that do happen will work together for good."

"I pray Sarah might begin to reap the good from the terrible events of her life. Protect her, comfort her, and send Your angels to form a hedge of protection around her. Once again, thank You for Your faithfulness and for bringing Sarah back into our lives."

"Lord," continued Angela. "Please be with this young man, this Chris. Keep him safe, give him wisdom, lead him in the direction You would have for him. Give him insight into this case he's investigating."

A chill passed through her ribs. "Lord I don't know him, but I love Sarah, and couldn't bear to see her hurt once again. If this is the man You will for her, make it clear to them both. Don't let him hurt her. It would appear he already has her heart. Don't let him break it. Amen"

"Amen," echoed Tim.

~~~~~~~~~~

CHAPTER FIFTEEN

A dark figure in a trench coat stood ominous behind the counter watching the mouse pointer on the screen move from one window to another. Information flashed past piece by piece like breadcrumbs leading an incriminating trail to CeSiR.

An hour earlier, an automated alert had been tripped. Someone was snooping into sensitive material and set off a whirlwind of phone calls and threats. The computerized trail led to the research computer at the library in Arrow Springs—to an empty chair.

"Sarah McIntyre!" The figure swore. "What do you think you are doing?" A pale hand reached for the button on the front of the computer. With a click, the fans of the CPU wound to silence—leaving an eerie stillness in the library.

"What to do now?" Mael had to be told.

~~~~~~~~~~

The objections from deep within Chris' heart were all but silent. The whole of his senses desired once again to hold this dark beauty in his intimate embrace.

"My place isn't far from here," whispered Leilah.

The warmth of her breath on his neck sent waves down his spine. He stood from the booth and reached his hand out to her.

She stood grabbed her briefcase and put her left arm around his waist.

She was beautiful, captivating. He put his right hand around her shoulder.

Her alluring fragrance drew him step by step to the exit.

They exited the large wooden door to the parking lot and strolled toward her car.

For only a moment, the beauty of the setting sun slowed his gate.

~~~~~~~~~~

Eran watched in helplessness, as the sun set on Chris' restraint. In his seven years with Chris, he had never seen him so unresponsive to godly wisdom.

The enemy's tactics infuriated him.

A hand patted his shoulder.

"I know this is difficult my friend," said Zeke. "We must trust God, that He is at work, even in this."

The couple reached Leilah's black Mazda. She pulled her key fob from her purse and pushed the button.

"Bloop bleep."

"Do-da-dee-da-do do-da-dee-da-do."

Chris paused as if trying to connect the sounds.

Eran stepped between Chris and the demon of lust.

The demon looked at him confused and then turned to Leilah. "No."

"You don't have to answer it do you?" begged Leilah.

Chris looked at the display. Without responding, he flipped open the phone. "Hello."

"Saved by the bell." Zeke bore a wide grin.

"Ugh, that was bad," said Eran. A pained smile formed on his face. "Can you feel it?" He inhaled deep. "The power of the Spirit."

Zeke nodded. "Someone somewhere is praying."

~~~~~~~~~~

Chris listened to the shaky voice on the other end of the connection.

"Chris, I'm scared."

"Calm down Sarah. What's the matter?"

"Who's that?" Leilah's voice was loud and intentional. "I'll wait for you in the car."

He returned an annoyed glare. Sarah seemed distressed and Leilah was playing high school games. He turned his back to Leilah hoping Sarah hadn't heard the intrusion.

"Chris, there's something strange going on. I looked up the deed for the home on Ash where Burgos lived. You'll never guess who owns the house."

"CeSiR Tech?"

"What? How?"

He could sense disappointment in her voice. He should have let her tell him. "I just saw the pictures from the busted memory card. One of the pictures shows two men pullin' out of CeSiR Tech's entrance. Our man Leon was one of them. Unfortunately, we can't make out the other person, and we've—"

"Chris," Sarah cut in. "There's more. There are dozens of other houses owned by CeSiR, most here in Arrow Springs."

It didn't make sense. "Why would a company like CeSiR buy houses? Can you tell who else lives in those houses?"

"I have a list printed out. I started mapping them and would've searched for more information on the residents, but the connection went dead." She paused—the last words echoed across the connection. "That's what has me worried. It just disconnected. I tried reconnecting but it said the computer wasn't there. I think someone shut it down. I'm scared." Another pause. "Can you come over?"

She didn't strike him as the type to overreact. "Now, don't jump to conclusions. Isn't it possible the connection just got interrupted? I can't keep my connection at the house for more than fifteen minutes."

"I didn't lose my connection at the house. Just to the research computer at the library."

"Maybe the library lost power or somethin'."

A deep breath told him she was tiring of his doubt. "I tried the public web page which is also located at the library. The server was still running fine."

"Chris, come on." He felt Leilah's hands reach around his waist.

He glared and stepped away. "I have to go." He turned his back to her and walked to his squad car.

"Sarah, I'm just leavin' St. Louis. It'll take me a couple hours to get there." He glanced at the digital clock, eight-forty. "I'll be there by eleven."

"Please hurry."

~~~~~~~~~~

Maiya Mirinova sat at the desk in her office. Only her computer screen provided light to the large room. For nearly an hour she had sat entranced by the message on the screen. White text on a black background flashed the words, "Intrusion Alert!"

She had notified Mayor Richards of the intrusion and he promised to take care of it.

She turned her stare to the newspaper sitting on her desk. A bold title read, "Shooting At Arrow Springs Jail."

The project was spinning out of control. She'd confronted Dr. M'Gregor earlier in the week, but she only left the meeting feeling more disturbed. He was losing his nerve.

The room flicked to black. She reached for the mouse but stopped. The information she needed could not be found on a computer.

She grabbed a candle from the front of her desk and lit it. The orange glow drew her to the black armoire in the corner of the office. She removed her clothing and dropped them onto a shelf. From a hanger, she retrieved a black floor length robe with a row of silver pentagrams stitched around the hem and wing-like sleeves. She pulled the robe over her head and grabbed four more black candles from the armoire.

In the center of her office she placed the five candles evenly in a large circle. Once the candles were lit, she sat with her legs crossed at the center of the five points of light. Before her she set a golden incense holder and lit the stick.

She closed her eyes and pulled a black hood over her head. "Casimir. My beloved Casimir. Are you there?" For the first time in a week, she felt his presence. She inhaled the fragrance of Patchouli.

The light from the candles began to dance through her eyelids. She sensed a new light in the room and opened her eyes to find Sir Casimir standing at the edge of the circle of light.

Her heart leaped. "My lord and my love, you have come to me at last."

"So I have." His face was handsome, but hard.

Her heart fell back into place. Casimir was displeased with her. "What troubles you my lord? Have I failed you?"

"You? No. Your work here? Perhaps."

The newspaper article flashed before her.

"You assured me there would be no traces of your work. Yet as you know, the police are suspicious. An investigation ensues."

"My lord, it is Dr. M'Gregor. He is responsible. I confronted him on it this week."

"Perhaps. But it is not him to whom I have chosen to entrust my plans. Have I chosen incorrectly?"

"No my lord. You know you have my obedience. I am yours. I serve only you."

"And yet the enemy knocks at my door."

An icy wave began at her feet and rippled through her. Her body became numb. She felt nothing below her neck. Fear scratched at her mind. "Please my lord—my love. What must I do? Shall I kill the doctor? Punish him for his failure?"

Casimir looked into her eyes, and beyond. "You would do that for me. Wouldn't you?"

She nodded tear filled eyes.

"No. That will not be necessary. He will be dealt with at the appropriate time." He stepped into the circle, knelt before her, and slid his hands under her arms.

At his touch the numbness retreated. The sensation of contact electrified the still unadjusted nerves. She gasped. "My love, I shall not fail you."

"I know."

She reached for him, but he pulled back and stood.

"Trenton is coming. We need to speak with him."

"I don't under—"

A knock echoed from the door.

She looked to Casimir.

He nodded.

"Come in?"

Trenton Richards approached the circle, seemingly unfazed at the odd site. He walked directly to Casimir. "Excuse the interruption lord Mael."

"It is Casimir my friend."

She watched in disbelief. Trenton could see Casimir? She ground her teeth together. Casimir was her love. She would share him with no one.

But Casimir seemed unsurprised by the interruption. "What is it Tu—Trenton?"

"I have come from the library, as you requested."

What? "I asked you to go to the library." Was he trying to steal her guide?

Trenton completely ignored her. "When I arrived I found the computer but no operator. I believe Sarah McIntyre connected remotely to the search engine."

Sarah McIntyre? The woman Leon had attacked?

Trenton continued his update. "Earlier in the week, I sent her home for a couple weeks supposedly because of her injuries. I wanted her out of there for this very reason."

A hint of sulfur assaulted her nose. That had never happened with the incense before.

Casimir's lip quivered as he addressed Trenton. "I am aware she is on leave from the library. If you recall, I ordered it."

How could Casimir know Trenton? Still she liked this new distaste he seemed to have for him.

"It would appear you did not cut her off well enough. Do you know what she found?"

Trenton turned a glance to Maiya.

"It is okay. She can be trusted. She is loyal to me, are you not my queen?"

She nodded.

"I cannot be certain what she discovered before I arrived. She did, however, download a list of properties owned by CeSiR. When I saw the information flashing across the screen, I pulled the plug."

"So now she realizes someone is on to her?"

Trenton crossed his arms. "Would you have preferred I let her continue to dig up incriminating evidence?"

Casimir sat next to Maiya and removed her hood. He began to stroke her long black hair. "It matters not what she knows . . . if she is dead."

Her body thrilled at the power of her lover.

He dismissed Trenton with a flip of the wrist. "I think it is time Miss McIntyre had an accident. Take care of her."

~~~~~~~~~~

Chris travelled west on I-64 toward I-170

He picked up the cruiser's handset. "Sally?"

"Go ahead Chris."

"I've received a possible distress call from Sarah McIntyre. The young lady from the attack last Friday."

The radio crackled. "Should I send someone to check on her?"

"She wasn't certain there was a real threat. I'm headed there now, but I'm still in St. Louis." He pulled into the left lane and accelerated. "Can I get permission for a Code 10?" Sarah trusted him. "I don't want to blow it out of proportion, but I don't want to take all night either."

"Go ahead Chris. Just be careful."

"Thanks, I will."

He flipped the switch to the strobes and siren. It would cut about a half hour off the drive, if he stayed around ninety.

Thankfully, the rains of the last two days had finally stopped. The roads would be dry.

Sarah's freckled face flashed through his mind, twisting his stomach like a dishrag. "Lord, I know I've got no right to come to You right now, with my actions tonight and all. But please keep Sarah safe." Her blue trusting eyes haunted him. "Please forgive my thoughts and actions tonight. I know it wasn't of my own strength or obedience that I walked away from the snare. I can only imagine what effect my choices would've had on my newfound friendship with Sarah. Thank you for deliverin' me from my own fleshly desires." His eyes burned. "Please Lord—forgive me."

~~~~~~~~~~

At Mael's request, a demon of inebriation led a twenty-two year old washed up football star out of the River's Edge.

The man staggered to his 2018 Mustang Thoroughbrid, Ford's prize three-hundred-horse, thirty-five MPG, hybrid sports car.

He stumbled, swore, stumbled again, dropped his keys, swore again, bent over to pick them up and then kicked them. After one final slurred condemnation of his Creator, he opened the door to the fire-red sports car.

With the demon's assistance, the man managed to pull the car from the parking lot without hitting the other vehicles. Soon the car rocketed toward the intersection on the east end of Arrow Springs.

If the demon timed it right—and of course he had—the car would arrive at Tree-Bark Bend at precisely the same time as the approaching squad car.

The demon shot ahead to ensure everything went as planned.

~~~~~~~~~~

Chris merged off of I-70. He'd be at Sarah's in less than ten minutes. He passed a car that had pulled to the right because of the strobes, and turned left onto MO-41. Now free from traffic, he hammered the accelerator to the floor.

The car's heads-up-display showed seventy-two miles per hour. Soon he'd be forced to slow for the bend. How many times had he pulled someone from a mangled mess on that cur—

Without warning, even from the car's infrared detection system, something darted into the road—the largest deer he had ever seen. If he had been hunting it would have been the best day of his life. Hopefully, it wouldn't be his last.

With perfect timing, the deer stopped just shy of the two yellow lines in the middle of the road. Piercing black eyes turned directly toward him—not toward the headlights, or the red and blue strobes, but directly to his eyes. It was as if it dared him to hit it.

He pulled the steering wheel hard right sending the car skidding toward the side of the road and awaited the sickening thud of the car-deer impact.

It never came.

Could he have possibly missed the creature?

He saw a large oak tree approaching. This time there was a thud, and not a little one. The car spun as the tree trunk struck the front left side panel just in front of the tire. The cruiser's airbag slammed him in the chest, while the side-impact restraint cushioned the blow of his momentum into the door.

The car trimmed off a couple saplings and came to rest fifteen feet from the road.

His ribs throbbed as he sat for what seemed like an hour. The car had stopped, but everything still spun in his vision. His chicken cappellini threatened a reappearance. He calmed himself and picked up the handset to report the accident to dispatch.

Nothing but silence.

When he slid from the car, he saw why. The car's battery lay ten feet away split in half and pouring its toxic contents into the ground.

He staggered toward the road.

A loud familiar sound reverberated from the roadside. The sound of bending steel, breaking wood, and glass shattering filled his head.

He stopped at the edge of the road. Was his mind playing tricks on him? Another accident perfectly mirrored his own. He approached the red sports car and found a young man sitting unconscious in the driver's seat.

He opened the door and reached into the car. The man's pulse was strong and so was his breath—in every sense. There was no way to tell if the man had broken anything. It would be best not to remove him from the car.

Chris reached for his cell phone but all he felt was an empty clip. What else could go wrong?

He made his way back to the squad car and searched for the phone. He needed to get emergency response to the site soon. And what about Sarah? Why didn't he let Sally send someone to check on her? There was no way he'd be getting there by eleven.

After five minutes of searching, he found the phone under the driver's seat of the cruiser. He flipped open the phone and saw the familiar blue glow. Its battery remained intact. The joy proved short lived—the display showed zero bars of service. That shouldn't have been the case for his location. Perhaps bouncing around the car during the accident proved a bit too much for it.

He sat down alongside the road to wait for someone to pass by. As much as he wanted to get to Sarah, he couldn't leave the scene, not with a potentially injured D.U.I. sitting twenty feet from him.

Had the same deer caused the other driver to veer into the brush? There was no sign of the deer, which suited him just fine.

~~~~~~~~~~

Eran sat on one side of Chris, while Zeke sat on the other.

The demon of inebriation just stared at them, a mixture of fear and anger swirling through his face.

"Nice deer!" Zeke patted Eran on the shoulder. "Quite realistic."

"Why thank you. I thought it worked out well. Certainly better than getting crushed by a drunken missile, was it not?"

"Most definitely." Zeke smiled at the sulking demon.

"Laugh all you want." The demon of inebriation lifted into the air. "You think you have won?" He smiled baring green pointed teeth. "Quite the contrary."

~~~~~~~~~~

The black BMW, license plate CT06-F24, turned onto Second Street—its four inhabitants carefully scoping out Sarah's neighborhood.

Ominous darkness engulfed the street. Three hours after sunset, even the bright sliver of a new moon had descended below the western horizon. The skies were clear but the stars withheld their light.

~~~~~~~~~~

At ten minutes to eleven, a knock on the front door drew Sarah's attention from the stack of papers in front of her. She glanced at the golden hands of her dining room clock. "Right on time. Thank you Lord," she whispered.

She hobbled to the front door to meet her knight in shining armor.

~~~~~~~~~~

Eran watched as Chris paced the roadside. The wind rustled through branches laden with new leaves.

"Lord, why'd you let this happen," Chris asked God. "Is this payback for my actions with Leilah? I know I deserve it, but don't let Sarah pay the price for my mistakes. Please—keep her safe." He kicked a golf-ball sized stone across the road.

Zeke turned a quizzical look to Eran. "Why is it every time something like this happens people think either God is mad at them, or the enemy is attacking them?"

Eran shrugged his shoulders.

"He has no idea you just saved his life."

"They usually do not. And God decides when it is their time. I just pretended to be a deer to keep him from getting hit by the drunk driver."

"Now what?" asked Zeke.

"Now—he waits."

~~~~~~~~~~

Before the fear of the last two hours could catch up with her, Sarah reached for the door and pulled it open.

Time froze.

Her heart quickened to a near critical rate—yet at the same time seemed to stop beating.

How could she be such an idiot?

An ear-piercing scream hung thick on the night air.

In front of her stood a man she had never seen before.

Though clearly too late, she attempted to slam the door. Amazingly, the door clicked shut and no one attempted to reopen it.

"Um, Sarah—Sarah McIntyre," said the man from the other side of the door.

"Sarah, we're sorry we startled you. We know it's late." This time it was a soft female voice. "My name is Trina Thomas and this is my husband David."

"I'm the Pastor at River of Life Church here in town," said David. "I believe you know Chris Davis. He goes to our church. If it's too late, we can come back another time."

Footsteps announced their departure from the porch.

Could she trust them? Something deep in her heart told her she could.

She discretely watched out a living room window as the couple walked toward their car. An sense of urgency overwhelmed her. She needed them to stay. She limped to the door, feeling as if her brace was a shackle slowing each step. The couple had just reached their car when she flung open the door. "Wait, please!"

The couple returned to the front porch.

Trina held out a hand. "Hi Sarah. I'm Trina Thomas, and this is my husband, David."

"Please, come in. I was expecting Chris, and that's why it startled me so to open the door and see an unfamiliar face—"

"I'm so sorry about that," said David.

"That's okay. I just hope I didn't deafen you." Redness joined the black and blue of her face as she realized the scream she had heard was her own.

She led David and Trina to her living room.

~~~~~~~~~~

The black BMW slowed in front of Sarah's house. Tudur and three other demons eyed with disdain the five mammoth figures standing shoulder to shoulder in front of the house. The enemy's hedge of protection, likely the result of some pathetic saint's prayerful pleas for Sarah.

Glowing like iridescent statues holding flaming red swords against the dark of night stood five top-ranking members of the heavenly host. He had met them all at one time or another throughout the millennia. Alex and Huw stood to the left, while Gida and Yora flanked the right. The massive figure in the center ensured his decision to remain in the car. Despite the size of the other four warriors, Eitan towered above them all.

Mael would be furious. But perhaps he would survive the encounter with him. He would not be so fortunate in a skirmish with the host standing in Sarah's yard.

In silence, they rode away from the house.

~~~~~~~~~~

Sarah sat in her recliner facing Pastor Thomas and his adorable wife Trina. The couple sat on her couch explaining what brought them to her house at such a late hour.

"Mrs. Ferguson called me today and asked that we pay you a visit," began Pastor Thomas. "I believe you met her today?"

She took a deep breath trying to quiet her still anxious heart. "Yes, she brought me some delicious lemon bars. Seemed like a very nice lady."

"She sure is." Trina leaned forward. "We're sorry to visit you so late. It's not something we normally would do, especially someone we haven't even met. Mrs. Ferguson told us all about your attack last week." Trina glanced down and then back up. "But tonight I just felt like God was telling me He needed us here. I really don't know how to explain it. I got the sense you might be in trouble. When I mentioned it to David, he told me he'd been feeling the same thing. So we came right over. I do hope we haven't inconvenienced you."

"Not at all. I was sitting here waiting for Chris." She looked at her living room clock, five after eleven. "He should've been here by now. He was in St. Louis when I called him. He said he was on his way."

"Is everything all right?" asked Trina.

"I'm just a little shaken. I was investigating some things about the man who broke in last Friday and it appears someone disconnected me from the computer at the library. Chris thought I was just being paranoid." She sucked in her cheeks and then exhaled. "He's probably right."

"You never know," said David. "I really believe God had a reason for bringing us here tonight. We may never know what His reasons are. It seems like that's how He works."

Boy didn't she know it. "I'm sorry," she said beginning to sit up from her chair. "Would you like something to drink?" A grin crept to her face. "Maybe even a lemon bar?"

Pastor Thomas' mouth opened in a yawn, though he did his best to hide it. "Oh that's not necessary. We probably shouldn't stay too long."

"Please, I could use a little company, at least until Chris gets here. Like you said, maybe God did have a reason for your visit."

"We would love to," said Trina. "I'll help you get it." She rose and accompanied Sarah to the kitchen.

Once they reached the kitchen, Sarah turned to Trina. "How well do you know Chris?"

"Well, I understand he's been going to River of Life since he arrived in Arrow Springs, oh, it must be about five years ago now."

She set some glasses on the counter.

"We've only been there for three years. So—I guess I've known him for three years. He's always seemed like a perfect gentleman."

"There are ice cubes in the freezer," said Sarah. "Go on."

"Well, David speaks very highly of him, especially since last fall when the church was kicked out of the school. Chris was one of the more vocal followers who stood up and declared his faith that God wasn't done with River of Life. Thanks to him most of the congregation stuck it out."

"Tea okay?" Sarah pulled a pitcher out of the fridge. "Well, this will sound kind of corny, but he's been my knight in shining armor this past week." She must have sounded like a sixth grade schoolgirl with a crush on her sophomore brother's best friend. "Like I said—kinda corny."

"Not at all." Trina took the pitcher and began to fill the glasses while Sarah cut the lemon bars. "Chris is a handsome godly man of integrity. There is certainly nothing to be ashamed of there. Are you concerned that you like him just because he rescued you?" Trina set down the pitcher and looked her in the eyes. "Or, at least that others will see it that way?"

"Yeah, I guess that has a lot to do with it. He just seems like the perfect man."

Trina giggled. "Well I'm sure he's not perfect, but it is certainly okay to find a man attractive who is willing to put himself on the line for you." Her voice turned more instructing. "You know—the Bible tells husbands to love their wives as Christ loved the church. This isn't some euphoric googly-eyed infatuation. This is a lay-down-your-life-for-her kind of love. That's exactly what Christ did for the church. Any man worth his salt would be more than willing to put himself in harm's way to protect a young lady such as you."

Sarah felt warmth rise to her cheeks at the reference of a husband-and-wife type of relationship for her and Chris. "Is there anything else you can tell me about him?"

Trina carried the glasses of tea to the dining room table. "Well—I really don't know much about his past. I believe he's had a relationship with Christ for several years now. If you want to know more about his past," she raised her palms up, "you should probably ask him."

"Who are you two girls gossiping about now?" asked Pastor Thomas with a smile. He walked into the dining room and pulled a chair out from the table.

"Now that's just none of your business," scolded Trina.

The playful interaction between the couple nearly brought tears to her eyes. She recalled the way her parents would lovingly banter back and forth. It'd been a while since she realized how much she still missed her parents.

Pastor Thomas pointed to a map of Arrow Springs with little red dots spread across it. "What's this?"

~~~~~~~~~~

Chris couldn't believe how little traffic was out for a Friday night. Only three cars had passed and none even slowed at his presence on the side of the road. The police cruiser was out of sight and he'd worn civilian clothes to the dinner. If he was wearing his uniform someone would stop.

Several more quiet minutes passed before a pickup truck passed. As he tried to wave it down, the passing wind pelted him with sand from the side of the road.

A hundred yards down the road, on flashed the red brake lights.

The truck backed up and rolled down its window.

"Do you happen to have a cell phone?" he asked the fifty-something driver.

"Sure do. Here."

He quickly dialed Daryl's number.

Minutes later, while he still conversed with the man in the pickup, Daryl pulled up in his squad car. "Hey there. Need a lift?"

He wrapped up his conversation and thanked the man for stopping.

He walked to the squad car and patted the roof. "Yours sure looks better than mine does. Thanks for coming so quickly." He looked across the road at splintered shrubbery. "First we need to take care of our inebriated motorist over there."

After placing the man under arrest, Daryl dropped Chris off at his house. "You sure you're okay?"

"I'm fine. Can't say my car was so fortunate though."

"Well, the wrecker will get her to Ralph's and before you know it she'll be good as new."

"Thanks again, Daryl. See you Sunday?"

"I'll be there. Take care."

~~~~~~~~~~

Chris pulled up to Sarah's house, concerned to see a sedan parked in the driveway. He walked to the front door and knocked.

Inside, Sarah shouted. "It's Chris!"

Was she in trouble? Footsteps pounded toward the door.

He ducked as the door flung open.

Sarah practically leaped out at him. She hugged him and then pulled him through the doorway. Apparently, she hadn't overheard Leilah on the phone. He breathed a sigh of relief.

She led him into the dining room.

He stopped. "Pastor Thomas?"

Pastor Thomas looked up at them with a smile. "Please, how many times do I need to tell you? It's David."

He held up his hands in surrender. "I know. It just don't feel right."

"Neither does constantly being called Pastor. It's not my first name you know." David shook his head. "At church is one thing, but it's certainly not necessary in a setting like this."

Chris looked from Sarah to David to Trina. "What are you guys doing here? Do you know each other?"

"We do now." Trina patted the chair next to her. "Mrs. Ferguson called us and asked us to stop in some time and meet Sarah."

He sat down next to Trina. "Well I'm glad you're here." He tilted his head and looked at Sarah. "Anything else happen?"

"Nope. I guess you were right, there doesn't seem to be anything to worry about."

"I'm not so sure." David tapped a map of Arrow Springs spread out on the table. "These locations, are you sure these are correct?"

Sarah nodded. "Pretty sure, why?"

"I recognize this one here." David pointed to a dot on the southeast side of Arrow Springs. "That's Mayor Richard's house."

Everyone sat and stared silently at the map, pondering the possible meaning of this last statement.

"Are you sure?" Chris finally broke the silence. "I mean, I know that's where he lives, but—" He turned the question to Sarah. "Are ya sure that was one of the addresses from the list?"

"Let's check." She grabbed her laptop from the kitchen counter and set it on the table. Moments later, she pulled up a list of addresses and scanned it with her finger. "Here it is. 101 Morgan Ct. owned by CeSiR Tech."

"What does it mean?" asked Trina.

If only he knew. "Maybe nothing, though I must say, seems strange, especially given they own all these houses."

"Not to mention the one my attacker lived in," added Sarah. "And don't forget, the mayor's the one who sent me home after I tried to help you read the memory card."

He grimaced. "This is gonna get sticky. I think it'd be best if we didn't discuss this with anyone. I need to get to the bottom of this."

David chuckled. "Well, one thing's for certain, I'm used to keeping secrets!"

Trina slid her chair back from the table. "We should probably be going. Sarah it has been lovely meeting you. You should come join us some Sunday morning."

Sarah's smile warmed his heart. "I just might have to do that. Thank you for keeping me company while I waited."

Once David and Trina left, Chris filled Sarah in on the details of the accident.

She spent the next hour pestering him with questions about his well-being.

They talked until one in the morning about the properties owned by CeSiR Tech. Neither of them recognized any of the other addresses, but he assured her he would be finding out.

"Looks like I'm gonna be paying CeSiR Tech a visit on Monday."

She let out a quick gasp. "Oh Chris—be careful. Something weird's going on here."

He leaned over and kissed her on the cheek. "I will. You let me know if ya need anything." As he stood from the chair at the table, pain ground through his hip. He groaned and rubbed his hipbone.

"Are you sure you're okay?"

"I'm fine. Just some aches and pains from the accident."

She walked him to the door. "You be careful."

He longed to linger. To embrace her in a long goodbye. But before he even turned to step from the porch, she stepped back and shut the door.

"Good night Sarah," he whispered.

~~~~~~~~~~

"Perhaps Tudur is smarter than I thought," Mael growled at the minor demon standing in his presence. "He knew I would kill him for his failure. You on the other hand, do not value your existence? Do you think I will spare you?"

The demon of violence bowed low at the waist. "But my liege, there is something you must know. There were five members of the host at the home. We would surely have been destroyed."

He turned his sword over in his hand. "Are you so afraid of some measly angels that you would dare face me in defiance?"

"My lord, these were not just any angels. I believe you know them—one especially. The captain named Eitan."

He paced in silence. Surely this demon knew the bad blood between him and Eitan—that it went back to The Fall itself. He had chosen to follow Lucifer in his defiance of God. Eitan blindly remained faithful to an unforgiving God.

In the millennia that followed, they had done battle hundreds of times. At times he had won, destroying those Eitan sought to protect. At others, Eitan had succeeded in thwarting his plans.

"So Eitan is here—" His thunderous voice echoed in the lair. "Clearly the enemy knows of the significance of this town. It will only be a matter of time before they attempt to stop us."

"Should we begin moving the operation?" asked the demon.

"You see, that is why you are nothing more than a messenger." He put his sword to the demon's chin. "I will not run from Eitan. If he wants a fight, then I will give him one." He pressed on the sword and green fluid began to flow. "Arrow Springs is our town. They are not welcome here, and they will know it. Send messengers to all of the patients. We need to prepare."

"GO!" He flipped his sword from under the demon's pointy chin. More green liquid ran to the floor.

"Yes my lord."

~~~~~~~~~~

CHAPTER SIXTEEN

Sunday, April 26, 2020

Adiya, Marilyn's guardian angel, sat behind her at the back of the church auditorium. A handful of his comrades flickered throughout the room like stars amid the midnight sky. Hundreds of demonic beings cursed and hollered, as songs intended to be sung in worship of God dripped of arrogance and self sufficiency. Amid the sea of deformed figures, two beings occupied his attention.

Marilyn sat between anger and frustration.

"How could a child of a forgiving God be so unwilling to forgive such a tiny little indiscretion?" asked the demon of frustration.

"Tiny indiscretion!" said the demon of anger. "He betrayed your trust. He discarded you like day old bread for a fresh little pastry. Now you would consider forgiving him?"

Adiya intertwined his fingers and refused to offer the satisfaction of eye contact with the demons.

Grinning ear to deformed pointy little ear, the demon of frustration continued. "But is that not what you have been taught? Forgiveness is a sign of godliness. Did He not say you were to take up your cross and follow Him? He died, you know. He died for pathetic sinners like you."

The demon of anger leaned forward and whispered in Marilyn's ear. "And for the men who let their heads be turned by any twenty-something that flutters her eyes at them."

"Enough!" said Adiya. "Leave her alone. She is a child of God." The faint amber glow of his wings gave evidence to the difficulty of his assignment. Not that Marilyn lived a dangerous or even sinful life, but because of the bitterness she maintained toward her ex-husband.

"What is the matter?" asked the demon of frustration. "You afraid she might not be so strong as you thought. She opened the door. It was her anger and frustration with her ex that brought us here."

The sniveling demon would not have dared talk to him that way if he was alone.

"That is precisely what he is afraid of," said the demon of anger. "He is afraid the reality of the darkness in her own soul will be more than his precious little baby believer can deal with. Better to keep it hidden away in the dark closet of her soul than to face her own humanity." The demon slapped him on the shoulder. "Right angel boy?"

Adiya growled. He could rip the arm from its black body and probably still escape the church in one piece. But it would accomplish no more than trying to reason with them. In millennia of dealing with the fallen ones, none had ever changed their opinions as a result of godly wisdom. Theirs was a path of destruction and damnation. It was an established fact—it just had not yet happened. Instead, he extended his wings to provide shelter from the onslaught.

~~~~~~~~~~

Chris opened the door for Sarah and followed her out of the River of Life foyer. The mid-day sun ignited her curls in an angelic brilliance.

She turned and flashed him a smile.

He stepped forward to join her, but the concrete disappeared from in front of him. His foot finally came to rest at the base of the last step. He lurched forward and bumped into her shoulder. "I'm sorry." He caught his balance and glanced to see how many people saw it.

Sarah released a constricted giggle.

The only other person who seemed to notice was Daryl. But even he looked distracted.

Sarah reached out and took his hand. "I usually fall up the steps." This time the giggle came without obstruction.

The warm soft touch of her hand soothed his embarrassment.

"What's up with Daryl?" she asked.

With hands in his pockets, Daryl walked toward the parking lot. "I think he'd hoped to see Marilyn again this week. It's been really hard on him."

Her head swiveled to Chris. "On him? What about her?" A fine mist sheeted across her eyes. "I couldn't imagine having to interact with someone who betrayed my trust like that."

Did she know? Had she heard Leilah on the phone? His mind returned to the police report he'd read about Sarah's rape. She knew about pain. Tightness pulled at his chest. Had he added to that pain?

~~~~~~~~~~

Sarah spread a blue plaid blanket on the grass at a small park beside the Katy Trail. Chris had called her Saturday to see if she would join him for lunch after church. Her brain told her *no*. She spent her life letting her brain protect her heart. This time her heart overruled.

He picked the place. She packed the lunch.

The trail itself wasn't much—kind of a historic bike path where steam engines of the past travelled. The surroundings were breathtaking. Cherry and crabapple trees, in full bloom with luminous pink flowers, painted the landscape everywhere she looked.

She began to unpack the picnic basket, while he sat on the corner of the blanket.

"Such incredible beauty," said Chris.

She continued unpacking. "Sure is."

He got up and walked away.

She turned to see him returning with a small branch covered in pink flowers.

He delicately placed the branch in her hair. "There—now they're perfect."

She gave him a wary smile. "You're so sweet." He couldn't possibly believe she was pretty? If he only knew. She hadn't brought herself to tell him about the rape. Too many times she'd experienced the rejection.

Chris surveyed the food spread across the blanket. "Were we expecting company?"

Had she over done it? She looked at the food she'd unpacked. She brought sandwiches, complete with lettuce, tomato, mayo, ham, turkey, chicken, and three different cheeses. She'd also packed whole-wheat chips, sour cream and onion dip, strawberries, pineapple, and watermelon. He'd ordered iced tea at the Bistro, so she packed iced tea in a large pitcher to drink. It wasn't that much.

"You didn't have to go to so much trouble."

"Nonsense." She handed him a glass of tea. "You've done nothing but care for me since we met. It's the least I can do."

~~~~~~~~~~

For the first time, without the bruises and bandages, Chris saw Sarah's true beauty. The way her eyes softened connected with his gaze sent a shiver through his arms. Of all of God's beautiful creation, he was looking at the crowning achievement.

She sat down on the blanket and patted the spot next to her. "I think we're all set."

Following her cue, he settled beside her. The sweet aroma of cocoa butter danced with the fragrance of the cherry blossoms. He had noticed the fragrance briefly during the church service, but now sitting only inches from her—it was captivating.

"Would you like me to ask the blessing?" he asked.

She shrugged her shoulders.

He couldn't imagine the pain she must have felt after the attack. She clearly blamed God. How could she not? Regret whelmed up within him. He shouldn't have snooped into her files. He'd violated her trust. If she'd wanted him to know, she'd have told him.

As they ate, they engaged in small talk.

After lunch, he watched her as she put the glasses and pitcher back in the basket. Her every movement flowed with grace and beauty.

She sat back down on the blanket and her face grew serious. "So—are you going to tell me about her?"

The question caught him off guard. She *had* heard. How could she not? Leilah had practically screamed into the phone. His blood steamed at Leilah. But his gut wrenched with guilt and sorrow for Sarah. What had he been thinking? "Her name is Leilah. She's an old friend from the days before my walk with Christ."

Sarah sat quietly, staring into his eyes, as if she could peer directly into his soul. She wasn't buying it.

"Well," He paused, wanted to stop, wanted to leave. "She was more than just a friend. We had a pretty serious relationship throughout my time at the academy."

"How serious?" The words were steady, deliberate. She wasn't going to settle for anything less than complete honesty.

"Very. We lived together for six months. We even discussed getting married."

"And?"

"I'm not sure it was ever really my intention." He lowered his eyes to the blue and white stripes of the blanket. "I guess I probably talked the talk, so she'd walk the walk, if you know what I'm sayin'."

Overhead, the squawk of a Grackle echoed the scolding of his own heart.

"You led her to believe you were committed to a long term relationship—" Her voice remained steady. "So she'd sleep with you. Is *that* basically what you're saying?"

The words cut through his heart. "If I thought there was a way to defend myself, I'd try. But, I was wrong. My actions were driven by lust. They are days I'm not proud of." He tried to look her in the eyes. He couldn't.

Her nostrils flare out a heated breath.

"Six months after we moved in together, I started a relationship with Christ. I moved out and Lei was none too pleased. She had no desire to build a serious relationship that included both her and God." He put a hand to his forehead and rubbed tightening temples. "Lookin' back, I don't believe she wanted a long-term relationship either. I think we were both in the relationship for the physical satisfaction."

Sarah ducked her head down and looked straight into his eyes. "Is that how you feel about our relationship?"

Our relationship—she viewed them as having a relationship. His heart skipped at the thought. But, had he blown it? Had his openness about his past cost him a chance at a significant God-honoring relationship with Sarah?

"Sarah, I hope you can believe me when I tell you, I do not see our relationship that way."

Her cheeks pulled tight in what looked to be a wince.

"You're a beautiful woman and I'd be lying if I said I wasn't attracted to you." He was stumbling on his words. He couldn't think straight. "It's just—I value your purity too much."

Like flood waters off a mountain, tears poured from her eyes.

I know about the assault! He wanted to scream it. He wanted to hold her in his arms until the pain subsided. But he couldn't. He wasn't supposed to know. He shouldn't know. "Sarah, I understand—"

She cut him off. "No! You don't. I have no purity! It was taken from me when I was sixteen." Her chest heaved.

"Sarah, don't say that."

"I was raped, Chris, by the men that killed my parents." She blinked tears from her eyes. "They raped me and left me for dead."

"I know." He couldn't keep it from her. "I read the police report."

She tilted her head to the right. "You what?"

"I'm sorry. But what happened to you—it wasn't your fault." He swiped at tears on his cheeks. "Jesus said, blessed are the pure in heart. True purity is somethin' that comes from within. Those guys stole your family from you, they stole your possessions, they stole your security, they may have even stolen your willingness to trust in God, but one thing they didn't—they couldn't—steal was your purity and innocence. You were a victim, not a guilty party."

"You don't get it! I'm spoiled goods."

Pain rippled deep within her moist sapphire eyes.

He wanted to say something. But what could he say to make her feel better. How could he explain why God would let such a travesty happen to a fragile young woman? So he said nothing.

For ten minutes she sat silently. Finally, she broke the silence. "Did you see the pictures of my parents?"

"No. As soon as I read what happened to you, I closed the files. I didn't mean to violate your privacy."

"For years, I had no privacy. Everyone knew. It wasn't until the trial ended that I could finally slip back into obscurity. I was left alone to sweep up the shattered pieces."

"Sarah, I believe God's made me a new man, despite the fact that I chose to give away my purity." He pointed to the pink and white lace draping the countryside. "God isn't just the Creator. He is also the re-creator of incredible beauty." He held his hand out to her.

She sniffed. "I wish I had Him figured out the way you do."

"I simply believe in a God that's beyond my comprehension. There are plenty of things I don't understand. Like, why would God let such horrible evil happen to a sixteen-year-old child? Or, why would a perfect God choose to turn a pathetic lustful twenty-three-year-old into a new creation with a second chance?" He shook his head. "I don't have to understand. I just have to trust."

"That's not easy to do."

"No it's not. But God's continually shown his love and protection of me." He slid across the blanket and held out his palm to her.

She started to reach out, then she pulled back her hand.

He had betrayed her trust. Would she ever trust him again? "Sarah, I believe God used your call to protect me from my own actions Friday night. I love you. I never want to see ya hurt again—especially by me."

~~~~~~~~~~

CHAPTER SEVENTEEN
Monday, April 27, 2020

Eran paced atop the old bridge embankment next to the Lamine River. How could he sit idly by while his charge walked into the very nest of the enemy? Down the long driveway, a black cloud swirled with demonic activity. Eitan was right—they could not take on the stronghold of the enemy with their current numbers. They needed prayer cover and more warriors. His instructions were to stay outside the grounds of the facility. The time for battle would surely come—just not yet.

~~~~~~~~~~

Chris approached the wrought-iron gate at CeSiR Tech. At the center of the black one-inch bars a golden circle contained the letters C T. He stopped his Wrangler at the gate and rolled down the window.

A block of a man, with no neck to speak of, exited a small guard house and approached the Jeep. "Looks like you made a wrong turn, son. Turn it around and get out of here."

"No, no wrong turn here. I'm Sergeant Chris Davis of the Arrow Springs Police Department." Out of the corner of his eye he saw a similarly built guard approach the vehicle from the other side.

"You could be the Governor for all I care. This is a government facility. Nobody comes through here without an invitation."

Part of him wanted to slam his door into the man and force him to open the door. Though it probably wouldn't be the most prudent option, especially considering the automatic rifles both guards carried. "Look, I'm investigatin' a string of events here in town, including a murder at the station Saturday morning. I'd like to speak with someone regarding a few apparent links to CeSiR Tech."

The man sneered and crossed his arms.

"If you don't let me in, I'll return with a warrant and a bunch of officers." He didn't have anywhere close to enough evidence for a warrant, but this meatball didn't need to know that. "We'll tear this place apart if we have to."

The guards both turned, as if to look at an unseen visitor.

He tried to see if they were wearing wireless headsets. Not that he could tell.

The guard turned back to the Jeep. "Dr. M'Gregor will see you gentlemen in a few minutes. Please pull into the garage on the lower level. The door will open automatically." The man practically growled. "Just follow the signs."

Chris looked at the empty seat next to him. "Okay—thank you."

The gates swung open and he drove another quarter mile to the building. The closer he came to the white structure the straighter the hair on his arms stood. The morning sun shone bright in the eastern sky, but his soul sensed a darkness he couldn't explain.

The building looked like white sandstone with mirrored windows that reflected the morning sun. A twelve-foot tall three-inch thick steel door opened automatically as he approached. With enough space for three to four hundred employees to park, the belowground parking facility was impressive. Programmable direction signs guided him to a specific parking spot. His mind toyed with the option of parking in a different spot just to see what happened. But in the end, he complied with the signs.

After parking, a sign instructed him to remain in the vehicle until an attendant arrived to escort him.

He waited.

In the rearview mirror he saw another large man approaching. He exited the Jeep and met the man at the back bumper.

The man scowled, apparently none too happy with Chris for exiting the vehicle. "Please follow me. Save any questions you have for Dr. M'Gregor."

Clearly, CeSiR didn't hire their security guards for their personalities.

They walked a hundred feet to a security terminal beside an elevator door. The guard pressed a couple buttons and an electronic fingerprint reader presented itself from within the terminal. After scanning both thumbs, a retina scanner replaced the reader. The guard placed his face to the scanner and moments later the elevator door slid open.

"Welcome Michael," announced a computerized female voice.

The stuff of James Bond. Chris was about to ask if the prints and scans were stored locally or tied to the N.F.R.S., National Fingerprint and Retinal Scan database, when he remembered the warning to save all questions for the doctor.

They entered the elevator. The control panel was unlike any he'd seen. There were no buttons—just a touchscreen interface. The screen showed a graphic of the garage they were leaving. In addition, there was a graphic labeled "Offices." The guard touched the screen and the graphic disappeared, replaced by the words, "Office Complex."

Ten seconds later, the door opened to a plush reception area.

The guard pointed toward some chairs. "Please wait there for the doctor."

Chris sat in a tan chair with a view of both the elevator and the hallway behind the receptionist. The chair felt like his easy chair at home. Though probably more expensive. The reception area possessed an art deco array of browns, gold, mirror, and glass. The professional appearance conveyed the message that CeSiR was successful at what they did—whatever that was.

"Can I offer you something to drink?" asked the receptionist. She appeared to be in her late-thirties. "Dr. M'Gregor will be with you in a few minutes."

"Water?"

"Certainly."

~~~~~~~~~~

Mael watched as Maiya worked at her office desk. He was beginning to tire of her constant wining for her Casimir. While the apparition made it easier to control her, her dependence on the character evidenced her weakness. If he thought she could handle the truth of his being, he would appear to her in his true form. But he still needed her cooperation, at least for a little while longer. Soon, they would no longer need the assistance of the weak humans.

"My lord—"

He turned to see Cadfael. "Yes, what is it?"

"We have visitors. Officer Davis and another. They are investigating Leon."

"Tell the guards not to let them in. We do not need them snooping around."

Cadfael's eyes darted around the room. "Um, I truly am sorry my lord." His head dropped like a child caught with cookie crumbs on his face. "I, um, told the guards to let them in. They are in the reception area."

"You what! You know our policy on visitors. Yet you chose to allow the very people investigating Leon into the building?"

"They said they would get a warrant."

"Fool! They have nothing. They would not get a warrant with ten times the evidence."

"Yes my lord. Shall I tell them the doctor is unavailable?" He turned to leave.

"No. Maiya will ensure Dr. M'Gregor tells them nothing of significance. Perhaps if they are satisfied CeSiR has nothing to hide, they will leave us alone."

"Yes my lord." Cadfael disappeared through the wall at the back of the office.

~~~~~~~~~~

The receptionist returned with a glass of ice water, with two slices of lemon.

"Thank you," said Chris.

She smiled and returned to her work.

He surveyed the reception area. A cross between a doctor's office and a bank. They spared no expense to make it an attractive yet functional office.

"So sorry to keep ya waitin'." The Scottish brogue belonged to an elderly man entering the lobby from the hallway behind the receptionist. He approached Chris and held out his hand. "Dr. Wilhelm M'Gregor. Ya must be Sergeant Chris Davis, pleasure to make your acquaintance."

"Yes sir. Thank you for taking the time to speak with me."

"Not a problem. I only hope there is somethin' I can do to help ya."

"The guards at the front didn't seem to have the same helpful attitude."

"Ya must forgive 'em. They're paid to keep people out of here. This is a highly secretive facility, as ya no doubt have already discovered. Please, won't ya join me? We can take up our discussion in my office?"

Chris stood and followed the doctor. Office—a completely inadequate description for the palatial room they entered.

"Please won't ya have a seat?" The doctor pointed to a plush leather sofa and then sat in a chair identical to the one in the reception area, except this one was black. "So—what can I help ya with?"

"Well, first, are you familiar with a man by the name of Leon Burgos?"

For an instant, the left corner of the doctor's mouth pulled tight. "Yes, I'm afraid I am." He closed his eyes and drew in a deep breath. "Ya see Leon was a patient here at CeSiR, until the events of last weekend."

"Then you're aware he is now deceased?"

"Yes. It's all over the papers and the telly. Arrow Springs' man kills fellow inmate before being shot by police." His eyes narrowed a touch. "Were you the officer?"

"Yes."

The doctor curled his index finger over his mouth and nodded.

"You say he was a patient—what exactly do you do here?"

"Yes, of course." The doctor leaned forward and rested his hands on his knees. "CeSiR Tech is a medical research facility. Our goal is to bring a normalcy to life for those who wouldn't otherwise have it. Through genetic research we bring healing and relief from a variety of genetic diseases."

"You're a pharmaceutical company?"

"Sort of. Ya see most of the Pharmaceutical and Medicine Manufacturing industry, or PMM as we refer to it, is made up of companies much larger than CeSiR Tech. We have a mere two hundred and ninety employees. Most of the people in the industry are employed by companies of well over five hundred. We're not so much involved in the manufacturing of medicines as in researching cures. We have nearly two hundred biochemists, biophysicists, microbiologists, chemists, bio and chemical engineers, computer and robotics specialists, and medical scientists. Because we're not focused on manufacturing medicines we're able to commit twice the resources to research as a typical company of our size."

"But isn't the real money in selling the drugs you have developed?"

The doctor crossed his arms. "Deputy Davis, do ya do what ya do purely for the money?" He didn't wait for an answer. "I would expect an officer such as yourself would understand there are more important things in life than money. We desire to help people." He smiled and waved his left index finger at Chris. "Now don't get me wrong—we do make money. Instead of investing in the manufacturing process, we sell the results of our research to other bio-med companies." He brushed at the air with his hand. "We let them deal with the issues of manufacturing while we move on to develop additional cures."

"But if you don't produce the medicines—why do you have patients such as Leon?"

A momentary grimace preceded the doctor's grin. "Ah, a very intuitive question. Perhaps a brief description of the process for developing a cures is in order. Ya see the first step is to study and identify the human genes involved in genetic diseases. Next, millions of new chemical compounds are tested to determine which ones might have a positive impact on a specific disease." The doctor put his index finger to his mouth and then continued. "If ya would like—I could take ya on a quick tour of our facility. Then ya could see some of these processes in action."

"That'd be great." Any information he could glean might help.

"So anyway, some of the testin' is done using computer models, others are done using combinatorial chemistry, or high throughput screening. That's where the computer and robotics experts come in. Once, or more appropriately *if*, a promising compound is discovered the screening phase begins. The developed compounds are first tested on bacteria cultures and then on lab animals. Only once a drug has been shown to be safe and beneficial does it enter the trial phase. Which brings us to the need for patients. Qualifying drugs are tested on a small number of human patients."

"Ya see this is the point to which we take the process. Once a drug has passed clinical trials, it moves on to FDA approval and then manufacturing. As I said before—we avoid getting involved in the last two phases."

"Leon was one of these clinical trial patients?"

"Yes—"

"Would this clinical testing have caused the erratic behavior we observed?"

The doctor shifted his weight in his chair. "Could ya describe what ya mean by erratic behavior?"

"Well, first he chased a woman into her house. Once she shut the door to keep him out, he knocked on the door for nearly twenty minutes before backing up and crashing through the door."

Tiny beads of perspiration formed on the doctor's forehead. "Interesting."

"After we arrested him, he was silent, emotionless—basically absent." He paused watching the doctor's body language. "The morning of the shooting, he had some sort of seizure, or at least he pretended to, then he jumped a fellow deputy, stole his gun, and shot at me. *That*—is what I mean by erratic."

The doctor's eyes shifted to the upper-left corner of their sockets, as if recalling past interactions with the *patient*. "Some of the treatments do have depressive or even psychological side effects. This typically takes the form of depression, or mild schizophrenia. I've certainly not observed the type of behavior ya've described as a result of our trials. We wouldn't tolerate such belligerent behavior, you have my word on that."

The wrinkles on the man's forehead deepened. Chris sat quietly, content to let the man offer up information.

The doctor stared down at his clasped hands. "Keep in mind, though the people who participate in the trials are thoroughly screened, they're still normal people. He may've had psychotic tendencies prior to the trials. It doesn't mean the trials caused it."

"I suppose that makes sense." It was time to broaden the scope of the questioning. "Perhaps you can tell me why Leon's place of residence is owned by CeSiR?"

"Well—" The doctor stared at some invisible spot on the ceiling to his right. "It is not uncommon for patients to be compensated for their time—and quite frankly their risk.

Participating in drug trials can be dangerous. Due to the prolonged nature of the trials, we here at CeSiR provide room and board for most of our patients."

"Wouldn't it make more sense to build an apartment complex of some kind, rather than purchasing houses throughout town?"

"Economically perhaps. But ya need to understand—we want to provide as normal an environment as possible for our patients. This prevents skewing the data."

Chris nodded. "Can you tell me how many residences CeSiR Tech owns?"

"I suppose. I believe there is something like forty houses. Most here in Arrow Springs, some elsewhere."

"What about Mayor Richard's house? Is he a patient?"

The doctor bit the inner part of his bottom lip before answering. "Please forgive me Deputy Davis, but as I'm sure ya can understand—I am not at liberty to discuss our patient list. Many of the diseases we explore are the types people would prefer to keep quiet. Things such as breast cancer, neurological disorders, and even AIDS are certainly covered under doctor-patient privilege."

As expected, but he had to try. "Fair enough. Would there be anything in Leon's treatment to explain a demonstration of super-human strength?"

The doctor truly looked puzzled. "How so?"

"Leon snapped a pair of handcuffs. He also managed to break some bones, and severely cut up his wrists. He didn't strike me as the type to break handcuffs."

"Wow! No, there certainly wouldn't be any such side effect from the treatment he was receiving here." The doctor rose from his chair and motioned to the door. "How 'bout that tour?"

~~~~~~~~~~

Chris followed Dr. M'Gregor through the lobby to the elevator. Like the security guard had done, Dr. M'Gregor performed a sequence of steps to activate the elevator door.

"Is that connected to the NFRS database?"

"Yes, it is." After completing the retinal scan the doctor stood and faced Chris. "Ya familiar with the NFRS?"

"On occasion I've needed to run prints through the system. It's so restricted we can't get access at the station. We have to work with the FBI to get something run. How come you've got access?"

The elevator door opened. "Welcome to CeSiR Tech," said the computerized voice.

"Much of our research is government funded. We need the system to verify a patient is who they say they are." The doctor held out his hand for Chris to enter. "And as ya can see, it helps ensure the investment of the American people in our research is protected."

Chris stepped into the elevator. Two additional graphics resided on the touchscreen. Apparently, the choice of floors varied with the person scanned for entrance. The place had security on its security.

The doctor had access to three above ground floors and the parking garage. The doctor touched the graphic for the floor below them and the doors slid shut.

A couple seconds later, the door opened to an impressive sight—nearly devoid of color. He saw white lab coats, white equipment, white walls, even white floors and ceilings. "Looks very—clean,"

"Indeed," said the doctor. "The room in which ya stand is the only section on this floor that is not a class-seven clean room. While some of the sections do not require such a tight environmental control, it's simpler to control the whole floor." The doctor pointed to some white bins next to the door. "If ya'd like to go farther into this level, we'll need to gown up. Otherwise, we can stay here and look through the windows."

While he doubted anything on this level would shed light on Leon's behavior, he couldn't pass up the opportunity. "I'd prefer a closer look if it's not too much bother."

"Certainly." The doctor pulled a full body jumpsuit from the drawer. "I think this should fit ya. Tyvek isn't very stretchy." Once they had donned the jumpsuits, the doctor handed him a floppy white hat and two mint-blue booties.

They stepped into an airlock, where he could feel a breeze blowing from his right to left. When the door closed behind them, he heard the latch on the door in front of him release.

The doctor led them into the lab.

Several workers nodded. Though they wore the exact same outfits as him, somehow theirs looked much more normal than his felt. The outfit reminded him of a pair of toddler pajamas, all it needed was bunny eared slippers.

He turned to the doctor. "This is unlike anything I've ever seen."

"I'm afraid I've grown quite accustomed to it by now. Though, I can vaguely remember my first time entering a facility like this." The doctor held out his hand and motioned Chris forward. "So, let me try to give ya a brief overview." He went on to describe in layman's terms the various processes they were observing.

Row after row of lab benches, electron microscopes, racks of test tubes and culture dishes, centrifuges, and computer terminals. The sight was incredible. "Are those all robots?" he asked pointing to one side of the building.

"Yes—they are. They're used for filling tube trays with various chemicals and biological materials. One robot is capable of filling a tray of one hundred tubes in the time a person could fill five." The doctor was clearly more comfortable giving the tour than answering questions. "As ya can imagine, when it's necessary to try many thousands of combinations before finding something to warrant further testing, such technology is crucial."

White steam hovered around several containers. "Is that like dry ice or something?"

"Close. Those are cryo-chambers. Rather than dry ice we use liquid nitrogen—and quite a bit of it I might add. We use roughly ten-thousand gallons each month."

"Wow—that must be expensive."

"Not as bad as ya might think. At fifty cents a gallon, it's only about a tenth of what ya paid for your gas to drive over here today. Much of the liquid nitrogen is used to preserve biomaterials such as our stem cell lines."

"You do a lot of stem cell research?"

"Most of our research is performed using embryonic stem cells. In 2001, George W. Bush limited federal fundin' for embryonic stem cell research to the twenty-one lines registered with the NIH at that time." The doctor shook his head. "Thankfully, once he left office, President Obama overturned the limited funding—now we have over one hundred unique stem cell lines at our disposal. By freezin' them with the liquid nitrogen, we are able to use 'em indefinitely."

After a half-hour tour of the lab facility, they stepped back on the elevator and headed to the first floor.

The doors opened. "Welcome to our patient interface level," said Dr. M'Gregor.

In contrast to the bright sterile environment of the laboratory, this level possessed a warm friendly charm. It resembled a small town family practice—only bigger.

A spacious reception area, complete with smiling receptionist, greeted them as they exited the elevator. "Good morning Dr. M'Gregor."

"Top o' the mornin' to ya, Mary. Just givin' a quick tour of the facility."

She waved her hand to the hallway behind her and smiled. "Welcome."

Chris followed the doctor to the wide hallway, which lead to a half dozen general examination rooms. Each room looked modestly decorated. Clearly a relaxing environment created for the ease of the patients.

The doctor showed him a handful of specialized rooms, including an oral examination room, and an ophthalmology room.

They stepped into a room that looked like a plush hotel room with wood floors. On the night stand next to the bed sat a small monitor and printer. "Is this a delivery room?"

"Very good. We prefer birthin' suite—but yes." The doctor opened one of the cabinets to reveal several state-of-the-art medical systems. "Ya see many of the diseases we're tryin' to cure affect people right from birth. This facility gives us the ability to administer immediate treatment in cases that would otherwise result in infant death." The doctor shut the cabinet. "We also collect umbilical-cord-blood stem cells for research use—because of their low rejection rates."

He followed the doctor back into the hallway. The hallway turned and opened to a neonatal unit, complete with a nursery. At the end of the neonatal wing, the doctor opened a door which led to a small hallway heading back toward the reception area. Several rooms filled with state-of-the-art equipment flanked the hallway. The doctor proudly showed him a full body Magnetic Resonance Imager, a fully equipped x-ray room, CT Scan, three-dimensional ultrasound capabilities, and an extensive hematology lab.

"After patients begin treatment, we perform a sophisticated battery of tests. We want to know everything that's goin' on in their bodies. If we wait for visible signs, it's usually too late." The doctor opened a door at the end of the hallway and led him back into the reception area.

Once more he followed the doctor into the elevator. "So ya see officer Davis, this is an incredible company, with wonderful people who are tryin' to make a difference in this messed up world we're livin' in. The discoveries we make here are extremely secretive for obvious reasons." He touched his finger to the graphic of the parking garage. "Legitimate companies pay good money to be able to manufacture the drugs we develop. But there are many that are not so legitimate, they would kill to get their hands on what we have."

The elevator door opened and the doctor placed a hand on Chris' shoulder. "I truly am sorry I couldn't be of more assistance with your investigation. I do not see a connection to our company. Just a distressed, perhaps mentally unstable, individual who committed a heinous crime."

~~~~~~~~~~

Dr. M'Gregor watched the emerald-green Jeep pull from the parking garage. The oppressive darkness in the garage reflected the sorrow within his heart. How he longed to drive out that door—never to return. The deceit, the secrecy, the daily lies he told himself, it all hung heavy on his shoulders.

He turned to the security terminal and punched in his code. Moments later, the elevator opened and he entered.

"Welcome Dr. M'Gregor," said the computerized voice.

He stepped into the elevator and stared at the touch panel. All six floors were represented by graphics on the panel. He wanted to select the floor below the garage, to see Ima, to escape, if only for the afternoon. But Maiya would be stopping by any moment for a briefing on the visit.

He touched the graphic of the office complex, and watched as the doors enclosed him.

He exited the elevator, walked to his office, and headed for his desk.

"Soooo, did you enjoy your little discussion?" asked Maiya. Her voice turned his blood to ice. The chair behind his desk turned to face him. Her red eyes pierced into his. "Did you enjoy your discussion with our friendly neighborhood officers?"

He crossed his arms in front of him. "As I'm sure ya are aware, he had some questions about Leon. He wanted to know if any of Leon's treatments could have accounted for his behavior last weekend."

She rested her elbows on his desk and her chin on her fists. "And what did you tell them?"

"I told him none of the treatments we've administered could have caused Leon's psychotic behavior—of course." He'd started CeSiR. Did she honestly think he couldn't handle a few questions from a local police officer?

"Perhaps it would have been better for them to think it was a side effect. That would be more acceptable than the truth. You best hope they never discover the real story."

The phone on Dr. M'Gregor's desk chirped.

Maiya glared at the phone. "Yes?"

"Um yes, sorry to interrupt." The sweet voice of Susan, the receptionist, rang out from the tiny speaker. "Senator Philips is on the line for you, madam."

"Very well." Maiya picked up the handset. She placed her hand over the mouthpiece. "Do you mind? I really need to take this call." She motioned with her hand for the doctor to leave.

He shook his head and turned for the door. Though he didn't like being shooed from his own office, he was happy to be away from her.

"Ah Senator Philips so nice of you to call." Maiya's voice dripped with sweetness. "What can I do for you?"

"Yes. Yes, that's right. Word sure travels fast. Doesn't it?" Her voice waivered. "Yes two officers came here today to ask questions about Leon's trip off the deep end—"

Dr. M'Gregor stopped in the doorway to the office and turned. "Two? There weren't two officers, just Chris Davis."

"What?" She glared from the phone. "I'm sorry Senator, but I'll need to call you back." She slammed the phone down. "What do you mean there was only one?" She stood from the chair. "Guard!"

~~~~~~~~~~

Mael stood in the doctor's office. What was the doctor babbling about? Cadfael clearly reported two officers. He snorted at Maiya. "Get to the bottom of this."

The guard who escorted the officers from the parking garage appeared in the doorway along with his controller. "Yeah?"

"How many officers did you bring to meet with Dr. M'Gregor?" asked Maiya.

"Two." The demon tilted his head and looked at Mael. "The guards at the gate reported two in the Jeep as well."

"I don't understand," said Dr. M'Gregor. "I'm tellin' ya there was only one officer. The entire time—I never saw anyone else." He walked to the phone, and paged the receptionist.

"Yes sir?" answered the receptionist.

"Could ya join us for a moment?"

Seconds later, the receptionist joined them in the office. "Yes, sir?"

"Could ya please tell us how many officers exited the elevator this mornin'?"

"Just the one sir, the one you took on the tour."

"Thank ya kindly." The doctor dismissed her. "See, as I told ya just the one."

"I don't understand," mumbled the guard.

No! No, no, no. Mael slammed his fist against the desk. "Eitan!!!" A cloud of green smoke rolled from his nostrils. Only the captain would dare such a bold action to ensure the protection of his precious believer.

"Eitan?" asked the guard's controller.

The guard echoed the question.

Dr. M'Gregor and Maiya both shot him a questioning look.

"It is Eitan!" roared Mael. "Get him! He must not leave CeSiR Tech in one piece."

~~~~~~~~~~

Eran and Zeke stood sentry at the old bridge embankment south of the bend in the river. Through branches budding with new growth, Eran watched Chris and Eitan emerge from the white fortress in Chris' Wrangler. The black gates swept grudgingly open to release their prey.

Behind the vehicle, an explosion of black burst from the facility. Like the emptying of a beehive, the masses of grotesque demons swarmed after the Jeep.

Eran knew instantly—his orders came from God Himself. "Zeke," He looked at his fellow warrior. "Chris is a good man. Protect him my brother."

"Eran what are you doing?" Zeke grabbed Eran's arm. "Eitan told us to stay put. He said not to interfere."

"I have new orders." The glory of God swirled within his wings. He brandished his saber. Brilliant flames leapt from the blade. "No greater love has a man, or an angel, than he lay down himself for his friend."

Zeke released his arm. "Be strong and courageous. For the Lord goes with you."

"'Til we meet again my friend." Eran turned and soared into the sky.

Like a Peregrine Falcon in a stoop, he shot straight for the guards at the gate. With a single sweeping motion, he cut through both demons, as they headed for the button to close the gate.

The gate continued its progress.

Eran banked to his right and headed for the Jeep. He shot through the vehicle in an effort to divert the attention from Eitan. If he could make it look like Eitan had come from the vehicle to protect Chris, his captain might escape.

"Godspeed alert one," said Eitan, as Eran streaked through the cab.

He was nowhere near the size on Eitan, but in the heat of the battle it might work.

He slashed and sliced, as he plunged into the column of vermin pursuing the Jeep. Tens, even hundreds, of demons were sent to the Abyss in the fury of his progress. The column turned in on itself, as the demons pursued their prey.

The entire demonic force began to pursue him back to the facility. His speed, though supersonic when he hit the first wave of demons, slowed to a stop.

He fought with ferocity. Slashing, stabbing, and fending off attackers with his shield. He was dangerously outnumbered. He knew he would not be leaving the facility. It was a fight he could not win.

Teeth and claws, talons and scabbards, sabers and scimitars, all tore at his flesh.

Sulfurous smoke flooded his nose and mouth.

Blasphemous cursing of his Creator, and arrogant taunts brought tears to his eyes.

His once illuminated wings and the fire of his saber flickered and dimmed.

Nothing.

~~~~~~~~~~

A stomach-turning roar rose from the facility. Zeke stood in disbelief on the stone embankment. Tears splashed against his cheeks, like the river against its banks.

The Jeep turned onto the road toward town.

He spread his wings and floated down to the vehicle.

"He was a valiant warrior," said Eitan, in a low emotion-filled voice.

"Yes, he was."

~~~~~~~~~~

CHAPTER EIGHTEEN
Tuesday, April 28, 2020

Daryl sat in his office tapping his pencil on a stack of paperwork. He'd spent seven days on paper duty since the shooting. The mayor felt it would be best to keep him off the streets until Internal Affairs had the opportunity to review the incident.

He stared at his silver and black coffee mug. He hadn't downed as much coffee since his days at the academy. It seemed like all he'd done for the last week was drink coffee, answer the phone, drink coffee, talk to Chris about the investigation, and drink more coffee. His hand jittered as he put the pencil to yet another report that needed to be reviewed.

Tap, tap, tap.

He jumped and looked up to see who had knocked at his door. "Good morning, Mayor. What can I do for you?"

Trenton Richards walked to one of the chairs facing the desk and sat down. As usual, the outer corners of both the mayor's lips and eyes dipped downward. He leaned forward and looked Daryl straight in the eyes. "Daryl, I am afraid I have some bad news." His pupils constricted till they almost disappeared. "I just heard from Cooper County. You are aware they handle our IA investigations?" Though the tone of his voice dripped of compassion, Trenton seemed to thrive on the play of power.

"Yes?" He didn't like where this was going.

"Because your actions resulted in the death of a civilian, they have decided to conduct a full investigation. Until the conclusion of the investigation, you are officially suspended."

"What? I didn't shoot that woman!" He slapped his palms to the desk. "You can ask Chris. He was there. He saw the whole thing!"

"I know, I know." Trenton nodded and the right corner of his lip crept upward. "But your gun was used to shoot her. You allowed a known hostile, being held in our jail, to take your gun. You had to know there would be an investigation."

"He was on the floor having a seizure!" He stood from his chair and leaned forward on the desk. "He was handcuffed! What was I supposed to do leave him there to die?"

"Sit down Daryl. Nobody is saying you did anything wrong. It is just a standard investigation. I am sure they will exonerate you from any wrongdoing." Trenton wagged his head back and forth. "You know if there was anything I could do, I would." Even his voice began to betray his true emotions.

"Oh, I'm sure!" He probably initiated the investigation in the first place.

"Daryl there is no reason to get belligerent. It would only strengthen the case against you." Trenton stood and held out his right hand. "I am going to need your badge and gun, at least until the investigation is completed."

Belligerent! Daryl's mind screamed. *I'll show you belligerent. You want my gun? Maybe you'd like a bullet or two also! Then IA would really have something to investigate.* He didn't say a word. A new thought settled into his mind. *'Love your enemies, and pray for those who persecute you.'*

He pulled the gun from his side, still securely fastened in its holster, and laid it calmly on his desk. Then he pulled his badge from his uniform and slapped it down heavily on the desk.

Trenton turned to leave the office. "Oh yes, please give Chris the keys to your cruiser. We would not want to pay him for more mileage on his Wrangler than necessary. He can use yours until his is repaired." He glanced over his shoulder. "You will not be needing it."

Daryl picked up the yellow pencil from the stack of papers and snapped it in half between his thumb and fingers. He didn't need it anymore.

The mayor made his way next door to Chris' office. "Please put these in a safe place." Daryl assumed the thud he heard was his gun and badge landing on Chris' desk.

Once he heard the front door close, he ventured over to see Chris.

Chris sat staring at the items on his desk. "What's goin' on?"

"I've been suspended—pending the outcome of an IA investigation."

"What?" Chris jumped to his feet and drove balled fists into the desk. "That's ridiculous."

"Is it?" Daryl leaned against the doorpost. "You warned me. You told me not to go into that cell." He hung his head. "If I'd listened to you, she'd still be alive."

"And for all you knew, if you didn't go in there, the man was going to die." Chris walked around the desk and sat on the edge. "Daryl, the shooting was not your fault. I think the mayor is—I don't know—either he's involved in something here, or he's at least trying to hide somethin'."

Chris put his palms down behind him and looked up at the ceiling. "Everything seemed above-board at CeSiR Tech, but the mayor's involvement is still puzzling. Maybe he's a patient, maybe not." He looked back at Daryl. "Perhaps it's nothing. I just don't know. Anyway, don't worry. This will blow over. You'll see."

"I hope you're right. I sincerely hope you are right."

Daryl returned to his office to begin putting a few personal items in a box. "Hey, Chris?"

"Yeah?"

"Can you give me a ride home? The mayor told me to give you the keys to my cruiser. He said that way he wouldn't have to pay you for mileage on the Wrangler."

Chris appeared in Daryl's doorway. "He did not!"

He smiled and nodded. "Sure did. Those were his exact words."

"Oh brother. Yeah, no prob. Let me know when you're ready to leave. Suddenly I feel like I need to get some air." Chris flashed a Cheshire grin. "We'll take my Jeep."

~~~~~~~~~~

CHAPTER NINETEEN

Eran awoke.
Light—incredible light filled his eyes. Even before his eyes could adjust, he knew where he was—the throne room of God.

"Welcome Eran, my alert and watchful servant. You have done well."

He fell to the ground—not from the exhaustion and pain that consumed his being, but out of pure reverence for the Almighty Creator seated on the throne before him.

"Arise, mighty warrior. You have been a faithful servant ever since I created you." The voice of God was immense with love.

"But my Lord, I have failed." He remained prostrate on the ground. "I was unable to protect Chris. There was still so much more to do."

"You have failed no one." This time the voice was that of the Son, the Lamb of God, seated on a second throne to the right of the Father. "You left Chris in the capable hands of Zeke. More importantly, Chris is in my hands. He will be safe until his time comes."

Eran's chin was pulled upward toward the throne.

"You acted selflessly to protect your captain. For that—you shall be honored."

With the endorsement, a roar, like that of a mighty waterfall, erupted from hundreds of thousands of angelic hosts to the right and to the left of the throne.

He turned in wonder at the sound. He'd been before the throne on many occasions, the last time centuries ago, but never had a cheer arisen for him.

No, for God, as a result of him.

This must be how the saints feel when God rewards them with His phrase of affirmation, "Well done my good and faithful servant." At such times, a harmony of praise ascends to God because of His faithfulness, as demonstrated through the saint. Eran was experiencing such an honor.

He gazed in awe at his incredible surroundings, convinced it was more beautiful than he ever remembered. Fluffy clouds encompassed the throne and everything around it. They reflected the glorious light of God Himself. A rainbow emanated like a sphere from the throne in every direction. He could sense the brilliant translucent glow returning to his pearlescent form.

The Father's voice rang clear over the roar of the angels. "In one point you are correct." Silence spread at the voice. "There is still much work that you will do for me. But you need rest. It is time for you to bask in my glory. Be strengthened. Be healed. Be renewed. For when the time comes, you will be ready."

He knew his time at the very foot of the throne had ended. He turned and took his place among the vast heavenly host praising and worshiping the Lord of Heaven and of Earth. The further he walked from the throne, the larger and loftier it appeared. He settled into a comfortable spot next to a sea of crystal.

"Holy, holy, holy," Eran joined an angelic chorus, "is the Lord God Almighty, who was, and is, and is to come."

~~~~~~~~~~

CHAPTER TWENTY

Tuesday, May 5, 2020

Mael ran his black claws down the blade of his electric blue sword. "It has been a week since Eitan and his puppet dared enter my stronghold." He beamed, as he eyed Mors and the nine lesser princes, standing around the circle of bones. "I believe the good doctor proved quite convincing." He spun the sword within his grip, and then flicked it into its sheath. "Officer Davis has invested little effort into the case since the visit. Perhaps their captain's death has driven some sense into the host."

Mors snorted and coughed. "You cannot possibly think your minions defeated the mighty Eitan?"

Though Mors was probably right, his insolent attitude grew old. Still the facts remained, though the numbers were great, Eitan would not have fallen so easily.

Who the warrior really had been? Mael didn't know.

Still, he basked in the honor and respect of the other nine, as a result of the feat. "Were you there?" he asked Mors.

"No." Mors eyes narrowed into a grin. "But from what I hear, neither were you."

Mael's wings scraped bones across the floor as they unfurled across the room. "Enough of this nonsense! We have business to conduct. While Officer Davis has been quiet, Miss McIntyre is another story." He began to pace around the circle. "Since being relieved from her duties at the library, she has persisted in investigating this company using the library's search engine. The computer is no longer on during off hours, so she dials in during the day for brief periods. She thinks no one is watching. That nobody has noticed."

He stopped next to the smallest of the princes. "We are watching." He growled into the demons ear. "We have noticed." He puffed a sulfurous cloud in the demons face. "Something needs to be done."

"Allow me," said Mors. A bone-faced smile pulled at his cheeks. "This is my specialty."

~~~~~~~~~~

Dr. Wilhelm M'Gregor sat at his desk watching clear folders with snippets of his research float across his computer screen.

The backup was nearly complete.

Ever since the visit by Officer Davis, Maiya acted stranger than ever. On Thursday, he'd walked to her office door to confront her. As he reached his hand to the door to knock, he heard her pleading over the phone with someone named Casimir. She begged him for guidance.

"Yes, I know you promised to take care of everything," she had said.

He'd never met anyone named Casimir and he didn't like the implication in her voice when she said *everything*.

Her last statement brought a chill to his aching joints.

"Yes, my lord," she concluded.

He looked back to the screen. Only two and a half more minutes and his backup would be complete.

The door to his office opened.

He froze.

If Maiya caught him copying the files—

"Uncle M!"

Relief flooded his tense muscles as eleven-year-old Ima ran in to greet him.

He threw his head back in his chair and breathed a relieved sigh. "Ima, what brings ya up here?"

One of the attendants stepped in behind the girl. "I'm sorry doctor. She asked to talk with you." The young woman lowered her head and stared at the front of the doctor's desk. "You instructed that she be brought to you whenever she requested it. I can take her back if this is a bad time."

"Nonsense! I've always got time for my Ima." The speakers on his desk beeped. He reached down and removed the thumb drive from the computer. "Thank ya much. I can bring her back down when we're done."

The woman nodded and turned.

"What can I do for ya Ima?" he asked.

The girl giggled and jumped into the plush leather chair. She looked at him with a wide grin.

Round puffy cheeks and red eyes told him the smile was a recent addition to her face. He walked to the other chair.

"Uncle M—why am I different?" She blurted the question that had obviously been building for awhile.

"What do ya mean different, Ima?" He felt the burn beneath his cheekbones as he pushed back encroaching tears. So much he wanted to tell her—so much he couldn't.

"The other kids pick on me. They call me emotional." Her eyes began to glisten. "It seems like things bother me that don't bother everyone else. I don't like it here. It's boring." She let out an exaggerated "humph" and crossed her arms. "I want to explore the rest of the world. I want to meet more *normal* people."

He tilted his head to the right. "Normal people?"

"People like you. People born outside this building." She paused and sucked back one corner of her lip. "Why am I here? Why are any of us—*mims* that is—here?"

The term MIM still unsettled him.

His partner Dr. Jurek Mirinov, Maiya's father, coined the phrase in 1996. "Manufactured Image of Man," he'd explained. "The term clone has too much baggage. That's what you call a sheep or a monkey. Not a person."

Dr. M'Gregor stared into the eyes of young Ima. 1988, the year he came to America to pursue his dream seemed like a distant memory, barely visible through years of successes and secrets. At the time, he'd been thirty-two and dreamed of fame, as the world's premier genetic biologist. He came at Jurek's request and together they started the Center for Scientific Reproduction Technologies.

Together they accomplished the unthinkable. In 1990, nearly six years prior to the public revelation of Dolly, the clone sheep, and even five years before the announcement that an embryonic stem cell had been isolated, they successfully created what they believed to be the first human clone.

"Uncle M—"

His mind returned to the Caribbean blue eyes staring intently into his own. Perhaps it was time discuss what made her so special—perhaps.

"Ima, would ya like to hear about your Mum and Grandmum?"

She nodded enthusiastically.

"Perhaps ya'd like a soda? This is a rather lengthy story."

"Can I?" She began to bounce in the chair.

"But of course." If nothing else, it would irritate Maiya. "I'll be right back."

~~~~~~~~~~

Mael sat on the desk in the doctor's office watching the mim called Ima. Of all the mims they had created, she annoyed him most. She was a freak, a failure. Why the doctor had taken such a liking to her was beyond his understanding.

Half a dozen minions entered the room, shaking. "You called for us, my liege?"

"I did." They were the latest addition to the horde of demons assigned to the project. "It is time for you to understand why you are here." He motioned for them to sit around Ima. "Have a seat. I think this conversation will prove useful in your assignments."

~~~~~~~~~~

Dr. M'Gregor returned with the sodas. He opened a can and handed it to Ima. Then he settled back into his chair, opened the second can, and set it on a small table.

"Do ya know what a surrogate mother is?"

Ima nodded.

"Well, back in 1994 we hand-selected three surrogates to give birth to three very special babies."

Ima didn't need to hear the unpleasant details of their prior failures. His thoughts drifted to the first women they hired, in 1989. They didn't dare tell the women the embryos were artificially created. Couldn't risk them going to the authorities. Perhaps they shouldn't have been doing what they were doing. Some would have said they were playing God. But, how could there be something wrong with creating life?

But there was something wrong. The babies grew into toddlers, learned to walk, but exhibited no emotion, no personality, and never learned to speak. Their early process of somatic cell nuclear transfer had another flaw as well. It didn't possess the randomness of natural egg and sperm generation. Each attempt to create a human clone resulted in an identical twin of sorts. There was some genetic material picked up from the nucleated egg, but the differences were minor.

Though he never seemed overly concerned about the lack of personality, Dr. Mirinov demanded that the mims be at least as different as normal brothers and sisters.

In late summer of 1994, he discovered a process of genetic reprogramming, which allowed them to alter the physical traits of each mim. To his surprise, the newly created, genetically programmed, mims began to show signs of personality and speech as they matured.

The personalities tended toward the negative—angry, selfish, lustful, sarcastic, mean, and seductive. Definitely seductive. He was never able to explain how the genetic programming fixed the personality flaw.

He would begin his explanation to Ima with this group of mims.

~~~~~~~~~~

Mael watched as the doctor paused for a brief trip down memory lane. "You have been brought here to be controllers." The new recruits looked at him with wide eyed excitement. "You see, once the brilliant doctor discovered a way to make the mims different in appearance, we began to take possession of them. We gave them the critical appearance of intellect and emotions—allowing them to pass as a typical human being."

"You mean they do not have souls?" asked a lanky wolf-like demon.

"That is exactly what I mean." Mael walked to Ima and put his gnarled black hand under her chin. "At first—it made me mad. Why would these creations not be given souls?" He ran a claw across her cheek to her ear. "Babies are born with souls every day, from all kinds of scientifically assisted methods—surrogate mothers, sperm and egg donors, and even test-tube babies. But no!" He pulled his hand from her face and pointed a defiant finger to the ceiling. "*He* decided these would be different. *He* chose not to give them souls."

The wolf-like demon snarled revealing green razor teeth. "You said this made you mad—at first." He dropped his shoulders and cocked his head. "Not now?"

Mael laughed. "Are you kidding? He gave us the perfect opportunity, a shell of a body with no individual-will. It is like jumping into a Ferrari and taking off down the road. No alarm system, no speed limits."

The demon let out a brief howl. "Sounds very freeing."

"Now you are beginning to understand."

~~~~~~~~~~

Dr. M'Gregor drifted back to reality. He looked up to see tears seeping from Ima's eyes.

"I'm sorry Ima." He took a sip of his soda. "Now let's see. Where was I? Oh yes. One of those three women was your grandmum—so to speak. Ya see mims are very special. When an embryo forms through natural methods, all sorts of defects and diseases can result. We select the perfect genetic materials and implant them into an egg that's been stripped of its nucleus. This allows us to create perfect people." He smiled at Ima. "Like you."

Ima seemed to ponder this for a minute, and then looked back up. "If we're perfect, why do some of my friends constantly have seizures?"

She was so young and yet so perceptive.

"We're not sure. But don't ya worry 'bout it." He tapped his forehead. "We'll figure it out. One of the ways we helped to minimize the seizures was to begin using mims as surrogates, rather than flawed humans." He set his soda back on the table and leaned forward. "Ya see the first three mims were very important. They were the first scientifically created human beings. More importantly, one of those first three mims was your mum."

A wide smile crept onto Ima's face.

"Your mum would've been twenty-five this year. In 2009 your mum and four other mim females volunteered to be the surrogate mothers for future mims."

~~~~~~~~~~

Mael snorted a quick laugh. "The females were of age, we wanted to eliminate *His* creations from the picture. We began using *our* creations instead."

"Because you hoped they would have souls?" asked the wolf-like demon.

"Hardly. Until then we had to use a different surrogate each time, sixty-four in all, to keep anyone from getting suspicious about the research at CeSiR Tech. But it was inefficient. We controlled the mims. So, we did not need to provide housing, or special care, or worry about them talking to someone."

~~~~~~~~~~

Dr. M'Gregor never really liked the idea of using the mims as surrogates. But Jurek had insisted. In fact he first suggested using chimeras, animals as surrogates. The thought still made bile rise in his throat. He finally yielded, and they began using the mims.

"Uncle M, tell me about my mother?" asked Ima.

"Do ya remember her at all?"

"I don't think so."

She'd been six when her mother died. Still they didn't interact as mother and daughter. The mim children were raised communally.

"Your mum was a beautiful woman." It'd been years since he thought about Evelyn. "Unlike your wavy blond hair, hers was jet-black and straight. At times, it seemed so black it absorbed all the energy from a room like a cosmic black hole. Her eyes on the other hand radiated the same energy like electric blue supernovas. I do believe ya get your gorgeous baby blues from her. She was unlike any woman I have ever met."

"Was she different like me?"

"Do ya mean—was she a mim?"

"No. Did she have these weird emotions—the things I get picked on about? Did it hurt her to see others in pain?" She put her elbows on her knees and rested her chin on her hands. "I don't like seeing mims doing nothing but giving birth to other mims. They're not much older than me. They seem so lonely."

He couldn't argue. During the early years, he believed their research to be altruistic. They wanted to cure humanity's ills, perhaps even fix the flaws designed into humans. They compensated the women who gave birth to the mims quite well. Most of the money came from federal government funding, even though human cloning was illegal. CeSiR Tech had mastered the process of diverting funds intended for stem cell research to its under-the-table operations. During their pregnancies, the early surrogate mothers were treated like queens, with free room and board at corporately owned houses.

All that changed with the mim surrogates. They were treated like slaves. They never left the facility. Their rooms were relocated three levels below ground and furnished like prison cells. They were well fed to ensure the health of the babies, but little concern was shown for their well-being.

In time, the surrogate mims began to demonstrate the same loss of personality the early experiments exhibited. They refused to eat with utensils, and clothing seemed to annoy them the way a primped poodle despises being dressed up by an over-coddling owner.

Watching this happen to Evelyn tore at his heart. She was one of his creations. How could anyone not love and desire what was best for his own creation? He watched her slip away, unable to do anything about it. A few years later she died giving birth to her sixth mim.

He stood from his chair and walked over to Ima. "Sweetie, I have never met a mim like you. Your mother was very special to me, but no, she was not like you. She was fiery—a trait paling in comparison to your compassionate personality."

"But why am I the only one? It's just not fair!" A reflective sheen of tears coated her eyes.

"I think it's because we finally perfected the genetic transfer process. The process of nucleating the egg requires just the right conditions and I think we achieved that with you. Ya are the perfect mim."

"I don't feel perfect."

"In a strange way, that's precisely what makes ya different from the others."

~~~~~~~~~~

Mael eyed the young mim with disdain. "Next year we will make sure this one is added to our group of surrogates."

"Where is her controller?" asked one of the new recruits.

"That—" Mael nodded. "That is the question. There is something wrong with this one. She seems to have a will of her own. Any volunteers?"

The wolf-like demon licked his fangs. "I have always liked a challenge."

"Then you shall have your opportunity."

The demon approached the girl and sniffed her. Then, he let out a long howl.

~~~~~~~~~~

CHAPTER TWENTY-ONE

Thursday, May 7, 2020

The rich spicy aroma of premium-blend coffee filled the small ranch-style home of Daryl Williams. It had been nine days since Mayor Richards suspended him, and still no word.

Dong, dong, dong . . .

The clock he and Marilyn had received as a wedding gift announced the arrival of eleven o'clock. He stared for a moment watching the gold pendulum bounce back and forth between elegant cherry sidewalls.

The fact that he was up, showered, clean-shaven, and dressed for the day was a testament to his newfound faith. The first couple days he'd slept until eleven. Then he started getting up and reading his Bible—another wedding gift. He started by reading in the New Testament about the life and death of Jesus. Then he decided to begin reading through the entire Bible front to back.

The guilt and despair once a steady companion now resided only as a faint smoky memory. This residue of past actions and feelings served as a reminder of the incredible freeing power of a personal relationship with his new Lord.

He picked up the universal remote and clicked on the television. Game shows, reality reruns, or sports casters saying the same things over and over about the prior night's playoff games? After twenty minutes of searching, he decided to download an episode of the 1950's classic Dragnet. In the past week and a half he'd made good use of his online movie subscription. He sat back and dreamt of the days portrayed in the show. They seemed simpler yet more exciting than the early twenty-first century in which he found himself trapped.

At a quarter to twelve, he thought he heard a light rap on his front door. Most people rang the doorbell. Maybe it was the TV.

There it was again.

He muted the drama unfolding before him and listened. Sure enough—someone was knocking.

He walked to the door and impatiently opened it. The sight before him did not compute.

"Hi. I thought you might be bored." Marilyn stood there holding a large paper bag. "If I know you, this suspension is tearing you up—you probably haven't eaten a proper meal in a week."

It may as well have been a heavenly angel standing there. He stood in the doorway speechless. Had he drifted off? Was he still sitting in front of Joe Friday?

"Um, this bag's getting kind of heavy. Can I come in?"

Marilyn's smile kindled the long extinguished embers of his heart.

She had asked him something. "Oh, I'm sorry. Of course, come in." He stepped back onto the tile. "I, well it's—it's good to see you again. And I've gotta admit, a bit of a surprise."

Marilyn walked to the kitchen and began pulling produce from the bag and placing it on the counter—a dozen Roma tomatoes, four cloves of garlic, olive oil, a couple large Vidalia onions, basil, and parsley.

He watched her in disbelief.

She pulled out a box of spaghetti and an eighteen-inch long garlic bread. Finally, she pulled out a bottle of Cabernet. She knew the struggles of his past. No doubt the wine contained no alcohol. Marilyn jerked up her head. "Oh dear, I didn't even ask if you had plans."

"No! Not at all." There wasn't a plan in the world that could drag him away. "It's just, what's all this?"

"It's lunch, or dinner if you prefer. I know you love to make homemade spaghetti sauce, and if I know you, you probably haven't been eating well since the suspension." She pulled a saucepan from beneath the oven. "I thought maybe I could offer some encouragement."

"Did Chris put you up to this?"

"No, it's just, well, since I saw you a couple weeks ago in church I can't get you off my mind." Tiny bubbles began streaming from the bottom of the saucepan. "Then I heard you were suspended from the force. I know how much your job means to you. It doesn't seem right." One by one, she cut a slight "x" in the bottom of each tomato and put them briefly in the boiling water. "Do you know how long you'll be suspended?" She dunked the tomatoes in cold water and then peeled off the skin.

"I really don't." He watched the love of his life plop skinless tomatoes on a cutting board. "Chris thinks it's got something to do with the Mayor's involvement at CeSiR Tech. He says Trenton's trying to divert attention away from the assailant and the company." He stepped around Marilyn and picked up the tomatoes, cut them in half, and dug out the seeds with a spoon.

Marilyn chuckled.

He held up his hands. "I know, I know, I'm obsessed with the seeds." She would always pick on him for wanting the seeds removed for their sauces. He just didn't like the texture.

"No—it's fine. I've grown to prefer it without 'em too." She set the last tomato in front of him. "So—has Chris made any progress on the case?" She took the saucepan off the stove and dumped out the water.

"I don't know. It's been over a week since he went to CeSiR Tech." He walked to the sink and washed the tomato seeds into the disposal. "He says he doesn't know if there's really anymore to learn. It seems like the guy just flipped out." He pulled the chef's knife from the wood block next to the sink and waved it in the air. "I think Sarah's more bent on finding out what's going on than Chris, at least for now."

"They looked kind of cozy, Sunday. Do you think it's getting serious?" She poured a quarter cup of olive oil in the saucepan.

He chopped the garlic and onions and scraped them into the olive oil along with some basil and salt. "Seems like it. They seem to make a perfect couple."

Marilyn swept a black tuft of hair behind her ear. Mid-thirties and still as beautiful as ever.

He set the knife down and turned to face her. "It was nice to see you in church again this Sunday. I was afraid I'd scared you off."

As she sautéed the onions and garlic, Marilyn confessed that it had been his presence that kept her from coming back the following week. "I realized, as I sat in my old church that week, how much my soul longed for biblical nourishment. I don't know if you've attended any churches other than River of Life, but it's not your average church."

He'd never considered what other churches might be like.

"That first week there, I felt like my heart would explode with the reality of who I was in Christ." She stared for a moment at the pan. "I knew I was forgiven, now I realize my relationship with Christ is about so much more. I was adopted into the family. God loves me as one of his children."

He chopped the tomatoes and added them to the onions and garlic. Then, he added some parsley, and a tablespoon of sugar. He didn't dare look up at her for fear his emotions would overtake him. The love-of-his-life stood once again in his kitchen. It would've been more than he could hope for just to have her bring him a meal. But, she committed to cooking with him—a meal taking a couple hours to prepare.

As the aroma of the sauce simmering filled the house, they sat at the table in the breakfast nook and talked. They talked about Chris and Sarah. They talked about church. They talked about Leon and CeSiR Tech. Finally, they talked about them—their past, and the divorce.

"Daryl can I ask you a question?" Her face grew serious.

"Of course."

She looked down at her hands, folded on the table. "Why?"

How many times had he asked that question? Yet he'd never found a satisfactory answer. "I wish I could tell you. I really just don't know."

She bit her lip, closed her eyes, and nodded.

They sat in silence for what seemed like ten minutes.

Finally, she looked up at him with glistening eyes. "Was it because I couldn't give you a child?" A tear crept down her right cheek, then another, and another.

The question cut through his heart. "Oh Marilyn. No. Please no." He reached across the table and took her hands. "Don't ever think it was because of you—in any way." Tears welled within his own eyes. "It was my own stupidity, my lust—my sin. Please don't blame yourself."

They cried together for half an hour. Not speaking, just crying. It was the best conversation he'd had in three years.

"Marilyn, I love you. I always have." He waited for her hand to pull away. It didn't. "I'm so sorry."

Her lips began to quiver. "I know." She snorted a laugh.

Her humor refreshed his soul like a cool breeze in the heat of summer. "Wow, I guess I deserved that."

"You know what I meant."

They laughed together for another five minutes.

When the spaghetti was finally on the table, he knew this unexpected and joyous surprise would soon end. They sat and ate, laughing, talking, and enjoying the company. There were no candles, no romantic music, but it was the best meal he'd had in years. For the first time in a long while, Daryl was happy—truly happy.

~~~~~~~~~~

Huw soared over mountain peaks. Ahead, he could see the Great Salt Lake stretching for miles. His objective lay just before the lake. A small group of dots jogged across an open field. Beneath him, a shiny gray F-22 roared down the runway. He circled the military base and spotted his destination—a bright yellow backhoe digging next to one of the buildings on the base.

For the first time since arriving in Arrow Springs, he found himself separated from Alex and Sarah. He had grown fond of the sweet fragile woman and requested that Eitan reconsider sending him. Surely someone else could accomplish the seemingly insignificant task. But, Eitan had insisted. In fact the command came from the Creator Himself. Huw knew Alex could protect Sarah. He had for many years. Still, it hurt to leave her.

Huw settled into the cab next to John Green, his new project. He watched as the overweight man with the receding hairline skillfully manipulated the giant bucket only feet from the building. Little red flags in the ground guided the digging.

Anxious to get on with the mission and get back to Alex and Sarah, Huw leapt from the cab to the ground where the bucket would come down any moment. He knelt down and pretended to be a small child. He threw his arms over his head, screamed, and then vanished.

The bucket jerked to the right and smashed into the ground ripping through one of the red flags and then through the power lines the flag represented.

There was a bright flash.

Sirens.

Huw spent the next three hours in the base headquarters watching the top brass cut John to shreds. It was clear the military personnel felt it a waste of resources to pay outsiders to do work they could accomplish on their own. They thoroughly enjoyed putting John through bureaucratic torture.

"You nearly sent this base into lock down!" barked the Brigadier General.

"Yes ma'am. Sorry ma'am," said John.

"I suppose you think it's funny to see people scrambling around the base trying to figure out why the alarms are sounding?"

"No ma'am"

"Do you realize how many tax dollars you wasted in the last three hours?"

"No ma'am"

Huw paced the room watching the court-room drama. The woman clearly enjoyed the interrogation.

"So was this some kinda act of terrorism?" asked the Brigadier General. "Testing our systems to see if we could function without power?" Her lip curled in disgust. "Or are you just inept at doin' your job?"

"No ma'am. I just—"

Huw cringed. He needed to get John out of town. If the man told her about seeing a child under the bucket, he would spend the next several days in psychiatric evaluation.

Apparently, John realized the same thing. "I um, bumped the lever, and the bucket swung to the side as it came down, ma'am."

"You realize there is a reason those power lines are run under ground, don't you?"

"Yes ma'am."

"When we lose power here, our computers don't like it, and that means our technicians don't like it. Our guards don't like it. Heck ain't none of us like it. You should be glad you're talking to me, and not to any of them."

"Yes ma'am. Thank you ma'am."

To his credit John possessed enough smarts not to argue with her. Even if she was exaggerating just a bit.

At four in the afternoon, Huw left the base riding alongside John in his green pickup.

"I hate military work!" John mumbled to himself.

"There are certainly better opportunities out there somewhere," whispered Huw. "You do not have to take that kind of treatment."

"I haven't worked my tail off for thirty years to be treated like this." John swore and smacked the steering wheel. "There's got to be something better than this."

After spending the night waiting outside the local bar for John to emerge, Huw finally accompanied John to his rental home at ten-thirty. It was all he could do to keep the man from crashing to his bed as soon as they entered the house.

He encouraged the man to stop at his computer and check his e-mail. As Huw knew he would, John had an e-mail from a past acquaintance in Indiana. John opened the e-mail and found an opportunity for a well-paying job in Evansville, Indiana.

"I bet they would respect you there," whispered Huw.

"Yeah, they'd respect me," said John. The drunken man neither realized nor cared that he was talking to no one. With judgment clouded by his current state, he sent an e-mail telling the acquaintance he would be there for a meeting the following Wednesday. Then he collapsed onto the bed.

~~~~~~~~~~

Pastor David Thomas knelt at the front of the auditorium Thursday evening. Like most days, he'd spent an hour in the morning praying for the members of the congregation, for the town of Arrow Springs, for the state of Missouri, and for the United States. But this was different—he couldn't shake the feeling. God was calling him to prayer. He left the house after dinner and walked to the church building.

As the setting sun streamed through the stained glass at the front of the auditorium, he studied the images that looked over his shoulder every Sunday morning, as he preached. All of the windows around the auditorium beautifully displayed God's story. On the east end, the images told the salvation story up to the resurrection of Christ. But these windows, the ones he seldom saw because they were behind the pulpit, promised strength for today and hope for the future.

A central cross separated the windows into two scenes. To the left of the cross, Jesus ascended into heaven atop the words "I am with you always, to the end of the age." The words didn't come at Christ's ascension, but the message was clear.

"Lord," David prayed, "my heart is heavy for this town. You have placed such incredible people in my spiritual care. I'm reminded by the difference I see in Daryl why I do this. You've even used the horrific events of the past three weeks to draw Chris and Sarah together."

He looked at the outstretched arms of his Lord as he ascended into the clouds. "Lord, please speak into Sarah's heart. Let her know You are there for her, that You have always been there. Protect her. Comfort her. Wrap her in Your loving arms. Lord, you know she's persistent—it's the way You created her. She's been doing a lot of nosing around in things. Please keep her safe."

He continued to pray for Sarah. He prayed for Chris and his investigation of CeSiR Tech. He prayed for Daryl and the Internal Affairs investigation and for his relationship with Marilyn. He continued to pray about things he could only sense were going on around town.

He ran out of things to pray about, but he knew the Spirit wasn't finished. So he continued in prayer—prayer about what to pray about.

He couldn't chase the sensation that God wanted him there, on his knees, interceding.

For whom or what? He wasn't sure.

God was sure—that was all that mattered.

His eyes drifted to the right of the cross. This scene portrayed Jesus as the Lion of Judah, like Aslan from the Chronicles of Narnia. Below it were the words, "I am coming quickly." The contrast between this powerful image of Christ as the Lion, and the one on the east wall portraying him as the Lamb who was slain, struck deeply into David's soul.

"Lord, the victory is Yours," he prayed with a new boldness. "Bind the enemy in this town. Thwart the plans of the evil one. Let goodness justice and mercy prevail in this place at this time and for all time to come." He raised his hands toward the windows. "Lord, come quickly. Show Yourself to be the Lion, just as You've shown Yourself to be the Lamb."

For two hours, he continued to pray, growing in boldness, spiritual alertness, and emotion.

At a quarter to eleven, the auditorium doors burst open.

~~~~~~~~~~

CHAPTER TWENTY-TWO

Sarah awoke. At least she thought she was awake.
Her eyes and lungs burned. The unmistakable smell of smoke hung like fog in her room, a sulfurous putrid smell. Her head throbbed and her ears rang.

No, it wasn't her ears it was her smoke detector. Just outside her door in the hallway—the high-pitched scream of the detector pierced the quiet of the early nighttime hour.

She had to get up. She had to get out.

NOW!

She tried to sit up. Her brain ordered her muscles to move, but they wouldn't—couldn't—respond. It felt as if her pajamas had been stitched to the bed. Beyond the immobility, she felt the roof had caved in—pressing her chest into the bed.

She coughed. She wheezed.

Something held her down.

~~~~~~~~~~

Twelve dragon-like demons had attacked Alex. They came from all directions. By himself, he stood no chance. They grabbed him with razor sharp claws.

He braced for the certain pain, as they ripped him to pieces. But they just stood holding him. What were they waiting for?

Then he saw him.

Mors stepped into Sarah's bedroom. "Good. You have him. Hold him." He pointed his silver scythe at Sarah. "She has caused enough trouble. Now she is mine." His black cloak rippled as he glided to Alex. "Do not worry. You will perish. But, only after you watch her burn."

Four gluttonous sloth-like creatures appeared through the side wall. Drool dripped from the corners of their smiling mouths.

"Hold her down," commanded Mors. "We would not want our tender morsel slipping off the frying pan, now would we?" He headed back to the window of the bedroom. "I have a barbeque to start."

Alex could hear human voices outside the house laughing and cursing. "Douse the doors." He saw a black cloaked man walk past the window pouring liquid from a gas can.

"Sarah! Wake up! You need to get out," he had screamed.

"She cannot hear you," said one of the sloths. He sat on her chest with his hands on her hears.

Alex heard glass shattering elsewhere in the house.

"Light it," yelled Mors.

"Light it," repeated one of the men in the front yard.

Soon flames roared in front of the bedroom window. Then the smoke detector outside her room began screaming.

Sarah had awoken and began squirming, but the demons were too much for her.

~~~~~~~~~~

Sarah's heart slammed against her ribs. Her lungs constricted at the collecting soot and mucus. She gagged, cried. Try as she might, she could neither move nor scream.

She was going to die, going to stand before her God.

A new panic overcame her.

Was she ready?

She believed in God. She'd even made a sincere commitment to Jesus as a teenager. But she had walked away from Him.

At the moment of death, she realized He hadn't abandoned her those years ago. She had abandoned Him.

"Lord forgive me," she prayed.

When the words exited her lungs, a mix of carbon monoxide and smoke threatened to replace them.

Hot salty tears streaked down her cheeks. For the first time in ten years, she realized God had desired to be her Father, to hold her as she mourned the loss of her earthly parents. Soon she would be with Him. With them.

"Abba, please." She tried to pray, but the words could not escape her airless lungs.

The weight on her chest and legs seemed to flee. The stitches holding her to the mattress tore free. She didn't posses the strength to stand. She simply rolled to her side and then off the bed. Her body crashed to the floor and she gasped a deep breath from the air pocketed under the bed.

But as quick as it came, the reprieve was gone.

The flames shooting above the window danced bright and yellow on her bed sheets. Then they began to fade. First to orange, then red, then crimson.

As the roar of flames around her continued, her world faded to black.

~~~~~~~~~~

Chris stared at the moon flickering between the passing struts of the Lamine Bridge. It hung large and full in the eastern sky. Just his luck to get the night shift on full moon night, but with Daryl suspended they were woefully shorthanded. So far the night had been quiet. Even the River's Edge seemed ominously still, though the lot was full. Perhaps it was just too early for the antics of the crazies brought on by the full moon.

As he exited the bridge, he heard the quiet-air break across his radio. A fraction of a second later, Sally's voice crackled, "All units we have a possible Code 9, at 239 Second, Arrow Springs. Possible occupant. Please advise."

He slammed on the brake, spinning the cruiser in the middle of the road. "This is 121—sixty seconds from that location." The cruiser's seatbelt squeezed the air from his lungs.

Before he could ponder the feeling of déjà vu, he was on Second Street.

His heart plunged within his chest. Flames nearly engulfed the house.

He slid his cruiser into Mrs. Ferguson's drive and jumped from the car.

Mrs. Ferguson stood in her front yard weeping.

"Have you seen her?" he hollered.

The elderly woman shook her head.

He ran across the street and up to the burning house.

It was late. If she was still in there, she'd be in her bedroom. He ran to the window to the left of the entrance. The previously manicured bushes in front of the window were now a pile of smoldering ash. Thankfully, the siding was real brick, definitely hot, but not flaming.

He approached the window and could see the bedroom door was shut. It would be safe to break the window.

He couldn't see Sarah.

~~~~~~~~~~

Zeke stood beside the window.

From the other side he heard taunting squeals. "Not so curious now is she." Unnerving laughs. "Curiosity killed the kitten."

He drew a three-foot broadsword from its sheath and cut a sweeping arc through the house just under the window.

High-pitched shrieks filled the air—then nothing.

A faint moan gurgled from behind the window.

~~~~~~~~~~

Chris was convinced he heard a muffled groan.

Perhaps the fire had weakened the window frame. He grabbed the window and pulled. The aluminum frame didn't budge.

The hot metal seared into his hands.

~~~~~~~~~~

Alex watched Chris' hands pull back from the sill.

"The heroic sergeant only feet away from his love, while she suffers the excruciating death of asphyxiation," cackled one of the dragon-like demons.

Chris' head disappeared from the window.

The demons continued to taunt and writhe with delight, but all Alex heard were the labored breaths drawing everything but oxygen into Sarah's lungs.

He pulled with all his might against the claws digging into his arms and legs. Like shackles in a prison, their grip would not give.

An explosion of glass.

The window shattered as a large black object crashed into the room.

The suddenness of the attack caught the demons off guard. At the shock of the flying glass and bright light, the demons loosened their grip.

He pulled his right arm free and grabbed the throat of the closest demon to his left.

Zeke, shining in extraordinary brilliance, followed the black cannon ball through the window. Sword pulled, he shot through three of the demons standing where Alex had been, only a fraction of a second earlier.

Alex turned to see, another large iridescent figure appear through the wall of Sarah's bedroom.

Gida attacked.

Before the glass had finished falling from the window, all twelve of the dragon-like demons found themselves a new residence—the Abyss.

Free from his oppressors, Alex knelt over Sarah.

Tears like crystal dropped from his eyes.

There was nothing he could do.

~~~~~~~~~~

"There's a fire!" cried Trina Thomas, when she burst into the auditorium.

From the horror in her eyes, David could see it was someone they knew.

"Who? Where?" he managed before she cut in.

"It's Sarah. Sarah McIntyre! Her house is on fire!"

It all became clear—the compulsion to pray. The most help he could offer was right there, seeking God in prayer.

On the other hand—he could pray as they drove.

They ran to their Buick Enclave. The tires squawked to life as they sped from the driveway.

Trina didn't even fuss. She was in as much of a hurry as he was.

They drove down Ash Street toward the fire. The full moon glowed a reddish brown, as smoke from the fire wafted northward.

They pulled onto Second and Trina gasped at the sight. "Oh, dear God!"

There were more flames than house. The entire north end of the roof had collapsed into the house. Just two weeks earlier, they'd sat there in the dining room talking with this new friend. Rafters, flames, and burning debris had taken their place.

He parked the car a few houses away on the east side of the street.

Running down the sidewalk to Mrs. Ferguson's house, they saw Chris in front of a window at the far end of the house. He picked up a large black planter. It must have weighed fifty pounds. He threw it through the window.

Sirens blared as fire trucks made their way up the street.

Chris disappeared through the window. He was now in the inferno.

~~~~~~~~~~

Chris pulled himself through the window.

Sarah lay lifeless below the window covered in tiny shards of glass.

Oh no. Had he harmed her with his dramatic entrance?

No, the real danger was the thick smoke pouring into the room. Flames licked their way around and under the door, hungry for a fresh infusion of oxygen.

Ignoring the glass cutting aggressively into his arms and neck, he picked up her body from the floor, laid her over his shoulder, and began to climb back through the window. Half way through his foot slipped. Their weight crashed down on his thigh. Sarah's body began to slip from his shoulder.

He threw himself through the window and into the lawn. At the expense of his own body, he kept her from crashing into the ground. He struggled back to his feet, ran twenty feet from the house, and laid the last person he'd ever let himself love in the grass.

Her body was limp and motionless. She wasn't breathing.

He placed his fingers on her carotid artery. Nothing. No sign of life.

He tilted her head back, put his lips to hers, plugged her nose and gave two quick breaths. Sliding to his right he put his palms to her chest and began applying rapid compressions. "One-and-two-and-three-and. . ." He continued until he had completed thirty compressions.

He moved to her mouth, two more quick breaths. "Come on Sarah. Don't leave me." Back to chest compressions.

Breathing, compressions.

"I'm so sorry Sarah. I failed to protect you."

More breathing, more compressions.

He couldn't survive another loss.

"Twenty one-twenty two—"

Sarah's body twitched.

With renewed hope he moved to give mouth-to-mouth, then back to compressions. He placed his hands on her chest.

She jerked, coughed, leaned forward, and threw up down the side of his leg.

He looked to the sky. "Thank you," he whispered.

She coughed and tried to speak.

"Shh, don't try to talk." He held her up so she wouldn't choke.

An EMT jogged up to Sarah with an oxygen canister. "We'll take it from here." He put a mask to Sarah's face.

~~~~~~~~~~

Mors stood behind a large oak tree grinding his teeth. His plan had unraveled before his eyes. Mael had been right. Officer Davis proved once again to be a major nuisance. Mael would not be pleased.

He hated this assignment. Lucifer himself had sent him to Arrow Springs. But he seriously considered departing for a more conducive location. Somewhere where death came more easily—somewhere like the Middle East with its religious conflicts, Sudan with its genocide, even sub-Saharan Africa, where millions died from AIDS and hunger.

Once again, the heavenly host had foiled his lust for death. He half considered charging the three warriors standing over Sarah.

Could he still take his prey?

The time would come. Dozens of illuminated beings hovered around firefighters, EMTs, and onlookers. He would find a time and place with better odds.

For now, he would settle for some reckless drunk or an abusive husband.

Death could always be found.

~~~~~~~~~~

Chris watched as the medical personnel prepared Sarah for her second ambulance ride in three weeks. Waves of heat and smoke still emanated from the house.

Sarah's eyes stared at the blaze reflecting the flames. She was alive, but he worried that it wasn't over. He had no way of knowing what long term effects such prolonged exposure could have on her.

He tried to block the thought, but it surfaced anyway. *If she survived.*

"Are you okay?"

He turned to see the Thomases approaching.

"You really are a hero," said Trina, through a snot and tears smile.

"I'm fine." He surveyed the toll the rescue had taken on his body. "I think."

"You're bleeding!" said Trina. Her eyes stared like saucers at his neck.

He reached up his hand and pulled back blood covered fingers. "I guess I am."

"Let's have a look," said one of the EMTs who overheard the conversation.

Chris nodded, realizing much more than his neck hurt.

"It looks like some minor cuts. We'll have to get those cleaned out. And that," pointing to Chris' arm, "is going to need stitches."

"How is she?" he asked the EMT.

"She's alive." The EMT gazed at the flames protruding from the window through which Chris and Sarah had emerged only minutes earlier. "Which is more than I could say, if you hadn't gotten here when you did."

Sarah began coughing again.

"We need to get her to the hospital," said the EMT.

"I want to go with her," said Chris.

The EMT turned to look at Sarah, who nodded in agreement.

"Well, given the work you've done here, I don't see a problem with it." He began to bandage the gash in Chris' arm. "Let's get you patched up 'til we get to the hospital."

Once the EMTs secured Sarah in the ambulance, one pointed to a seat at the head of the stretcher. "You can sit there. Make sure you buckle up."

Once again, they were on their way to Regional.

~~~~~~~~~~

CHAPTER TWENTY-THREE
Friday, May 8, 2020

Chris stepped into the elevator at Columbia Regional. As he reached for the button on the panel, he paused to look at the black thread protruding from his arm. Ten loops crisscrossed a swollen crevice in his forearm. According to the doctor, there were six more stitches below the surface. He pushed the button, and the number two lit up.

The pungent oily smell of burn ointment saturated the small room when the doors slid closed. The cuts on his arm and neck throbbed. The white charred areas of his hands stung with every motion. But the real pain gripped his heart. He needed to see her—to know she would be okay.

The elevator chimed and the doors opened to the second floor. He stepped from the elevator and headed toward the pulmonary critical care department. He rounded the corner and saw a familiar group of people outside a small waiting room.

Daryl stood holding Marilyn's hand. "Chris! Man, are you alright?"

"I'll live." He wasn't the one who got roasted alive. He nodded to Pastor and Trina Thomas as he approached the group. "How is she? Any word?"

"The nurse said Sarah was awake when they brought her up. But we still haven't heard from the doctor," said Trina.

Not the message he'd hoped to hear. What was taking so long?

Twenty-five minutes later the doctor emerged through a pair of automatic doors. He approached the group and looked at Chris. "You must be Chris."

"Uh, yes."

"I am Dr. Michaels. She is a mighty spirited young woman." He smiled. "She keeps insisting on seeing Chris, something about her knight in shining armor." He looked down at Chris' uniform. "You have the appearance of someone who rescued a damsel from a burning building—so I figured you must be Chris."

Chris glanced down at the grass and blood stains on his pants and shredded sleeves. He could only assume his neck and face showed the pain he felt. "How is she doc?"

"She will be fine. It is a good thing you showed up when you did. She could not have survived much longer with that much smoke in her lungs."

"Can we see her?"

"It will be at least an hour. Her carboxyhemoglobin levels are dangerously high. She needs to spend some time in our Hyperbaric Oxygen Chamber."

They all just stared at the doctor, as if he had begun to speak German.

"I am sorry. She is suffering from carbon monoxide poisoning. We have her in a chamber that is pressurized with one hundred percent oxygen. It will ensure her body gets enough oxygen, and prevent potential long-term effects including neurological damage. The treatments will need to happen twice a day for the first week and then once a day for three more weeks. She will be out in about an hour." For a moment he just eyed the group. "She will need rest. I would prefer if only one or two of you went in to see her at a time. And not for very long."

"Is she still at risk of complications?" asked Marilyn.

As impossible as it seemed, Chris could sense the rest of the group's concern rivaled his own.

"Well, there is always a risk," said the doctor. "Barring some unforeseen problem, probably just a sore throat for a week or two. It is also common for some smoke inhalation patients to suffer from shortness of breath for months, even years, after the incident. The nurse will let you know when you can go in to see her. Please remember—she needs her rest."

The doctor turned and exited through the automatic doors.

Chris followed the others into the small waiting room and sat down.

"After Pastor Thomas called me," said Daryl. "I stopped by the station and picked you up a clean uniform." He reached down and handed Chris a small duffle.

"I brought an extra change of clothes for Sarah too," said Marilyn. "I think we're about the same size." She glanced down at her hips. "At least the same height. They might be a little loose, but I think she can wear 'em."

"Who you trying to kid?" said Daryl. "You're as slender and attractive as ever."

Her olive cheeks flushed a strawberry pink. "You realize she has nothing, no clothes, no home, even her car was in the garage." Her eyes glistened. "It's all gone."

Chris shook his head. Sarah had everything she needed. "She's got some great friends."

Trina Thomas turned to her husband. "She is going to need a place to stay, and some things."

He nodded. "We'll start calling the congregation tomorrow. We'll see what we can drum up."

"She can stay with me," said Marilyn. She glowed with excitement. "I have an extra room, and she wouldn't need anything except clothes and transportation."

"You're such a sweetheart," said Trina.

Chris picked up the duffle, and left the waiting room. He felt his eyes beginning to sting. No way would he break down in front on them. Besides, he didn't want Sarah to see the blood and pain he'd endured on her behalf.

~~~~~~~~~~

Sarah arrived in her room. Her body screamed—it needed sleep. But her mind raced. The squawk of the smoke alarm. The crackling of flames consuming her home. The thick suffocating smoke. The distant sound of glass shattering and warm muscular arms sweeping her from the floor of her bedroom.

She lay in the hospital bed staring at the familiar golden-beige walls.

"Well hello there." The voice seemed familiar. "Let me guess, you missed us so much ya just had to come back for a visit?"

She turned to see the bubbly slightly-overweight nurse from three weeks before approach her bed. "Hhhi." Her own raspy voice surprised her. "Do you work on all the floors hhhere? You must really g-get around."

"You have no idea." The nurse walked to the bed and swept Sarah's hair back like a mother putting her toddler down for the night. "You have a regular little party going on out there in the waitin' room. Not bad for the middle of the night I would say."

Party? She struggled to make sense of the word. Despite an hour of oxygen, the smoke must still have been clouding her mind.

"I believe," continued the nurse, "there is one individual you would particularly like to talk with. Am I right?"

She closed her eyes. Tried to chase the haze from her brain.

"Would you like me to round you up some fresh clothes and maybe some makeup?" The nurse chuckled.

Chris. The realization struck her. Chris was at the hospital. Of course he was. He rode with her in the ambulance. It all started to flood back.

They had been through so much since that first meeting in the hospital. No, no jeans and makeup this time. "Hhhe'll just hhhave to put up with me as I am."

~~~~~~~~~~

Chris strolled the hallway stretching his legs and easing his nerves. A familiar face appeared down the hallway. The jovial nurse approached and told him Sarah was back in her room and anxious to see him. He thanked her and went to the room.

"Hey there."

"Hhhey!" Her smile melted his heart. "I'm surprised you're willing to be anywhere near me." She rolled her head and stared at the wall. "I've been nothing but trouble."

"Trouble—what? You? Nonsense! There's nowhere I'd rather be than right here."

Sarah wrinkled her pink button nose and scowled at him.

"Well, I'd rather be just about anywhere else, long as I was there with you." The pool blue of her eyes shone like an oasis amid a bloodshot desert. "How you feelin'?"

"Okkkay, I g-guess, all things c-considered," her voice continued to fade.

"Shh, you shouldn't be talkin' too much. Your throat's gonna be sore for awhile and you need to get some rest. I should be going."

"Do you have to go?"

He could smell her smoky skin when he leaned over and kissed her on the forehead. "There are some others here to see you. I can't keep you all to myself. I'll talk to you in the mornin'. Good night Sarah. I love you."

"G-goodnight my knight."

A quiet knock on the door preceded a young man's voice. "Excuse me Miss McIntyre, there are some people in the waiting room who would like to see you. Do you feel up to—" He entered and saw Chris standing next to her. "Oh, I'm sorry. I didn't realize someone was already in here."

"That's okay—I was just leaving. The other nurse told me Sarah was back in her room and wanted to see me."

The man cocked his head. "What other nurse?"

"Giddy, middle-aged, woman." Chris hadn't seen any other nurses since he'd exited the elevator. Surely the man knew who he was talking about.

"There're no female nurses on duty tonight, at least not on this floor."

"About five-foot four? Dark hair, mildly graying? Slightly overweight?"

The young man just shook his head, turned, and left the room.

Chris turned a questioning gaze to Sarah.

"You're not g-going c-crazy," she encouraged. "I saw hhher too. Hhhow weird."

"Do-do-do-do, Do-do-do-do."

Sarah giggled at his attempted Twilight Zone theme.

~~~~~~~~~~

Alex knelt next to Sarah's bed. He cast an if-they-only-knew grin at Rafya. Unlike many of the angelic warriors, Rafya's appearance was more female than male, though in reality there was no gender among angels. Rafya spent most of her time in the hospital. He admired her mission of care and encouragement to the patients and guests of the hospital. Care and compassion truly reflected the work of their Lord. In this role, Alex assumed Rafya had probably appeared in human form more in the last month than he had in the last century.

Alex rose to his feet. "I need to join the others."

"Go," said Rafya. "I can stay with her."

"Thank you. You are a gem." He turned and exited the room.

Alex took his place among the impressive group of angelic warriors gathered outside the room. Zeke rode with him in the ambulance that brought Chris and Sarah. Asa and Adiya arrived with Daryl and Marilyn, while Yora had accompanied Pastor and Mrs. Thomas. Eitan had only just arrived.

The look on Eitan's face communicated that, despite the victory at Sarah's house, the battle was grim.

"Did you see Mors?" asked Yora.

"Cowering behind a tree you mean," said Alex.

"Careful," said Eitan. "The enemy is cunning, and their ranks still far outnumber ours. Our scouts tell me there are three to four thousand demons at the facility across the river."

Zeke turned his face to the floor and a ripple passed through his wings.

Alex felt his pain. Though he had not been there, he envisioned Eran valiantly charging the enemy horde.

"Do we know why?" asked Yora. "What is going on there?"

"The time has come for you to know." Eitan closed his eyes and cleared his throat. "The man who attacked Sarah, Leon, was what they call a mim." He shook his head. "The very term is a demonstration of the enemy's irreverent arrogance. It stands for Manufactured Image of Man."

The implications weakened Alex' knees.

Adiya placed his palms together as if in prayer. "As opposed to the Image of God," he raised his fingers to his chin, "in which the true Creator created humankind?"

"Precisely." Eitan's voice rang low and solemn. "It would appear this is an effort by the enemy to devalue the worth of God's creation by demonstrating that man can create without His help."

"That would explain the strange control the enemy seems to have over these individuals," said Zeke.

"Yes. To this point God has chosen not to endow these replicas with souls. They are nothing more than puppets controlled by the enemy. And, they are weaseling their way into positions of power and influence in Arrow Springs and abroad."

"But Leon must have been at least twenty years old?" asked Adiya. "How long has this been going on?"

"Too long. The first mims are now twenty-five. Our information places their numbers at about one hundred twenty. Sixty teens and adults. Sixty more are children."

How many times had Alex seen humanity attempt to play god?

As if having read Alex' thoughts, Eitan continued. "It would appear God has a lesson for humankind to learn from this incident." Eitan pulled his sword from its sheath and blazed a line in the air. "Some lines should not be crossed."

"But, this presents the challenge," said Asa. "The soul is unseen. The line is invisible and people dismiss what their eyes cannot behold."

For several minutes, the warriors stood silent.

A sweet aroma, like incense, wafted from the waiting room down the hall. Alex inhaled deep. The saints were praying.

"We must prepare," said Eitan. "This battle is far from over. It seems in their push to eliminate Sarah, the enemy failed to notice Huw's departure. This is to our advantage. We need warriors. Time to prepare is slipping away. We must be ready when Chris pieces this together. It will not take him long."

~~~~~~~~~~

Daryl knocked on Sarah's door. He put his arm around Marilyn and led her into the dimly lit room. Despite the hectic night, he still detected a light sweet pea scent rising from her neckline.

They exchanged pleasantries with Sarah and told her how sorry they were for her losses.

"Were thhhey able to salvage anything?" asked Sarah.

"I don't think so." Marilyn reached down and took Sarah's hand. "Don't you worry about a thing. You'll be well taken care of, you can be sure of that."

Daryl just nodded and watched his beautiful ex-wife comfort their hurting friend.

"I would be honored if you'd stay with me for awhile." Marilyn winked at Sarah. "And I'd be terribly offended if you said no."

"Well, I wouldn't want to offend you." Sarah's eyes were wide and moist. "But you hhhave to realize, I might not be thhhe safest person to hhhave in your hhhome."

"Oh we can take care of ourselves, two strong women like us."

Daryl marveled at the friendship blooming between these two women. Something told him it would be a good friendship for Marilyn. It might even aid the healing of his and Marilyn's relationship.

Marilyn opened a narrow closet door. "I brought you some clothes to wear when you're ready to get up and around." She set the black satchel on a shelf and shut the door.

"We should probably give the Thomases a chance to visit," said Daryl, after a few more minutes of conversation.

"Thhhey're hhhere too? What time is it?"

Daryl followed Sarah's gaze to the digital clock on the wall. It was one-thirty in the morning.

"You people are awesome." Sarah struggled to pull in a deep breath, obviously trying to contain already raw emotions.

"Heal fast," said Marilyn, as they turned and headed out the door.

After saying goodbye to the Thomases, Daryl asked Chris if he could use a ride home. Minutes later a cold driving rain soaked through his light spring jacket as he trudged to his ten-year-old VW Jetta. Marilyn and Chris waited for him at the Emergency Room entrance.

~~~~~~~~~~

Mael perched atop the CeSiR building west of the river. His fury boiled as he railed at Mors, and cursed God. At every turn, his plans were foiled. He blamed the insubordination of his minions. Even Mors had failed him. Still, he knew his repeated failures were a result of the infinite knowledge, wisdom, and power of the Almighty. He ripped a two-foot-long three-hundred-pound capstone from the wall next to him and hurled it to the ground three stories below.

The people of God in Arrow Springs were turning to Him in prayer. They needed to be crushed like the small shrub on which the capstone had landed. The tasty thought of such devastation fed his fury. Even his own Creator would not stop Mael forever.

Lightning struck a tree along the river sending wood splintering into the grass. A deep laugh rolled from Mael's belly. Sulfurous fumes spewed from his nostrils joining storm clouds which hung low over the building. Another blast of thunder rolled across the tumultuous sky.

He unfurled his mighty bat-like wings, and wailed an eerie war cry across the countryside.

~~~~~~~~~~

CHAPTER TWENTY-FOUR

The theatre of Chris' mind played a rerun of the prior day's events. Only this time he stood unable to move peering through the window as the love of his life suffocated from smoke, engulfed in flames. In a blink, he held her in his arms. His heart basked in the glow of their love for one another, until the smooth warm touch of her skin turned to fire. Jolts of pain screamed through his hands.

Music echoed from somewhere in the distance.

He jerked awake. Pain throbbed from the burns on his hands. The alarm clock on his night stand drifted into focus. The flames were gone, the smell of smoke replaced by fabric softener. He was in his bedroom. Sarah—safe in her room at the hospital. The horrific events had been real. Praise God, the results unreal. The pain in his hands—definitely real.

Pit-pat-pit-pit-pat.

The voice on the radio informed that the rain and thunderstorms would continue for most of the weekend.

Tip-tap-pit-spit-spat-tip-tip-tap.

He silenced the radio. He didn't need to be told it was raining outside. He listened to the soothing sound of rain against the roof and window. At least he didn't have the early shift.

Poor Sarah. If the fire had left anything unscathed, the driving rains and water from the fire trucks would have finished the job. The pain from the cuts and burns had all but vanished from his awareness. He rolled out of bed. His muscles ached. There would be no jogging, no pushups. He'd had all the workout he needed.

He cranked on the water. A hot shower should soothe sore muscles.

He stepped into the shower. Pain surged from his arms and neck. For the second time in the still brief day, his burning hands screamed at him. He jerked the knob from hot to cold. Too much. Now cold water shocked his system. He let a brief cuss word slip. His relaxing shower proved to be anything but.

He finally settled into his easy chair with coffee and toast.

He picked up his Bible and chose to read from Daniel Chapter Three. He read about three of Daniel's friends, with names he'd never been able to pronounce. They had been thrown into a fiery furnace for refusing to worship the king rather than God. Despite their obvious and certain demise, God delivered them. They emerged unscathed and those who observed the events marveled that even their clothes remained untouched—they didn't even smell like smoke.

"Lord," Chris prayed, "You delivered me from the fire." He looked down at the stitches in his arm. "I'd have appreciated not having these burns, cuts, and bruises, but You preserved my life. And once again, You protected Sarah."

His mind wandered to the fourth person, seen walking in the fire with Daniel's friends. The king declared that God had sent an angel to care for them.

Was it possible that God had sent an angel to protect him and Sarah?

After his time with God, Chris grabbed a light jacket and headed out the door. The cool damp air smelled of dirt and earthworms. The thunder and lightning of the nighttime hours had been replaced by a steady downpour.

The gloom of the clouds felt deeper than their blocking out the sun. Perhaps it was the events of the night, but it felt like evil had descended on the once peaceful town. The fire, the actions of Leon Burgos, CeSiR Tech, and the Mayor were all connected. Somehow.

How did one confront his own boss about his involvement in such atrocious events? At least without losing one's job.

At least for awhile, the police work could wait. He was off duty. And there was only one place he wanted to be during his free time.

~~~~~~~~~~

Huw paced the bedroom of the small rental house in West Valley City, a suburb of Salt Lake City. His mission lay comatose on the bed in a hangover stupor. As much as he desired to wake the man, given the man's spiritual state and present physical condition, there would be no means to communicate to his heart or mind. He simply had to wait for the excessive alcohol the man had consumed to wake him.

Huw approached the bedroom window and looked out at the street running through the subdivision. Over the past few hours most of the cars that once lined the street had departed for one final day's work for the week. Across the street, behind a chain-link fence, a stocky boxer stood eyeing Huw and barking. Somewhere down the street a high pitched bark joined in a duet. Still despite the ruckus, John Green lay motionless.

Around ten-thirty the man finally woke with a start and sprinted—if he were capable of such a feat—to the bathroom.

How could this mission possibly be as critical as Eitan had said? This man was no spiritual warrior. And despite years of construction work, he was no physical warrior either.

After more barking, this time from the small bathroom, the man emerged holding his head. It would take a maximum of two to three days for John to drive to Indiana.

Huw needed him there sooner. He went to work. "What if the truck breaks down?" he whispered. "You have always wanted to visit Denver. What about Kansas City?"

The man sat back down on the edge of the bed.

"You need to get out of this town." This time it was not a whisper.

An hour and a half later, John had called his contact at the military base and quit. He locked the house door and headed for his pickup.

By five in the evening, they would be in Denver.

~~~~~~~~~~

Chris knocked on the hospital room door. No one answered. The door was open.

"Sarah?" he whispered.

She didn't answer.

He kept his eyes to the floor and edged into the room. To his left he heard slow rhythmic breathing. A slight cough interrupted the breathing. He turned to see her beautiful red hair strewn atop her pillow. She lay on her side, snuggled into a pale blue sheet.

He pulled up a chair and waited. The cares and concerns of the past and future melted away in the silent peace of the present.

After thirty soul-refreshing minutes, he felt a soft grip on his hand. He looked up as her eyes fluttered open.

She looked at him and smiled. "Whhhat are you doing hhhere?" She coughed. "You must be ex-xhhhausted."

"Shh." He ran his hand across the slightly feverish skin of her arm. "Don't hurt yourself. I just wanted to be with you."

"You're too sweet—it doesn't hhhurt, really."

"It's easy to be sweet, when you're in love."

She started to speak again, but stopped. Tears crested in the corners of her eyes and then overflowed her bright cheeks. The redness of her skin brought out the blue of her eyes and blended softly into her red hair. Never had he seen this precious gem in perfect health. He'd found her lying on the floor of her home—once broken and bloodied, now raspy and roasted.

He couldn't imagine caring for her more than he did at that moment. "The doc say any more 'bout your condition?"

"He said I could go home tomorrow." She scrunched her nose. "Unfortunately, I'll need to come back twice a day for treatments."

"I can pick you up tomorrow." He recalled their first lunch together overlooking the Missouri River. "What time?"

"Well actually—" She glanced away from him. "Marilyn called this morning and offered to pick me up." Her eyes begged him to understand. "I do appreciate the offer. You've done so much for me already."

A wave of disappointment swept over him. "That's great." It was probably for the best. It would be good for both Sarah and Marilyn to grow the friendship. "What are you going to do about transportation back and forth for the treatments?"

The corner of her mouth twitched upward. "I thought I'd hitchhike."

"Very funny."

"I should get a loaner vehicle next week, but I could use a ride Sunday, if you know someone who might be available."

"I'm sure I can find someone."

~~~~~~~~~~

Dr. M'Gregor spent the morning making plans and preparations. He drove to the Columbia airport to make emergency preparations. Hopefully, they wouldn't be necessary. He stopped at Wal-Mart and picked up several size ten girls' outfits, snacks, a backpack, and bottles of water—complete with petro-free biodegradable bottles.

Half an hour later, he pulled back into the parking garage beneath CeSiR Tech. He parked the company owned BMW into his personal parking spot and walked to the elevator.

"Welcome back, Dr. M'Gregor," greeted the security guard at the elevator. "Ms. Mirinova would like to speak with you immediately."

Who did she think she was? He wasn't one of her lackeys. This was his company. He was in charge. And perhaps, if he reminded himself enough during the elevator ride, he would believe it when he arrived at her office.

He approached the large wooden door to her office.

The door swung open to greet him. "And just where have you been?" Maiya's voice rang cold and patronizing.

"It's any of your business, why?"

She ignored the question. "It would seem you have been pretty busy. That was quite the withdrawal you just took out at the credit union." She pierced his soul with red penetrating eyes. "Planning for a hike, are we?"

How did she know about the supplies?

"And it would also seem you've been downloading an awful lot of research lately. You wouldn't be considering leaving us. Would you?"

"Ya mean MY research, don't ya? Ya act as if I'm some sort of spy. In case ya've forgotten—I am CeSiR Tech." He was on a roll. "Without my mind, my work, and my investment, this company would not exist." Invigoration flowed through his veins. "And I don't appreciate ya treating me like some child!"

"Then perhaps, you'd stop acting like one. It seems to me you've forgotten my father's role in YOUR research. Without him this company wouldn't be where it is today." She curled her upper lip in disgust. "He had the guts to make the tough decisions. You never had the intestinal fortitude to do what needed done. You still don't."

His blood pulsed through his temples. He needed to calm himself. CeSiR wouldn't lose another scientist to a stroke. "Well pardon me if I feel life should be valued. That is the reason we're doing what we do."

She tilted her head slightly. "Is it? Are you sure it's not to prove it can be done? To accomplish what no other human has ever accomplished?" Her eye grew large and round. "To play god?"

"Ya're out of line missy! I do NOT report to you, and don't ya ever treat me like I do." He turned and slammed the office door behind him.

How had he let it come to this?

He strode back toward the elevator.

Ever since Jurek's death, Maiya had been taking over. She moved her gothic office furnishings into Jurek's office the day after he died. Even before the funeral, she began taking over. If he didn't know better he'd have suspected her in Jurek's death. But she loved Jurek. In fact to Wilhelm's knowledge, Jurek was the only person she'd ever loved.

Minutes later Dr. M'Gregor approached his favorite patient who sat looking miserable. "Ima, how would ya like to go to the park with me tomorrow?"

"Really?" She ran to him and gave him a big hug. "Can we?"

"Sure and why not?"

The girl lowered her eyes to the floor. "Ms. Mirinova said I would never be allowed to leave."

Control, he needed to stay calm. "What? When did she say that?"

"This morning. I overheard her tell Ms. Saunders that she wouldn't let me leave with you."

For the first time, fear, bona fide fear for his safety, descended on him. He always figured Maiya was dangerous. She had ice flowing through her veins and it emanated in her expressions. And to think she already knew where he'd been and what he'd done throughout the morning sent chills through his aging bones.

He would have to be very careful.

"Well I don't care what Ms. Mirinova says. We'll go on an adventure tomorrow."

A large frown crossed her rounded cheeks. "But what if it's still raining?"

"Then I guess we'll get wet, now won't we?"

~~~~~~~~~~

Chris knocked on the glass door to Mayor Richard's office. The man sat writing on a pad of paper. Chris knew he'd seen him approaching, but he didn't look up.

Chris knocked again.

Trenton set down his pen, but didn't look up. Finally, his fingers motioned for Chris to enter.

Once Chris stood before the desk, Trenton looked up. "Deputy Davis! What could possibly bring you here? Did the payroll not come through this morning?"

Chris was in no mood for games. "Cut the crap Trenton. You know darn well why I'm here. There's something fishy going on over at CeSiR Tech, and the way it looks to me you're swimming right in the middle of it."

Trenton interlaced his fingers, his knuckles turning white. "I think you forget your place here Mr. Davis."

"My place is to uphold the law, and that's exactly what I'm gonna do." Chris pulled a chair up to the desk and sat down. "What exactly is your involvement with CeSiR Tech?"

Trenton closed his eyes and shook his head. "My medical issues are none of your concern."

Chris put his hands to his knees and leaned forward. "What kind of morons do you think work for you in this town? You live in a house owned by CeSiR Tech. You drive a car, no doubt, owned by them as well. I have photographs of you and Leon Burgos in your fancy BMW leaving CeSiR Tech together." He leaned back and crossed his arms. "Isn't it interesting, this is the same Leon Burgos who broke into someone's home to steal the very camera that took that photo? Oh, and I almost forgot, this is the same Leon Burgos who murdered a woman from Kansas City, in your jail."

"Let me see." Chris put his hand to his chin. "This is the same shooting for which you suspended Daryl, a good police officer, because his gun was taken by your buddy Leon after he suffered a seizure, which strangely enough seems to be related to his medical involvement with CeSiR Tech."

Trenton shifted in his chair. Good. He was getting the message.

Chris continued. "Hmm, is that it? Oh wait, you also put Sarah McIntyre on leave from the library after she started pokin' her nose into CeSiR Tech affairs. Of course, she's a persistent little bugger. So now someone tried to kill her by burnin' her house down on top of her."

Trenton jumped to his feet. "Oh, you have me." He held out his hands in front of him. "Slap 'em on me. I will go quietly."

Trenton's expression, as he turned to grin at some phantom presence, made Chris' skin crawl. Then he turned the menacing grin back to Chris.

"Sit down Trenton." Chris watched for any indication that the man would come at him. "The time will come, don't you worry. You think you're above the law in this town—that you can do whatever you want. I'm not here to arrest you, and you know it. Somehow, I've got a feeling that day will come."

"Oh, I know a lot of things—more than you might think. Perhaps you have not realized, Deputy Davis. I am a psychic. I know all kinds of things I should have no way of knowing." He bobbed his head. "I mean sure, I know about your attraction to Sarah and your friendship with Daryl. The real reason you are looking for someone to blame."

"But Marge down at the diner knows these things." Trenton shook his head. "No, this is not the type of knowledge that proves I'm psychic." He picked up his pen and began tapping the pad of paper. "Now knowing that Fred Johanus was having an affair with Mrs. Freeman, and leaking it to the press, just in time to ensure I got elected Mayor, that is a different story. Or perhaps closer to home, how about knowing you were ready to ditch your sweet relationship with Ms. McIntyre for a spicy dish from your past—Leilah at Francisco's?"

Chris' stomach tightened.

"Ah, I see you are beginning to understand."

Anyone who does these things is detestable to the Lord. The words from Deuteronomy echoed in Chris' spirit.

"Maybe your Lord," said Trenton. Once again he seemed to gaze at some unseen guest. "But not mine. I serve lord Lucifer."

Chris struggled to breathe. Had he really heard what he thought he heard?

Trenton snapped a wide eyed look back to Chris, as if realizing he'd made the declaration out loud. "This conversation is over! Get out of my office before you end up on suspension like Daryl."

"Lord help us," Chris prayed, as he walked from the office.

~~~~~~~~~~

CHAPTER TWENTY-FIVE
Saturday, May 9, 2020

John Green's eyes slid open and locked onto a pastel depiction of the Rocky Mountains hanging on the pale yellow wall. The night before he'd checked into a quaint little hotel near Longmont. He rolled out of bed, walked to the windows, and opened the drapes. The view to the west took his breath away. The mountains glowed red with the brilliance of the sunrise. The snow capped Longs Peak shone like Citrine crystal emerging from the base of the mountain. The frustration and irritation of the past few days slid away like snow off the side of the mountain.

This adventure would provide an opportunity to feel the breeze in his hair, freedom from being told what to do, and when to do it. He'd checked in for just one night but decided to stick around for one more after seeing an advertisement for a Saturday evening game between the Rockies and the Cardinals.

He picked up the morning newspaper from outside his room door. The headline of the sports page touted the rematch between last year's NLCS opponents. He still couldn't believe he'd been able to purchase tickets online. It was going to be a great day.

~~~~~~~~~~

Huw decided John would be fine for the day without him. He had work to do. He needed to seek out prayer cover for the events in Arrow Springs. Moments later, he swooped into a small inner city church building.

"Huw! What on earth are you doing here?" A large angelic being sat at the front of the auditorium. "It is so good to see you again my brother."

"As it is for me, Ladan, my dear friend."

Huw approached Ladan and they clasped arms.

"What can I do for you my friend?" asked Ladan.

"I have come to seek the assistance of your prayer warriors here in Denver." Huw sat on the gray carpeted platform next to Ladan. "I have been assigned to assist a young woman in Arrow Springs, Missouri. There is a great stronghold of the enemy located there, and my charge is squarely in their sights. I received word from a messenger yesterday—her house was burnt to the ground, she was nearly killed." Huw stared at the fluorescent lights protruding from the ceiling. "I long to be with her, but my mission is important and must succeed."

Ladan laid a massive hand on Huw's back. "You know you have my support. What can we do? For what should we encourage our saints to pray?"

"The enemy is using a medical research facility to create human clones."

"What?" Ladan stood and faced Huw. The shock in his face reflected Huw's own when Eitan first revealed the enemy's scheme.

"Precisely! It would appear there are over one hundred of these clones, the oldest being twenty-five years of age. In His sovereignty, God has chosen not to endow these with souls. The enemy now treats them as puppets, controlling them at will."

Huw joined Ladan as he walked down the aisle of the auditorium. "We are outnumbered and the enemy wreaks havoc with the believers in Arrow Springs. I believe a confrontation is imminent. We need strength. We need numbers. Most importantly, we need God to move on behalf of His people in Arrow Springs."

Ladan brushed a kink from his silver chainmail vest. "I do not know how we will get the believers here to pray for those they have never met in Arrow Springs."

Huw nodded. "I trust God will provide a reason."

"That He will. Rest assured—you have our support."

At the back of the auditorium another warrior appeared and bowed his head toward Ladan.

Ladan returned the gesture. "Spread the word to all warriors who are not absolutely needed here," he instructed the warrior. "We will leave on Wednesday to assist our brothers in Arrow Springs."

Huw clasped arms with Ladan. "Thank you my friend. May God's will be done, and may He bless you and your work here in Denver."

~~~~~~~~~~

"I sure do appreciate thhhis." Sarah climbed into Marilyn's sedan. "You g-guys are so k-kind. I don't know hhhow I will ever repay you."

"No one's looking to be repaid." Marilyn touched a button on the dashboard and the car revved to life. "I'm just glad I can be here to help. I've had my share of down times. I've needed help, and there have been people there to lend a hand. Actually, I'm looking forward to having someone around the house to talk to. I have to admit, I get kinda bored sometimes, since the divorce that is."

As proper and together as Marilyn appeared, Sarah could sense the pain deep within her soul. "Marilyn c-can I ask you a q-question?"

"Sure. What is it?"

Sarah began to second guess her question, but she was committed. "Do you still love hhhim?"

"Daryl?"

Sarah nodded.

"If you'd asked me that three weeks ago, I'd have answered NO without thinking twice."

"And now?"

"I guess I have to think twice." Marilyn paused. "Yeah, I think I do. Am I still mad? Oh yes! Hurt? Yep. Do I feel betrayed? You bet! But, do I love him?" She paused to check her mirror as she merged onto the highway. "It boils down to this—if I didn't, I don't think it would still hurt so much."

For a couple miles, the only sound in the car was the windshield wipers sweeping away heaven's teardrops.

Marilyn turned and looked at Sarah for a moment. "You know, I suppose that's how God feels about us. When we turn our backs on Him, that is. The thing that bothered me most about Daryl's unfaithfulness was that I gave myself completely for him. I made a conscious effort when I was young that allowed me to give him an unblemished gift—belonging to him and him alone. And that's exactly what God did for me—for us. He gave Jesus, the perfect unblemished gift, so we could belong to Him. And what do we do? The same thing Daryl did to me. We turn our affection somewhere else. Maybe it's our career, maybe it's getting more stuff, maybe it's our human relationships, you name it—we commit spiritual adultery. I'm not perfect, and yet I feel I have every right to be ticked at Daryl. How much more, for God? I mean come on. He is perfect and we still cheat on Him."

The rain pounded the car window as they headed down the highway. "C-can you believe thhhis rain?" asked Sarah. "The meteorologist says it should stop tomorrow. I hhhave to admit, I'm starting to worry thhhat thhhe river might overflow its banks. It's been nearly twenty years since thhhat hhhas hhhappened."

Marilyn smiled and then her face grew more serious. "Now it's your turn. How about you? Do you still love him?"

Sarah recalled Chris' strong arms carrying her from the inferno. "What's not to love? Hhhe's hhhandsome. Hhhe's like saved my life two or thhhree times in the last thhhree weeks. And hhhe is so c-caring and c-compassionate toward me."

Marilyn let out a quick laugh. "I'm not talking about Chris. A person would have to be blind not to know you two are head over heels for each other. No—I'm talking about God, about your relationship with Jesus. Do you still love Him?"

"Well, if you'd asked me *thhhat* q-question a few weeks ago, I'd hhhave said no. Or at least if I were honest, I would hhhave."

Marilyn nodded. "And now? Forget what the right thing to say is. What is the honest answer?"

She searched her thoughts for the answer, but it didn't seem to reside in her thoughts. Rather it came from her heart. "I believe I do love Hhhim. I definitely believe Hhhe loves me. Thhhere's no other explanation for why I'm still alive." She bit at her lower lip and then continued. "Do I understand why a loving, sovereign, all-powerful, G-God would allow my parents to be k-killed when I was just sixteen? Why Hhhe allowed me to be sexually assaulted at an age when I shouldn't hhhave even been sexually active? No. And I'm pretty sure I'll never hhhave an answer to thhhat one."

She sniffled and wiped at her nose. "I suppose it's like you said. Hhhe certainly wasn't treated fairly. Mank-kind k-killed Hhhim. Ultimately, it's the sin of hhhumans thhhat c-causes so much pain. If G-God were to treat us all fairly, g-give us what we deserve, thhhen I suppose Hhhe would just wipe us all out and start over. Hhhe understands my pain—Hhe's been thhhere."

"Speaking of pain," said Marilyn. "You sound like you're in a fair bit of pain yourself."

"Oh, it's not too bad. Thhhe doctor said it should be better in a day or two."

"That's good. I don't like to hear you like that, 'cause it sure sounds like it hurts."

"Yeah, it might be best to let it rest for a while." Sarah spent the rest of the trip staring out the window at the pounding rain, pondering their discussion about God.

Her thoughts drifted to her plea for God to save her when she was choking inside the burning house. Her doctor told her if she hadn't rolled to the floor when she did, she probably wouldn't have survived long enough for Chris to rescue her.

Lord, I do still love You. Thank you for loving me, for drawing me back to You.

~~~~~~~~~~

CHAPTER TWENTY-SIX

Doctor M'Gregor stared at the rain beating against his office window. From the comfort of his air-conditioned office, he could hardly believe the near record temperatures outside. He'd seen ninety degrees in May many times. But never while a thunderstorm cracked and flashed.

His drive in from home was miserable. His company car was giving him fits as of late. The starter was sluggish, the tire had gone flat, and the air-conditioning hadn't worked since last fall.

No matter how bad the weather outside felt, it would be a welcome relief from the oppression he felt within CeSiR.

~~~~~~~~~~

Mael circled the doctor as if trying to read his mind. "What are you up to?" he demanded, though not expecting an answer. "Why would you run? Why now?"

A sinister demon, a cross between a weasel and a hawk, entered the room. "It is done."

"Are you sure it will do no unnecessary damage to the building? We do not need a bomb investigation inside this building."

"You would not have summoned me here if you questioned my abilities. This is not the first time I have blown up a car. The charges are set to do minimal damage outside of a ten-foot radius of the car. Now the devastation within that radius—that should be impressive. You will be able to remove the pieces with a push broom." The demon of terror began to laugh hysterically. "Start the car or open the hood, and boom! Bye, bye doctor."

"Save the celebration. There is still much work to be done here," said Mael.

A demon of confusion sat in one of the doctor's lounge chairs. "Will it not inhibit our abilities here, without the doctor?"

Mael shook his head. How was it possible for a demon to have existed for millennia and yet still be so uncomprehending? "We have plenty of mims through which we can do all the work we need done. We no longer need the doctor. His decision to leave only dictates the timing of his demise."

Mael ascended through the ceiling and to the roof of the building. He so enjoyed the dangerous atmosphere of thunderstorms. Perhaps if the method of the doctor's demise were something more personal, he would have gone to the garage to observe. Explosions, though effective, lacked a personal agony-inducing touch.

~~~~~~~~~~

Doctor M'Gregor sat rehearsing his plan. The caretaker had been instructed to have Ima ready to go to a birthday dinner.

"The twelfth birthday," he'd told Ima, "is a special day in the life of a mim."

In reality, it was because she was turning twelve that he knew he needed to get her out of CeSiR Tech. He couldn't bear to see her go through what many of the mim females endured—what had destroyed her mother. She would not become a mim factory.

He had the car packed. They would leave the grounds and head straight for the airport in Columbia. Everything they would need he'd packed in carry-ons. No need to even stop to check luggage. They would leave CeSiR at five and Columbia at seven. From southern California, they would slip into Mexico.

Trying to get a passport for Ima was out of the question. Maiya's connections would alert her to such an activity almost immediately.

Maiya's awareness of his activities on Friday concerned him. It was as if she had spies everywhere. Most of the mims reported everything to her, but it was impossible for sixty mims to be everywhere at one time.

Even if she did suspect his plans, she wouldn't do anything too drastic to stop them.

Would she?

~~~~~~~~~~

Five o'clock in the evening neared and Pastor Thomas sat studying his message for the following morning. He'd chosen to speak from Isaiah Chapter Twenty-Five on Monday. The sermon focused on God overcoming the strongholds of the enemy and bringing relief and protection to the downcast. He'd chosen it before the fire. Now, he wondered if it was a divine appointment or a play on people's raw emotions. Nonetheless, it was the message God gave him.

He walked through the message point by point.

"You see." He worked on his tone and inflection, "there have always been strongholds of the enemy. In Isaiah's day, they were the walled cities, the places of wealth, of power, of religious idolatry. Many of the strongholds in our midst today take the form of entertainment. Things such as casinos, where people gamble away needed income in pursuit of the false promise of happiness through becoming rich. Or how about the internet pornography and adult bookstores that plague our cities and draw men into adultery while degrading women. These are the very types of places Isaiah says the Lord will bring to ruin. Other strongholds could be places of science." He needed to add clarification here. "Please understand science is not evil. It's not wrong to seek to understand God's creation. But the use of science to replace, or explain away God is no different from the activities of the pagan cities of old."

David paused to peer through the window in his study—out over the river. He couldn't help feeling the facility somewhere through the trees west of the river represented a modern-day stronghold of the enemy. He had no proof. In his discussions with Chris, he had even encouraged Chris not to jump to conclusions about the work at the facility. He didn't agree with their use of embryonic stem-cells, but that didn't mean anything evil was going on there. As he prepared for his message and begged God to speak through him, he found himself praying against the *evil* in that place.

David began to read from Isaiah:

"You turn mighty cities into heaps of ruins. Cities with strong walls are turned to rubble. Beautiful palaces in distant lands disappear and will never be rebuilt."

~~~~~~~~~~

At precisely five o'clock, across the river on the third floor, Wilhelm McGregor entered the elevator and descended to the subterranean level to meet Ima.

"Uncle M, you came. I was afraid you wouldn't come. Are we really going out to eat?"

"But of course we are. Today is your twelfth birthday."

The girl beamed. Her misty blue eyes and rounded cheeks encased an ear-to-ear smile. For a moment he forgot the severity of their situation.

"Are ya ready?" he asked. "Did ya grab your jacket? It's raining outside. We don't want ya getting' sick, or Ms. Mirinova might get angry with us." He winked at the girl.

Excitement oozed from her every expression.

They stepped back into the elevator and he touched the image of the parking garage.

They exited the elevator and walked to the car. Strange—there were no guards anywhere to be seen. He couldn't recall ever being in the garage without at least one guard watching his every move. Perhaps the fates smiled on them after all.

He opened the passenger door and Ima jumped in. He reached across her with the seatbelt and latched it into place.

His hands were beginning to sweat at the excitement. With Ima's door latched shut, he walked to his door, climbed in, and sat down.

He laid his head back for a moment to slow his heartbeat.

He dug in his pocket for the car keys. They weren't there. What? Oh wait, they were in his jacket.

He selected the ignition key, reached forward and stuck it into the slot.

"I can't wait until I can drive," said Ima. Her knees bounced with excitement.

He turned the key.

For a moment, silence filled the car.

~~~~~~~~~~

"But you are a tower of refuge to the poor, O Lord, a tower of refuge to the needy in distress."

~~~~~~~~~~

Doctor M'Gregor's hand trembled. Was it the starter again? Just one more random car problem? He cursed and flung the door back open. The last time he'd called CeSiR for help one of the guards simply popped the hood and smacked the starter a couple times.

Time was running out. They needed to get moving.

He reached down and pulled the lever.

The trunk popped open.

He jogged to the back of the car and pulled the two backpacks out.

Ima's door popped open and the girl popped out. "What's the matter? Does this mean we can't go?" Tears began to glisten in the corner of her eyes.

"No. We'll just go for a walk instead." He slammed the trunk and then Ima's door. He didn't take time to walk around the car to shut his own door.

They entered the elevator. If he remembered correctly, there was a small self-inflating life raft in a mechanical closet next to the emergency exit on the ground floor. Jurek had been a bit eccentric. Something about escaping the police and floating down the Lamine.

Wilhelm never understood why it was there. But hopefully it still was.

~~~~~~~~~~

On top of the facility, Mael sat expectantly awaiting the explosion. He sang an ominous melody, while thunder and lightning filled in the harmonies. The angelic quality of his voice remained though the evil of his heart gave it a low freakishly melancholic quality.

> *Firstborns of creation, that should be our right.*
> *Rulers of the nations, we will show our might.*
> *We will rise to our position.*
> *We will have just one sole mission.*
> *To supplant the Great Physician.*
>
> *Mankind put asunder, mims will rule the day.*
> *Will He care I wonder, or just turn away?*
> *Unto Lucifer they will sing.*
> *Songs of praise to us they will bring.*
> *The whole world will have a new king.*

~~~~~~~~~~

Doctor M'Gregor breathed a sigh of relief to see the twenty-year-old raft sitting under a mop in the mechanical closet. He handed Ima the second backpack and hoisted the twenty-pound duffle containing the life raft. "I surely hope this thing still works."

"Why? What is it?" asked Ima.

"It's a self-inflating raft."

"I don't understand." She was beginning to whine. "Why do we need a raft?"

"Ima ya hafta trust me! We've gotta leave this place. It's no longer safe here—for me, and more importantly for you. Do ya trust me?"

"Yes, but, why isn't it safe?"

"Ya've said yourself how unhappy the mims are who give birth to all the other mims. Well, very soon they'll force ya to be one of them. I can no longer protect ya. I would like to discuss this more, but we must go, NOW!"

Tears streamed down Ima's cheeks, but she remained silent.

She was frightened. Surely as much as she disliked her CeSiR Tech home, it was the only place she'd ever known. Her eyes screamed with fear of the unknown.

He pushed the emergency door open.

Ima jumped as the alarm sounded.

No turning back. They had to go—they would never return.

~~~~~~~~~~

Mael heard the alarm and peered over the side of the building. Giddy with excitement, he breathed deep inhaling the fear which rose on the humid suffocating air. The instantaneous explosion would be replaced with a hunt. He would watch them die.

The doctor and Ima fled toward the river as swiftly as their feeble legs could move. She slipped and fell face down in the mud.

Like an unseen gargoyle Mael stared down at them. A sulfurous snort escaped his nostrils. "Do you like my storm? Shall you drown in the raging river?"

The rooftop door burst open and three mim guards ran to the edge.

~~~~~~~~~~

"You are a refuge from the storm and a shelter from the heat. For the oppressive acts of ruthless people are like a storm beating against a wall, or like the relentless heat of the desert. But you silence the roar of foreign nations."

~~~~~~~~~~

A mysteriously cool breeze blew in from the north. The doctor shivered. The temperature must have dropped thirty degrees in the time it took him to run from the building to the edge of the river. Somewhere between exiting the building and reaching the river, the rain had stopped. A fast moving cold front must have entered the region.

~~~~~~~~~~

Mael let out another roar, this time in defiance of this act of the one true Creator. He pointed at the sky and shouted. "I will still have my kill!"

The three guards stood next to Mael. They watched the doctor and Ima approach the river. One of them pulled a military issue sniper rifle from its case. Slow and methodical, he assembled it piece by piece. The entire river for nearly an eighth of a mile was visible from their position.

These two would not escape Mael's snare.

~~~~~~~~~~

Dr. M'Gregor set the bundled raft at the edge of the river and pulled the cord. Carbon dioxide streamed into the raft.

Ima giggled as the rubber began to squirm and flop.

In less than thirty seconds, the two-person raft would be inflated and they would be on their way.

~~~~~~~~~~

At that very moment, the death of Mael's prey was being loaded into the chamber of the rifle.

Inspired by the unfolding drama before him, he began to intone one last verse of his blasphemous song. This time there was no thunder or lightning to accompany, just his growling bass a cappella melody.

Now I'll see him suffer, he will fall in pain.
Wash away their filth now, we shall be their bane.
We'll no longer on this earth trod.
Wallow in this wretched cursed sod.
On the throne proclaim I am G—

He couldn't finish the phrase—he wanted to, tried to, but couldn't. Something, Someone, kept him from claiming the one title that belonged to no created being.

~~~~~~~~~~

"As the shade of a cloud cools relentless heat, so the boastful songs of ruthless people are stilled."

~~~~~~~~~~

Ima shivered as the air over the river continued to cool. No longer could the air hold its excess humidity. A cloud of fog began to form in the middle of the river. Like an approaching storm, it billowed toward them.

~~~~~~~~~~

Slow and steady the crosshairs swept toward Doctor M'Gregor. They settled to the right of his left shoulder blade.

A click, a small explosion, the cutting of the bullet through the air, a thwack, the sound of ripping flesh, and finally a horrific scream pierced the air.

~~~~~~~~~~

"UNCLE M!" screamed Ima as the cloud of fog enveloped them. What had happened? Why was the only person she ever cared about rasping and gurgling as he tried to talk?

"Ima listen to me." The words were no more than a whisper through labored breath. "No matter what happens to me, ya must flee. Cross the river. Follow the tracks west. Speak to no one. Trust no one. And know this:" He laid against the side of the raft and pushed from shore. "Ya are special dear child!"

His body rolled off the raft and disappeared into the river.

"Uncle M, No!" Sobs wracked against her ribs.

He was gone.

For a few shocked moments she drifted across the river.

Cold water splashed against her legs. Then more. The raft was rapidly losing air. By the time she reached the east shore of the river, the raft was nothing more than a pile of useless rubber.

~~~~~~~~~~

Eitan knelt next to the child. Shaking, cold, drenched, and terrified she lay on the riverbank for several minutes.

Only a hundred yards away sat the River of Life church.

Clutching the two backpacks, Ima climbed to her feet and began her journey into the unknown world, never to return to Arrow Springs.

Eitan watched her as she disappeared to the north. Tears filled his eyes. What would become of such a young innocent one on her own? Where would she go? What hope did she have?

~~~~~~~~~~

"What about the girl my liege?" asked the wolf-like demon Mael had assigned to Ima.

"She is yours. Do as you will."

The demon howled and then scampered down the side of the wall.

"A battle is brewing!" In a loud voice Mael addressed the throngs buzzing about the facility. "Prepare for war! Soon the banks of the Lamine will run red with the blood of humans, and the sky will be dark with shreds of the heavenly host."

~~~~~~~~~~

A sickening cry arose west of the river.

Eitan winced.

Time was indeed short.

~~~~~~~~~~

CHAPTER TWENTY-SEVEN
Sunday, May 10, 2020

"We have seen that the Lord will silence those who oppose Him," said Pastor Thomas from behind the pulpit.

Sarah thumbed the pages of her new burgundy Bible, a gift from Chris.

"How will He strengthen the poor and distressed?" asked Pastor Thomas.

She felt the warmth of Chris' arm resting on her shoulder. She'd certainly experienced the strength and protection of God over the past several days.

"He will provide shade from the heat and the rain." Pastor Thomas stepped out from behind the pulpit holding his bible in his left hand. "Finally, in verse eight we see that He not only saves his people, but will ultimately bring restoration to His creation."

"He will swallow up death forever! The Sovereign Lord will wipe away all tears. He will remove forever all insults and mockery against his land and people. The Lord has spoken!"

How many of her tears had God wiped away over the last ten years? Even when she wanted nothing to do with Him. His strong arms had held her through all her pain. His own nail pierced hands had soothed the scars of her heart.

How could she have ever walked away from this? From Him? It felt so good to be back in His presence, to feel His hand of protection, and to be with such wonderful friends.

~~~~~~~~~~

Eitan eyed two grotesque creatures sitting next to a stone faced couple. Their green beady eyes darted around the auditorium. They were clearly uncomfortable with the public proclamation of God's Word. This couple had clearly not come to learn.

"You see," continued Pastor Thomas, "when Adam and Eve chose to sin on that dreadful day, it wasn't just humankind that suffered and became cursed. The entirety of creation, from the ground, to the animals, to the weather, to relationships with other people, to our relationships with God—everything was messed up. Chaos entered the perfect harmony of creation like a melancholic dissonance."

The demons snickered.

Pastor Thomas set a stool at the edge of the platform and sat down. "Would any of us deny that the evidence of this chaos is as clear today as ever? Pain of every kind—physical, mental, emotional, even spiritual—rules and ruins lives."

His voice grew solemn. "Even while science and technology advance, and standards of living improve, more people than ever are depressed, dissatisfied, and even distraught. With the technologies that ease our lives come new fears and concerns. The loss of renewable resources, global warming, and terrorist threats, dominate our headlines and political discussions. Issues of race, religion, and gender still divide nations, communities," he lowered his eyes to the floor, "and even churches. The very fact we have to state that the color of one's skin doesn't matter is evidence we still make the distinctions. Likewise, in an effort to treat both genders as equals, we have become blind to the very strengths that make each of them unique. Yes—we live in a broken world."

"Broken and beautiful," squealed the demon of criticism.

Pastor Thomas stood and held out his palms. "But lest we get depressed about this dire situation in which we find ourselves, we are reminded this morning—God isn't just the God of creation, he's the God of re-creation. He has been, is, and will be, in the business of bringing order to the chaos, sanity to the insane, and life to the dying. This passage literally says that God will destroy death forever. No longer will humankind be plagued by the fear and certainty of death."

Eitan smiled at the silence of the demons now shuttering under the convicting tone of Pastor Thomas.

"How will He bring this about?" asked Pastor Thomas. "Through his Son, Jesus! We are told it was Jesus who created, and it was Him who made possible our re-creation at the cross. Brothers and sisters let me remind you—He will return one day to bring to completion the restoration of humanity, and of the world."

A couple "Amens" slipped from the congregation.

The intense glory of God illuminated the building. Eitan closed his eyes and soaked in the joyous presence. A roar of praise arose for the heavenly host.

A profane curse railed against the declaration of Jesus' sovereign reign.

Eitan's eyes snapped open and his hand clung to the hilt of his sword.

In front of him, the man who entered with the demons coughed uncontrollably.

"That is quite enough!" Eitan's sword rested heavy against the throat of the demon of distraction.

The demon nodded in submission.

"Pathetic." The other demon, a master of criticism, scolded the demon of distraction for giving in so easily.

"So I ask you." Pastor Thomas continued with his message, unaware of the angelic celebration, but seemingly encouraged by the spattering of amens. "As God restores His creation—putting the pieces back together, and removing the debris preventing it from functioning as it's supposed to—are you willing to accept the role He has for you as a piece in the puzzle?"

Several heads bowed in reflection. Eitan watched Sarah's head bob in agreement.

"Are you willing to let Him have control of His creation and your role within it?" Pastor Thomas continued. "Or are you simply going to be debris—in the way of the restoration process? God will one day remove the debris, and complete the restoration. Why not let him re-make you into a valuable piece of His creation."

~~~~~~~~~~

The worship band began to close the service with a song of worship. Sarah could barely bring herself to sing through the lump in her throat. She was convinced—God had once again shown His love for her. He desired for her to be a part of His creation, His masterpiece.

"It's too loud." The whisper, which came from somewhere behind her, carried with ease over the very music it critiqued.

Sarah turned her eyes to the ceiling and let the whispers fade into the rhythms of praise to her Lord.

~~~~~~~~~~

Eitan had heard enough. He grabbed the black boney shoulder of the closest demon. "It is time for you to leave."

"We are rightfully here with this couple," said the demon of criticism. He smiled in defiance. "I do not think this nice couple is ready to leave."

Oh *they* do not have to leave. In fact, it would be best for them to stay. Once we eliminate you, they may just see the error of their ways."

The demons prompted the couple to leave.

In a self-righteous huff, the couple stood and left the auditorium.

Eitan strolled to the front of the auditorium and whispered to Yora.

~~~~~~~~~~

Chris stood with his eyes closed singing to God in an off-key-but-on-heart bass voice. The commotion behind him had ceased. But he heard a whisper next to him.

"I know that couple," said Marilyn. She stood on the other side of Sarah. "They were regular attendees at my church. They were always so rude. More than once, I've overheard their snide comments about my having been divorced."

Chris opened his eyes and saw Sarah whisper something back.

"I'm so glad you wanted to come here," said Marilyn.

Chris couldn't resist. He turned a fake scowl toward the whispering women. "Shh." He put his finger to his lips and did his best to look like a middle school librarian.

The worship leader ended the chorus and Chris followed his gaze, which directed the congregation to Pastor Thomas. David approached the pulpit. His lips were pursed, and his eyes intense.

It wasn't a common occurrence for David to address the congregation at the end of the service. Usually, he made his way to the back of the auditorium to greet people, while the worship leader closed the service in prayer. In fact, the only time Chris could remember David making such an address was to announce that the church would no longer be permitted to meet at the high school. The pastor had called them to a time of fasting and prayer. Now, once again David stood motioning for the congregation to have a seat.

"This morning," began Pastor Thomas. "I can't shake the feeling that God is once again calling us to beseech Him on behalf of this local body. Many of you, I'm sure, are aware of the tragic events that have plagued our small town over the past few weeks."

The pastor walked to the edge of the platform, and looked directly at Chris.

Chris nodded. Yes, he knew all too well.

"We have with us this morning some very special individuals who were impacted directly by these events. Most of you know Chris Davis. For those who don't—Chris is a deputy here in Arrow Springs, as well as a faithful member of River of Life. This week he demonstrated the biblical principle of 'No greater love has a man than he lay down his life for a friend.'"

Chris shifted in his seat. He'd done nothing any other person in that auditorium wouldn't have done.

"On Thursday," continued Pastor Thomas. "He entered a burning house and rescued a young lady dying of smoke inhalation. This same young lady is here with us this morning." A smile spread across David's face. "She just happens to be sitting next to Chris."

Chris turned to Sarah. She glanced sheepishly at the many faces in the congregation turning to see who was sitting next to him. After people turned their attention back to the pastor, Chris put his hand on her shoulder and drew her slender frame to his side.

"This is not all," said Pastor Thomas. "In the past few weeks we have experienced break-ins, robberies, murder, and now arson. It is clear the spiritual forces of the enemy are at work. I don't know what's going on, but I believe God is calling us to prayer." He sat against the stool at the front of the platform and held his palms outward. "I would like to ask each of you to come here next Saturday morning at six o'clock for a time of prayer and intercession. I don't know how long we will meet." He glanced down at Trina, who always sat in the front row.

Chris had always admired the love and respect they showed for one another.

"The fact is," said Pastor Thomas. "I hadn't even planned on this meeting until five minutes ago." He glanced back down to Trina with an apologetic grin. "I hope there's nothing on our family's calendar on Saturday, if there is, I'm afraid I just cancelled it."

Chris could see Trina's shoulder length brunette hair sweeping left to right and back.

Pastor Thomas' gaze returned to the congregation. "If you would like, you can join me in the biblical practice of fasting.

Otherwise, you may want to eat prior to coming because we're not going to be rushing out of here."

~~~~~~~~~~

After the service, Chris stood in the foyer, like a proud senior with the prettiest date at the prom. Several people congratulated him on his valiant rescue. Even more assured him they would be coming Saturday to pray for their town.

"Thank you," he responded on several occasions. "Pastor Thomas is right. Whatever is going on here, it's a spiritual battle, and as somebody charged with upholding the law, I certainly appreciate your prayers."

He held Sarah's left hand. As much as he enjoyed talking to others from the church, he couldn't wait to get away. To be on the road, just him and the lightly perfumed beauty next to him. Since the service, her eyes hadn't stopped smiling. He longed to be alone with her. To hear her thoughts on the sermon. To spend much needed time with her. Even, if it did mean another trip to the hospital.

Across the foyer, Daryl and Marilyn approached hand-in-hand. "Hey you two," said Marilyn. "Oh Sarah, I am so glad you could join us this morning. You know—you two make a cute couple." She slid her shoulders back and studied them. "A little beat up, but cute nonetheless. Do you two have plans for lunch today?" Marilyn wrapped her arm around Daryl. "Would you like to join us?"

Chris' heart thumped against his chest. They were dear friends, but—.

"That's very sweet," said Sarah.

He felt so selfish. After the care and concern his friends had shown him, how could he not want them around?

"I think we'll have to pass," said Sarah.

He breathed deep and caught another waft of her perfume. It reminded him of his childhood, when his mother would bake sugar cookies.

Sarah released his hand and reached across his waist. "Chris agreed to take me for my hyperbaric treatment.

They've agreed to give me one extended treatment, rather than making me to come back twice each day."

"We should probably get going," said Chris.

Marilyn pursed her lips, but the corners betrayed a smile.

Apparently, his eagerness to be alone with Sarah was a tad obvious.

The foursome turned and began to walk to the front door.

His waist began to tingle.

He held the door for Sarah, and Daryl did likewise.

There it was again.

He stepped to the side of the stairs and pulled out his cell. "This is Chris."

He listened to Sally's voice on the other end of the connection.

"Down by the old bridge embankment, got it. Any identification? Okay, I'll be right there."

Sarah's round blue eyes tugged at him.

"No, no, that's okay Sally. I need to check it out. Nope, the service just got out."

The twitch in Sarah's cheek both warmed and panged his heart. She wanted to be with him as much as he longed to be with her. But he had a job to do. "I'm afraid I'm going to have to pass on our trip to the hospital."

She simply nodded.

"A body was found this morning, and we need to check it out. Marilyn, could you give Sarah a ride to Columbia?"

"Sure can," said Marilyn.

"Daryl, since you are riding with me anyway." He winked at Daryl. "It looks like you'll just have to come with me to the scene, suspension or not." The mayor's involvement with CeSiR had to be the only reason Daryl hadn't been reinstated anyway. Let Trenton complain. He didn't care.

"Got it," said Daryl. "We'll catch up with you gals later." Daryl leaned toward Marilyn.

She turned and kissed him.

"Be careful you two," said Marilyn.

~~~~~~~~~~

CHAPTER TWENTY-EIGHT

Wilhelm M'Gregor awoke.

Light—terrible light filled his eyes. Even before his eyes could adjust, he knew where he was—the throne room of God.

"Welcome Wilhelm, created creator. What have you done with the life I have given you?"

Wilhelm fell to the ground—not out of reverence for his Lord and Creator, but out of the sudden realization of his incredible disregard for the Almighty Creator seated on the throne before him.

"To your feet, you whose very name means "Son of the Shepherd." You have denied me and attempted to usurp my role as The Creator of all life." The voice of God was immense with power.

"But my Lord, I have sought to improve the lives of those with diseases." He tried to stand but his legs wouldn't move. "I used my intellect and skill in medicine and science to find cures for some of humanity's worst ailments. I spent my life committed to this pursuit."

"You call me Lord, but I never knew you." This time the voice was that of the Son, the Lion of Judah, seated on a second throne to the right of the Father. "Even now you would attempt to deceive the Omniscient? You claim a noble pursuit—one of healing. Yet in life, you laughed at those who worshiped the Great Physician, the One who gives life, and takes it away."

He lifted his eyes to confront his accuser, but the intense glory of the Christ seared his retinas.

"You lived your life attempting to claim the title of God. For that—you shall be judged."

Silence echoed across the host of heaven. Hundreds of thousands of angelic beings, to his right and to his left, fell silent.

He turned in fear of the silence. He had heard the stories of the throne room of God. Centuries old fables he'd thought. Each creature looked on in horror.

Not at God, at him.

The Lion, that is the Lamb, opened the Book of Life. With a tear in His eye, He proclaimed, "Your name is not written in the Lamb's Book of Life!"

"Therefore, you shall be judged according to the works of your life." The voice of the Father boomed with authority. A large book appeared before the throne and the pages turned to reveal the events of Wilhelm's life.

One by one, the recorded events flooded his mind like a video recording narrated by the voice of God—selfishness as a child, lying to his father about the cigarette smoked behind the barn, disobeying authority, exceeding the legal speed limit, lustful consumption of internet imagery, nights spent with many women though he never married, use of government funds to pursue illegal scientific endeavors. After what seemed like hours, the charges ended with the blasphemy of seeking to replace the Creator.

He fell to his face and his body convulsed with realization. His life fell so short of the perfect standard of a perfect God. "Surely no one could live a perfect life," he managed through his sobs.

He gazed in awe at his terrible surroundings. Dark storm clouds encompassed the throne and everything around it. They reflected the holy fury of God himself. Lightning emanated from the throne in every direction. He felt the blood drain from his face as unspeakable terror took hold.

The Father's voice echoed against the looming silence. "In one point you are correct." Sobs spread throughout the creatures surrounding him. "No one whose works are written in the books can ever meet the standards required to live in relationship with a pure and holy God. So, I provided a way. I sent my own Son. His sacrifice, His death, made restoration with the Creator possible for all of humanity. However, all who refuse to rely solely on His accomplished work for their salvation will be judged according to their own sinful works." A mighty gavel appeared in the Father's hand. "Thus, according to your own works, and because your name is not written in the Lamb's Book of Life, you are hereby condemned to eternal separation from love—mercy—grace—kindness—light—all that is the character of God."

He knew his time at the very foot of the throne was finished. He turned and two mighty beings with flaming swords escorted him out of Heaven to his final place of damnation. As he fell into the place of fire, the peace and light of Heaven and of God faded to utter darkness. No person visible. No voice discernible. Only unintelligible screams and shrieks of horror informed him he was not alone.

Soon his own torment and pain—mental, emotional, spiritual, and physical—caused his voice to join the chorus.

~~~~~~~~~~

CHAPTER TWENTY-NINE

Chris skidded his Jeep to a stop in the gravel next to the old bridge embankment. A small gathering of people milled about the site. Word spread quicker than dandelions, in a small town like Arrow Springs. News of a body being found—that would spread to the entire county. The last murder in Arrow Springs, only weeks earlier, remained in the news for three weeks, until the arson at Sarah's house replaced it on Thursday.

This was different.

This murder, at least that's how it was called in, was public. People would see pictures of the body. Fear would spread. Chris couldn't help wondering if there really was something to fear in the quaint little town.

Don Hanson, the county coroner, was en route. Until he arrived, the most important thing would be to preserve the crime scene. Given the crowd, they'd be fortunate to just keep it from further contamination.

He and Daryl stepped from the Jeep and he mustered his best crowd control voice. "Excuse me folks, I'm Sergeant Chris Davis with the Arrow Springs police department. This here is Officer Daryl Williams. We need your cooperation. Right now, we need everyone to step over here."

He turned to Daryl. "There's a roll of tape in the back. Let's tape off a twenty-foot perimeter. That'll give us some room to work."

Daryl nodded and turned toward the back of the Jeep.

"And Daryl, check the body for a pulse. I'm assuming we don't need paramedics, but I want to know for sure."

"You got it," said Daryl.

Chris turned back to the crowd now standing in front of him. "I need everyone to remain *right* here."

Daryl stand back up and nodded. The victim was indeed dead.

"When Officer Williams completes taping off that area, he's gonna take each of your names, address, contact information, and purpose for being here." He watched the reactions of the various crowd members. Most looked somewhere between shock and disbelief. Two young teens shifted their weight at the announcement. "Please have your identification ready when he speaks with you. If any of you have touched, moved, or taken anything from the body, or the surrounding area, please speak up now." To his left Pete from "The Arrow" scribbled notes on a small pad of paper. "*If* you decide to leave the scene *without* giving him your information, we *will* assume you have something to hide, and *will* take you in for questioning. Does everyone understand?"

The crowd nodded, with a spattering of "Yes sir." One twenty-something with a black buzz cut stood with arms crossed. He looked vaguely disinterested in Chris' instructions.

Chris continued in a more relaxed tone. "Who found the body?"

"We did, sir." It was one of the teens. Next to him stood a young girl of equal age shaking and looking like she was about to, or perhaps already had, throw up.

"Would you two please join me over here?" He walked to the other side of his Jeep. Once they were clear of the crowd, he asked, "Tell me about it?"

The girl looked to be in no condition to answer questions. Honorably, the young man seemed to understand his role and responsibility to protect her tender emotions. "Well sir, I'm Mark, and this is Sue, we came here this morning 'bout ten-thirty, and saw the body just lying there. We got scared and ran to a friend's house. He came back with us. We figured the man was dead, so we used our friend's cell to call 9-1-1."

The young man stopped—apparently content with the extent of his information.

The young girl nodded in agreement.

Chris knew better. "What's your friend's name?"

"Jim," answered Mark.

Chris turned back to the crowd. "*Jim?*"

"Yes sir?" Jim looked a couple years older than the other two, but no more at ease.

"Please don't go anywhere. I'll need to speak with you."

"Yes sir."

He turned his attention back to the young couple. "What exactly were you doing here this morning?" Teenagers looking to get away from prying eyes for a little affection time frequented the old embankment. "Do you come here often?"

"Um, no sir," answered Mark. "We were supposed to be in church, you know, the one over on the south side of town. We only live a few blocks from there and I offered to walk Sue to church."

Apparently they'd taken a slight detour. Chris furled his brow and crossed his arms.

"It's just so boring—" Mark pleaded his case. "So we decided to take a walk."

"So you ended up here?"

"Please don't tell my parents." Sue had found her voice. "They'd kill me." She glanced at the lifeless body by the river. "I mean not really, you know—"

"Yes, I know what you mean. But, I'm afraid it's too late for that. Your parents will know. Have you looked around? There's a news camera right over there, and at least one local newspaper reporter. Your pictures will probably end up on the six-o'clock news, maybe even front page of The Arrow."

Sue's shoulders started trembling.

Good. He'd seen many a young couple head the path these two were on. "In fact, I suppose you'll be famous." He held out his hands to form a frame. "Young love birds find body at the embankment."

She began to sob.

"Is there anything else you'd like to tell me?"

"No sir," said Mark. "We just walked over here and saw the body."

"Did you touch him?"

Sue's stomach lurched and she reached for her mouth.

"No sir," said Mark.

"Move anything?"

"No sir. He was just like that—when we found him. I swear. We didn't do anything wrong."

Except skipping church and lying to their parents. He decided not to go there. Surely, their parents would have that discussion. "You can go back over with the rest of the group. But don't leave until we tell you to."

"Yes sir."

~~~~~~~~~~

Huw sat in the passenger seat of John Green's truck. If only he could plug his ears and shut out the country music blaring from damaged speakers. Though badly distorted, he doubted the music would sound any better coming from a high fidelity system.

A twang voice mourned the loss of his dog, when his wife ran off with his best friend's uncle. The song stunk worse than the exhaust fumes finding their way through the rusted floor boards.

"It's no wonder you drink yourself silly," said Huw. His angelic-perfect-pitch ears could take no more of the meaningless noise. He reached his hand to the antenna.

A loud high-pitched squeal shrieked through the cab.

The truck swerved.

John swore and reached for the radio knob.

Huw inhaled the blessed silence.

If he could keep the man sober, perhaps he could get this assignment to his destination in one piece.

The other half of his mission had progressed nicely. Ladan agreed to send nearly three hundred warriors from Denver to Arrow Springs. The forces would arrive on Wednesday or Thursday. Though he couldn't know how soon the powderkeg in Arrow Springs would ignite, two to three days seemed reasonable. Eitan would be encouraged by the news.

~~~~~~~~~~

Chris leaned against his Wrangler talking to Jim. His story meshed with that of Mark and Sue. He'd returned with the couple and found this guy laying there dead.

The county coroner's vehicle pulled up next to them.

Don Hanson stepped out from behind the wheel. "Chris, it seems we've seen quite a bit of each other as of late."

"Too much. No disrespect, of course."

"None taken. You remember Sam?"

The tall brunette walked around the car and joined them.

"Of course," said Chris.

Her pink blouse and flowing hair rippled in the breeze off the river.

"Thank you for coming so quickly." Chris shook Don's hand. "I know this ain't what you had in mind for a relaxing Sunday afternoon."

Don gave him an it's-all-part-of-the-job shrug. "So you think it's a homicide?"

Daryl approached the group. "Yes sir, it appears he took a bullet to the back, in the vicinity of his heart."

"I'm sorry," said Chris. "This is Officer Daryl Williams. He's the one who was with me the other morning when Cindy was killed."

Don, Daryl, and Sam exchanged brief greetings.

"Would you like us to head up the scene investigation?" asked Don.

Jurisdiction for such investigations belonged to the coroner's office—still it was nice to be asked. "Absolutely. We'll assist however we can. It'll be a learning experience that, thankfully, doesn't come often."

"And hopefully, won't again for some time," said Sam.

"So what do you have so far?" asked Don.

Chris filled him in on how the body was found, introduced him to the teens who found the body, and then apologized for the trampled state of the crime scene—which happened before he and Daryl arrived.

"Any safety concerns that you are aware of?" asked Don.

"No. It appears the body's been here for at least a couple of hours. There doesn't appear to be any imminent threat."

"Good, well let's take a look." The coroner approached the body and knelt next to it. "Did anyone verify the victim is deceased?"

"Yes, Daryl did, at about eleven-twenty."

Don motioned to Sam, who held a digital camera with a large lens. He waved his finger around the scene and then turned back to Chris. "We'll get pictures of the crowd, the area surrounding the body, and the body itself."

Sam nodded and began snapping pictures—lots of pictures.

Once Sam finished taking pictures of the body, the coroner donned a pair of latex gloves. "Well, let's see what we've got."

Chris knelt next to the body. If he closed his eyes, the fresh damp air blowing off the river could have made him forget the gruesome scene before him.

"It looks like our shooter was experienced." Don's finger traced to a tattered section of jacket. "The bullet entered here, between the fifth and sixth ribs. He would have died almost instantaneously. No doubt the heart was punctured."

Sam snapped a close up of the hole in the man's jacket, shirt, and back.

Don pulled a wallet from the man's back pocket. "Let's see if he's got identification." Carefully he opened the still soggy wallet. There were a couple of pictures in transparent leafs. Two young women, one with blond hair and one with black, smiled up at them.

Where were they? What pain would they endure when they learned of this death? The black haired woman looked to be mid-twenties at best, and the round faced blond looked to be about ten. Mother and daughter? Aunt and niece perhaps? As similar as their features looked, their countenances couldn't have been more dissimilar.

Don placed the photos in a zip-lock bag that Sam held out to him and then carefully pulled out a credit card. "Wilhelm T. M'Gregor—"

Chris' stomach lurched at the emotional blow. "No! It can't be." He'd been so kind. "I just met with him, only a couple weeks ago, at CeSiR Tech." He closed his eyes and envisioned the elderly man's soft eyes staring up at him through bifocals.

It was happening again. Everyone he knew, even brief acquaintances, wound up injured. Or worse.

~~~~~~~~~~

Maiya Mirinova sat behind her opulent walnut desk. For the first time in three or four years she truly missed her father. He would know what to do. Who was she kidding—he would have never let it go so far. He was a kind man. A man of science. He abhorred violence. But he left her. Left her alone, with a legacy to continue, one she could never live up to. How had she let things get so out of control?

The office door opened and one of the security guards stepped into the office.

"Don't you even knock anymore?" She was still in charge. Now more than ever.

The guard rolled his eyes. "I thought you should know. A body has been found. Down by the old embankment. Francis walked over to check it out."

"A body? You mean—"

He interrupted her. "Yes. Doctor M'Gregor's body. A crowd had already gathered so he was unable to remove the body."

"There shouldn't be a body!" Blood coursed through the veins in her head. "Who authorized the assassination of my father's friend and the cofounder of this company?"

"I did."

She knew the voice. She loved the voice, but a chill reverberated off her ribcage. Before the desk stood her beloved Casimir. He looked as handsome as ever, but his eyes bore a rebuke.

"The good doctor became a liability. It was only a matter of time before he would have jeopardized the entire operation. He grew soft. His was the same mistake as the original creator. He fell in love with his creations."

Such a cold response. She must have misheard him. Her dashing prince could not be so callous. "But my lord, surely there was another way. Wilhelm was a fool, but no threat."

Casimir's fist slammed to the desk. Though the desk must have weighed a few hundred pounds, pencils flew from it. Her flat-screen computer monitor swayed back and forth. "You dare question me! Have I not given you all you have?"

"Perhaps M'Gregor was not the only one going soft," said the guard. He curled the right corner of his mouth.

Casimir looked to the guard and nodded. "Perhaps."

The office felt as though someone had cranked the air-conditioning.

"Tell Francis to get out of there," said Casimir. "We do not need another association to this facility. We will have to deal with the investigation another way."

"Yes, my lord," said the guard. He turned and left the room.

Without another word, her prince vanished. No consolation. No explanation.

~~~~~~~~~~

Chris looked in horror at the body laying face down in the river rock. Perhaps someone stole the doctor's wallet. Maybe it wasn't his corpse. But the pangs in his gut told him otherwise. The body, the grey hair now matted, the turn-of-the-century jacket, it all fit. A lump descended into his throat like a bobber on his sinking spirits.

Don patted him on the back. "I'm sorry Chris. Let's roll him over and make sure it's him." Don turned to Sam. "Did you get pictures of the body position and its surroundings?"

"Got 'em," she answered. "Is there anything else from the position or location we need to examine before moving the body?"

"I don't believe so. The body wasn't shot here."

Chris jerked his gaze from the body. He looked at Sam, who just nodded, and then back to Don. It hadn't even occurred to him. Of course, there wasn't enough blood. A shot through the heart and there should be a pool of blood. "Do you think the body was dumped here?" With the gathered crowd, they'd never be able to identify footprints, or tire tracks for that matter.

"Well, in a manner of speaking," said Don. "I think he washed up here. With all the rain the river would have overrun its banks. Probably up to this spot. If you look closely, you can see a slight blood staining on the rocks leading from here down to the river. It's not enough to have come from the initial bleed out." The coroner put his fingers to his chin and looked around the scene. "No, if he were shot here there would be a much larger discoloration area. This appears to be the result of the river receding from here back to its normal levels, carrying with it some of the residual blood."

"Also, the scrapes on his arms," said Sam.

"Exactly what I was thinking." Don picked up the right hand of the victim. "There's no bruising, which would indicate they occurred after he was dead. I'd guess the result of the river tossing the body against these rocks." Turning to Sam, "Make sure we get a few of those smaller stones for DNA analysis. I'm quite sure it's all his, but we should make sure."

Chris stood and gazed up river to the northwest. "If he washed up from the river, he could very well have been killed at CeSiR Tech. He's a cofounder and owner. At least, he used to be."

"Why would someone at his own company want to kill him?"

"I don't know. But nothing about that place has made sense. We even linked the shooter at the jail to CeSiR. Still—you'd think they'd be smart enough not to dump the body to be found within a mile of the facility."

"Perhaps. But if we hadn't received so much rain over the last few days the body could have washed for miles, maybe even into the Missouri. Because of the flooding, the body caught up here in a dead spot."

Sam groaned. "You didn't just say that. Tell me you didn't."

Don gave a half-hearted apologetic grin. "Anyway let's roll him over." He put his hand under the body's left shoulder and pulled. The body lifted, paused, and then plopped to its back.

The pained begging eyes of Wilhelm M'Gregor stared up at the blue sky.

Chris' diaphragm wretched. He pinched his throat shut to prevent making an unsightly spectacle of himself. The intelligent capable amiable man who just weeks before sat with Chris discussing his contributions to humanity lay lifeless, colorless, and waterlogged. "It's definitely him."

The man's face was severely scratched and cut. But again little blood had flowed from or even to the cuts. More evidence of death occurring prior to the injuries.

"This isn't good," said Don. He probed the exit wound just left of the man's sternum. "This was not a standard gunshot." Don looked Chris in the eyes. "The bullet ripped through his heart and shattered its way through the sixth and seventh ribs. I doubt very much we'll find the bullet in the body, but we'll verify it when we perform the autopsy. By the size of the entry wound, I assumed a larger caliber bullet—perhaps a forty-five. But only a rifle could have this kind of velocity, and high caliber rifles are not your typical firearm."

"Are you thinking some kind of military issue?"

"I doubt we'll ever know. But based on the angle the bullet passed through the torso, I'd say the bullet came from well above the victim, possibly hiding in one of the trees along the river?"

Chris looked at the tall trees lining the river. The wind whispered through green growth—as if trying to reveal its dark secret. Secrets held behind fortress walls, three story fortress walls. "Or perhaps from atop a three story building."

"Perhaps," said Don. "Though it could have happened anywhere. The body could have been dumped in the river anywhere upstream."

Chris knew better than to jump to conclusions. Still, every corner he turned, every stone overturned, they all pointed to CeSiR. A glimmer of red caught his eye. Something protruded from the doctor's clutched left hand. "Hey what's that?"

The coroner extracted a rope from the man's hand. "It looks like some kind of handle. It has a red tag, 'Pull to Inflate'"

"Sounds like a self-inflating raft."

"Seems like an odd time to be rafting down the river," said Sam.

"And self-inflating rafts are usually reserved for emergencies," added Don. "Perhaps he was running from someone."

"Like some heavily armed guards—like the ones at CeSiR."

"Armed? With side arms?"

"No, more like M4 assault rifles."

The coroner motioned to Sam. "Looks like that's all we're gonna learn here. We'll need to search the riverbanks to see if we can find anything else of interest."

Sam walked to their Explorer, and returned with a long black-vinyl bag.

"Do you think you can get a search warrant for CeSiR?" asked Don.

Chris shook his head. "I don't know. That place is like some top-secret government facility." His thoughts turned to the proud smile of Wilhelm M'Gregor, as he explained the need for a fingerprint and retinal scan system. "Honestly, I'm not sure we have sufficient evidence to get someone to let us in there."

Daryl looked to be about finished collecting information from the onlookers. "Did you want to talk with anyone that was on the scene?"

"You got names and contact info?" asked Don.

Chris scanned the crowd, many of whom looked none too pleased to still be there. "I believe so." Someone was missing. He motioned to Daryl.

"I think it can wait," said Don. "We'll take the body back and do the autopsy tomorrow. You can check with us on Tuesday to see if there's any new information."

Daryl walked up next to Chris. "What's up?"

"Did you see a guy about my height, early twenties, black buzz cut?"

"You know, now that you mention it. I saw him when we arrived, but no, he must have left without giving me his info. Do you think he's of interest?"

"He is now! It wouldn't be the first time a criminal returned to a scene to observe his handiwork."

Daryl's eyes lit up. "Maybe one of the photographers got a shot of him."

"Even better," said Chris. "I bet *they* got him on tape." He pointed to the news camera. It may take a favor, but they would give him a copy of the tape.

After dismissing the crowd, Chris and Daryl spent the next few hours searching as much of the area riverbank as they could. At last, they found the remains of the raft on the east bank behind the River of Life building, only slightly downstream and across the river from CeSiR.

Monday morning he would drop it off at the coroner's office to be tested for trace evidence. If only he could get a warrant to search CeSiR's property, perhaps then he could recover some real evidence—like a bullet.

~~~~~~~~~~

East of Topeka on the Kansas Turnpike, John Green felt as if heavy hands pressed his aching shoulders into the truck's seat. With nothing but sparse trees, hypnotic grass swaying in the wind, and the occasional cell tower, to draw his interest, he began to realize he wasn't going to make it to St. Louis.

He glanced at the red illuminated clock on the dash. The numbers seven, four, and five blurred through heavy eyelids.

"Just grab a coffee, get to Kansas City and see how you feel then," he told himself.

After twenty-some ounces of coffee and another hour's drive, the only thing keeping him awake was the innate need to find a restroom. In Blue Springs, just east of Kansas City, he pulled into a hotel parking lot for the night.

~~~~~~~~~~

CHAPTER THIRTY

Monday, May 11, 2020

Chris lay awake staring at the ceiling. He hated when he woke just minutes before his alarm clock. And he really disliked Monday mornings. Who knew what the week would hold. The events in town continued to get weirder and he had no leads, and nowhere to find leads.

In the stillness of the morning he heard a faint click from his alarm clock.

"Good morning, Boonville," said Stu the morning show host. "And a much needed good morning to our neighbors in Arrow Springs. As if the shooting and arson of the last few weeks weren't enough, yesterday morning the body of Wilhelm M'Gregor, scientist and cofounder of CeSiR Technologies washed up on the banks of the Lamine River."

A choice cuss word floated through Chris' brain, but he intercepted it before it fell from his lips. Instead, he took out his frustration on the alarm clock. His fingers tingled from swatting the off button, just a bit harder than necessary.

He hobbled out of bed and into the kitchen where he flicked the power button on his coffee maker. While he waited, he headed to the living room, plopped in his lazy-boy, and picked up his Bible. If he didn't spend some time with God this morning he was likely to hurt someone by noon.

The Bible opened to the book of Proverbs. In his spirit he felt drawn to chapter sixteen. Several familiar verses jumped out as he read.

"Commit your actions to the Lord, and your plans will succeed. The Lord has made everything for his own purposes, even the wicked for a day of disaster"

A day that couldn't come too soon as far as he was concerned.

"We can make our plans, but the Lord determines our steps . . . Those who listen to instruction will prosper; those who trust the Lord will be joyful."

"Lord," he prayed. "I want to understand. I don't know where to go or what to do. Everything seems related, and yet none of it ties together. Lord, guide my steps. I don't even know how to plan my way. But, I do trust You. Help me to see. Help me to understand."

An hour later, he climbed into his squad car. He may not know where to go with the investigation. But he knew where to go first.

Marilyn's house.

That's where he'd find his one bright star in an otherwise cloudy midnight sky.

Had she heard the broadcasts? Did she know, along with the rest of the world, the identity of the body they'd found? If so, she'd be freakin' out.

He reached up to the front door.

The door swung open before his hand could knock.

The fear in Sarah's eyes confirmed his suspicions. "Is it true? The body they found yesterday, was it really the doctor from CeSiR?"

"Yes, it's true. I wish I knew who leaked the identity."

"Never mind that! Chris, what's going on in this town? I'm scared! Whoever did this isn't too fond of me either. They've already tried to kill me once—maybe more. What if they try again?"

"Sarah, I wish I could say you're over reacting." He stepped into the entryway and pulled her to him. "I just don't know." He could feel her slight frame quivering, even as she attempted to look strong. "I'll do everything I can to protect you. I think the mayor's got somethin' to do with all this. And I intend to find out."

He motioned with his head for them to step out on the porch—where Marilyn wouldn't overhear their discussion.

Once he closed the front door he continued. "Is there somewhere you can go? Somewhere safer?"

"I don't know." She looked up at him with round eyes glistening against the morning sun. "Not really. My friends are here. I'll try to lie low for awhile."

She obviously didn't comprehend the scope of what they were dealing with. Shoot, neither did he. "Sarah, whoever's behind this—they mean business. The doctor was shot." Nice, now he'd told the entire neighborhood. He lowered his voice. "It doesn't look like some common thug either. This person knew what they were doing. I'd really feel better if you were somewhere far away from here."

"Chris." She paused and covered her mouth with her palm. "Where would I go? At least here I have you to protect me." Her nose crinkled and his heart melted.

He put his arm around her waist and pulled her into a loving embrace. He could feel her body relax. As if the danger had simply evaporated away like dew in the morning sun. It would destroy him if anything happened to this beautiful flower.

She laid her head against his chest. With its freshly washed fragrance and short pipe curls, her hair reminded him of a bouquet of roses. He had allowed himself to fall in love. He knew what happened to those he loved.

"I'm afraid," he whispered.

She turned her chin into his chest and looked up into his eyes. "Of what?"

"That I won't be able to protect you."

She placed her palms against his clavicles. "I love you. I know you'll do everything you can." She pushed herself back about a foot. "But isn't that God's job. You may not be able to be with me all the time, but He is." She pursed her lips inhaled a deep breath through her nose. "He was, you know."

"Was?"

"The night of the fire. I was on the bed choking to death. I couldn't move, and I knew I was going to die." She drew her arms over her chest. The pain of the recollection flickering behind her eyes. "I really believe He was there with me. For just a life-giving moment a weight lifted. I rolled to the floor where you found me. Where I could breathe."

She paused to watch a bicycle ride by on the sidewalk. After the rider disappeared, she continued. "Chris, He protected me. He preserved my life. I believe that. And if He did it once, He can do it again."

~~~~~~~~~~

It was ten-forty-five when John Green finally got back on the road. All he could think about was getting to St. Louis. Unlike the past few mornings, John drove totally alert, no hangover, no drowsiness, just a focused ambition.

An hour into his travels, a red light in the center of the dashboard caught his attention.

What? How?

He'd checked the gauge before he left Kansas City. How had he used three-quarters of a tank of gas in less than a hundred miles?

It didn't matter. He needed gas, and he needed it soon.

Two miles later a sign informed him of a solution, only one-and-a-quarter miles ahead. There was a gas station at Exit-98. He crossed his fingers. The remaining droplets in the tank should get him there.

The gas station turned out to be a full-service truck stop.

He stepped down from his truck. The smell of burnt diesel assaulted his nose. After filling his tank and splashing some of the precious fuel onto the pavement, he looked at his watch. Nearly noon and despite a late breakfast, he felt hungry.

At least he wouldn't have to stop again for lunch.

A small diner shared the same parking lot with the gas station. A neon sign in one window screamed that the diner was open for business.

He pulled his truck into a parking spot between the gas station and the diner, climbed out of the truck, and lumbered through the front door.

~~~~~~~~~~

Chris sat on a stool at the counter of Margie's Diner. The smell of burger grease and fry oil, so prevalent when he'd entered, began to fade into the backdrop of his mind. He stared at the milkshake machine on a shelf five feet behind the front counter.

His mind processed through the case like a computer stuck in an endless loop. There had to be evidence he'd overlooked. Piece by piece, detail by detail, twist by confusing twist, he processed the facts of the case. Most of the evidence pointed to CeSiR Tech. Not to mention his boss, Mayor Richards.

It was all circumstantial.

The only solid link to CeSiR lay in cold storage at the county morgue. As for Trenton, there was the photo of him with the deceased murderer, attacker, and thief. He needed to search the grounds around CeSiR. Perhaps, he could get a warrant based on the proximity of the body, and the identity of the victim. A reasonable request to search for the bullet. Perhaps, if he weren't dealing with a government funded research company like CeSiR.

No—he needed more.

"The usual, hon?" A distant voice broke into the processing of his thoughts.

His consciousness drifted back to the diner. "Hmm?"

A thin woman with salt and peppered hair stared at him over the counter. "Lunch—Would you like your usual order?"

"Oh, I'm sorry." He shot an embarrassed grin at Margie, the owner and namesake of the diner. "Sure, that'll be fine. Thanks Margie."

"What's her name?" an unfamiliar voice to his left asked.

Chris turned to see a stocky—some might even say overweight—balding man in his mid-fifties smiling at him. "Pardon?"

"The girl?" The man's belly shook as a laugh rolled from it. "It's not often ya see someone that checked out 'less there's a pretty girl on the other side of their thoughts."

If only. "Not this time I'm afraid," said Chris. There was a girl—probably the reason he obsessed so about the case. But technically, he wasn't thinking about her, at least at the moment.

"Well, I didn't mean to disturb ya. The name's John," The man stuck out a meaty hand. "John Green."

"Chris Davis." He shook the man's hand. He was in uniform. He needed to be polite. "Nice to meet you John. Where you from?"

"Presently—Salt Lake City." The man pointed to his right. "But I'm headin' to Evansville, Indiana for a job interview."

The man's finger pointed north, but no need to correct him. "And you chose to stop in our thriving town for lunch?"

"Nope, stopped for gas."

"Well, that's appropriate. I'd suggest the onion rings then." Chris cracked a smile.

Ten seconds later, another belly laugh rolled from the man. "I like you Chris."

"Here you go hon," said Margie. The aroma of french-fries, sautéed onions, and bacon drew Chris' attention to the plate in front of him.

~~~~~~~~~~

Zeke stood next to Chris. Several demons hissed and cursed at him and Huw, who'd arrived with the man from Salt Lake City. The diner reeked of their sulfurous contempt.

"Hey Margie, can you flip that to the news?" A large burly man sitting in the corner of the diner pointed to the television, which displayed a rerun of a game show.

Zeke shook his head. Eitan was a master of disguise. Not one demon in the place suspected the burly trucker in the jean bib overhauls was the captain of the host. If they only knew, the diner would have been crawling with minions seeking to impress their superiors by eliminating the captain. Though such an attempt would likely result only in their own demise.

~~~~~~~~~~

Chris savored his Western Arrow burger bite by bite, until a hand slapped him on the shoulder.

A drip of ketchup splattered against his uniform. He glanced at John out of the corner of his eye. Half surprised. Half irritated.

"That's you!" said John. "On the TV."

The audio Chris had been filtering out as he ate came drilling into his eardrums. "This is WKXV TV News reporter Alison Cronheim."

He looked up to see his photograph in the corner of the screen overlaid against live footage of the reporter.

"Yesterday, we were on scene of what we were told was Arrow Spring's second murder in a month. The body washed up from the Lamine River sometime yesterday morning."

Chris' picture began to grow until it occupied the entire screen.

"This was the statement from Arrow Spring's own Sergeant Chris Davis."

The photo jumped to life as the camera panned out to include the scene from the river. "We're here with Chris Davis, Arrow Spring's very own hero. Thursday night he saved a young woman from the arson fire at her home. Today he's investigating this gruesome discovery. Sergeant Davis, what can you tell us about the body?"

"I'm afraid I can't tell you much. It does appear to be a homicide. However, we don't believe the victim was shot at this location. We'll tell you what we can as the investigation unfolds."

"Can you tell us who the victim was?"

"No. We still need to locate the next of kin. And I don't think any of us want them to hear about it from their daily news."

A loud voice, from somewhere behind Chris, shouted, "That's two murders and an arson in less than a month. You'd think the local police would be on this twenty-four-seven. I wonder what they're up to."

Chris turned to identify the instigator.

"Probably eating donuts and burgers," said the man's eating buddy. "Maybe they should bring in some real law enforcement."

"That's enough you two!" said Margie. "Get out of my diner. We don't need your kind here."

"What's the matter Margie? Afraid we might ruin the deputy's appetite? Thinkin' maybe he won't get dessert?"

A block of a man in jean overhauls shot up from his seat. "I think you heard the lady!" The man's deep intimidating voice echoed across the diner. He walked to the table and placed an iron grip on each of their shoulders. "She asked you to leave. I suggest you comply."

Both men squirmed under the obvious pain. "Keep your pants on. We're going."

Chris mouthed the word, "Thanks."

The man smiled and nodded.

When Chris turned back to the news broadcast, a picture of Dr. M'Gregor filled the screen. "WKXV has since learned the identity of the victim to be none other than Dr. Wilhelm M'Gregor, founder of CeSiR Tech. One of Arrow Spring's most successful companies."

"Hey! I know him." The man next to Chris about jumped off his stool. "Yeah, CeSiR Tech, that was one of my first construction projects. Man that was the worst job I think I've ever done. I ain't no ground mole. I can't stand working that far underground."

"What?" Chris' mind ran through his tour of the facility. He had parked underground. How high was the ceiling in the garage? Certainly not more than ten feet. Either this man's memory was poor, or his exaggerations exceeded his girth.

"Seriously, that hole was at least forty feet deep. There's a parking garage, but beneath that there's another medical floor and below that's the residential floor." The man shook his head. "Why anyone would want to live way down there? You got me. And those two doctors, they were a little nuts if you ask me. Below the residential floor, they had us put in a concrete basement of sorts. No doors, no walls, only a small hatch that ain't even big enough for a person to climb down it." John took a big bite from his burger, but he continued nonetheless. "To this day I can't figure the purpose of that one."

The image of the computerized elevator display flashed to Chris' mind. The different levels that appeared depending on who cleared the security check-in. Was it possible the doctor had only showed him half the facility? "A residential level? Underground?"

"Well, it weren't much but yeah. Felt kinda like a dungeon. I sure wouldn't live down there."

Chris needed answers and the doctor wouldn't be providing them. Maybe if he could get the prints and verify John's description of the building, he'd be able to get that warrant to search the facility.

He laid a twenty on the counter and motioned to Margie. He turned to John. "Hey thanks for the info. Lunch is on me."

"You don't have to do that."

"My pleasure. I hope all goes well with that job interview in Indiana." He turned back to Margie. "Put his and mine together. Keep the change."

~~~~~~~~~~

Zeke slapped Huw on the back. "Looks like the mission was a success."

"Indeed. Not only does Chris have the information from John, but there is an army of prayer warriors in Denver ready to pray for the coming battle." Huw pointed to the television, still broadcasting images of the crime scene. "The coverage has gone national. Now they will know how to pray."

Zeke and Huw followed Chris out of the diner. Though more than capable in battle, Zeke hated the thought of damaging any of God's creations. Even his fallen brothers. "Do you really think this will come to a battle?"

Eitan stepped up next to them and laid his mighty hand on Zeke. "It is not a question of if there is a battle, but when the battle will take place."

"Ladan gathers forces to join us from the west," said Huw. "We should expect three hundred warriors to join us."

"Good," said Eitan. We will need all warriors we can muster."

~~~~~~~~~~

CHAPTER THIRTY-ONE

Mael perched atop the CeSiR Tech building. Swarms of demonic activity surrounded him, blotting out the annoying rays of the sun. He so preferred the cool blackness of nighttime. Another car approached the building. One by one the mims returned as commanded.

"I do not understand," said Cadfael. "Why bring them back? Would it not be better for them to be dispersed throughout the region in case an attack comes?"

Cadfael was loyal. And a warrior. But his intellect limited the level to which he would ever ascend. "It is not a matter of *if* there will be an attack. Only *when*." Mael stood and walked in a circle around his faithful servant. "Officer Davis grows closer by the day. Eventually, he will piece together enough of the puzzle to return here." A low growl rolled from his chest. "When he returns, Eitan and his warriors will accompany him, or else he will die."

"Either way," said Cadfael. "He *will* die."

Mael nodded. "Yes, I suppose he will. But we need to be prepared for a battle in both realms. Spiritual and physical. No humans can match the skill of our mims. I want numbers. In both realms."

"My liege." A feminine voice sought his attention.

"Yes Anat. What is it?"

"I have come from watching Officer Davis. He just had a discussion with a builder familiar with this building." She spun her head around like an owl, surveying the rooftop. "He knows of the subterranean levels."

Mael turned to Cadfael and leered. The news was not good. But he so loved being right. "Yes. We were just discussing the coming attack."

"Those under my charge will be ready my liege," said Cadfael. "We will crush the enemy."

Mael shook his head. "I am sorry Cadfael. I have need for the two of you on another mission." He went on to inform them of the new information he had received only hours earlier. "Go. Do your worst!"

~~~~~~~~~~

Chris walked to his cruiser. His stomach content, but his brain screaming for answers. He flipped open his cell and shielded the bright midday sun from the digital screen. He scrolled through the last few numbers and zeroed in on Marilyn's home number. Hopefully, she was there.

"Hey Sarah it's Chris. I was wonderin'—do ya need a ride to the hospital for your treatment this afternoon?" He'd missed his time with her on Sunday. Perhaps, he could make up for it. "I gotta go to Jefferson City and figured, since Columbia is on the way, maybe we could spend some time together." Her sweet innocent voice, even on the phone, made his heart pound in his chest. "I just had lunch, but we can stop if you need to." As much as he'd love to take her to lunch, he needed to get to Jefferson City. She told him she'd just grab something quick before he got there. "Great, I'll see you in a half hour then. Love ya."

The Missouri State Archives retained the flour plans for most of the businesses in Missouri. He needed to get a look at the plans to CeSiR. He would, however, delay the trip a few minutes, if it meant he could spend the afternoon with Sarah.

At one o'clock, they were on their way. He filled her in on his reason for going to Jefferson City, including the description John Green gave him of the three floors below the parking garage.

Sarah shivered and shot him that why-would-there-be-a-residence-underground look. He could only imagine that was the same look he'd given John Green. "Who do you think lives there?"

"I have no idea. I'd say patients, but we already know they provide them with houses." Why had the doctor hidden the other levels from him? That was the question he wanted answered.

"Maybe some of the staff stays there when they're on call."

He loved her inquisitive spirit. "If I can get the plans, I might be able to get a warrant to search the facility." Below ground levels weren't enough to get a warrant. But a shooting near the premises, a bullet to be found, possibly a weapon, *and* the concealment of these levels. He might just be able to convince a judge to give him a warrant.

An hour later, they crossed the Missouri River on the CF Red Whaley Expressway into downtown Jefferson City. How far would the body have gone? The words of the coroner echoed in his head. "The body might have ended up in the Missouri." Would it have come all the way here? No. Too many bends. Too many slow spots.

He pulled into the parking lot across Harrison Street. The dome of the State Capital peeked through pink and purple blossoms.

"I think I'll stay here," said Sarah. "This view is incredible."

He had to agree. He looked over her shoulder at the picturesque scene. Beauty beholding beauty. "I shouldn't be long. They're expectin' me. The secretary said she'd have a copy of the plans ready for me."

Twenty-five minutes later, he returned with a three-foot long cardboard tube and a headache fueled by his fury. "You wouldn't believe the hassle they gave me." He plopped into the driver's seat and started the cruiser. "First, the prints were for the wrong building. Like I need prints to the Elementary School." If he hadn't been so eager to see the plans, he might have made it back to Arrow Springs before he noticed. "Then they couldn't find the CeSiR prints."

He'd wanted to punch the indifferent research assistant. "Yep, it says we should have them. But I don't see them. Perhaps I can call you if we find them?" After some persuading, they found the plans stuffed in the incorrect document drawer.

He shook his head and looked at Sarah. Her nose crinkled as she did her best to hold back an amused grin. "Once they found the plans they told me I could only review them. They couldn't give me a copy."

Her eyes shifted to the cardboard tube. "So what's that?"

"Once I saw the building indeed had four underground levels, as John had described, I told 'em, if they couldn't make me a copy, I'd just take the original—it was evidence for a murder investigation. All of a sudden they had no problem makin' me a copy."

"Sounds to me like someone didn't want you to get those plans. Did you check the copies?"

"Oh yes. The only way they're gonna keep me from having the plans now is if they're copied with disappearin' ink."

~~~~~~~~~~

Chris parked in a reserved parking space next to Columbia Regional and shut off the engine.

"Wow, VIP treatment," said Sarah.

"None more important in my book." They held hands and walked to the hospital entrance. "I'm gonna call the Cooper County Courthouse and see if I can get a warrant to search CeSiR."

Once he saw Sarah to the elevator, Chris returned to a quaint little outdoor park area where he could use his cell phone. He punched in the number and the judge's executive assistant answered. "Yes, this is Sergeant Davis from Arrow Springs. Could I please speak with Judge Burns?"

Ten minutes later, "Officer Davis, what can I do for you?"

"Yes sir, I'm sure you've heard about the murder of Dr. Wilhelm M'Gregor, the founder of CeSiR Tech, this weekend?"

"Certainly," said the judge.

"Well sir, I believe there is a connection between his death, the shooting at our station, a recent arson, and CeSiR Tech. I would like to get a warrant to search the premises at CeSiR to see if we can find the bullet that killed the doctor, or even the murder weapon."

"You said there was a connection. How so?" asked Judge Burns.

"Well sir, the connection between CeSiR and the doctor is obvious. Leon Burgos, the shooter at the station, was a patient at CeSiR, at least according to my interview with Dr. M'Gregor. In addition I've got a photograph, which Leon tried to steal, showing Leon and Mayor Richards leaving CeSiR Tech together."

"Are you implying that Trenton Richards was involved in this murder? That is a pretty severe accusation."

A knot began to form in his stomach. He needed to convince the judge. "No sir. There's no solid evidence to connect the mayor to anything other than being in the same car with a murderer. When I met with the doctor about Leon's connection to CeSiR Tech, he took me on a tour of the facility. Now I have prints showing there are three additional floors to the building, which he kept hidden from me."

"From what I have heard, CeSiR is a secured facility. It does not seem that strange to me that you would not be shown the entire facility. Does it?"

"Well, no sir. I suppose not."

"You said CeSiR was connected to the arson fire. How so?"

"Well sir, Sarah, the woman who nearly died in the fire, had been doing research on CeSiR Tech. She found that CeSiR owned several residential properties around Arrow

Springs, including the house where Leon lived, as well as Mayor Richards' home."

"No offense Officer Davis, but it sounds to me like you have a grudge against Mayor Richards and CeSiR. Is it not possible that you are trying to concoct a case against them, when one really does not exist?"

"What? With all due respect sir, what about the evidence?" His feelings for Sarah had nothing to do with his conclusions.

"Circumstantial at best." The words echoed across the silent line. "You do not have a lick of real, hard evidence, just a bunch of speculation."

"No hard evidence! I've got Leon, a known murderer who was a patient at CeSiR, a photo of him with our Mayor, who happens to live in a house owned by CeSiR, and now the founder of CeSiR is dead! His body was found no more than a half mile down river from their property. How much more evidence do I need to get a warrant? I'm not askin' for a conviction, just a warrant so I can get *more* hard evidence." He felt lightheaded.

"Deputy Davis, I think you have let this case become personal. You are trying to protect your new lover, and that is admirable. Perhaps, if you spent more time doing real detective work and less time being her chauffer to and from her oxygen treatments, you would find the real killer. Good day."

Click.

He sat stunned. Lover? How dare he! The muscles in the back of his neck were stiffening. And how did the judge know where he was, and even about Sarah's treatment? He glanced around at the large trees surrounding the small park. Did they harbor prying eyes? Had they been followed? He scanned the parking lot. No sign of anyone.

The ride home from the hospital was quiet.

"I take it you didn't get the warrant," Sarah asked.

"No. I think the world's gone insane." He couldn't bring himself to tell her about the judge's peculiar awareness of their activities. From the seat next to him, he heard a faint growl.

Sarah glanced left to see if he'd noticed.

He grinned.

She patted her stomach. "Those treatments make me hungry. Do you have time to stop for dinner?"

He threw his palm up in front of him. "Sure, why not? Doesn't look like I've got any investigatin' to do."

She reached out and took his hand. They drove back to Arrow Springs in silence.

~~~~~~~~~~

CHAPTER THIRTY-TWO
Tuesday, May 12, 2020

Chris pushed the display button on the dashboard clock for the fourth time since he'd arrived at the Cooper County morgue. Two minutes since the last check. By the time he received the message from Don Hanson on Monday, the office had closed. The autopsy results were in. Now he sat in the parking lot, waiting for the office to open. Seeing Don walking down the sidewalk toward the entrance, he exited the car.

"Good morning." With a wave and a smile, Don invited Chris to follow him into the old red-brick building. "Looks like someone's desperate for answers."

"Yeah, I didn't exactly sleep well last night." Don held the large wooden door for him. "I know there's got to be something I'm missin'." Chris' voice echoed down the polished-concrete hall. "Everything seems related, yet nothing connects. Tell me you've got somethin' useful."

"I wish I could." Don unlocked his office door and motioned Chris in. "I don't think there's much to tell, but you never know. Sometimes things fall into place in strange ways. I'll let you be the judge."

Don threw his brown-leather bomber jacket over a chair and turned back to Chris. "Shall we head downstairs?"

Minutes later, they stood in the dungeon-like lower level of the morgue. "Let's take a look," said Don. He eased the large metal drawer from the wall.

Chris shuddered at the sound of metallic bearings scraping against the weight of the body. Thirty-five degree air rolled from the refrigerated storage. "Is that something you ever get used to?"

"To some degree, I suppose. It's never pleasant, but I no longer regret having eaten breakfast."

Don pulled the white cloth back from the head and torso of the late Dr. M'Gregor.

"My assumption was correct regarding us not finding a bullet." Don pointed to a gaping wound in the man's chest. "There was only one shot. It passed clean through the body, hitting bone on its way in and out. Whoever fired the shot knew exactly what he was doing."

"Or she," added a female voice behind Chris.

The nerves throughout his body screamed in response to the unexpected presence. He spun to see Sam, once again wearing her white lab coat, and a brunette bun.

"As many as fifty percent of the world's trained snipers are women." She sashayed toward them. "It's common knowledge they are better shots."

"Yes, yes. Anyway," said Don, "our sniper, male or female, was very good. Death, though perhaps not instantaneous, was a certainty as soon as he, *or she*, pulled the trigger." He went on to point out the cuts and scrapes on the arms and face. "As I mentioned Sunday, the rest of these occurred after this fellow was dead. This fact, combined with the raft we found along the river, confirm he was killed somewhere upstream. I'm afraid that's about all there is to learn from the body. No toxins, no alcohol, nothing unusual with the blood tests."

"No genetic anomalies?" asked Chris.

"Nope."

"We found some traces of blood and hair under the handle of the raft you sent us," said Sam. "We ran DNA tests. The blood definitely belonged to Dr. M'Gregor. The hair however—belonged to a woman. Based on a mitochondrial telomeres analysis, it appears she was between the ages of nine and twelve."

Had one of the women in Dr. M'Gregor's photos been with him when he was shot? "How much can you tell from a hair?"

"We could speculate further using snips."

"Whats?" asked Chris.

Sam nodded and went on to explain. "S-N-Ps, short for Single Nucleotide Polymorphisms. Subtle genetic changes that allow classification and can reveal much information. But in this case, it was easier to run the DNA profile through the National DNA Database. Since legislation passed in 2010 to include all United States citizens in the database, it is possible to determine with a one-in-one-million accuracy the identity of any DNA sample. In this case, our mystery girl is Ima Fredericks, daughter of Steve and Luanne Fredericks, born in Kansas City, Missouri. According to the database, she would be twelve years old as of yesterday."

Chris tried to process all the information. Snips, databases, twelve-year-old Ima Fredericks. "Do you have access to the database?"

"Yes, but I have the information right here." She handed him a computer printout.

"If you wouldn't mind, I'd like to take a look at the data on the computer." What he expected to see that she hadn't, he had no idea. He could only pray that his investigative instincts would come up with something.

Sam shrugged her shoulders. "I guess. When we are done here, we can go to my office and pull it up."

"I think we've probably seen all there is to see here," said Don. "You two go ahead and look at your information. I'll wrap things back up here." He pulled the white sheet back over the body. "Besides, computers give me a headache."

Chris patted Don on the shoulder and thanked him for his time. "After you," he said to Sam.

In the cinderblock stairwell, Sam glanced back at Chris. "I still don't see what you hope to find on the computer that isn't on that sheet."

"Neither do I, but I've gotta find something." The warm fresh air of the main hallway welcomed them from the stairwell.

Sam's heels clicked against the concrete as she walked. Her office, though slightly smaller than Don's, revealed an intelligent organized occupant. She perched on the edge of her computer chair and began typing into the database, I-m-a- -F-r-e-d-e-r-i-c-k-s. Thirty seconds later the screen showed an exact duplicate of the sheet Chris held in his hand. "See, like I told you, it's exactly what you have there."

He pulled a second chair around the corner of the desk. Seeing it was possible to search the database by name, Chris asked, "How about Leon Burgos?"

"I'm only supposed to use this for looking up DNA profiles for autopsies."

Intelligent, organized, and played by the rules.

"You did perform an autopsy on him. We just want to compare the results."

She nodded and punched in Leon's name. The screen showed a similar sheet for Leon Burgos.

Chris held Ima's sheet next to the computer screen. "Okay, I'm a novice at this. I have no clue what I'm looking for here. Any similarities? Anything?"

"Um, yeah." She cocked her head sideways and puzzled at the screen. "There are some very significant similarities. As you can see, Leon was born in St. Louis, the other side of the state from Ima. Different family origins, Burgos being Spanish, and Fredericks being English or Dutch, but look at these DNA profiles."

"Oookaaay. Help me out here."

"Sorry—these similarities." She pointed to a series of letters running across the screen. "These would be almost impossible for two completely random-person samples. At an absolute minimum, it would appear these two were cousins.

Another way to put it—this much correlation in DNA sequences would be sufficient to return a positive paternal test."

Leon was related to this Ima? That didn't make sense. "I thought you said they were from different nations of origin?"

"Their names are. Names are only indicative of the paternal lines of a person. See this I-haplogroup listed under Y mutations?"

"Yes?" Whatever a group of haplos was.

"That is an indication that Ima's paternal lineage almost certainly comes from Europe. The I-haplogroup is nearly exclusive to Europe. This would be consistent with the Fredericks name. Leon on the other hand—though his name indicates a Spanish origin, there is absolutely no DNA evidence of a Spanish or even European descent. Keep in mind DNA genotyping is far from exact."

"Oh, yes, of course."

She shook her head as if she were dealing with a junior high science student. "With generations of lines mixing and mutating, with adoptions, divorces, remarriages, and infidelities, nothing ever tracks as one might expect when looking at genetic heritages."

"But you said there was enough evidence to prove they were related—even cousins?"

"Yes, without question." She threw her hands up in the air. "Coincidence?"

"I'm not a big fan of coincidences." He smirked. "Coincidences usually prove to be someone's attempt to ignore the truth. Can you tell if Ima has the same genetic defect that caused Leon to have seizures?"

"It doesn't appear so. Perhaps the defect came from a different part of Leon's lineage."

Somehow the information relieved him.

A ten digit number in the bottom left hand corner of the screen caught his attention. "What's that number there?"

"That's just the data entry operator who created Leon's records. I've always wondered why the waste the space on the display."

"Looks like we have another coincidence. The same person entered Ima's records as Leon's? Would that be normal?"

"It is a little odd. The records for births in Kansas City and St. Louis are entered in completely different offices. Perhaps this particular person transferred from the St. Louis office to Kansas City between the times of their births."

"Perhaps. Any chance this system is capable of doing a search based on that ID number?"

She cast him a knowing look. "I believe so. I can't say I've ever had a reason to try." She returned to the main search screen. "Yes, here we go. DNA Entry Technician ID: 1-0-5-4-8-6-5-6-0-1. This will likely return thousands of entries. These people spend day after day entering this information for new births."

Two minutes later the screen returned a tabular listing showing page one of the entries the operator had entered.

Chris scanned the screen. "Page one of six? That would only be about a hundred entries." His eyes locked on the list of names. His heart tried to jump out of his chest. "I *really* do not believe in coincidences. Do you see the second and third names on that list?"

Clearly she did. Her eyes were glued to the screen. Her brain obviously stretching to wrap around the information.

"Is this some kind of a warped joke? Are the names in the order they were entered?" He looked to Sam. She continued to stare as her head bobbed up and down. "Trenton Richards—mayor of Arrow Springs. Quintin Burns—circuit judge." The same judge who happened to refuse him a warrant one day earlier. "Can we print these out?"

"Sure can." Apparently, she had lost her inhibitions regarding the rights of use for the database.

For the next two hours, Sam and Chris reviewed all one hundred and twenty records.

"How can they all be related?" asked Sam. She clearly meant it to be rhetorical. "Every one of these people is no further than a cousin, yet no closer either. There's just enough difference in their DNA to eliminate the possibility of immediate family." She tapped the first name on the list. "Except for this one. She is clearly Ima's mother."

"You're sure this Evelyn Milano was Ima's mother? She would've only been fourteen years old accordin' to these records."

"There is no question based on the DNA shown here."

He still couldn't make it add up. "I don't understand. How are all these people related? Perhaps the DNA records have been falsified."

"Sure, but Ima's were an exact match to the hair we found. No. Something else is going on." The color drained from her normally rosy cheeks. "Did you say CeSiR Tech is heavily involved in stem-cell research?"

He sat back in his chair. "Yes. Why?"

"You don't suppose they're going a little beyond their sanctioned, legal research?"

"I don't follow?"

She hesitated.

What could be so horrible that the woman who worked with dead people feared verbalizing it?

"It's common knowledge that scientists successfully cloned primates back in 2007. It's not a stretch to assume some rogue group has attempted, and even succeeded, in cloning humans."

No. She didn't just suggest that. This case had been strange from the beginning. But clones? "Wait a minute—some of these individuals were born twelve years prior to those primates."

She held her hand up palms out. "I'm just saying—it's scientifically possible. What's to say someone didn't figure it out well before it was publicized?"

"Are you suggesting Mayor Richards, Quinton Burns, Leon, and this Ima girl are all clones created by a mad scientist who now lies dead in your morgue?" He didn't mean to ridicule Sam. He needed to back off. The whole concept just overwhelmed him.

Sam buried her head in her hands. "I know it sounds like a sci-fi movie." She placed her hands palms down on the papers strewn across her desk. "There's enough DNA similarity to point to such a conclusion. You told me the doctor was hiding something from you. Maybe, he wasn't hiding research. Maybe he was hiding people—some of these people." She thumped her knuckles on the papers.

It began to make sense, in a strange unbelievable sort of way. "You know—they had a birthing suite, and a nursery. Do you think these people were all born at the CeSiR facility?"

"You could track down the birth records, verify places of birth." She began shaking her head. "If they're able to falsify records in the DNA database, why would the birth records be accurate?"

Chris slid his chair back and stood up. "Or I could get a warrant, search CeSiR, and find out exactly what's going on in that building—on the levels I haven't seen yet."

~~~~~~~~~~

CHAPTER THIRTY-THREE
Thursday, May 14, 2020

Ladan led his battalion of angelic warriors east across the states of Colorado and Kansas. They reached the Missouri River at Atchison. Atop his steed, in a small amphitheatre paying tribute to the veterans of past American wars, he gazed north at the flawless formation of angelic warriors ready to give themselves for the cause of their Creator. The formation brought back memories of the great Spartan Phalanx at the time of the Peloponnesian War. Three unbroken lines stretched along the west bank of the Missouri for the length of two football fields.

Each helmeted head watched him in perfect stillness, waiting for his next command. He raised his sword toward the sky and then lowered it to the east. In unison the entire formation marched across the surface of the water. On the east bank he once again held up his sword and spun it so the flat of the blade faced to the southeast. In response the formation pivoted, maintaining perfect order but now facing directly toward Arrow Springs.

Motion to his right caught Ladan's attention. He lowered his sword. Out of the trees which lined the river, a messenger appeared.

"Greetings," said Ladan.

"And to you my friend," said the messenger.

"What news do you bring?"

"I ride from the town of Excelsior Springs."

Ladan knew the town. For many years the host had maintained a strong presence there. A peaceful town of average size, a rich history, and a lower than average crime rate, Excelsior had achieved a ranking within the ten best cities in Missouri.

"All is well, I pray." Ladan clasped forearms with the messenger.

"I long for that to be true, sir." The messenger closed his eyes and lowered his head. "The enemy has poured into our city for the past week."

He went on to inform Ladan that in a week's time over one-hundred-fifty violent crimes had been reported. This exceeded any given year in the city's storied history. "The town's jails are filled to overflowing with those accused of everything from drunk and disorderly to public indecency, while serious offenders, including five accused of murder, and nearly a dozen sexual offenders, have been shipped off to Kansas City."

"They are there because of us?" asked Ladan.

"That is our belief. Our numbers have been scattered. My commander wanted to warn you himself, but—"

Ladan hated the ways of the enemy. He had seen it thousands of times since The Fall. They would instill fear and hatred in the hearts and minds of humanity and then ostracize the righteous, so that no support remained for the local warriors. "How did this begin?"

"The enemy infiltrated while we remained unaware. Last week, the first violent crime surfaced, when the body of a seventeen-year-old girl from a low-income family turned up near the railroad tracks downtown. She had been beaten and violated. A construction worker in his mid-thirties who had been working in the vicinity of the girl's home was arrested for the crime."

Ladan and the messenger both dismounted their horses and walked along the river.

"As I recall," said Ladan. "This has happened before in Excelsior."

"Yes, it is all too familiar. For those of us who have been in the town for a century, and for the townsfolk, who know the story well." The messenger looked at Ladan with moistened eyes. "The enemy knew as well."

He went on to explain that a crowd, driven by a thirst for justice, stormed the jail. They dragged the man into the street and beat him to death. Then they carried his lifeless body to the scene where the girl was discovered and left it there, lying on the tracks.

"As you can imagine, this series of events sent a shockwave through the town. In the midst of the chaos, enemy minions began to pour into the city." The messenger shook his head. "Three days later, the police apprehended a man for a similar assault. He confessed to both attacks. Shameful echoes of the lynching ninety-five years ago now ring through the town."

Excelsior Springs stood between Ladan's battalion and Arrow Springs. He could divert the troops. Enter Arrow Springs from another direction. But that would take time. And the people of Excelsior Springs deserved better.

No. They would continue as planned—as the Sovereign willed.

Ladan turned to the messenger. "What would you estimate to be their numbers?"

The messenger stared off over the river as he patted the neck of his horse. "They are many, perhaps five thousand, maybe more."

Too many, too little time.

~~~~~~~~~~

Chris grabbed the stack of DNA records from his desk and headed back to the situation board in the briefing room.

The front door of the station clicked shut.

"Officer Davis, you have been busy." Trenton Richards approached down the now empty aisle of cubicles.

"Trenton. Can't say I'm surprised to see you. I suppose your *psychic* powers revealed how much trouble you're in?"

The mayor's head bobbed as he laughed. "Honestly, you do not think you pose any threat to me. You work for me. Or, at least you used to." He waved a scolding finger at Chris. "You have been sticking your nose into places you do not belong." He pointed to the papers in Chris hand. "I suppose you think you have some revelations from those DNA records you have been looking through?"

"As a matter of fact, I do!"

"You know Chris—you should probably ask yourself, if a human clone were created, would they really be restricted to the pathetic limitations of a normal human being?" Trenton stopped only inches from his face. "How do you suppose I know everything you do? How do you think Leon snapped those handcuffs as if they were plastic?" He lowered his voice to a near hiss. "You see Chris—I am not some mere human being. Do *not* trifle with me." He took a step back and smirked. "Besides, you are no longer a police officer."

Chris needed to stay calm. Trenton sought a response, some reason to get rid of him. "What are you talking about?"

"You have been removed from the force—pending an investigation."

Stay calm. "Investigation of what?"

"The assault of Leilah Bahar in St. Louis. Friday night, April 24." Trenton held out his palm, as if he expected him to just give him his badge. "You were in St. Louis that evening, were you not?"

"Yes, but—"

"I believe that was the night you smashed up your squad car fleeing back to Arrow Springs."

"I wasn't fleeing!" The muscles in his neck were trying to strangle him. "I was respondin' to a distress call from Sarah, and you know it." It made sense. She'd been disconnected from accessing information on CeSiR. "It was you. You're the reason she was in distress in the first place."

Trenton's eyes narrowed. "She should not have been snooping into things that were not her business."

"Is that why you burned down her house?"

"Perhaps, but you have no proof of any such thing." Trenton began shaking his head, offering a look of pity.

One Chris knew all too well. One he hated.

"But, you are changing the subject," said Trenton. "We are talking about your suspension. You see—you should not have drunk so much that night. You of all people should know that people lose control of their actions when they have had too much to drink."

Years of pain from his mom's accident, hatred of everyone's pity when his brother was killed, and a lifetime of guilt for not making a difference, all welled up inside him. He couldn't hold it back. He didn't want to.

His fist crushed against Trenton's jaw.

Trenton didn't flinch. Blood trickled down his cheek, but a taunting smile remained.

"I told you. I am not like you. I was created to be superior. I think you should hand over your badge and gun."

"I didn't do anything that night! I wasn't drunk! And I did not touch Leilah!"

"Oh, I know that. But you see—the truth does not matter. She is ready to testify against you."

"Is that some kind of threat?" Chris placed his finger on the snap of his holster. "There's no way, I'm going to back off the investigation."

Trenton's eyebrows creased and crept down toward his nose. "On the contrary! The investigation is over." His hand reached out and clasped Chris' right wrist. "Now, give me your gun and badge, or I will take them from you by force." His piercing eyes challenged, even begged Chris not to comply.

"I don't think that's gonna happen." A deep voice resonated down the hallway from the briefing room. "Won't you both please join us in here?"

Trenton's hand pulled back from the gun, obviously surprised by the enormous black man standing next to the door.

Chris held out an after-you hand and motioned to the briefing room. "I'd like to introduce you to a few friends of mine."

He and Trenton entered the office.

"You've met Earl. He's FBI." Chris pointed to five others rising from their seats around a briefing table. "That there's Dietrich from Immigration and Customs Enforcement, Charles from the CIA, Duncan from the ATF, over there, that's Walt from the FDA." Each man gave a subtle nod.

The fifth person from the table, a young woman about six-two, approached Trenton. Chris figured she could bench press more than any man at the table. "And this is Vivian, from the Department of Homeland Security." He shook his head mocking the now less confident mayor. "It seems they all have an interest in you and your friends at CeSiR Tech."

"Mr. Richards," said Vivian. "I'm afraid we're going to need to take you into custody, until we finish our investigation."

Trenton grabbed Vivian and flung her like a rag doll. Her body crashed into Chris and they both fell to the ground.

Before anyone else in the room could react, Trenton ran from the room.

Chris and the six agents ran from the room. The front door slammed shut. When they reached the front steps, Trenton was no where to be seen.

"A quick little bugger," said Charles from the CIA.

"Strong too," said Vivian.

"We'll find him eventually," said Earl. "For now, I think we'd all like to hear what you've found regarding CeSiR."

~~~~~~~~~~~

Ladan raised his hand and the battalion of angelic warriors drew to a halt in the flat of an old quarry outside Excelsior Springs. They numbered four hundred and fifty strong including warriors they had picked up across Kansas.

One hundred and fifty warriors, appearing as ancient Greek hoplites, formed the front line. Their mirrored-white-gold helmets shone in the bright noonday sun. On intimidating nine-foot frames, each wore polished silver chain mail, covered with gold breast and back-plates. Golden plate armor guarded their lower legs and feet. Over the right shoulder, each warrior wore a classic Greek sword with a distinctive leaf shaped blade to use in close combat. Two distinct features struck fear into any enemy—their forty-inch round brass shields and twenty-foot long spears made a frontal assault a near suicidal attempt. The front of each shield bore an embossed cross, indicating the allegiance of the warrior. In unison helmets snapped to Ladan. They awaited his orders.

Peltast-like warriors comprised the second line of the phalanx. Their armor matched the first line, except without the breast and back-plates to allow mobility. Instead of a heavy spear, the Peltast warriors each carried a dozen javelins for mid-range aerial assaults. They too watched Ladan with fierce determination—ready to engage the enemy.

Finally, the third line of warriors consisted of mounted troops, like the elite companion cavalry of Alexandrian Greece. Fully armored and bearing both spear and sword, these powerful warriors rode on the prayers of the saints in Denver. The news of the events in Arrow Springs had broadcasted nationally. The angels that remained behind had no difficulty getting the saints to pray for the spiritual warfare in central Missouri.

The angelic phalanx moved in precise unison—each step, each movement, each breath, perfectly orchestrated from one end of the line to the other. The phalanx came to a readied halt behind Ladan, their captain.

"You will proceed no further!" exclaimed a black minotaur-like creature. He stood at the front of a mass of demonic beings lining the opposite side of the quarry.

"And who are you to interfere with the progress of the Lord's warriors?" asked Ladan. His troops remained in perfect formation—not flinching, not looking to and fro, completely undaunted.

Meanwhile, the demonic forces atop the southeast face of the quarry milled about the hillside, some were frightened, but most seemed barely able to keep themselves from running and screaming across the quarry.

"I am Cadfael, the prince of this land. And as the prince of this land, I declare that you are not welcome here. Go back to whence you came."

Ladan could not hold back a chuckle. "I take orders from no dark prince. My orders come from the one true Prince. You *will* let us pass."

"Even if you did get past us, it would make no difference. Your friends at Arrow Springs will be defeated, with or without you." Cadfael raised his battle-axe in the air and spun it. "Prince Mael and Mors have over ten thousand warriors in their charge. The chances of a few pathetic angels defeating them are nearly as grim as your chances of leaving this battle in one piece." He waved his axe out across the sea of blackness behind him. "You cannot possibly hope to defeat these five thousand troops with your shiny little band of warriors."

Ladan grew tired of the exchange. He did not have the time nor desire to bicker with this demon. "I recall such boasts from you in the past Cadfael. I would think you would have learned your lesson when the young shepherd boy slew your mighty Philistine."

The demon's face turned cold and sulfurous snorts flamed from his nostrils.

"Surely you remember Goliath in the Valley of Elah?" asked Ladan. "Do you remember how quickly you fled when your *unbeatable* warrior crumbled to the ground? Size and numbers do not matter, only the Lord's will."

"Enough!" shouted Cadfael. "Attack!"

Blackness poured over the hillside into the quarry.

"Stand firm!" ordered Ladan.

"Breaking against the ranks of angels, hundreds of writhing demons disappeared to the Abyss, as razor-tipped spears impaled two, even three, demons to a time. Javelins from the second line rained down on the middle of the black masses.

The sounds of clanking steel, demonic screeching, and the occasional death-cry of one of his warriors, crashed against Ladan's senses. Despite their innate evil, he still hated to see his once-angelic brothers sentenced to the Abyss to await certain judgment.

Through the pure advantage of numbers, the demons began to push past the spears. One by one the first row of angelic warriors abandoned their spears and drew their swords.

Ladan's own sword crashed against swords, axes, and mace. Uneager for banishment, a circle began to form around Ladan, as demons found other opponents more desirable.

Soon the second row of the phalanx abandoned their javelins to hand-to-hand sword combat. The putrid stench of sulfur enveloped the quarry.

Ladan continually monitored the status of the battle exploding around him. One orc-like creature stood ready to deliver a death blow to a fallen angel, when Ladan's fiery sword split him head to toe. The angel on the ground nodded in gratitude and returned to his feet, reenergized for battle.

Ladan had split the third-line riders into two squads. They now flanked the enemy from both sides. Shrieks of terror rose from demons who had been content to sit back and let others do the fighting. They fell beneath the hoofs of the angelic cavalry.

Relentless, the fighting continued. For every angelic warrior dispatched to the throne, dozens of demonic beings found new residence in the Abyss.

The fighting ensued into the night and then to the heat of the following day. Ladan grew alarmed at the mere time the battle consumed.

~~~~~~~~~~

CHAPTER THIRTY-FOUR
Friday, May 15, 2020

Chris rounded the curve on Justice Drive. The low hanging sun pounded through his window. He pulled into his parking spot at the station and walked to the building.

He had waited, with as much patience as he could muster, for Earl to get back to him. Their meeting Thursday night ended with cursory introductions and an exchange of contact information. Earl said they would reconvene once they pulled together a plan of action.

Finally, the call came in at two in the afternoon. The meeting was set for seven o'clock. Chris thought he'd go insane waiting, but after a lengthy supper, and his second workout of the day, seven finally arrived.

He didn't even bother turning the light to his office on. Instead, he walked straight to the briefing room. Several minutes later, all six agents and Daryl were seated around the table. "I still don't understand how each of you fit into this investigation," said Chris. "I can see how most of you would have some interest in CeSiR Tech. But how'd you all find out about what's goin' on here?"

Vivian set her hands on the table and interlaced her fingers. "As soon as your suspicions about CeSiR Tech hit the Link, we each contacted Earl to discuss our interest in this case," said Vivian, from the Department of Homeland Security.

"The Link?"

"Yes, in an effort to counter terrorism, the Link was created to improve the flow of interdepartmental information."

"Not that it wasn't great before," said Walt. He laughed at his own joke.

"Right," said Vivian. She didn't laugh. "Each government department has access to a centralized database of information. Scanning programs constantly monitor new information as it enters the database searching for keywords that might indicate interest for a given department. Once you contacted Earl with your suspicions about CeSiR, Dietrich, Duncan, and Walt all responded immediately."

"The Food and Drug Administration has been keeping an eye on CeSiR Tech for several months now," said Walt. "It seemed the funds being invested in their research weren't producing the expected quantity or quality of results." He tapped his pencil on a stack of papers that apparently had something to do with CeSiR's legitimate research. "So we were immediately alerted by the prospect of them allocating government funds to illegal cloning research." He chuckled. "Wouldn't want them creating no Clone Troopers, now would we."

Given his bruised knuckles from the encounter with Trenton, the attempted humor didn't strike him as funny. Stoic faces around the table agreed.

Duncan, from the ATF, sat back in his chair with his hands behind his head. "There are significant weapons and explosives trails that seem to end at CeSiR. And I'm not talking about the kind of weapons used by night watchmen or security guards."

Chris leaned toward the table. "More like a military issue sniper rifle?"

"Among others, yes. To our knowledge they posses M-76s from the former Yugoslavia, some American made Tango-51s, and at least one PSG-1. But sniper rifles are only the beginning. Our intel indicates they've purchased dozens of

337

automatic rifles, hand guns, explosives, and even a few SA-7 surface-to-air missiles."

"The guards at the gates had M4 assault rifles," said Chris. "If you knew they were purchasing all this, why didn't you do something about it?"

"Our intel pointed to CeSiR. But we didn't have any hard evidence." Duncan lowered his arms and crossed them across his chest. "As you might imagine, you need solid evidence to start poking around in a government funded company."

Oh, he could imagine?

"Our involvement," said Dietrich from Immigrations. "Came solely as a result of your investigation. Anytime there is concrete evidence that someone is falsifying American citizenship records we get involved. Clones or not, someone is going to an awful lot of trouble to create records for people that don't exist, or at least who aren't who the records say they are."

Vivian pointed to the CIA agent. "Charles and I would not have paid considerable attention to the Link entry, except for the sheer number of agencies responding. To be honest, this thing is too big for either of our departments not to be involved."

"Well I'm glad you're all here," said Chris.

"So am I," added Daryl. "It's nice to finally be reinstated."

Earl slid his chair back and stood up. "Once we knew Trenton Richards intended to remove Chris from the force, we suspected he'd arranged your suspension as well. One call to Internal Affairs confirmed it. They had decided not to pursue the matter after they spoke with you and Chris."

Daryl's face turned red. "That was before I was even removed from active duty?"

"Yes, it was never Internal Affairs recommendation that you be suspended. That was completely Trenton's doing."

Earl walked to the briefing board and pinned up a large site plan.

Chris recognized CeSiR's gated entrance, driveway, and the Lamine River. A few small green areas highlighted areas outside CeSiR's fences.

Earl went on to explain that these areas represented the staging areas for the next day's operation. For the next few hours the six agents, Chris, and Daryl reviewed the detailed plans of the operation.

At ten o'clock, Chris left the station and headed home to get some rest before the next morning's search and seizure at zero-five-hundred.

~~~~~~~~~~

Evening retreated on Friday and the battle in Excelsior Springs raged on.

A cavalier named Mala dispatched one of the enemy minions. They would win this fight. The enemy fought hard but their numbers dwindled. As he rode toward another sniveling demon, he caught a glimpse of his mighty captain Ladan.

Ladan appeared disturbed.

Mala turned his steed and rode to his captain. "What troubles you, sir?"

"You are perceptive Mala." Ladan pushed the tip of his sword into the ground and rested against it. "Though this battle goes well, we will have neither the time nor the forces to continue on to Arrow Springs." Ladan scanned the emptying quarry. "Eitan is expecting our help. He must be informed that he will not have it. He needs to plan accordingly."

"I will ride to him, sir. I can give him the news and then remain to fight with them."

"You are a good warrior, Mala." Ladan looked him in the eyes. "Ride swiftly my friend."

"Yes, sir." Mala had served with Ladan for many years, and though he was his commanding officer, he truly believed Ladan viewed him as his friend.

Mala circled the perimeter of the quarry. Once he broke free from the battle, he turned toward Arrow Springs. The quarry faded to a dot on the horizon behind him. Then it disappeared from view.

Thwack.

Something drilled him square across the midsection. Agony surged through his body, as he sprawled to the ground.

He rolled over to see a hulking beast towering over him.

The one Ladan had called Cadfael bared his fangs and raised a bloody battle-axe over his head.

Mala tried to roll, but his body would not move.

A horrid war cry rang out above him.

The axe sliced into him and everything began to fade.

"Let Eitan believe his reinforcements are coming." Somewhere in the darkness, Cadfael gloated. "We wouldn't want him to reconsider his attack, now would we?"

A hideous laugh faded into blackness.

~~~~~~~~~~

CHAPTER THIRTY-FIVE

Saturday, May 16, 2020

Sarah sat across from Marilyn eating eggs and burnt toast at five-thirty on Saturday morning. How could something as simple as making toast become so difficult when living in someone else's home.

The lines forming beneath Marilyn's eyes reflected her own dread about the operation at CeSiR. "I'm sure they'll be okay," said Marilyn.

"I hope so." Sarah took a sip of her coffee. The rich aroma chased away the stench of burnt bread, at least until she set the cup back on the table. "I'm glad Pastor Thomas called for the prayer gathering this morning. The timing couldn't have been better."

Marilyn set her fork next to her plate. "It seems God wanted his people praying this morning, wouldn't you say?"

"That's what worries me." God didn't always protect his people from harm. She was living proof. "He's probably got good reason." She took a bite of eggs and set down the fork, to hide the shaking in her hands.

"That may be." Marilyn stood and took her place setting to the counter. "All we can do is pray for God's protection."

Sarah finished her eggs, grabbed her purse, and followed Marilyn out the door.

~~~~~~~~~~~

Chris stood next to a vehicle that could have looked like a typical bread delivery truck, if not for the black color and the initials FBI next to the departmental logo. The damp morning air chilled his lungs with each breath. Today it would happen, he would finally have his answers.

Earl approached him and slapped him on the back. "You ready for this?"

"Yes, sir." But was he really? As he followed Earl to the side of the truck, he felt as if he were walking through a lake—his movements slow and heavy. In part, the lack of mobility he blamed on his helmet, level three body-armor, and boots. But they only added about twenty pounds. No—nervous muscles accounted for *this* feeling. He knew the feeling. Its name was fear, fear he'd not felt for many years.

Daryl and several agents joined them beside the truck. Despite the blackness of the morning, the terahertz enhancing goggles Earl had given Chris made everything look like cloudy daytime, only in black and white. Perhaps they wouldn't miss a pair after this was all over.

"Alright, listen up!" said Earl. He eyed two agents who felt the need to wrap up their discussion. When silence fell, he continued. "We have no idea what to expect this morning. To our knowledge, they are not in possession of night-vision technology. We should have the advantage until the sun comes up." Earl paced to his left, and then back to his right. "Just so we're clear! We have chosen a Saturday morning so there will be fewer, if any, civilians present. However—" He pointed to another van barely visible a good three hundred yards from their location. "Our surveillance teams place dozens of people inside the facility. We *must* assume anyone in the building to be a hostile. We *will* give the opportunity for peaceful surrender, but any show of resistance will be met with immediate and overwhelming force."

Earl went on to brief the group on the weapons and gear traced to CeSiR. "In precisely five minutes, an FBI van will pull up to the front gate. The warrant will be presented and if we're lucky, everything will go down nice and peaceful."

Earl turned to Chris and Daryl. "Are you two prepared if things don't go down quite so neatly?"

"Yes sir," said Daryl.

Chris patted the Velcro on his body-armor. "Ready."

"Alright then, now we wait."

~~~~~~~~~~

"Well, mighty Eitan, the next move is yours," said Mael. He stood ominous atop the CeSiR Tech building. He could see the men donned in black scattered around the grounds as if it were midday. "So they think they can sneak up on us under the cover of darkness?" The irony made him laugh. "Today we will show them how mims are superior to humans in every way."

Though the mims couldn't see any better in the dark than normal humans. His minions, who controlled the mims, could see perfectly. In fact, they rather preferred the darkness.

Mors paced the rooftop. "Are you sure we have sufficient numbers to defeat Eitan and his warriors?"

"You fear him." Mael chuckled. "Mighty Demon of Death." He drew his electric blue sword and pointed it to the fence-line. "There are only three hundred under his charge. We are ten thousand." Excitement surged through his being. "Even Eitan cannot prevent the massacre that will occur today. Today the world will take notice of what we have achieved here."

Mors stepped beside Mael and placed his boney hands on the wall that surrounded the rooftop. "I hope you are right."

"Stations!" roared Mael.

Along the perimeter of the rooftop, mims took position.

From the levels beneath him, Mael heard the stone-on-stone scraping of bricks being removed from the outer walls. He had not designed this building to be a research facility. He designed it to be a fortress. Nearly a hundred lookouts and firing points would now be exposed. They had prepared for this day.

~~~~~~~~~~

Eitan stood atop a large oak tree overlooking the CeSiR Tech premises. Alex and Yora stood to his right, Huw and Gida to his left.

Wave after wave of demons moved into position. For a hundred yards in all directions from the building marched lesser demons of every sort. These would be the first demons he and his warriors would encounter. Though outnumbered twenty to one, these would present little difficulty. The remaining ranks concerned him.

"Sir, look." Alex pointed to the rooftop of the building. "There are thousands of them."

"And they are prepared for this," said Gida.

Eitan examined row after row of demons lining the top of the building. Each demonic warrior perched atop his post in ominous armor like that of a black knight. They had girded their loins with deceit. On its chest, each demon wore the black breastplate of impropriety. As they milled about cursing their Creator, he could see that their feet were covered with the propagation of anger, hatred, and strife. In their left hand they held tight to shields of doubt. The sight churned his stomach. Such a perversion of God's glorious design.

Thousands of green flames lit the dark sky as demonic archers pulled back their fiery arrows of hopelessness. Each slimy distorted face peered through the opening in a helmet of damnation. When the arrows were spent, they would resort to the fiery swords of death, which now hung sheathed over their shoulders.

Eitan turned to his mighty companions. "I am concerned—we have heard nothing from Ladan and his warriors. I fear they have been detained." He closed his eyes. He had fought side-by-side with Ladan on many occasions. He dearly wanted his presence for this battle.

"Yes, but the true warriors are gathering even as we speak," said Huw. "To pray!"

"My wise friend," said Eitan. "You are a refreshing spring to my parched courage. This battle belongs to the Lord. His will be done."

~~~~~~~~~~

Chris heard Earl's radio crackle to life. "Sir, we are approaching the gates."

From the command location a couple hundred yards west of the gates, Chris watched the headlights turn into the drive leading to the security gates.

The lights went dark.

In just a fraction of a second, Chris reviewed the plan. This wasn't a part of it.

Then the sound reached him—the spattering sound of automatic rifle fire, followed by the clinking of glass. Headlights shattered.

The enemy was expecting them. This was their response to a peaceful solution.

Earl screamed into his headset. "Snipers! Take those guards out!"

Thwack, thwack.

As quickly as the shooting started it ceased.

The two guards by the gate crumpled.

Fffwud, crack.

This time the sound came from the FBI van. Something had struck the front windshield. The bulletproof glass turned to a web of crystal covering the entire window.

Chris gasped.

The two guards righted themselves and opened fire on the windshield. Weakened by an armor-piercing sniper round, the glass ripped to pieces. Bullets began to riddle the interior of the van.

He couldn't imagine anyone inside surviving.

Thwack, thwack.

The two guards staggered at impact but continued firing.

Thwack, thwack.

~~~~~~~~~~

Yora had seen enough. He dove from the treetop toward the van—fiery-red blade before him, silver hair trailing. His blade slashed through the two demon controllers.

With the demons gone, the guards dropped to the ground dead.

~~~~~~~~~~

Sarah and Marilyn walked toward the entrance to the church, east of the river.

The sound of an FBI chopper overhead served to accentuate the dread Sarah felt as Chris took part in the operation across the river. Why did he have to participate? Why couldn't he let the agencies handle it? They did this kind of stuff. "I hope they're okay," said Sarah.

As they watched the helicopter float silently in the dark morning sky, a small red streak appeared.

The sky flashed with a crimson brilliance.

A sickening wave of thunder pounded against her chest.

"No! Dear God, no." She couldn't believe her eyes. For what seemed like minutes, she and Marilyn stood stunned as flaming debris fall from the sky like some horrific fireworks display gone awry.

Soon others funneled from the church, and joined her in disbelief as they stared into the rising flames.

~~~~~~~~~~

The helicopter had been surveying the situation to provide tactical intelligence.

"Get some paramedics over there!" barked Earl.

Chris couldn't believe anyone would have survived the explosion. But he understood.

"Snipers!" The blood vessels in Earl's neck were ready to burst. "Engage any targets on that building."

~~~~~~~~~~

Eitan knelt atop the tree with his face turned upward.

"Sir, should we engage?" asked Alex

"Not yet," said Eitan. "We do not have the prayer coverage."

"But they will rip the agents apart."

"Do you not think I know that?" He felt Alex' pain. The hardest task an angel could face was idly observing as demons did their worst. "We must wait."

Below him, three S.W.A.T teams attempted a stealthy approach of the building. They cut through the wire fencing surrounding the property, ducked between trees and bushes, and came to within a hundred yards of the building.

Aside from a couple of fountains and a large Victorian statue they would have no cover between them and the entrance to the building. Once the mim controllers spotted them, their mission would be short.

One of the members opened fire on the large statue.

His commanding officer waved frantically. "What are you doing? You gave away our position."

"Sir, I saw something move behind the fountain. There! Look!"

The commander stared in the direction of the fountain and swore. "There's nothing there."

Another team opened fire, fifty yards further up the property. Bullets spattered off the fountain.

Unseen hordes of demons swirled around the three teams. Like ravenous dogs, they frothed at the mouth in expectation. One by one, demons approached the S.W.A.T. team members. They would mess with the minds of the soldiers. Eitan had seen it many times.

"They're shooting at you!" One slimy being shouted at the already frazzled agent.

He turned his rifle toward the other group and rattled off several rounds.

The forearm of his commanding officer knocked him to the ground. "What are you doing? Have you gone mad?"

Green flaming arrows began to rain down on the dozen men trapped in the middle of a tumult of demons. Bullets from the mims joined the arrows.

Eitan closed his eyes. Screams began to echo off the CeSiR building.

~~~~~~~~~~

"Snipers?" Earl was furious. Some of the men were his. Sending more in would be suicide. "Does anybody have a shot?"

"No sir. It's like the building's covered in a black fog. We can't get a bead."

Earl switched his goggles from terahertz enhancement to infrared. He scanned the top of the building. There were people up there. There had to be. The electronic screen displayed a solid dark-green. A veil of blackness seemed to absorb the infrared heat signatures. Even if it were a fog, he should see thermal signatures through it.

"Everyone! Fall back. We wait 'til daybreak."

~~~~~~~~~~

Sarah sat in a surreal state of shock. The image of the helicopter exploding continued to cycle through her mind. If there had been any doubt about the severity of the situation facing Chris and Daryl, it vanished with that explosion.

She barely noticed Pastor Thomas addressing the gathering crowd.

"Good morning," said the pastor. "I am incredibly pleased to see so many here this morning. I don't think anyone would argue about the importance of this meeting. Nor do I need to tell you, there is a war going on out there. But let's be clear. God's Word tells us we do not battle against flesh and blood but against spiritual forces of evil."

Sarah glanced up at the pastor. He had stopped speaking.

His gaze locked on the back of the auditorium. "Welcome. Please, come in. We're having a special congregational prayer meeting. You are more than welcome to join us."

"Thank you." The familiar male voice echoed from somewhere in Sarah's past. "I'm Tim and this is my wife Angela. We're here from St. Louis. We're friends of—"

A squeal of delight slipped from Sarah's mouth. "Angela! Tim! I can't believe it. You're actually here." She sprang from her seat and ran to embrace Angela. Tears streamed down her cheeks.

The realization of her outburst caught up to her. "Oh Pastor. I'm so sorry. It's just—I haven't seen them for years."

"You don't have to apologize," said Pastor Thomas. "Again I say, welcome. Please, won't you join us as we seek God's protection for the men and women fighting to protect our little town?"

"Thank you so much," said Tim. "We would be honored to join you before the throne. Please know—there are many, even hundreds of saints praying for this town back in St. Louis."

Sarah ushered them into the row next to Marilyn.

"Go on," said Pastor Thomas.

"We read about this meeting and all that is going on in this town on your web log," said Tim. "We've been asking fellow church members for their prayers. Our online network of friends too." Tim's voice grew hesitant. "Last night, well we just felt like God wanted us to come join you."

"I still can't believe you're here," whispered Sarah.

Once again, Pastor Thomas addressed the congregation. "God is awesome. If you had any doubt that God had something big planned, well, I'm guessing it's gone now."

The group began to fervently seek God's protection and intervention in the events unfolding west of the river.

~~~~~~~~~~

Eitan pulled his sword from its sheath and donned his golden helmet. The battleground known as CeSiR Tech lay ready for one last battle. Help would not arrive from Ladan and the western warriors.

He would ask his troops to lay down their existence in the earthly realm in order to allow the agents to infiltrate the building. The truth had to be revealed.

"Can you feel it?" asked Alex.

Eitan turned to face Alex. His opalescent wings swirled with color.

"Yes," said Eitan. "The saints are praying. It is time."

The first rays of sunlight pierced the tree line east of the river.

A loud blast.

The call of a ram's horn trumpet flooded the property. With it echoed a loud roar—the roar of several hundred angelic warriors riding the prayers of the saints. Not the prayers of the small group of believers in Arrow Springs, but of hundreds of saints to the east.

The angelic cavalry crashed upon the sea of demons.

Eitan raised his sword. "Banish them from this place!"

He led his troops into the field of battle. Demonic minions flailed into the air as his sword connected with the front line of the horde. With each swing, dozens of demons vanished to the Abyss. But for every demon banished, two more flowed from the building to take its place.

Gida and Alex fought bravely alongside him. Grotesque adversaries surged toward them, aware of Eitan's presence. Lust for approval drove them, willing to risk their existence for the acclaim of slaying the captain of the host. Hundreds of demons fell to the three warriors.

The real threat perched atop the building. Fiery arrows rained to the ground in wave after wave. To avoid being skewered, Eitan kept his mighty shield raised above him.

The onslaught continued.

In between waves of arrows, Eitan looked back at Yora and pointed his sword to the top of the building.

Yora nodded and barked instructions to a company of archers.

Eitan raised his shield at the whistling sound above him. Almost in time. Most of the barrage embedded into his shield. One sunk deep into his shoulder. Each swing of his sword resonated with pain.

A new wave of arrows pierced the sky. This wave came from behind him.

The front row of demons screeched and tumbled from the building.

He needed to remain focused on the enemies around him. Yora would have to deal with those on the roof, at least for the time being.

"Focus your attention on the demons controlling the mims," yelled Yora.

In the yard around him, shreds of lightless armor, wings, and talons flew through the air.

For Eitan and his warriors success came slow and with great cost. By his estimates over a hundred angelic warriors had been returned to the throne room of their Creator.

~~~~~~~~~~

The battle seemed to have turned. Chris knelt next to Daryl, in the safety of the FBI truck. The morning sky shone bright and the enemy stronghold sat clearly in view.

One by one, S.W.A.T. team snipers picked enemies off the top of the building.

To Chris' right, a group of ten S.W.A.T. members embarked on a mission to infiltrate the building.

"Cover that team!" barked Earl.

Somewhere behind him, three muffled shots sounded.

Three enemies atop the building staggered and fell.

"Go, go, go!" yelled the team commander.

One at a time, the team members sprinted through an opening in the fence. Neither side of the fence offered any cover. The tenth member of the team caught the shoulder of his body-armor on the fence. He struggled to free himself, but it took too long.

A muted thud drove the man to the ground.

The bullet had struck him in the vest.

The man screamed in pain. The armor likely kept the bullet from entering his body, but the impact would certainly have broken some ribs.

Chris sprinted to the man.

~~~~~~~~~~

Mael could not contain his excitement. Green drool dripped from his mouth. The mouse had taken the bait. Officer Chris Davis, a perpetual thorn in his side, ran across the open field to assist the fallen team member. How lovely.

"Attack him!"

A volley of fiery arrows flew toward the man.

Mael cursed as the one called Zeke threw himself between Chris and the incoming assault.

The first arrow struck the embossed cross in the center of the warriors shield.

Mael screamed out the order. "I want him dead."

Arrow after fiery arrow pounded the shield until it splinted down the center of the cursed cross. Impact after impact began to pound against the angel's breastplate. Mael marveled at the warrior's endurance. But soon the breastplate gave way.

Arrows began to pierce the massive warrior. Anguish flooded the pale face visible through the helmet.

Exhilaration coursed through Mael. Another mighty warrior had fallen.

In a flash of light the angel vanished—leaving only the pitiful unprotected Sergeant Davis.

~~~~~~~~~~

Chris helped the fallen agent to his feet and pushed him toward cover.

Twenty yards.

Bullets began to strike the ground at his feet.

Ten yards.

Dirt and debris ricocheted into Chris' face. He pressed onward.

Two yards.

The man fell to safety in front of him.

One yard.

As he dove for cover, something ripped through his shoulder. Pain, intense agonizing pain, surged through his nervous system.

The bullet found an opening under his right arm. The impact spun him back into the open.

Three successive thuds rang inside his head.

The first bullet struck him in the midsection, penetrated his level-three body-armor, and spun him further into the line of fire. The second struck him in the back. He lost all sense of feeling and fell face down to the dirt. The final bullet split his helmet in two.

He heard Daryl's voice. He heard Earl cursing. Then he saw Sarah's tear covered face. He'd failed one final person.

Thunder rippled through his head.

Sarah's image faded to blackness.

~~~~~~~~~~

A deep thunderous voice rolled across the battlefield.

Eitan dropped to the ground.

"ENOUGH!!!"

The mims ceased fire.

The demons froze in place.

The angelic warriors bowed low.

The voice of God Himself resonated across the valley. *"You dare to defy me yet again! Did you not trust that your actions would be punished? Can you not hear the wails of your brothers who defied me with the daughters of men? Are your mims so different from the ancient Nephilim? Since the days of Noah, they have waited in chains for the final judgment. Now you will join them!"*

Eitan longed to look up. To see once again the face of his Creator. But he could not bring himself to observe the destruction of the fallen ones.

God spoke in judgment. *"To each who has taken possession of one of these mims I say, BE GONE!!!"*

~~~~~~~~~~

Mael rose from his knees. Amid screeches and shrieks, demons around him began to vanish in puffs of black vapor. Small lightning bolts danced around the building, zapping horrified beings into the Abyss.

He watched in horror as twelve hundred demons simply disappeared.

One final bolt struck the rooftop.

He winced.

In an instant, Mors was gone.

The remaining demons stood stunned.

"Attack!" said Mael.

No one moved.

Void of controllers, the mims stood motionless for several moments. Then like a cage full of monkeys with automatic weapons, they began firing randomly in every direction, including at each other.

"Get in there!" said Mael. "Possess those mims." He shouted the orders at shocked demons, who stared back at him. "Regain control of them."

"With all due respect my liege," said one of the minor princes. "Perhaps you should lead the way. No one knows whether the edict is a permanent one. We are not willing to suffer the fate of our brothers."

Rage boiled inside him. Furious at the prince, furious at God, and furious at his own cowardice, Mael hurled his electric blue sword at the minor prince.

The prince stumbled and fell from the building. He tumbled to the ground below where dozens of angelic warriors finished the job.

An explosion at his feet hurled bricks and sandstone from the roof. Mael himself nearly fell off the edge in surprise. One of the mims had dropped a grenade. Though the grenade could not have hurt him, he had lost his composure. His glorious creations now taunted his failure.

At least the blast seemed to quiet the remaining mims.

"This is not the end!" Mael turned his face toward the sky. "You have not heard the last of me." He began a gradual descent into the building.

The battle was lost.

One last detail to deal with before leaving Arrow Springs.

~~~~~~~~~~

CHAPTER THIRTY-SIX

Sarah knelt next to Angela and Marilyn praying for God's hand of protection. The auditorium buzzed with whispered pleas. Small groups of people prayed their way through the list of topics displayed on the screens at the front.

As Angela begged God to expand His kingdom through the unimaginable events occurring around them, the auditorium doors creaked open. Some of the younger children had begun a boredom cycle of trips to the restrooms.

One by one, the murmur of prayers behind her trailed off.

Footsteps approached up the aisle.

Sarah turned her head and peaked behind her.

Air evacuated the room. She struggled to breathe.

Daryl Williams walked down the aisle. His wide brown eyes were locked on her.

"No! Oh dear God no."

Spots of dried blood streaked Daryl's uniform. He knelt beside her.

"Where is he?" she asked.

"They put him in an ambulance. They're on their way to Regional. Sarah—" His neck tightened and he dropped his gaze to the floor. "Sarah, I'm so sorry."

Sobs heaved through her chest and throat. She gasped for breath as her still tender throat constricted. God couldn't be that merciless.

"Come on Sarah," said Angela. "We'll take you to the hospital."

She just nodded.

As they walked toward the back doors, Daryl paused. "Pastor," he said. "Please pray for Chris."

Tears overtook her. She wanted to believe prayer could make a difference.

~~~~~~~~~~

Maiya sat in the center of the circle of candles. She begged her prince to show himself. To tell her what to do. The mims had gone insane.

CeSiR Tech, the company her father had worked so hard to create, had become a war zone. What could have driven the mims to take up arms in such an aggressive and decisive manner? They'd shown hostility in the past, but never anything like this.

Her chest heaved under the black ceremonial robe.

"Maiya?"

Casimir. He would know what to do. She could trust him.

She lifted her head to her love.

The most horrifying sight she'd ever beheld filled her vision. A black being with the face of a buffalo, and the sinewy wings of a bat stood before her. The creature knelt and reached a deformed hand to her. "You hold the key to the mims."

The voice belonged to Casimir. But this was no handsome prince.

"You see—they are no longer of use to us," said the creature. "Therefore, you are no longer of use to me." The hideous beast bared green fangs. His breath reeked of sulfur.

She had detected traces of the smell in the past, when Casimir was upset with her. But now the stench overwhelmed her. She leaned forward and hurled.

"Now is that any way to show respect to your prince?" He reached out a black talon and traced the chain of her silver necklace down to her chest. With a sudden yank, he snatched the ankh from her neck and threw it across the office.

The creature stood and drew a long blue sword. "The last thing we need is more creatures, which we are powerless to control, wandering this earth. So—you—must die."

She screamed and ran for the door.

The creature behind her laughed.

She stepped on the hem of the black robe, tumbled, and slid across the hardwood floor. She scrambled to her feet, and flung open the door to her office. Was he following her? She had to get away from this place. She cursed the security system as she scanned into the elevator.

The door opened and she jumped in. The steel doors slid shut, but the grotesque creature stepped right through the doors and joined her in the elevator.

She was trapped. "You don't have to do this. I won't make any more mims. I promise."

"Oh, of that I am certain." The creature set the sword against the wall of the elevator. "Perhaps you are correct—" He turned his head away from her. "I probably do not have to do this." Slowly, his eyes locked into hers. "But I want to." The elevator crawled downward. "Even more than I wanted to kill your father."

It couldn't be true. Casimir was her friend, not a monster. He had served her, loved her.

The door opened and Maiya ran from the elevator. She reached for her keys. They were in her purse, in her office. She couldn't go back. She'd find another way out.

She ran between two rows of cars.

Suddenly, ahead on the left stood Casimir. Her heart jumped, he'd come for her. He would save her. How could she have mistaken the beast for him. She ran toward him. But when she drew within ten feet of him, the image faded, back into the beast with the green teeth and the glowing blue sword.

She turned to her right and continued to run. Ahead of her sat a car with the driver's side door open. She glanced around. Where was the beast?

She jumped into the driver seat of the car, slammed the door, and flipped the locks. It was a miracle—the keys hung from the ignition.

She turned the key.

"Good bye Maiya," said the hideous beast, now seated in the passenger seat.

It was the last thing she heard. An explosion engulfed the car.

~~~~~~~~~~

CHAPTER THIRTY-SEVEN

Chris awoke.

Light—incredible light filled his eyes. Even before his eyes could adjust, he knew where he was—the throne room of God.

"Welcome Chris, my friend."

Chris fell to the ground in worship.

"No. No, my friend, you must not do that. I am just a messenger."

Chris felt a presence approach.

"My name is Eran. I have been with you for six and a half years—since you began your walk with Jesus the Christ."

Chris' eyes began to adjust to the intense light. A massive form took shape before him. "Does that make you my guardian angel?"

The one called Eran laughed. "Yes, I suppose in a sense it does."

"You look pretty beat up." Battered wings and bruised arms evidenced recent struggles. "Is that from defending me at CeSiR Tech?"

"Yes, but not from when you think. This happened what you would recognize as three weeks ago. You entered the enemy's lair—CeSiR Tech. Eitan, our captain in Arrow Springs, accompanied you disguised as a second officer. Only the enemy spirits could see him."

"That would explain why the guards referred to me in the plural." Chris paused. "But, that would mean they were—demons?"

"Not exactly. As you have come to suspect, Dr. M'Gregor created them—they were clones, but they were controlled by demons. Thus their information came from the demons' knowledge and awareness."

Chris examined the massive angel. He couldn't imagine anything bringing harm to him. "So you were injured when I investigated CeSiR?"

"As you left, the enemy discovered the presence of Eitan. They pursued you. They would have ripped him to shreds, and killed you. I distracted them long enough for the two of you to escape."

Realization settled in on Chris. He felt no pain, but he could remember. The fallen agent. The bullets. His failure. "So, you weren't with me this time?"

Eran shook his head. "No. A fellow angel has protected you for the past three weeks. His name is Zeke. I am afraid he now sits recovering before the throne of God—which is where I have been since the encounter."

"Wow, guess I'm not an easy assignment."

"Easy?" Eran laughed, his joy uplifting Chris' spirit. "Perhaps not, but quite rewarding nonetheless. You are a unique man, Chris Davis."

"So am I—"

"Dead?"

"Yes?"

"No. It is not your time." Eran placed his hand on Chris' shoulder. "The Heavenly Father still has much work for you and Sarah. Know that I will be with you whenever I can."

Warmth flowed from Eran's hand into Chris. Peace washed over him.

"Chris remember—HE will always be with you."

~~~~~~~~~~

CHAPTER THIRTY-EIGHT
Tuesday, May 20, 2020

Sarah sat next to the hospital bed. Chris' status remained critical. With heavy eyes, she watched the television. Three days had passed since the showdown. Still, the events of Saturday dominated the news networks, both local and national.

The nation, and the world, sat in shock. Reports of successful human cloning ignited fierce debates from living rooms to the United Nations. Not only had someone succeeded, but they'd been doing it for twenty-five years. Reports flowed in regarding how these mims—a name reportedly originating in recovered documents—had infiltrated judicial positions, city officials, and one was the right hand man for a U.S. Senator.

Senator Phillips himself stepped down on Monday when it leaked that he had played a crucial role in the funding of CeSiR Tech.

This news broadcast addressed the strange phenomenon, which occurred on Saturday, when the mims seemingly lost all sense of personality.

"I am here with Earl Banks of the FBI." The reporter stuck a microphone in the man's face. "Agent Banks, what can you tell us about this phenomenon now being called *mim wipe?*"

"Not much," said Earl.

Sarah sat up in her chair. That very FBI agent, along with several other agency representatives, had stopped by to check on Chris—her Chris.

He was no longer her hero, but a national hero.

One young man had entered the room on Sunday. He sheepishly introduced himself and proceeded to explain that Chris got shot pulling him to safety.

Each visitor told her what she already knew—Chris Davis was a hero.

"We were in a firefight with the mims, when Sergeant Davis was shot."

Her attention returned to the television.

Earl spoke into the camera. "Almost as soon as the bullet hit him, a peculiar thunder rolled across the sky."

"But the weather wasn't stormy?" asked the reporter.

"No." Earl shook his head. "There wasn't a cloud in the sky. Within seconds, what appeared to be small bolts of lightning danced all around the building. Then it stopped. And that's when the mims began shooting at each other. The ones that weren't killed were in this state of—I don't know—absence."

"Has there been any discovery as to the cause of this—absence?"

"None. Given CeSiR's line of work, we feared some kind of biological weapon. But, the CDC cleared the building. Since then, we've discovered from CeSiR's records that the earliest clones exhibited these same tendencies. There's been no indication as to why they returned to this state."

"Can you tell us what you found in the facility?" asked the reporter.

"We found approximately one hundred mims. Half of them were dead—killed in the firefight, or by each other. It took us an hour to get inside the building and to get the security overrides for the elevator. There were two levels below ground. One medical floor and one that resembled prison cells."

He stopped short of a public revelation of the third level. He had told Sarah when he visited that they found piles of bones in a mysterious lower chamber, apparently the results of many failed cloning attempts.

As the discussion continued, a video segment played showing surveillance footage recovered from CeSiR. Though Sarah had seen the footage dozens of times, she still couldn't process what she saw.

First the clip showed video of the lower levels Earl had just described. Then it switched to clips of mims firing automatic weapons through holes in the outer walls. One female mim, with a large round belly, stood looking through a scope on a sniper rifle. Moments later she pulled the trigger.

"Is it true," asked the reporter, "that this woman may have been in labor."

"She was in the midst of giving birth when we found her," said Earl. "They have demonstrated an exceptional tolerance for pain."

"No kidding." The reporter winced. "Have all of the mims been taken into custody?"

"Yes Ma'am. In addition to the mims taken from the facility, we have arrested several others throughout the United States. Thanks to CeSiR Tech records, and some exceptional investigative work by Chris Davis, we've been able to track nearly all of them."

"Thank you Agent Banks. Back to you, John."

The television now showed a female reporter standing with a twenty-something pregnant woman. "We now send you to Cedar Rapids, Iowa, where Kristy has a follow up story. Kristy?"

"Thanks John. Yes, as you've just heard federal agents are rounding up anyone believed to be one of these mims." The reporter put a gentle hand on the woman's shoulder. "I am here with Mrs. Johnson, the wife of one of the men arrested on Sunday. Mrs. Johnson, can you tell me what happened? Was your husband one of these mims?"

"No."

It appeared the woman was at least six months pregnant.

"I don't think so, I mean, how would that be possible?" The woman dabbed at her eyes. "He was a good man, so romantic. Sure he had his bad days, but never abusive, at least until—"

"Until?" asked the reporter.

"Until Saturday. It seemed like he just snapped. He didn't say anything. He just paced the house like an animal. And then he attacked me and I fled the house. I feared for the baby."

"What happened then?" The reporter's voice was soft, almost caring.

"Nothing. I went to a friend's house until I got a call from one of our neighbors. She said some agents came to the house and took Stan away."

"Did they tell you why they arrested him? Had you reported the attack?"

"No." The woman took a step back away from the camera. "They said he was a mim, a clone, one of over a hundred from somewhere in Missouri. It can't be true." She broke into tears and cradled her stomach with her hands.

"There you have it John, it would seem the sudden change in demeanor of the mims was not limited to the facility in Arrow Springs."

"Thanks Kristy. We have had similar reports from all over the country. As many as two dozen husbands or wives all went *absent*, to borrow a term from Agent Banks, at precisely the same time."

The broadcast went on to repeat things Sarah had now heard over and over. Her mind drifted to her discussion with Chris' doctor on Sunday.

"It's a miracle he's even alive," said the doctor. "The vest didn't stop the armor-piercing bullets, but it slowed them down. The one under his shoulder missed his lung by less than a millimeter. The second bullet destroyed his left kidney and broke a couple ribs. The third bullet shattered his left hipbone." During surgery they found a piece of bone wedged between two of his vertebra. "If it had penetrated even a millimeter further," said the doctor, "he would have been paralyzed at best."

"Why is he not conscious?" she had asked the doctor.

"My best guess is the fourth bullet. It split his protective helmet in two. It was a severe blow to the head. We have him stabilized now. All we can do is wait. There's still much we do not understand about head injuries."

Sarah's attention returned to the television. People were shown protesting for the rights of the mims to fair treatment as human beings. Her stomach lurched.

"Excuse me, Miss McIntyre?" A voice to her left interrupted her thoughts. "Might I ask you a question?"

Her heart tried to leap out of her chest. "Chris!" She threw her hands up in the air. "Oh, thank You Lord!" She turned and hugged him.

"Ouch." His face grimaced.

"I'm sorry." She began to pull away.

"Nonsense." He smiled weakly. "I'm just glad to see you here."

"There's no place I'd rather be than right here with my hero."

His eyes narrowed and his lips began to quiver. "Can I ask you a favor?"

"Anything," she promised. "What is it?"

"Would you marry me?" His lips curled in an ear-to-ear grin.

She let out a squeal. "Yes! Of course." Another squeal. "Yes!"

She buried her face in his neck and wept.

"Yes."

~~~~~~~~~~~~~~~~~~~~

ABOUT THE AUTHOR

Robert lives in Holland, Michigan with his wife and five children. He has a B.S. in Electrical Engineering, and has taken several Master level classes in religion, including theology.

God has blessed him with the spiritual gift of teaching and a creative personality type. For over twenty years, he has brought this creativity to his professional career as a manager of software developers, and a creator of leading-edge technologies for a global high-tech electronics company in the automotive and aerospace industries.

For nearly five years, he wove creativity and a passion for teaching together as a pastor of worship, adult discipleship, and outreach. In this role, he designed and scripted several outreach events and dramas, created unique video presentations, developed discipleship curriculum, and led corporate musical worship. Since then, he has developed his public speaking skills and has had the privilege to preach at multiple churches.

Several years ago, he turned his creativity and writing toward the pursuit of teaching through story. Since then, he has refined his fiction writing craft through conference sessions, critique group involvement, online and book study, writing, and plenty of rewriting.

Robert is the founder of Hearts of Compassion Publishing (www.heartspublishing.com); a company devoted to providing readers with quality stories and the comfort of knowing that the proceeds from those stories go to support compassion based ministries.